Praise for the Gyrford duology

'Warm and dark and wonderful'
Francis Spufford, author of *Light Perpetual*

'[*All The Hollow of the Sky*] reintroduces all the characters [from *In The Heart of Hidden Things*], is a warmly polished execution of the voice, and – crucially – is a story directly about the family themselves, which raises the stakes considerably'
Niall Harrison, *Locus*

'It's a joy to return to the world of Gyrford and its fairy-smiths, where magic stalks the hillsides and encounters with the fey can be as perilous as their gifts. Settle in with this book and prepare to be enchanted!'
Alison Littlewood, author of *The Crow Garden*

'A gripping multi-generational family saga of surreal folk magic, with memorable characters, detailed worldbuilding and a satisfying plot'
Fiona Moore, author of 'Jolene'

'As tart, dark and juicy as a summer pudding . . . combines power and poetry to serve up the perfect slice of folk
Daily Mai

'Engaging, believable chara
into a world of walking bramb
fire-breathing hounds . . . stands out for its depiction of a family deeply connected to a community, helping those who need it the most, regardless of the danger to themselves'
The Guardian

'An immersive and rewarding read'
ParSec

'Warm, witty, compassionate'
Francesco Dimitri, author of
The Book of Hidden Things

'It is refreshing to find a novel where the ordinary people take centre stage . . . a very engaging novel'
SF Crowsnest

'[I was] gripped by the sheer entertainment of finding out what would happen next . . . [Whitfield] creates believable characters that the reader cares about'
British Science Fiction Association

'Whitfield studs the tale with artful digressions, which provide useful backstory without interrupting the story. The prose is skilful and appropriate to a fairy tale'
Isn't Life Strange

'Power struggles, violence, mistakes and responsibility are threaded throughout the story. John is a strong, nuanced protagonist whose sound heart gives this book its warmth, even when things start to go wrong. Whitfield's world-building is detailed, the magic of this story is enticing and I found plenty to enjoy in this book'
Beth O'Brien, ***Disabled Tales***

ALL THE HOLLOW OF THE SKY

Kit Whitfield was born in West London and brought up in Wiltshire and London, where she now lives with her husband and son in a neurodiverse family. She is the author of *Bareback* (published in the US as *Benighted*), which was shortlisted for the Authors' Club Best First Novel Award and longlisted for the Waverton Good Read Award, and *In Great Waters*, which was nominated for the World Fantasy Award. You will find her on X @KitWhitfield.

Novels by Kit Whitfield

THE GYRFORD DUOLOGY
In the Heart of Hidden Things
All the Hollow of the Sky

In Great Waters

Bareback

ALL THE HOLLOW OF THE SKY

Kit Whitfield

First published in Great Britain in 2023
This paperback edition published in 2024 by

Arcadia
An imprint of
Quercus Editions Ltd
Carmelite House
50 Victoria Embankment
London EC4Y 0DZ

An Hachette UK company

A CIP catalogue record for this book is available
from the British Library

PB ISBN 978 1 52941 495 0
EBOOK ISBN 978 1 52941 496 7

10 9 8 7 6 5 4 3 2 1

Typeset by Jouve (UK), Milton Keynes

Printed and bound in Great Britain by Clays Ltd, Elcograf S.p.A

Papers used by Arcadia are from well-managed forests
and other responsible sources.

To Andreea Grigorescu
who I can never thank enough

Our eager fancies noted all they brought,
The glorious, unattainable delights!
But always there was one unbidden guest
Who cursed the child and left it bitterness.
The fire falls asunder, all is changed,
I am no more a child, and what I see
Is not a fairy tale, but life, my life.

Amy Lowell, 'A Fairy Tale'

And the cuckoo's sovereign cry
Fills all the hollow of the sky.

William Wordsworth, 'The Sun Has Long Been Set'

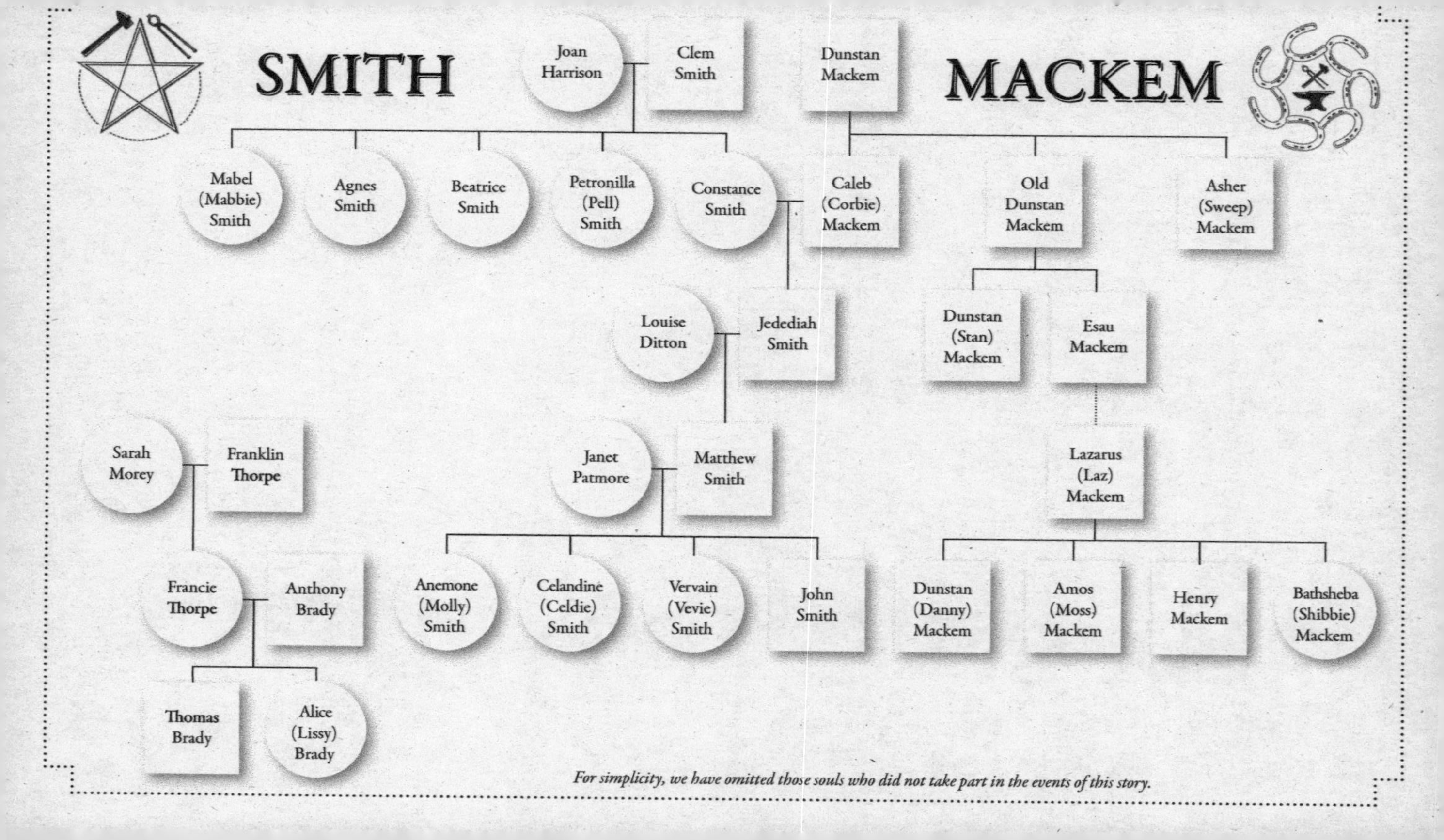

For simplicity, we have omitted those souls who did not take part in the events of this story.

FAMILY TREE

The Smiths and Mackems, and indeed, the other fairy-smithing clans of this time and place, were a network of families linked by intermarriage. While they tried to avoid uniting close relations – spend enough time around horses and you develop views about inbreeding – it was sometimes necessary to arrange a match between distant cousins. Farriers needed to be trained from early childhood, so when an elder farrier had only female heirs he would be obliged to choose a suitable son-in-law from another farrier clan, usually a younger brother from a family with a surplus of boys. A full family tree of the Smith clan, or indeed any fairy-smithing clan, would be immensely complicated. We have, therefore, reproduced only such branches of the tree as are relevant to the tale told here.

PROLOGUE

Jedediah

It took him an hour to write, and when it was finished, the letter said this:

To be kept at Tinsdowne forge for Corbie Mackem and read aloud to him by any who can read.

Dear Father,

Louise is dead of sickness and Matthew is with me in the smithy. He learns quick and I think will make a skilled man. He is a big boy for his years and should he be spared I think he will be tall. For now he is well. He is fine looking and not naughty. This is all the news from,

Your respectful son,

Jedediah Smith

There is no need for you to come, I do all and the work is done.

There were things it did not say. Corbie did not believe that fairy-smiths should be lettered, and Jedediah only learned from his grandfather when he got old enough to be stubborn; as a result, he could read better than he could write. But that was not why he left them out.

It did not say: I watched my wife die. I saw fever seize her lungs and drown her on a dry bed. I have heard my son cry and cry and I cannot give him what he cries for. He shivered as the earth touched his hand and the village waited to see him throw dirt on the coffin of his mother, and I whispered to him that it was like tucking her into bed while she slept, and I thought I should burn in Hell the moment he believed me.

It did not say: My heart is broken. What would be the point? Broken hearts still beat, and the work has still to be done, and Corbie Mackem's strengths, however numerous, had never included consolation. Jedediah just wanted to be left alone, to hold his grief steady so no one would jostle it into overflowing, and to stand between the world and his little boy. What was left of his family was his alone, and his to protect. If Corbie came, there would be nothing to do but take Matthew and leave Gyrford and never look back.

That was the last letter he sent. He did not hear from his father again until one day, when Corbie Mackem should have been nearing fourscore, he came back younger than his son.

BOOK ONE

MATTHEW

Corbie Mackem came twice to Gyrford.

To understand what it meant the day he came aged eight-and-thirty, you have to understand what it meant the day he came as a bridegroom, seventeen years old and already too bold for his father's liking.

And to understand why he came as a bridegroom, you have to know that once upon a time, his father-in-law Clem Smith tried to do the right thing, and if he was rewarded for it in heaven, his life on earth was a plague of friendship ever after.

This is the tale as it was told to John Smith three generations later, when his great-great-grandfather Clem's bones still lay in peace beneath the soil. It was told by John's father Matthew, who was the closest his clan had come in nearly in a century to producing a normal-minded man; he felt rather worried by that responsibility, for John was not entirely steady in his nature and had a way of looking at things that made everyone nervous. Matthew had to tell the story to explain certain facts about the family, but he made sure not to tell John where the Ab-tree grew. John, with the best intentions in the world, could make things worse – and what making this tale worse would look like, Matthew and Jedediah quailed to think.

Well now, Johnny love, once upon a time there was my great-grandfather Clem, Grandpa's grandpa, and he was a good man and didn't mean any harm. But this isn't a pretty tale, and you must promise you won't trouble Grandpa with it.

Why? Because it's about his own grandpa, and he says he was always very kind. You know how much care he takes of the grave, and it's not just because there's no grave for his father Corbie to care for. Grandpa says Great-Grandpa Clem did his best and isn't to be judged, and after all, you wouldn't like it if the tale told of your own grandpa after his time was all of his mistakes, would you?

No, Grandpa isn't dying, he's very well for his age.

No, that doesn't mean you need tell him every mistake you think he makes. There's never any need for bad manners.

Johnny, dear, do you wish to hear the tale or not? Just leave the hart's-tongue alone, there's a good lad; whatever's under it is doing no harm to us. Here, hold my strike-light; if you must play with something, play with something iron. It's a tale that calls for it.

So: Clem Smith was the fairy-smith of his day, and once upon a time he was called to a case up by the Lenden lands. Yes, hard by where Aunt Pell lives. Back before the business with the Sarsen Shepherd, cunning men liked to live there, and one of them was a man folks called Elder Samuel. Though if he was elder of any craft, it wasn't licit.

Cunning folk can be among the best of men and women – just think of Godfa Tom. But Elder Samuel's neighbours took against him because they thought he'd witched them. His crops grew mad; he had corn-stalks tall as May-bushes, and anyone who quarrelled with him found their cattle wouldn't milk for anyone but him, or all their bees flew off to drink from his flowers alone and wouldn't nest back in their own hives, but built in his trees till their branches were all clotted with comb and dripped honey beyond all sense. And one man's sheepdog grew so fond of this Elder Samuel—

No, I don't reckon he was the head of any coven or the like. I reckon such stories are mostly grown in the telling. I've known cunning men and women who worked harm, to be sure, but they were mostly poisoners, which is murder more than it's uncanny business. Or they tried to cast love spells, which would be no good if they worked, for you shouldn't force a heart any more than a body, and in any case, I reckon love spells would be wickeder than they sound if they worked, but I've never known one that did. Not now, Johnny, but we will talk about it later – yes, tonight, then – for that's important too, but not to the point just now. As to covens, I reckon if folks get hungry enough they might gather together and try to work marvels, but unless one of the People decides to help them, that's just wishing, and I'd say the greater wickedness is in their lords and neighbours who let them starve in the first place.

Where was I? Oh yes, the neighbour's sheepdog, poor thing, for I'm sorry to say that this dog scratched its belly until the skin on its flanks came loose and stretched out into wings, and it flew right over to Elder Samuel and circled him round. Folks took it for a witch's familiar, although Elder Samuel was heard pleading with it to leave him alone.

So in the end, Johnny, I'm sorry to say, this is a tale of wicked murder. Elder Samuel's neighbours got together one night, and they dragged him from his sleep, and they took him to a crossroads, and they hanged him.

No, love, the dog didn't follow him. I heard that Elder Samuel sent it back to its master, and the man put it out of its pain.

Me? I reckon I'd have knocked it on the head with an iron-braced club, poor thing. Let's just hope we never come to that with anything, for even if it's the kindest thing to do, it's not pleasant. But do you wish to hear what befell Elder Samuel?

All right then. So these men, his neighbours, they didn't ask the farriers for help; instead, they hanged him from a tree at the crossroads, and when he was quite dead they cut him down and buried him there, pinned down in his grave with an iron railing through his heart to keep him in place.

Yes, they should have called the farriers in, for it does sound more like the People at play than witchery, and Clem would have known fey trouble when he saw it. But Clem was known to be a gentle man, and the neighbours were angry and afraid, and the ones who hanged poor Elder Samuel were fellows without much regard for the rights of things.

Now, after Elder Samuel's murder there were shrieks and yells of a night at those crossroads. Men were afraid to ever set foot upon that road in case Elder Samuel's body heard them from under the earth and recognised their step, for he might rise up and shake off the earth and catch them.

So in the end, they did what they should have done before: they called in Clem to look at the grave.

Clem was no coward, and he said there had been wicked murder done, and that if there was trouble on the road, it was no wonder. And now, Clem said, Elder Samuel's body was to be taken to the churchyard and laid in holy ground.

It wasn't a comfortable job to dig up a man not long buried and look upon his mouldering corpse, and it's my belief that the smell must have put Clem off his stride a little, for he didn't pay full attention. But they had to haul up the corpse and move it – yes, I reckon it must have been maggoty, though that's not the thought I'd like to dwell on, Johnny love. Can I tell the tale without we dwell on all the nastiest parts? I know a farrier can't shirk ugly work, but he needn't harp on it either, and you know you'll have bad dreams later.

All right, love. Clem saw it through, but he didn't trouble to take the iron stake out of Elder Samuel's heart, for he was afraid the corpse might fall to pieces, and that would have been a terrible mess.

So that was that. And with the smell and the wondering whether any of the men around him had done such dreadful murder to Elder Samuel, Clem didn't think to fey-test the grave for aught but Elder Samuel's body. And he was a kind man, but as farriers go, he didn't have as strong a sense of things as some. So if anything did whisper up from the grave, he didn't notice.

★

Clem headed home. He'd sent his horse off to bear the body, but he didn't mind, for it was only three miles in the clean fresh air.

So he walked the first mile, and as he walked, he heard a flutter overhead and he looked up to see something like a quarrel of rags and ribbons thrashing down towards him. He rubbed his eyes, and now he was gazing at what had always been a great black crow.

'Well, now, good Crow,' he said, feeling that it was one of those days and it would be best to mind his manners, 'I hope I find you well this noontide.'

'Well, now, good Man,' said the crow, 'you hope you find me well, but hungry is what I am. Empty as a straw is what I am. Be good to me, sir.'

Now, Clem might not have heard a crow speak before, but he knew better than to offend the People. So he said he only had a bit of bread, and it mightn't be the freshest since he'd had some dirty work this morning, but the crow might have it if the crow liked. And when the crow agreed it would like, he tossed it on the path. He didn't see it land, nor hear a beak snatch it away, but the crow was gone without a sound, and the bread with it.

Clem walked the second mile, and out of the woods came a big spider, its back glowing bright as bronze, rolling along like a crumpled rag, although there was no wind to propel it.

'Good morrow, sir,' said Clem, who by good luck was not afraid of spiders.

No, I'm not either, I love them; all their hinges and fine legs – we could never work so fine. Marvellous little engines of God.

Grandpa doesn't like them so much, but of course you won't say that to him.

Good lad. So, where were we? Clem said to the spider, 'Well now, is aught amiss, good Spider?'

'Well, now,' said the animal, 'tangled in my feet is what I am. Knotted together with webs I am, and cannot walk. Be good to me, sir.'

For all Clem reckoned that a true spider would no more come to grief in its own web than a man would come to grief in his own skin, he bethought himself and said, 'A sorry thing, Spider. Perhaps I can untangle you.' And the webs came loose at a touch, melting away like mist, and so too did the spider.

Clem walked the third mile, until he came to the River Byde, and when he reached its banks, he found it had turned wild, all veined with white and flying along fast as a hawk.

And in the shallows, there was a woman, with her hair black and glossy as wings, wound around with great garlands of russet and gold, and she smiled at him a little too wide.

No, Johnny, she wasn't naked. She was clad in something like a dress, and that hair, Clem said, went all the way down to her toes. I didn't give you any look, Johnny, love. Women are lovely and it's natural enough for a young man to see that, but it's not to the point just now. And however lovely a woman, there's no excuse to forget your manners with her, always remember that, for she has a soul just as much as you, and feelings to hurt if you aren't kind. It's a great sin to hurt a woman; only silly men think otherwise.

Can we get back to the tale? Clem was kind, and that matters here – though don't take from this tale the lesson that kindness does you harm, for likely he would have suffered worse if he hadn't been. Maybe.

'Well, now, Mistress,' Clem said, and I can't blame him if he was daunted at the turn the world was taking, 'I hope you don't catch cold in this wet place.'

'Well, now, sir,' she said, and they say her voice rang like a struck bowl, 'I hope I shall not be cold. I must cross, good sir, is what I must do. Be good to me, sir.'

Clem sighed, and hoped she wouldn't mind if he said his prayers before they crossed, and she flapped a dainty hand and said he might. He said later there was something just a little talonish about the bend of those fingers.

He knelt and prayed, then hoisted the woman on his back. She landed on him quick as a swallow, but as he stepped into the water the weight of her pressed down, bending him low so the waves slapped at his face like hands and his muscles burned, and he staggered till he thought he'd fall and drown.

When he reached the other side, he was nothing like as wet as he should have been, at least around the legs, although his shirt was drenched with sweat. 'Will you light down, Mistress?' he asked.

At that, something lifted off his back, and he turned to find himself by the Byde, as steady as usual, and there was nothing beside him but a crow, a little copper-streaked around the edges.

'Well, now, well, now, well, now!' it sang in delight. 'Good to me, sir! Good to me, sir! As your kindness has no end, this one likes to be your friend!'

Clem swallowed. He'd reasoned with the People before, of

course, but it wasn't usual for them to take such a fancy to him. 'That's quite all right – have you a name, kind friend?' he asked.

'Well, now, have I a name?' it carolled. 'Have I a name? A name have I need of. Be good to me, sir.'

Clem didn't know what to say. The thing might be man or woman or both, for it had worn its woman's skin with an air that made him think it reckoned the stuff much as it regarded crow feathers or spider silk. So he suggested 'Ab', thinking that it might be either Abigail or Absalom, and besides, he was feeling much too tired to search through the alphabet for a better idea.

'Well, now, Ab!' The creature clapped its wings. 'Ab, Ab, Ab shall I be. You are good to me, sir. Your kindness has no end.'

'I don't reckon I did much out of the common,' said Clem. 'No need to thank me.'

Listen to the words they spoke, Johnny: the exact words matter here, that's why we took the trouble to remember them generations down.

So Ab tolled out, 'Quite all right you must be, kind sir. What will you have? I would be good to you!'

'Thank you,' said Clem, 'but if I'm honest, I'd like just to go home. I'm new-married and I wouldn't like to worry my wife. It's better when the girls are happy.'

He meant it as a rule for husbands in general. He did not mean it to go the way it did.

And that was the way of it. Ab decided it loved Clem, who was the best friend in the world, and that Clem must delight in Ab's friendship as Ab delighted in Clem's, and Clem didn't dare disagree. But it soon became clear that Ab's gifts were – well, that Ab thought as the People do, you see.

There was one day his wife Joan was out of temper with Clem, for he had awakened her when he came to bed late. Ab grew very angry with Joan and said to Clem that if he liked, it would turn her to smoke and ash and fetch him a better bride from the other side of the wind.

Clem said no thank you, that he liked his wife very well and he didn't blame her temper for she did need her sleep – and the next thing he knew, she was asleep in their bed, which was all laid over with a fine pallet woven in swirls that made your eyes cross to look at them, and the warp was chamomile and the weft valerian root, which are good herbs for sleep, but Godfa Tom will tell you, they're not a smell you want over your whole bed, at least not the valerian. Joan slept for seven days and seven nights before Clem could wake her at all, and though he was but three-and-twenty, his hair started to go grey, for he thought she might die.

And it was like that with many things. Ab wasn't there all the time, but you never knew when it would show up. If Clem should mention that he liked cheese, he'd find his kitchen so full of it you couldn't open the door, or if a customer wouldn't pay Clem's prices, they'd find everything they owned heaped on Clem's doorstep the next day, and it would be a day's work to persuade Ab to let him give them back.

Nobody thought the farrier was a witch, no, of course not, but Clem started to see why folks had thought that of Elder Samuel, who Ab must have liked very much. I reckon it had hid in the grave and meant to spring out at his murderers, that it had been in just the wrong place when they ran the iron stake through his heart. But now, of course, Clem had had them pull the stake up.

Well, nine months later, Joan bore Clem their first child, a daughter, healthy as could be. That was my Granny, Granny Constance, God love her, and Ab was there, all eager to give a blessing and good luck to the girl. Now, Clem was doubtful, for it doesn't do to chance your luck on what the People think will help you, but before he could say much, Ab cried out, 'She will have beauty beyond all other women!' And she'd been a pretty enough babe in her mother's arms, they say, but when it said those words, something came over her. Her eyes, that had been grey before, were deep silver, and she looked up at her Mama and cried as if something cramped her, and the cry puckered her little face up, the way baby faces do when they squall. And her mother held and soothed her, and when her face settled smooth as snow over stone, and you could see something in her, something that was just a pretty moppet now, but that had bones beneath the skin as perfect as ice-flowers.

Joan and Clem looked at each other, and they weren't quite sure if this was truly a blessing, but Clem said to Ab, 'Well, now, this is kind of you, but maybe there's no need. It doesn't help a girl to be vain, after all.'

And Ab cried out, 'As you ask, my friend! She shall have beauty beyond all, and know not of it!' and so pleased was it with itself for this clever thought that it jumped right up into the air and wasn't seen again for weeks.

So that's how it was, that was Granny Constance. She was

lovely, though a kind of lovely that looked queer on a face still in a cradle bonnet, but Clem and Joan grew ill at ease as the years passed, for she was slow at everything but gazing. She smiled bright as a star if she was happy, which was always, unless someone was hurt – anyone, sometimes even a fly, or a stick someone stepped on and broke. But she was bewildered.

Well, Johnny, you've met Granny Constance, though she looks different now. She was a lovely girl, lovely in her heart, too; she was the dearest woman to me. But she was – 'simple' isn't the right word; no one's simple, not really. But she thought everyone in the world was beautiful, because she was. And if someone was hurt, she thought she was too, because she had trouble telling the difference between herself and anyone else. And she had trouble understanding things. Think how easily puzzled you'd have to be, not to know you were as beautiful as she was.

Well, Clem and Joan, they fretted and they worked and they coaxed to her face and wept behind her back and blamed themselves and Ab, but they couldn't send Ab away, for it wouldn't go. It wouldn't pass the smithy door, but it popped up when he spoke to neighbours and curled up between him and Joan in their bed like a cat – well, mostly like a cat, although Clem said it could never get the jaws right – and Clem, well, he was a good man, but he wasn't the best at solving tasks outside what he already knew.

Then along came another baby, my Great-Aunt Mabel – Mabbie, they called her. All the time she was carrying Joan wore an iron ring, and Ab didn't trouble her. They warned the midwife, and gave her an iron ring as well, but when Mabel was born, the midwife, who was a foolish woman, took off the ring to wash her hands. And she took off Joan's ring, for Joan's fingers had swollen, as women's fingers will when they're carrying, and the midwife thought it bad for her.

So before they knew what they were about, Mabbie was in the midwife's ironless arms and Ab cried out from somewhere, 'She will have the sweet voice of a bird!'

Well, Joan shrieked for the midwife to fetch Clem at once, for Ab never listened to any soul but him, and Clem covered his face and said to Ab that it was a kind thought, but that he did not understand the tongue of birds and he would like to be able to understand what his daughter had to say, for if she just piped all day life would be full of confusion. And indeed, Mabbie was trying to squall, for she seemed to have something about her face and throat that pained her, but she couldn't cry; she just trilled, a high, clear note to make your ears ring.

So Ab cried out, 'As you ask, my friend! She shall know the tongues of air and earth! What clever fellows are we!' And it jumped up into the air again, and Clem said he thought he saw it shred like spiderwebs in the wind before it vanished, but he couldn't swear to it, as his mind was on other things.

And there they were. Mabbie didn't cry; she peeped. And she grew up with her wits untouched, and she spoke English well enough, but she had an ill temper, for she felt a terrible dislike of dawn. She woke every morn to hear the chorus, and while it sounds sweet enough to the likes of you and me, Johnny, to Mabbie it was all talk and fight, for the song of the birds in her ears was an endless cry of, 'Mine! Mine! Stay far from me or I shall hurt you!' And to wake every day in a world where matters go on so does not give you the best view of life. Mabbie had a beautiful voice to sing with, it's true, but she used it most when she was angry, and she never would join the church choir, not for shyness, but because she said she heard in the notes of the music the most addled thoughts and dirty suggestions and brutal insults you could imagine. I can't blame her for her nature, but she took to a hermit's life in the end, when she grew up, I mean, and it was most likely for the best. She never was the friendly sort.

Clem and Joan were grieved to the heart, and Clem gave Joan talismans a-plenty and the midwife a long piece of his mind. And a year later, there was another baby. That was my Great-Aunt Agnes.

Well, you know Auntie Agnes too, and you know how gentle she is? Well, she was always a dear woman. Clem put horseshoes on the door of the bedroom and pinned a charm to the apron of the midwife and swore he would kick her himself if she took it off, which did not make him much liked in the village, and she wore it all right. But she was so busy watching out for Joan and looking around the room to see if anything fey might have slipped in that she forgot to warm the water, and when she put Agnes in, the girl wailed and thrashed, and one of her little limbs caught the pin and knocked it flying, and so busy was the midwife that she didn't notice. It was only when she wrapped Agnes up and went to carry her out to show her to Clem that Ab appeared and clapped its claws, and cried out, 'She is a mighty one and shall have the strength of a hundred men!'

Well, the midwife was afeared indeed, for now she had to tell Clem what had befallen. But there was no hiding it, for already Agnes was squirming in her arms and wanting to go back to her Mama, and so hard did she push that the midwife dropped her right then and there, and she had bruises on her chest that lasted a fortnight after. She tried to pick her up again, but Agnes was weeping from the fall and knocked her away, and she fell, and in the end there was nothing to do but beg Clem to have a word with Ab, who was a-float over the baby and chuckling with delight at how well it had wrought what it meant for a blessing.

Clem rushed in and saw Agnes, who had not yet found out how to walk and wished very much to get back to her Mama, and was knocking holes in the floorboards trying to make some headway there. He fell to his knees and pleaded with Ab, 'You see what has become of my floor! I beg you, protect us and her from this harm!'

Ab was not one of those who understood that folks don't like to have their things broke, for it was an outdoor spirit by nature and did not see that snapping one twig mattered more than another, but it was pleased by its generosity and said to Clem, 'Harm she shall not nor cannot do!' Then it scuttled out the window and ran up the wall to the roof.

So that was my Great-Aunt Agnes. She was strong, indeed; she's five-and-seventy now and could still wrestle me to the ground.

No, I don't reckon you did know that of her, but it's true, she could, if she was sure she wouldn't hurt me by it. But she needed much care, for Ab had been thorough. She could never hurt anyone, so she could never protect herself; if children in the square teased her she had to stand mute, and if Mabbie smacked her in temper, which I'm sorry to say did happen, Agnes could never hit back, nor even stop her hand. Not so much as a fly could she swat, and she needed someone to cook for her, for she couldn't so much as gut a fish.

Well, Mabbie was ill-tempered, but Constance and Agnes loved each other from the first. Granny – Constance, that is – was a sweet girl, if confused, but she took a lot of caring. She loved Agnes, who couldn't hurt her, and Agnes was a queer-looking girl with great arms and shoulders before she was steady on her feet, and folks looked at her in doubt, if they didn't know her. Those around the village grew used to her, of course, but with strangers coming to the smithy all the time, she had many look at her with a wary eye, and it doesn't make a lass feel welcome in the world if so many folks act shy of her, so she clung to Constance, who saw nothing queer in anyone. Constance saw great beauty in Agnes, and Agnes sorted sense from nonsense for Constance, and they kept each other company and didn't let the other cry. Mabbie was more out of temper than ever, for she said that each of them might as well perch on the other and shout, 'Mine! Mine!' and let the world go hang, and there was no sense in either of them and one day the world would send a cat to eat them both.

And all this time, there was only Clem to work the smithy, and he grew greyer and more tired all the time.

It was two more years before they knew another babe was on the way, and this time, Clem called Ab to him beforehand. He said that what he'd like most was a child left to take its own way, for he was a common man himself and it'd be company for him to have a child born with no more blessings than a baptised soul, and that, the parson could do for them. Ab said it was a fine thought in Clem and if he wished, he should have the commonest child ever seen, and was gathering itself to bless the babe unborn, but Clem at that moment grabbed an iron poker and Ab backed away, all flustered at its edges, and Clem said he begged Ab's pardon but he feared the fire would go out and needed much attention, and Ab's thoughts turned in another direction and the fire in their hearth did not go out for a year and a day and blazed so high that the chimney gave out sparks of white and gold, which was not quite comfortable in summer, as I'm sure you can picture.

Just to make sure, when Joan was near her time, Clem said to Ab that he had a great curiosity to try a fruit grown in the Ethiop fields, and perhaps Ab would fetch him one, and enjoy the sunshine and take his time. Ab took this as a great courtesy, and off it hied, and by the time it was back, Beatrice was born, with an iron chain put round her neck the moment she drew breath, and Ab did not trifle with her.

No, she died some time ago. She married young and moved far from Gyrford as soon as she could, for she wasn't . . . well, once Corbie Mackem was in the family, she wished to leave Gyrford. She didn't live long, I'm afraid; she married a man who wouldn't go for the midwife when she was bearing her first child, and that was the end of her. The baby lived, though not with her father; she went to live with the Fabers. Your Cousin Letty is Beatrice's granddaughter – you remember Letty?

Yes, Ab did bring a fruit. A loamy, it called it, something like that. It was yellow as a daffodil and smelled as fresh, and it looked very fine, but inside it tasted sharp like vinegar. I suppose Ab had not thought to pick a ripe one, or else it had odd ideas of how to make it to a mortal man's taste – it was in slices inside like a cut cake, so my guess is it tampered with the fruit on the journey.

Yes, it could be they like different things among the Ethiops, but I can't think they'd like to eat a whole sour fruit as big as a pear. I've heard it's a grand country, and I don't see how it could be if all its folks carried on like that.

For a while, things went on. There were four daughters to fret over and Joan and Clem were like folks running ahead of the rain, and before you knew it there was another babe on the way. Clem and Joan agreed that the family had enough of fairy blessings, but they still needed a son to 'prentice. Clem said to Ab he was so well pleased with Beatrice that he'd like another child untouched, and what would be a very great favour would be to fetch some fruit from the moon.

I don't know what Ab was about that time, for it brought nothing but ash, which poor Clem had to eat and make Ab think he was glad to do it. Perhaps it was easier for Ab to run up a moonbeam than it was for it to run across the earth, and that caused trouble, for it was back with the ash when Joan still had the babe within her, so Clem called the midwife – yes, the stupid one, may she rest in peace. He had to, Johnny, none of the other midwives would come.

So there they were. Joan needed a midwife with her lest she should die, for some of the other births had gone hard with her. So Clem went to the midwife again, and he told her plain that this time she must wear iron bracelets on her wrists and iron bands around her ankles, and she should wash the sheets in quench-water, and iron the babe the very second she saw it, and for good measure he nailed horse-shoes around the bedroom doorway and window – yes, those same ones that your mama painted pretty colours. So when the babe was to come, there was no way for Ab to take to get in to bless it. It might try later, Clem thought, but by then he could speak to Ab and tell it how perfect the babe was, how it couldn't be changed but for the worse.

Oh yes, it worked. Aunt Pell was born and ironed and mortal as anything. Petronilla, they called her, but having given her such a long name, they found that with running after all their children, they never had time to say it full. She was always fond of Grandpa, and kind to me too, in her way. She liked to say she'd seen enough of the trouble marriage caused and wanted none of it herself, and we were what she had for children.

So there was Pell, with her little iron chain around her neck, and Clem, having seen her safe and kissed Joan and made sure all was well, headed back to the smithy. But as he stepped into the square, he found someone there, or rather, a great whirl of pieces of someones: a monstrous ball of wind dashing itself against the cobbles and smashing off walls, and within it were the sharp stings of crow-feathers and the sharp fangs of spiders and the sharp spines of salamanders and the sharp blades of thistles, and it howled with a great shrieking fury that was heard seven miles away, and it lashed all around Clem, crying out, 'Trickster friends have ye, have ye, and Ab has failed to keep ye free!' It was weeping in rage, weeping great shining drops that spattered across the square and shone a day and a night after, a cold light like the winter moon, and folks who saw those drops felt their hearts sink and went home to rail at those they loved best; over what, they never could say.

'Now, now, Ab,' said Clem, but before he could say anything else, Ab screamed, 'Free from enemies I'll make ye—!'

And it was gone. Not with a bang, or a blaze of light, but just gone, the sudden silence sharp enough to set you reeling.

And for a week and a day there was nothing; things went on as they went on . . . until they saw a mist come rolling down from the north, tumbling over itself as if it kept tripping on its own skirts, faster and faster. It was upon Gyrford within a few hours, and they say it tasted of cold honey, sweet on the tongue and choking to the throat.

It was beautiful, but something walked in it.

You could glimpse it from a distance, walking slow. Folks thought it might be a carthorse, at first, but it had no ears atop its round green head, and its legs weren't made for trotting or cantering; they curled, as if kneading the air, and at the end of each limb was a great hand. And its coat, great locks as thick as your fist, swayed to and fro, but too slow for its gait, a swish and swing that almost made your eyes cross.

You've never seen a drowie, Johnny, and that's no bad thing. Yes, I can tell you what I know of them, but whether there's

People who are always drowies, or it's just a form they sometimes take, no one's got close enough to find out – or at least, if he has, he hasn't lived to explain himself. But a drowie's a terrible thing, Johnny. It's pretty girls they like, and children, and midwives especially: they like the spring of life, and those who bring it. And that's what Ab chose to be that day. Clem reckoned it had gone north to find a true drowie, to learn from it how to be one itself, and it did a thorough job. When folks went inside to escape that uncanny mist, they found their skins wet, but it wasn't sweet any more. Ab's mist smelled of blood and womb-water and the other stuffs that go into making life, and life's a blessing, Johnny, but it's not a smell you want raw on your skin.

Ab walked slow, grasping the mist with its paws, feeling it out like a tailor feels cloth. It had forgotten to give itself eyes and its long head never turned from one side to the other.

The midwife's house was not far from the middle of the village. Ab walked its mist right up to the place and stood outside, while that poor silly woman closed up her windows and prayed, and Clem ran out with iron-tipped arrows and fired at Ab, but the mist set his aim askew. It stood still out there, its great locks swinging to and fro, and though you'd think it'd be hard to miss so great a creature, none of Clem's arrows went home.

Ab leaned down and put its mouth to a crack in her window, and it sucked out the air. It had a mouth like a girl's, Clem said, sweet pink lips stark against the pond-green of its skin, and it sucked and sucked until the midwife had nothing to breathe.

All the time, Clem was firing and missing, and before he

could think of aught else to do, she had run to another window, and for all Clem shrieked out that she should keep it closed tight, she was choking for lack of air, and you will remember, she wasn't a clever woman.

Yes, that's just what she did, Johnny: she opened the window, just a crack, but it was enough for Ab to peel it open with the lightest of touches, and it reached in and picked her up and clutched her to its heart, before at last it turned and padded away.

Clem ran after it with an arrow in his hand for a dagger, and he stabbed at its foreleg, the one that wasn't holding the midwife, and Ab shuddered all over, and it gave a howl that was like the howl of a woman in childbirth, so they tell me, a sweet voice wrenched and racked, and it turned and *stamped* . . . It was still holding that poor woman close, dandling her and stroking her, and as it did so, her body cracked in its grip, and at last, it went on its way.

And then it was gone.

Outside, there was still the mist, but some of the braver folks ran from their houses to see what had become of Clem, who was lying there, his arrow in his hand, with his leg crushed like a cherry all across the cobbles.

Well, there was nothing to do but cut it off, what was left of it. Agnes carried him in – she was five then, and well up to his weight, and Constance, who was nine, cried and cried and clawed her own legs, and Mabbie carried little Beatrice out of the way and slapped Constance for crying. Joan was upstairs with the newest babe, Pell, still not quite on her feet.

No, you're right. Clem was never quite on his feet again.

It's a hard enough life for a farrier, Johnny, and Clem worked as well as he could, but you know, there's always fetching and carrying to do, and an anvil to stand over, and some People it's best to run away from, and Clem was growing a haggard man. Of course, there's one-legged farriers who do all right, for the skill in the hands and wits in the head need no leg to make them work, but they will need some help about the place, and after the business of the Ab-drowie, Clem found his neighbours not inclined. He had five daughters and a wife to feed and no 'prentice nor journeyman – and there was Ab, who was sure as sure that it was Clem's best beloved friend who had done him such a good favour by ridding him of the midwife it had overheard him lament for a stupid woman.

What could Clem do? To iron Ab, he'd have had to be quick on his feet or quicker with his wits than he was, poor man. The most he could think to do was to tell Ab that he'd enough daughters and would like no more, and Ab said that as its dear friend liked, so should it be. It was a desperate thing to do, but he needed a son, and as Aunt Pell says, if you expect folks not to try wild things when it comes to childbearing you'll only be disappointed in mankind.

When, two years later, Clem asked Ab why there were no sons, it explained, so pleased with itself, 'Why, dear friend, you told me, on that first delicious day, so tasty a day, my dear friend, how it is better when the girls are happy. So the girls are happy and all is better. What best of friends are we!'

And that was the end of all their child-bearing, for Ab had, that first day, given Clem its first favour: he would have only girls to father. He had five daughters and one leg, and that was his lot in life.

No, Ab didn't fret about the loss of Clem's leg. Ab added and took limbs from itself all the time, so it reckoned that if Clem hopped on a crutch now, it must be because he liked to wear his legs that way. Clem had a hard enough time keeping it persuaded that there was no need to tack on some fins or feathers to his skin just to give him variety.

Folks said the Smiths were an unlucky line – no need to huff, remember, this was before Grandpa's time – and it was soon clear there'd be no heir to the smithy. Clem wouldn't complain, and Joan hated to see him suffer and quarrelled with him for bearing it so patiently. But his back pained him now, and when he woke in the mornings he was frozen to the bed, quite unable to bend, and the hammer strokes on the anvil must have rung his backbone like a bell.

After ten years Clem finally relented and agreed with Joan that he needed help. And since there'd be no son of his own getting, there was only one other choice.

Mind, there weren't so many lads to choose from, back then. There'd been some marrying between the Smiths and the Fabers three generations or so back, and he thought that too soon to try it again, for it's good to keep a mix of things going when it comes to blood – well, you've seen overbred horses, haven't you? And the Gowans had no one of an age for the Smith girls, no men under forty or boys over twelve.

But the Mackems had three boys. The eldest was married

already, with a babe on the way, and he and the next eldest were the best of friends and liked to work together, but the youngest, Corbie, was seventeen and said to like the girls, and his father reckoned that to get him settled in his own place with his own woman would be good for him.

So he married Constance, the eldest and the fairest of the daughters. He was told she wasn't clever – although I'm not sure that was the right way to describe her – but he just laughed, for at least that way, he said, it'd be easy for him to win when they quarrelled.

Well, when Ab knew Clem had a son-in-law coming it offered all sorts, about how it could keep him true to Constance and be sure he didn't wander, and when Clem thought of how it might bring that about, he could only cross his legs and pray and tell Ab that instead he had a yearning to taste fruit from the depths of the sea, and then he had to eat what Ab brought and so he was quite sick when Corbie arrived, for whatever grows in the depths of the sea, it isn't what we'd call fruit trees.

But the wedding went ahead. Agnes begged that she be allowed to stay after they were married, for she said she could help around the house. Yes, Clem and Joan and their daughters moved out, just as when you marry one day, if you would rather have this house to yourself, Mama and I would leave for you. Yes, Grandpa could have done so when I married Mama, only we thought we'd like to have him live with us instead, and none of us regrets the choice, for you see how happy we are together. You can decide for yourself nearer the time; you mightn't like us under your feet so much when you're a man.

Well, Corbie, he laughed and said he would gladly take two

women for the price of one if she liked, and Agnes thought she didn't quite like him, but for that reason she felt the more that she'd better stay by Constance. Well, Dada doesn't talk of it much, and it's best not to ask Granny Constance herself, for it upsets her. I think she was willing to be married, for Corbie paid her compliments and gave her kisses, and she was a woman grown and she liked that.

But Dada doesn't talk of it much, so all I know is fourth-hand. But the women told your mama that for a year or so, all was well enough and Constance was quite cheerful. But then she had Grandpa.

I may be no midwife, but there's only one way to bring a baby into the world and it's never an easy one on women. But after that, if Corbie ever tried to touch her, she screamed and screamed until he went away.

Well, you know how babies are made, and she couldn't bear the thought of having another. Corbie wasn't pleased with her after that. I don't know that he cared so much about having more children – he had the son and heir, and while children can die, your grandpa was always healthy, thanks be to God – but . . . well, he didn't marry Constance because he loved her, and I don't think he was a man who liked women around just for their company. Yes, I do, don't you? It's a pleasant thing to come into the house and hear your mother and sisters chattering away; there's nothing more cheering than a happy woman. But I don't think Corbie was good to his wife. That's an ill thing, Johnny: a man who won't be kind to his wife is no man at all, though it's true not all folks think that way.

What folks did care for was that he was a fine farrier, finer than Clem by far, peace to Clem's memory, and folks around here were just glad to have a man hold the forge who knew what he was about.

And young Corbie, he had an idea of how to rid Gyrford of Ab.

Clem had been harried by Ab all these years and he didn't dare try to iron it, for when the People turn against those who betray them, it's not a thing you want to see. But Corbie went up to the grave of Elder Samuel – both graves, in fact, the place in the churchyard where he lay now, and the place at the crossroads where he'd lain with Ab. He dug up bones from the first and earth from the other, and he ground them into the charcoal. He hunted down a crow and plucked the feathers from it living – yes, it really was alive, poor thing – and . . . do you want to hear this? All right, I'll be quick: there was a set of spider legs, and yes, the poor spider was alive too.

Ah, well remembered, my man: it was indeed a crow, a spider and a woman Ab had tested Clem with.

No, he didn't flay a woman alive; Corbie was not quite that formidable – but he did find a girl in a village beyond Gyrford who had hair as black as crow wings, and he spoke her so fair that she let him pluck some of the hair off her living head, tug it out by the roots, a whole long hank of it, and he trimmed her nails as well and kept the trimmings, and some say he visited her so often that in the end she let him razor away a little slice of her skin. Then he mixed up these things, Ab's shapes and the pieces from where Ab had lain, and with them all in the fire, he forged a new stake.

This one wasn't for spearing; it was a great needle, with a chain at the end, though not a common chain; it had flat links, and he called it a jess, like you'd put on a hawk.

Then he made Mabbie come out with him.

No, Mabbie didn't wish to go. She was out of temper with the whole business; she said Constance might as well have been married to a crowing cockerel, for he had nothing to say that wasn't a cry atop a dung heap.

She went with him, even though she didn't like him. He was married to her sister, after all. If a man's not kind to his wife, and you love that wife, you don't want to put him out of temper.

So he took Mabbie with him, and he watched the crows around the place, and he made her tell him what they said.

So when one day Ab came to Clem, when Clem sat outside his smithy, with a pipe to smoke and a weary look upon his face, Ab asked if he would like a bed of phoenix feathers to sleep upon, thinking, I suppose, that as Clem spent his days around hot coals he might like to sleep upon flames as well. Clem said no, he was tired of the world, for midges bit the horses and the snakes abandoned their young and the cats beat the mice from paw to paw for sport and yet the mice never rose against them, and it seemed to him that there was nothing, bird nor beast, that had any feeling of justice. If he could just see one proof of it, he said, he could endure the world, but there was no proof and he was beset with sorrow.

Of course Ab believed him at once, for this is the kind of tale the People understand. Ab said it would fly around the world to find him justice, be it the elegant slime-fish that winked their coloured stars in the deep, or the sailing spiders that scudded through the sky on white silk, and Clem said thank you very much, and while Ab was at it, perhaps it could fetch him some bread from the baker in Middle Latchton, for he liked that bread better than the Gyrford stuff.

Off Ab went.

And after him, down the road, went Clem – slower, but he went.

Ab came to a field and there, in its midst, was a great gathering, the green speckled with black and the trees full, for all the crows of the country had, it seemed, come to pay tribute. There in the middle was a dead crow, and it was dead badly, Johnny: its head was off and stuffed into its belly, which was slit open, I'm sorry to say. Corbie Mackem had a strong stomach.

Mabbie sat beside the crow, singing a hard bird-sob, lamenting the fallen one.

The crows sat around, watching as she mourned.

You've heard tell that crows hold funerals, of course. They gather around a dead kinsman – yes, kinscrow, I suppose. At any rate, Mabbie had never had patience with such tales. She said that the crows thought of their future, not their past, and what they did when they gathered was not to bewail, but consider. They wish to know what killed the dead one, so they can avoid such a fate themselves. It's not a funeral they hold, she said, but an inquest.

But Mabbie sat and wept in song, and above her there flew, of a sudden, a great black creature with the wings of a raven and the face of a man, all crumpled up and glowing red as a firethorn berry, with a nose of flesh that snapped open and shut like a beak.

Ab asked in the voice of a crow, which Mabbie understood quite well, what had done this wicked deed? And when they heard the question, the crows all took it up, crying, *What? What? What?*

And down the road, a little out of breath for he'd had to hurry, came Clem.

Mabbie raised her hand and pointed, and, doing as Corbie had bid her, said that it was that man there, and she feared his cruelty and what was she to do?

Ab saw her pointing, and she pointed at Clem – and so did the crows, and at that moment, they all hurled themselves down from the branches like living spears, swooping and scolding at Clem, snatching at his hair and diving at his eyes, and if Corbie hadn't given him an iron mask to put on to shield his face, it might have been an ill day for him. The crows rose and mobbed him, and Ab rose up crying, 'There is justice in the crows of the air! There is justice in the crows of the air!'

And then it dived dagger-beaked at Clem, for it was very angry with him, though not, I think, because it felt tricked him seeming to be kind all these years; Ab's memory was much possessed by whatever thought it had last. It was so pleased with the justice of crows that that pleasedness took hold of its mind and it decided that they were in the right of it, that it would have nothing more to do with the wicked man who had wronged them.

So that was a beginning, but Corbie did more than that.

★

All right, Johnny, for this next part, I must ask your trust. Well, thank you, but you won't like this, for I shan't tell you where Corbie did his next work.

Because, darling lad, I'm afraid you would wish to go and look at it, and even if you did mean no harm, well, everyone makes mistakes.

No, I don't mean to bring up that time with the brambles, but you're a young lad still, and an apprentice, and this is master-work. When you're a master farrier – no, not a journeyman, but when you're a master, then we can talk of this again.

No, Johnny, truly, don't beg me. I can tell this tale or I can not tell this tale, but if you will not accept this one thing, we'll have to stop. I will make you this promise: I'll tell you where the place is when you're one-and-twenty, and I'll take you to see it – but I'll only do that if you never ask where it is, and never, ever try to find it on your own. If you do – and in particular, if you try to find it on your own – then the knowledge will die with me.

Yes, it does sound like something Grandpa would say, and that's because he made me promise to say these words if I ever told you this tale. Of course he trusts you, but – look you, Johnny, this is master-work and there's things you have yet to learn before you can do everything. You're a clever boy, but you're a boy still, and that's that.

Thank you. Let me have a smile?

All right, it's your own face and I won't order you to smile if you can't. I don't think it's a lie to smile just for manners' sake, at least with customers, and I'm not so sure as you that the parson would second your view of things, but I won't force you.

★

Here's what Corbie did next. He had spent weeks training the crows – of course, you can't man a crow the way you can a hawk, but you can teach them where they can find good things, and Corbie had taken the time to teach them that there were good things to eat in the hollow of a certain tree.

Well, I say Corbie taught them – it was his idea, but he made Mabbie do the training. He said he was a busy fellow, and no doubt he was.

After Ab joined the crows that day, they went as usual to gather treats from within the tree, and Ab went with them. And there Corbie waited atop the tree, his face masked so the crows would not know him. They carry grudges, do crows, and they remember faces. He waited until they'd all hopped inside the tree, the crows ahead of Ab, and then Ab itself.

Then he threw an iron plate over the hollow. It was a deep hole in the trunk, big enough to hold the crows, and the plate covered it completely. Then Corbie took a chain and he sewed it shut, dragged it through holes he'd drilled the day before, and stuffed them with moss and sawdust so the crows wouldn't see them.

Since that day he sewed Ab into the tree with an iron chain, Ab has never troubled us, Smith or Mackem. Only the harms done stayed with us, and those we just had to live with.

Yes, the crows went in too. I suppose they famished in the end, poor things.

So this is how Corbie Mackem became elder farrier of Gyrford, for he rid it of a problem that had plagued it for two decades, and he reckoned if after that the Smith family didn't think him the best fellow that ever lived, it wasn't his fault.

No, I'm sorry to say that they didn't. Dada doesn't talk much of his father; I don't think they got along too well. No, I don't suppose Dada was a dislikeable little boy; Godfa Tom said he was excellent company when he was young, for he was gamesome and clever, and bold enough to play at anything, and fond of any who were good to him, and that sounds like a boy any father would be pleased with, don't you think? He doesn't sound so different from you, in those ways at least.

No, I wasn't like that, for I was given to fretting, but I was lucky, for Dada was a kind father even when I went shy. But Dada, as a boy – well, he was fond of his mama, that's only natural, and Corbie Mackem wasn't too pleased with her as a wife, and that's not an easy way to live together.

Look you, there's a little more to the tale. There's a reason we lay Clementing wreaths on Clem's grave, and his dada's, and his dada's before him, but not on Corbie's. It isn't that he was buried with his own clan in Tinsdowne.

The truth is, we don't know where he lies. Not even his bones.

Dada grew up and learned his trade, and Ab stayed pent. But about the time he married Mama, there was a visit from the Mackem cousins, who came to the wedding, and while they were there, they quarrelled with Corbie. No, I don't know why, but there's some who say that around the time Dada and Mama wed, there were many crows in the sky. It's just talk, though. Mostly they told it as a pretty tale, for Mama was well-liked, and she had raven-black hair, so they liked to imagine the birds loved her for that. But really, it was just because she was fond of birds and beasts, and she'd always throw scraps out of the door for the crows, so of course they liked her. I remember we watched them together when I was little. Oh, your Granny was a lovely woman, Johnny. I wish you'd known her.

Well, now, Corbie didn't go to the wedding. Aunt Pell says that he wasn't well, which was a pity, but after that, he chose to leave Gyrford. He'd never been quite at ease here; he was a Tinsdowne man and perhaps he couldn't change his heart as to that. He went off to travel, they say, and there are tales told of his adventures, but Grandpa reckons they're mostly made up, or else folks hear this or that old story, like the Smith and the Oak-Eyed Giant or Tom-o'Catskin, and retell it using Corbie's name for the bold man, the way folks will. There's nothing to be sure of.

Yes, Corbie and the Little Fox is one of those; we've no reason to suppose it was truly Corbie who did that. Mind, I don't think anyone did; it never did ring true to me.

Well, Joseph Brawton says a great many things are true, but that doesn't mean they are.

Yes, Corbie and the Eight-Mouthed Maiden is another such, but I'd like to know who told you such a dirty story.

All right, never mind, but do you always remember that it's only rogues and swaggerers who cheapen women, and very young lads who think it'll make them look big.

But to return to the tale: no one heard from Corbie himself after the wedding. Dada thought he must stop in sometimes in Tinsdowne, and the Mackems thought he must stop in sometimes in Gyrford. And the Mackems don't read or write, not a one of them, so they couldn't send letters. Dada did send letters to Tinsdowne, hoping Corbie'd go by sometimes and find someone to read them to him, but he never had a reply.

So Dada became elder when he was a young man, and he held the forge well. He was married to Mama, and they had me, and nothing tried to gift me in my cradle. They didn't have other children, but I don't think that was anything fey, just one of those things that happens or doesn't happen as God wills. A pity, for I'd have liked brothers and sisters, but then I had Franklin, and no brother could have been kinder to me, so I was lucky, truly.

But then Mama died, you see, and Dada wrote to Corbie at Tinsdowne forge, and someone read the letter to Old Dunstan Mackem, Dada's uncle, he was elder farrier at the time. And he came to see Dada, and to visit Mama's grave and pay respects . . . well, it was a hard time, Johnny, I won't say it wasn't. I was only little, but I remember it. There was some talk of sending me to Tinsdowne, or to some other farrier clan with a farrier's lady still there to look after me, but I wanted to stay with Dada and Dada wouldn't part with me, so there were many visits from different clans.

No, I don't think I was such a perfect lad they all wanted to steal me away – that is, I was well enough, I suppose, but it was more that folks don't trust a lone man to bring up a child and Dada had no mind to remarry, and they all thought I needed a mother. Well, I wanted *my* mother, but she was gone, and after that I just wanted my father.

But the point is, there were many visits and talks, and from what was said, nobody had seen Corbie Mackem since the day his son married.

Yes, that's right: he walked down the road and was gone. Dada thinks he just went off somewhere; he was ever a restless man. But he won't be alive now, I reckon; he was – let's see . . . Corbie was only eighteen when Dada was born – well, it seems young to me; I was one-and-twenty when we had Molly, and I didn't feel so old myself – in any case, Corbie would be eight-and-seventy now, and if he is still alive I don't suppose he'd like to travel.

So I never knew my grandpa on Dada's side, only Granny Constance and Auntie Agnes. And Aunt Pell, of course; she trained your mama in midwifery. She's a wise woman – yes, she *is* wise. I know she thinks all men are foolish, but a midwife sees enough silliness from men that you can't blame her if she forms some views, and truly, Johnny, we are all silly sometimes. It only causes trouble to think we aren't.

And on that thought: Ab rests within a tree which you have promised you will *not* hunt down, and that is something you must remember. Farrier's promise, Johnny.

And Corbie rests somewhere, we know not where. And Granny Constance and Auntie Agnes are the way they are, and . . . well, we're well enough now. But if you have more questions, do you ask me, not Grandpa. He'd tell you, but it wasn't the easiest time for him.

Never fear, though. They say Corbie Mackem was a fine fairy-smith. There's no reason to suppose Ab would ever come back.

BOOK TWO

ANTHONY

There is a tradition among fairy-smiths: every November the twenty-third, they celebrate Saint Clement's day, remembering bygone ancestors who hopefully lie at peace in their graves. There is nothing in the tradition, unfortunately, about what you should do if it turns out they weren't doing any such thing.

It was late in October when the pig grew leaves, shook itself into verse and went on the rampage, and on that day, all John Smith meant to do was bring his cousin to the midwife. Many things in life were John's fault, but this really wasn't one of them.

Clementing was one of the great festivals in the village of Gyrford – any working village can boast a smithy, but few can boast a clan of fairy-smiths – and Saint Clement, the patron saint of metalworkers, was celebrated with enthusiasm. Apparently the sanctified namesake wasn't a smith himself; he had got himself drowned tied to an anchor, so why this had given him a liking for the smiths who forged such things, Jedediah couldn't say – and of course, his grandson

John had asked him; John was prone to impossible questions like that.

Jedediah had held the forge since the age of one-and-twenty, and he was the law in those parts when it came to fairy-smithing – but when it came to doctrine, he had no idea why life must be as it was. John thought – rather hopefully, it seemed to Jedediah – that the People under the sea might be so very fearsome that it was better for Clement to die with cold iron holding them at bay, but Jedediah's best guess was that Clement was one of those saints who went around forgiving everyone for everything. Though if that were the case, he was probably more Matthew's sort than Jedediah's. Matthew Smith had grown up as tall as a steeple, as burly as a bull and as gentle as a lamb; he was a man who felt the world to be a good place under the eye of a kindly God. Jedediah loved his son with all his heart, protected him with the sternest advice he could muster and didn't like to disabuse him of any notion so comforting.

And it was true that both John and Matthew enjoyed Clementing. At sunset you tested your anvils with little blasts of gunpowder, which produced satisfying showers of light for everyone to enjoy. John loved the bonfire feast too, with the roasted pig and everyone singing and eating cake, and if nobody was watching, his elder sisters might slip him a little bit of cider, as long as he asked Celdie and Vevie rather than Molly. The supper was always good; the pig came from the Lenden farm, and they kept the tastiest beasts in the county, and if Janet Smith was an indifferent housekeeper in most respects, she was fond enough of cakes to bake a good one. But the part of the celebration John liked best was the wreathing of the forebears' graves.

This was the private part of the day: you rose before sunrise on the twenty-third of every November and adorned the graves in the dark. Matthew loved it because he felt it was like surprising the village with a gift. For Jedediah, the deepest of farrier work was done in privacy, and walking through the starlit lanes with his family on those cold mornings, John's hand keeping warm in his own, he relax in the chilly hush and make some remarks to the effect that John had learned well this past year, that Matthew was a good man, that if the forebears had any objection to the work of the last year, then they would be an ungrateful set of fellows, which his grandfather Clem Smith, at least, was not.

(His father, Corbie Mackem, he never mentioned.)

And John loved it because there was nothing so festive as slipping out silent under a berry-dark sky, the night crackling cold around you and no one to stop you when you stared. The bushes burst with sound as they passed – a little flaming rustle of hedgehog scuttling its bristles beneath the leaves as it raced out of their way, the shrieks of foxes cutting across the dark, and by the time they reached the graveyard, John could never remember that he was cold.

The purpose of the visit was to mark the grass beneath which slept fairy-smiths of generations past. Like every farrier clan, the Smiths laid wreaths of wrought-iron flowers hammered fine as leaves. You laid down your skill, and the bones knew they could rest in peace. Farriers wrestled with the unkenned all their lives; they ran alongside the People from childhood, sometimes befriending, sometimes negotiating, sometimes fighting, but whatever course they took, it could be guided by the iron rule that mortal folks must be protected from the People. It wasn't fair for anyone to be overborne by those who could lay a lifelong curse, build castles in a night or turn your toes into carrots and root you to the earth. Iron kept the People at bay, and a farrier's grave with an iron wreath was a place of peace, within which the dust of those long gone could rest in the knowledge that those above still kept up the trade.

Exactly what might happen if this wasn't done was unclear; Jedediah told his descendants with brusque reassurance that the answer was probably nothing, except that other farrier clans would judge you, and they'd be right to do so. And, Matthew assured John that the forebears in the graveyard were doubtless good men whose souls were in Heaven and whose bodies were mostly gone. After all, Matthew added, he felt no desire to haunt any great-great-grandchildren he might have himself; on the contrary, he dearly wished them well. Family was family, wasn't it?

(Of course, what you might expect from those who didn't lie in family earth was another question. Corbie Mackem's body had never been found, or at least, not by any in Gyrford. But then, most men preferred their grave to be a final kind of going-home, and whatever Gyrford was to Corbie, a home was not what he made of it.)

For the village of Gyrford, however, it was the feast in the evening they remembered, and there was plenty of enthusiasm for the coming one – most of it, since Jedediah lived to provide good work, secret charity and unsweetened advice in about equal proportions, directed at Matthew. So that morning, Matthew had taken his son and knocked on Anthony Brady's door.

★

Matthew, at eight-and-thirty, was an honest man who examined his conscience with anxious care, addressed everyone from children to elders with tender courtesy, and was frequently mistaken by strangers for a fearsome, brooding hulk of manhood – something that can happen to very big men who get tongue-tied in the face of conflict. Those who knew him, though, found him patient and helpful under the shyness, and with Clementing coming, had been dropping in at all hours to contribute delicacies. This was something Matthew wished to enjoy – he loved the thought of so many generous neighbours – but there was a certain competition as to whose cheeses, pickles and preserved fruits would best honour the day. Matthew's Janet was in charge of the foodstuffs, and she enjoyed praising the most disputatious donors in each other's presence so they could concentrate on vying with each other, leaving their more amiable neighbours alone, while John would taste whatever he could and give frank opinions as to which he liked best, but Matthew had no spirit for such contests. Anthony Brady, who was very mild company, was a welcome change.

'That's most kind of you, Cousin Matthew,' Anthony said at the invitation, his face lighting up with the surprised pleasure it still showed at finding himself welcomed by anyone in Gyrford; he had grown up wealthy and secluded, and only recently had the Smiths been able to introduce him properly to the community and advise him as to the most charitable use of his funds. 'And Cousin John, too; I'll be glad of your company, I'm sure.'

The three of them set out at a good pace – officially to visit Pell Smith and consult her midwifery, but mostly just as an excuse to take a friendly walk. John felt himself rather too old to hold his father's hand, so Matthew, needing some outlet for his goodwill, clapped Anthony on the back instead.

Anthony and Matthew had only really got to know each other in the past couple of years, and they weren't strictly cousins. Anthony had married Francie Thorpe, the daughter of Matthew's best friend Franklin, and Franklin, while not exactly a Smith, had lived under Jedediah's unofficial protection for as long as anyone could remember. Even now, as a middle-aged forester who held at least as much authority as Jedediah – more, if you counted the opinions of the high and mighty, though most common folk didn't – Franklin was devoted to Mister Smith and honoured him to a degree Jedediah found slightly embarrassing. Franklin was family, so now Anthony was, and the Smiths called him 'Cousin' because he loved it when they did.

The three of them set off on foot, Anthony striving to keep pace with Matthew's long stride while John trotted beside them with all the energy of a twelve-year-old boy getting a few hours off work. It was a soft October morning, little skeins of mist tracing themselves around the edges of the hills and tangling in the hedgerows; at the corners of the fields, little white waves roiled to and fro, as if huddled upon a tiny shore.

John tried to feel it in the air, this white texture: with the mist still not quite burned off by the risen sun, it should have been cool and damp to the skin. But the air was crisp, a clean, wood-smoke cool, all quiet earth and bonfires and not a scent of rain anywhere. Matthew was clearly enjoying the weather: he took off his cap and shook his hair back, a habit of his on dry days that John rather envied, for being possessed of his mother's curls, it didn't shake out very much; he felt that straighter hair might act more like a cat's whiskers and bring new tingles of texture to his waiting scalp. But the mist peeled back around their boots, creeping away from their iron hobnails, and there was something about today that was not quite itself, and John couldn't stop paying attention.

He would have liked to say something, but the trouble was that John was widely regarded as a little touched. His mother had had a run-in with the People around the time he was conceived, and while she was mostly all right (as long as you didn't mind her sewing thread turning into bristling brambles), John had a way of becoming what his family called 'starey'. It was a private habit, or it should have been: Matthew had been making an attempt to interest himself in what John saw, but he never quite got the point when John tried to explain, and it was embarrassing to be caught gazing when nobody could understand why you were so very certain of something, even when you didn't know what that something was. If he mentioned it to Dada now, Dada would just ask a lot of questions, and Cousin Anthony would look politely uncomfortable, and in all the talking he wouldn't be able to pay attention to the mist. So John held his tongue, determined not to talk about it until he had to. He liked to stare, but he didn't at all like to be stared at.

So when his Aunt Pell came into view, her walking-stick clouting the earth with every step as if to remind it of its manners, he was almost relieved. Pell could be relied upon to command everyone's attention.

'Matthew, boy, there you are,' she said, addressing her great-nephew with brisk authority. This authority was directed upwards: she couldn't ever have been more than moderate-sized even as a young woman, and as an old one she had the tight density of a nut. Hair forthrightly white, skin weathered, Pell stood firm on her one remaining foot; a treetop hare had taken off one of her legs a few years ago, but she mastered her walking-stick with the same forceful spirit that leads some men to taking pride in their mastery of mettlesome horses. 'And I see you have your new cousin with you once again. Anthony Brady, I'll tell you plain: that wife of yours is a healthy woman, and she bore her first babe without trouble, so the second will come easier. All she needs is a husband who keeps his head so she doesn't have to hold it on his neck while she's busy holding up her own, and her baby's too. Go and trouble Matthew's Janet with your questions; she's been Gyrford's midwife long enough.'

Pell had never married, and was frank that she had thus spared herself a world of trouble. John felt her views on men quite unfair, but Matthew put a lulling hand on his shoulder before he could attempt any justice on behalf of his sex.

'Good day to you, Aunt Pell,' he said. Every Smith called her Aunt; Pell had no patience with longer titles. 'It's Janet sent us. She has dried raspberry leaves in store, but she swears your preparation is better, and with Francie such a favourite she hoped you might let us have some.' This was more tact than truth – Anthony was a worrier when it came to Francie's health and was soothed by second opinions – but Matthew's normally active conscience was quiet. Janet was an adoring wife with a fierce passion for her family and very little regard for the truth when it came to protecting them, and she would retroactively justify more or less any lie he told in her name.

'Never you mind that, lad,' Pell said, a certain amusement in the twist of her mouth. 'I'm too old to flatter, and when I wasn't too old, I had better sense. Save the honeying for your wife, if she wants it.'

'She does,' John said helpfully. 'She kisses him when he says things to her, and I think they oughtn't do it in the kitchen.'

'You and your views again, is it, young John?' she said, not without friendliness. 'Still up to your ways, I see.'

'I'm always up to my ways,' John objected. 'So's everyone. If they're up to it, it's their way, and if it's their way, of course they're up to it.'

Pell's grinning teeth were still white and strong. 'Good for you,' she said. 'Keep your wits awake, that's it. Now, did you just come to test an old woman's patience with lies about my raspberry-leaf brews – which the impudent Janet found fault with only last month, my boy – or is there aught I can do for you?'

'Anthony's a little troubled, that's all,' Matthew said, abiding Pell's '*Tcha!*', 'and Janet thought you might be the one to set his mind at ease.' This was another polite pretence: Anthony had great respect for Janet's opinion. He just always appreciated reassurance on all sides. 'You know the trouble Robbie Marsh has with his dogs?' Matthew went on.

Robbie Marsh herded his flock near Hawton Down, and the place was a problem. In Jedediah's younger days, the stone circle that crowned the mild slopes had become wolves at night, raising their sarsen snouts and howling to the icy sky, and heaven help any who heard them. Now they were tamed, you might say: a chalk wolf had been carved upon the facing hill and the stones had stopped wandering about. They weren't entirely still, though; they murmured under the moon, drank down any rain that fell upon them or wine poured into their crevices, and even after the wettest night, you could touch the top of any stone wolf and find it dry.

Such things had a way of affecting the land around. Robbie Marsh was a good shepherd, but every sheepdog he owned had ended up herding other things in its spare time. Sometimes it was chicks or goslings, the way sheepdog puppies do, but Brindle had herded them before they were hatched, the eggs spinning on their ends like tops and dancing across the yard in perfect order, while Pawsy had herded cats – actual *cats* – and worst of all, Steady had herded rain. She drove a shirring flood of drops in tight formation until they ran up against a wall, where they all collapsed at once, flooding an empty bin, but Steady, who was not a dog to abandon a job half-done, leaped in after them and drowned.

Blackie was still all right, and the Smiths had finally contrived an iron-studded collar that a dog couldn't worry off – for all dogs near Hawton Down all had a dislike of the collar and leash – but it was well known that a pregnant woman who brushed up against the fey could expect some of their eeriness to smudge off on the unborn child, and Blackie, last market day, had licked Francie's face. Janet Smith knew about the risks better than anyone; her own mistake with the People had been small, but John himself was – well, as Pell might put it, he had *ways*.

Pell favoured Janet and was ferocious against anyone who disrespected her. 'Never tell me your wife couldn't have answered that question,' she told Matthew; evidently addressing Anthony was beneath her, and it must be admitted that Anthony, underslept as only a new father could be, was at that moment yawning. 'She knows what's what. The dog's collared and showing no fey signs, and I'm sure Janet gave Francie quench-water to drink along with herbs as she saw fit, and she doesn't need me to tell her.' Quench-water, in which hot iron had been cooled, was a general failsafe for minor wounds and illnesses caused by the People.

Matthew said something conciliatory, but John wasn't really listening. The mists were plucking at his attention. Standing as still as they were, their feet were no longer sweeping the damp aside; in fact, his boots were oddly dry. But his arms felt damp; little puffs of breeze, thin as sheep-hanks on a thorn, were running to and fro over his hands, as if something was trying to tug at his sleeves.

Anthony was rubbing his eyes, Matthew was deferring to Aunt Pell and no one was watching, so John turned aside, just a little, and let the day take him.

There was Aunt Pell's land ahead of them and the Lenden farm beside, but while he knew the boundaries as well as any Gyrford man, the land itself didn't: in curve and fall, it was all of one piece. It was the little woodland that drew him the most; it spanned the border, and his attention flowed downhill towards it. Under the dead leaves nestled truffles, black and warty as deer spoor, with a dense fragrance the grand folks would pay any amount of money to get in their dinners. The Lendens were a nervy set: pigs could be led through the woods on an iron leash so that nothing fey might decide to drop upon their russet backs, but between the uncertain caprice of the People in a woodland they were known to favour and the uncertain tempers of a herd of pigs encouraged to dig out truffles but forbidden to eat them, the price for such delicacies was hard-earned.

The wood rested there, clear and dark in the morning light, self-contained as an apple cupped in a palm. John wished, as he always did, that he could go and visit it. He couldn't, though: he was firmly forbidden to enter. It was a great frustration to him; even on quieter days, there was a chill brilliance, a glassy heaviness of air between the trees, as if the whole place existed underwater, and he craved a walk there like an overheated man wanting to dive into a shimmering pool.

But Aunt Pell would have known. Every single time he had tried to climb the fence, she had known; he could never get more than one leg up before he'd feel a firm set of fingers on his ear. It was infuriating, especially as Pell had no shadow of the unkenned upon her, nothing that should have let her see things others didn't. She was as plain as earth, and glad to be so – and yet she always caught him. Knowing such things without a touch of feyness about her was *cheating*, somehow.

Even on the thought, Pell gave his ear a light tweak. 'Don't you stare at my wood,' she said. 'I'm too busy to chase you today.'

'Why can't I go in?' John demanded; it was an old argument, but she'd re-started it and he wasn't about to refrain. 'Are there child-stealers in there? Is it the Ab-tree? Are there troubled trees in there, Aunt Pell?'

'No,' Pell had said, unblinking. 'No to all three; there was a child-stealer on Lenden land in times gone by, but your grandfather killed it, and so he should have. You're not to go in because I say not, and so do the Lendens.'

'That's not a reason!' John protested. 'And the Lendens only say not because they do whatever you and Grandpa tell them.'

'It's the reason you'll get,' Pell had said, unperturbed, 'and if you think life owes you an explanation for everything, lad, I've a shock for you, and life no doubt holds many more.'

'I'm sure Johnny will mind you,' Matthew said with more loyalty than certainty. 'You're all right, aren't you, Johnny?'

'Yes, Dada,' John said. He kept his eyes very conscientiously on Anthony until the talk returned to pregnancy, birth and other matters that came under the heading of dull adult conversation. Within a few sentences, he was gazing again, for something was twitching the edges of his attention.

He couldn't wander down into the woods, not right before Pell's eyes. But if anything, the forest was less touched today than the world around it. John looked down again: there was a pool of clear air around his boots, and beyond it, across the fields, whiteness curled like milk in water. Only here and there were little spots of clarity: Jack Lenden, the old patriarch of the place, had been so fearful of the People that he'd placed cuckoo eggs on every fence post, and Jedediah had filled them with scraps and filings of iron for good measure. Jack Lenden had a particular horror of changelings; his notion with the eggs was that any People with a mind to replacing his children would decide that there was no point, for cuckoos had plundered the nest already.

This, of course, was pure hedge-witchery, and with another

man Jedediah would have been stern about the nonsense of it, but Jack had had a tendency to think his own children changelings when the mood was on him, so rather than let the man take out his feelings on his little ones, Jedediah had decided this was a case of customer-smithing. He had blown the yolks from the eggs himself, adding the shavings so as not to shame his trade entirely – although the quantity of iron was about equivalent to planting rue in a garden to discourage passing cats. Now, the eggs stood out, casting little halos of ordinariness around them like candle-flames.

It was no good; he was going to have to put up with Dada giving him a look.

'Dada,' he said, putting his hand on Matthew's arm, 'there's something queer about the day. Look at the eggs.'

It took Matthew a moment to change track; he'd been reminding Anthony that Thomas was a fine strong child, which was a subject they both enjoyed.

'What's that, Johnny?' he said.

'It's misty here,' John said, struggling a bit now. That was the trouble: what was obvious to his senses never sounded obvious when he tried to put it into words. 'But not in all the right places, and I don't think it's as it should be.'

Matthew turned and squinted. To his eyes, the day looked fairly ordinary: a little misty, yes, but that wasn't strange in October. He gazed over the fields, seeing what stood out to him: the Lendens had ploughed in good straight rows, but the fall of earth suggested that their harrow might be in need of repair; the horses were idling in a field beyond, all healthy and none with a shoe loose; it was a couple of hours till noon judging by the shadows, and the sky was pale and smooth, threatening no rain; there was toadflax blooming gold as summer in the verges, which would do the horses no good at all if they ate it, but Janet would be pleased if he gathered a bunch for her before reminding the Lendens to weed it out.

'What do you mean, the right places, Johnny?' he asked.

'Well,' said Pell briskly, 'if you're finished fretting, Anthony Brady, I suggest you take yourself off home. If this lad's in a starey mood it could take all day to get some sense out of him, and your wife might like you helping her rather than wandering the fields. Go and take your son off her hands.'

Anthony looked a little chastened. 'Thank you for your kindness,' he said, with a slightly self-conscious effort. 'No doubt you're right as always. You don't mind, do you, Matthew?'

'No, no,' Matthew told him. 'Kiss our little Thomas for me.'

Pell was evidently finished with him and John was distracted again, so Anthony headed off at a compliant trot.

'All right, Johnny love,' Matthew said, with a kind of careful patience that made John's eyes itch. 'Can you tell me what you meant about the mist?'

Anthony slowed to a walk as soon as he was out of sight. He was glad to oblige his cousins – the word still warmed him – but he was also truly tired. Francie was the dearest girl in the world, and being with her felt like coming home to a self who was better and happier than he'd ever thought he'd be. He was blessed in his father-in-law too: Franklin Thorpe knew pretty much everything and everyone in the county, but never seemed to find Anthony ignorant. Then there was his darling Thomas, who was adorable beyond all measure and possessed of every living virtue; it wasn't the boy's fault that he still woke at night.

It was true that he woke rather a lot, though. Francie was so far along in her pregnancy that getting out of bed took her some time, and Anthony was glad enough to go to Thomas instead; it made Francie call him wonderful, for one thing. But exhaustion soaked his muscles, weighing them down so that even lifting his feet was sometimes an effort.

Without the presence of Matthew and John to keep him alert, Anthony was more or less sleepwalking across the Lenden fields. He thought it must be part of a dream when he heard a soft murmur:

Darling . . . My sweeting . . .

Anthony stopped, rubbed his eyes. He was a little near-sighted, and the fields around him were always rather blurred. They were a bit more blurry today than usual, but perhaps he was dozing on his feet.

Precious . . . Come to Mama, heartling . . .

He looked around. The warmth brought by thoughts of his new family seeped out of his bones; he was so cold now that his eyes watered. Something was amiss, and he didn't know what it was. His mother had doted on him, it was true; she had used to call him 'heartling'. And she had been dead for nearly a decade.

Sweeting, heartling, come to Mama. Come here, pretty love.

Anthony cast about. He was growing more exhausted than ever; something was sapping his wakefulness. Everything was smudged around him; was he going blind?

'Matthew?' he called. Matthew would know what to do.

He'd given Anthony iron-nailed boots, and indeed, Anthony's feet were on solid ground and didn't feel quite so confused as the rest of him, but panic and sleepiness were at war in his breast. Something was terribly amiss, and Anthony felt himself what he'd thought he'd never be again: a trapped and lonely boy who didn't know what to do, who had no skills or wisdom and couldn't cope with the world.

'Matthew?' he called again; was he crying? Where was Matthew? Matthew would know what to do. Francie might know what to do, but she wasn't here, nobody was, and he couldn't see, and again, from out of the haze, a voice called to him:

Heartling. Baby. Come to Mama.

'All right, Johnny,' Matthew said in the end, 'I think I see what you mean. It could be we should go to the Lenden farm – I mean, survey proper. Aunt Pell, I reckon you'll have your own work to be about?'

He bit a nail as he said this, and John looked at him with suspicion. 'I think you have something in mind you haven't told me, Dada,' he said. It wasn't entirely a critical impulse: John was worn out from trying to explain and had eventually taken Matthew's hand and pulled him over to look straight at one of the cuckoo eggs. It was a robin-blue one, red-specked as if it had caught a spray of blood; the mist fell away from it like pipe-smoke, leaving a hands-breadth of dry air around the shell.

Matthew looked at it again and shook his head. 'I don't know how you saw it from that distance, old lad,' he said, giving John a pat on the shoulder. 'Through the mist? You must have eyes like a falcon.'

'That's all very well,' John said, not wanting his eyes interrogated, 'but I still think there's something you haven't said. Are there secrets here? Aunt Pell said the Ab-tree wasn't around here, but are there more things you hide from me?'

'Now, Johnny,' Matthew said, heading across the fields, 'there's no need to speak so.' He said it gently – Matthew was not one of nature's scolders – but he was feeling uncomfortable. There had been many things amiss on the Lenden land over the years, and he wished his father were here. Folks tended to assume Jedediah ruled his family with a fist of iron – folks attach many iron-related proverbs to the fairy-smiths – but in fact, Jedediah had always been emphatic that Matthew had a sound head on his shoulders and it wasn't there to hold up his hat. Their relationship, both working and domestic, was a comfort to both of them, and Jedediah's sureness relaxed Matthew more than many a milder man's courtesies.

Instead, there was Pell, giving them both a beady glare. Matthew was aware that she had always been good to him, in her way, but it was Jedediah she was fondest of, and if Matthew didn't get John away from her soon, one or other of them would become irritated. John meant so well, and he couldn't understand how heedless he truly was – but the boy could bicker affectionately with Jedediah for hours and still feel quite safe. Pell might actually hurt his feelings.

John, unlike his father, was not given to doubting his own opinions. 'I may speak rude or speak gallant, but either way I did ask a question, Dada,' he insisted, 'and Grandpa says it's my work to listen and learn, and I can't do that if you don't speak and teach, you know.'

'He tells you to hold your tongue five times a day too,' Pell observed, 'but I don't see you minding that bit of wisdom.'

John froze. For a moment Matthew thought the lad was upset and he felt a sinking of his heart: it hurt him to see John hurt. It was only when he put a hand on the boy's arm that he felt the tight muscles, strained and ready as a bowstring.

'What is it, Johnny?' he said softly.

John moved his mouth, shaped a word. It didn't sound aloud, but he didn't notice. His attention was filled, for he could hear it clearly now.

Hoofbeats.

It was something like a charge, but it was more than that: with each frantic step, the earth . . . *flinched*. That was the only way he could explain it; it was as if a tree had planted and uprooted itself all in an instant; there were twitches of unease shuddering through the ground, bending it like water beneath the sharp toes of a skimming beetle.

'Dada,' John said, trying for the firm tone his grandpa was so good at, 'there's a thing or two coming towards us.'

'Hm?' Matthew said, and then it rounded the corner of the lane.

Ralph Lenden, his shirt torn and his eyes wild, was running for his life. And there, after him, came what might once have been a pig, with bristles jagged and sharp and green as a spring leaf all over its pelt.

To Pell's credit, she was a fast thinker. 'By that tree!' she snapped to Matthew, and then, 'Ralph! That tree – there – Matthew will give you a shove!'

John's whole self caught light; he was too intrigued to think, just at that moment, that Aunt Pell was making rather free with his father's safety. As Matthew hoisted Ralph Lenden aloft into the sturdy beech tree, John leaped up to another branch, nimble as a cat: a boy very interested in and not at all afraid of the People has to be quick when it comes to climbing trees.

Matthew had lifted Pell into the tree beside them and was climbing up after her. When the tree creaked under his weight, Pell barked, 'Hold to the trunk, Matthew, you'll crack the branch.'

Before John could attempt any help there, the pig stopped to champ up at Ralph Lenden, who was staring in wild horror. The green spikes weren't still like the ordinary hairs on a pig's back, or even a hedgehog's; they rippled as if driven by a wind lashing the muscles beneath them.

'Stay where you are, Johnny,' Matthew called, doing his best to sound steady. He wasn't particularly afraid of pigs, but you had to respect the fact that even the common ones could be violent. This fey-looking thing was snarling with every bristle.

John cleared his throat. 'Now then, Sir Pig,' he said, doing his best to sound calm, 'What's all this about, eh?'

'Johnny!' Matthew hissed. Evidently, it hadn't occurred to John that 'Stay where you are' encompassed 'Don't try to befriend the slavering monster below you.'

The beast swung its head to consider John. From its furious chase and hulking pelt, one would have expected it to have the face of a wild boar, the terrible tusks and aquiline snout of some great patriarch of the forest. But no: the face beneath the seething green quills was as pink-nosed as a kitten's, with the sandy coat and big, cupped ears of any ordinary pig.

Johnny! it grunted. It was definitely a voice, a kind of husky, wet-slurred grumble that was quite intelligible, like the words of a man who'd soaked himself in strong drink for so many years his mind would never quite get dry. But it was words. Unmistakeably, the pig was talking.

'Pity me! Punish him! Push him down!

'Haul him for hanging! Have off his head!

'Skin him! Stew him! Sausage and shove him!'

'Er,' said John. This wasn't actually the first time he had addressed a pig – pigs were clever animals and he often stopped to exchange a few pleasantries when visiting a farmer's yard – but it was the first time he'd met one who'd addressed him back, and he wasn't quite sure what the form was. The beast was clearly of the view that he should be helping it murder Ralph Lenden, though, which he would have to respectfully decline.

The trouble was that the pig's voice didn't appear to be entirely fey. He'd heard an animal talk before – there had been an encounter with a loquacious cat that he'd just about managed to survive – but in that case, the voice had issued from the cat's throat like birdsong, a speaking spirit rather than anything from the body. This pig was rather slabbering its words, but it was forming them with its own mouth, and the groan and squeak of its tone wasn't that different from how pigs expressed themselves the rest of the time. Almost certainly the People were somewhere behind this, but its fleshly-sounding voice made him feel that he was, still, at heart, talking to a pig, with a pig's way of thinking – and unfortunately, he was a limited authority on that. 'Are you out of temper, Sir Pig?'

'*Fierce and fighty, I am, fellow!*' it husked.

'Now none of you holds a knife
'Am strong and sensible, not for slaughter!
'Not born to become bacon.

'*Bastards*,' it added, with a bitter snort.

Yes, there it was again: a sloughing of sound around the more difficult consonants, as if the pig's lips weren't really comfortable with words made for men. This wasn't so much a talking pig as a pig that was talking; it was a fine distinction, but it felt somehow important.

'Well,' John said, trying to gain its attention without giving offence, 'I see your point. Perhaps we can reason together.'

The pig's gaze was fixed so hard on John that Matthew took a chance and lowered himself from the tree. He could slip his knife out of the sack he'd dropped, and then if he could creep forward while John drew it into one of his endless wrangles . . . Matthew was not very fond of pig-killing, and usually found something else to do on slaughtering days, but the thing was grinding its chops at his only son.

The pig's snout and ears really did have a domestic look to them, John thought, almost sweet. This should have made the baring of its teeth less feral, but the things were as thick as thumbs.

John took a deep breath. He couldn't deny the creature's accusation: he did eat pork and bacon. Ironworkers need solid food, and that was the kind of meat they could afford. But it wasn't personal, and he felt a little annoyed at being treed for it by a beast that would gobble absolutely anything.

'Well, I bet you eat meat, or you do if you can get it,' he said. Without thinking about it, he gave his head an upwards jerk, a kind of nod as if to emphasise his point, but it also, once he found himself doing it, felt like a butting motion, as if charging the pig's opinion head-on. 'I saw a pig once, a little bird fell into its trough as it fed, and the pig ate it up alive, still cheeping. I cried over that.'

'Lying lad, you leave off!' The pig's outrage overspilled in a slime of froth, flowing either side of its working jaws.

'Don't you dare! That was your Dada!'

At that, John stopped. It was true: the boy who'd cried over the fate of the martlet had been his father. He had told him the story once when John was very small and had been unable to save a little mouse he saw trapped at the top of a rick the People had set alight after Thomas Jefcroft ignored their warning not to trespass upon the field he'd just bought for a suspiciously low price. The mouse had leaped in the air, dark and frantic as a flea, and John swore he could hear its tiny shrieks over the flutter and hush of the flames, and he'd cried his eyes out. Afterwards, Dada had taken him on his lap and told him the story of the hurt martin to prove that there was no shame in tears, for even big strong men had their moments. But there was no way the pig could have known that.

'Sir Pig?' John said, very carefully, 'how did you come to know—?'

But at that moment his father, coming up from behind, hurled himself upon the pig, his knife raised.

It would most probably have been the end of the pig had it not been for the spines. Greenery pierced Matthew's skin from a hundred sharp angles and he found himself caught, as helpless as if he'd landed in a bramble patch.

He gritted his teeth and took a firmer grip on his knife. If he could just slice himself loose . . .

The pig turned its head, a slow, furious light building in its gaze. Pig and man came eye to eye.

Pig expressions are mostly a question of ear and snout, but this one had a grin, almost human, rough-toothed and gleeful, and it was the most gruesome sight Matthew had seen for years.

'*Ha ha!*' it grunted. '*Hug a hedgehog!*

'*Spiny and spiky me, not to be stabbed!*'

And, with a massive, grinding snort, it bucked its body and tossed Matthew off into the verge. They watched it race down the road, its trotters slicing the earth at every stride.

'Well,' said Pell after the kind of long silence that follows an explosion of spit, greenery and personal remarks. 'That's not a thing I've seen before. Matthew, boy, are you much hurt?'

'N-no,' Matthew said, making an effort to gather himself. He was spiked all over, and speckled with blood so thoroughly that he might have been a cuckoo-egg himself. 'No, thank you, Auntie, I think it's just some cuts and bruises. Nothing that won't mend. I'll need some splinters taking out, but we've tongs for that at the—Johnny, love, are you all right?'

'Oh, I'm quite all right,' John said, landing with a jump and looking disturbingly cheerful. 'You just rest, Dada, you look sore. I'll help Mister Lenden down. Mister Lenden – there you are, down you get – when did this begin?'

'This morning,' Ralph Lenden said, descending with a groan. 'Got out of its pen last night. Always was a wanderer, that Left-Lop. That's its name,' Ralph added, evidently apologetic for giving the animal a title now it had proven itself so verbose. 'Always was one to break in and out of things, but I hadn't thought it was that clever. I mean – I'd have thought foreign languages weren't what a pig would wish to study, if it went to be a scholar. Not that English is a foreign language to us, of course, but I reckon it must know to speak Pig already.'

'Oh, for pity's sake, Ralph Lenden, that'll do,' Pell said. 'We've to catch that pig before it does any more amiss. It's a bad day's work you did for all of us when you let it out of that pen and you'll answer for it.'

John stared. Aunt Pell was a frank woman, but she wasn't usually outright unkind.

'I'm sure he didn't mean to,' he said, and then, at the sight of her face – white, drawn, her mouth tight as a pulled stitch – he added, a little quieter, 'I only mean, even if it hadn't gone talkative, he wouldn't set a pig lose on purpose.'

'John, lad,' Pell said, as sharp and fast as he'd ever heard anyone, 'close your mouth and move your legs. Matthew, you're well enough to ride, yes? Good. Ralph Lenden, let him have the use of one of those horses of yours; that pig needs catching, poor beast. John, you should get home. It's not a place for you.'

'I like that!' John burst out. 'I talked to it more than anyone! I'm an apprentice, not a baby – I'm all but thirteen!'

'You're twelve, lad, and a pig wouldn't need many bites to finish you,' Pell said, already drawing clean cloths from her sleeves and mopping the worst of Matthew's cuts. 'Get you home.'

'John, love, help us out,' Matthew said in soothing haste.

'That's a big beast and – thank you, Auntie – I reckon the more men we have on this the better. You run back to Gyrford – you know you're the quickest of us – and fetch Grandpa; maybe Franklin too, if you see him. It'd be a good deed for us all.'

'Well, I obey my father,' John said rather crossly, just at that moment feeling that he always did. 'I never heard that my great-great-aunt was a farrier or master, so perhaps you should get home too, Aunt Pell, as we're much of a size, you and me.'

'Glad to hear you talking sense,' Pell said, not bothering to take umbrage. 'I'll to my house and you'll to yours; off you go, boy, swift as you can, for you've two legs and both of them are young, so use what God put under you, now.'

It was a well-aimed blow, for John still remembered the night they'd had to cut off Aunt Pell's leg; her set face, her teeth clamped around the leather strap, the meaty smell of cauterised flesh. She hadn't screamed, not once. He'd had nightmares afterwards, but he'd made Dada swear he wouldn't ever tell her.

'I'll tell folks to be careful, Dada,' he said, already running.

John was fleet of foot and Matthew a fine rider with a pretty good eye for the ground, considering that he wasn't a trained huntsman. Given better luck, they would have found the pig first, and much could have been avoided.

Anthony Brady was lost.

He hadn't moved a step; he wasn't sure he remembered how. He was tired and thirsty, helplessly thirsty. Something was calling his name and it sounded like his mother, but he was too helpless and stupid to know what to do about anything.

He didn't want to go to his mother. Tears ran down his cheeks, smearing themselves into the mists that blinded him. He had loved her, but she had *adored* him. His feelings for her were tangled in guilt, for she had petted him in public, which had always embarrassed him; he blamed himself for looking weak before the other boys, and for being ungrateful to her. He had seen his brother's face tighten every once in a while, when she would turn from some real concern of his with a, 'Later, Ephraim,' to tend to some trivial need of Anthony's; Anthony was ashamed of her favour, and afraid that without it he might not be strong enough to face the world, for he'd never had to overcome any trial that proved he did have the strength. So he'd depended on Ephraim instead, and Ephraim had been feared and hated by everyone in Gyrford except Anthony, who hadn't even known the dread the Brady name carried until a couple of years ago.

He didn't want to go back, not to any of it: the dependence, the shame, the loneliness. Something in him just about remembered that there were other folks in the world who didn't treat him that way, that somewhere, some time, he had touched the edge of a life where he had been a respected man, but now he was a little boy crying in a field, and his mother was calling him, and in a moment, he'd have to go to her.

Then the mists broke apart with a grinding roar, and Anthony shrieked. Something was bearing down upon him, a great galloping hill of greenery with a wet mouth and ears a-flap.

The mist wavered a moment – and then it was a clear, bright autumn day, with a clean bite of cold in the quiet breeze.

Anthony found that he was shaking, but to his bewildered relief, the creature was not charging him but had stopped and stood a little apart, staring out of eyes that, now he looked, were set in the face of a pig. A large pig, yes, and one that was thorned over with some kind of leaf or husk, but it wasn't the most terrifying sight he'd ever seen: spend any time around the Smiths and you came across far worse. Anthony liked pigs; back in his isolated youth, chatting to the pigs in other folks' gardens had been a kind of company. He could fall back on pigs when nobody else would speak to him, and after a little shoulder-scratching, they were usually friendly beasts.

He was still chilled and he had no idea what had just happened, but he'd remembered that he had a wife and children and friends now, and it didn't feel the moment to refuse any more blessings.

'Well, my handsome,' he said, 'I don't know what you did to clear the mists there, but I'm glad to see you.'

The pig grunted. Then it opened its mouth and Anthony abandoned any expectations that the day would now make sense.

'*Handsome hog, you think, hey?*' it said, sounding a little comforted. '*Like the look of these leaves?*'

'Er . . . yes,' said Anthony. He had not been told the story of Ab and didn't think there was any danger in befriending the fey. All the warnings he'd had were about what happened if you offended them. 'Yes, I'm sure they suit you very well.'

Pig noises aren't very musical to the ears of a man, consisting mostly of snorts and squeals, but the pig managed a kind of chuckling noise.

'*The mists muddled you, man?*' It cocked its head on one side as if pleased with its efforts. '*Fighty and fine me set them to flight!*'

'Well, er, I thank you,' said Anthony. He reached out to scratch the pig's head before it occurred to him that perhaps he should ask permission, but the creature was still piggish enough that it accepted the courtesy with a contented grumble. 'How did you do it?'

The green spikes twitched in a kind of shrug. It didn't sound very interested in the question.

'*A fighty and fearsome fellow is me.*

'*Have I found a friend? Need a favour.*'

'Well,' said Anthony, 'I, er, won't be the one to deny it. Something queer was about to befall me, and I'm very glad that it hasn't. What can I do for you?'

'*Save me from slaughter! Free me from the feast!*'

Anthony Brady was not a stupid man, but he was kind-hearted. 'Well, I can see why you'd wish that,' he said. 'How may I help?'

When John came running into the square, Jedediah Smith was sitting at ease. It had been a quiet sort of day, and he cherished those. Or at least, it was as quiet as things got around his home: the farrier house overlooked the Gyrford square, with the church in sight and the green a few steps away, and beside it was the smithy. The forge was always alight, the doors always open – or at least, always in the daytime, except for a few minutes at sunset when you washed off the day's sweat, and even at night, anyone in need could knock and wake them if they had a need for his and Matthew's ironwork or Janet's midwifery. You were never entirely alone, never more than one voice's call away from your work.

Well, that was as it should be, and a man his age didn't need as much sleep as he once had. It was restful just sitting here, working quietly away while his Molly, his eldest granddaughter, sat on a stool beside the coals, her little knife busy stripping the skin from parsnip after parsnip.

That was a blessing too. Molly had always been a lovely girl: sensible as Matthew, which was to say, more sensible than anyone else in the family, and with a face that caught at his heart the moment he saw her. Janet always delighted in how much Molly resembled her father, but then, she'd never known Louise. Matthew took after his mother, but Molly was her living image. Her expressions were different – Louise had laughed at life where Molly frowned and pondered – but in moments of rest, he could be struck hard with a glimpse of his late beloved. It was a sweet kind of pain: Molly was a girl Louise would have loved so much, carrying her face into the future while the past held Louise in its unreachable embrace.

But no, Molly was her own; he felt his memories as a weight he mustn't place on her, and being stern with himself was a well-worn way of bearing the loss. He had been careful since her babyhood to listen out for everything Molly had to say that marked out her separate soul. Perhaps for this reason, or perhaps just because she was a good girl, she had always trusted him; when she was sleepy, it was his lap she crawled into and his shoulder she rested her head upon just as often as it was her father's or mother's. He was glad when she'd join him in the smithy; as a shy child she'd preferred the privacy of the back garden, but at seventeen, tall and thoughtful, she would quite often come into the smithy when Matthew and John were away. She'd settle herself down with her own task and the two of them would work side by side in silent peace.

The parsnips were for the Clementing feast, he supposed; it was like her to be ready ahead of time, though how she'd keep them preserved was some feminine mystery. He could hear, too, the voices of Celdie and Vevie; everyone had given up on disciplining the twins; they were happy as larks, blonde as corn-sheafs, impulsive as kittens and unshakeably contented with themselves. He couldn't say who they resembled; there was something of his prettier aunts, perhaps, and something of Janet's side of the family, but really there was no point seeking family likenesses, for the twins looked so like each other that they felt no need to compare themselves to anyone else. At the moment they were sitting in front of the house, embroidering with rapid, effortless skill, winking at any handsome lad who went by, and entertaining themselves in the ladless moments by singing a sweet song – or at least, it had been a sweet song to begin with, but they'd each wandered off on their own chiming harmony until it had become all harmony and no melody, giving it a haunting, slightly frustrating loveliness that was, Jedediah felt, a pretty normal expression of the twins.

He'd always loved music and today he could just listen to them sing, for his task was a quiet one: he was filing down the last details on the Clementing wreaths. Matthew had made them petal-thin and graceful; a breath would rust them away. Last time he'd looked at the family graves, the old ones were quite melted away. Fine work, they had been, very fine. And these new ones would rust just as well; they hardly needed any sanding, but his grandfather Clem deserved as pretty a wreath as they could make, and it was a pleasure to handle Matthew's ironwork and admire what a master his son had become.

Things were as he liked them, Jedediah reflected; everyone was safe. Matthew was off with his new friend Anthony Brady, who had intelligence rattling around in his head somewhere but needed a lifetime's experience of packing-straw to stop it falling apart at the least impact. John couldn't get into too much trouble under both their eyes. Janet was visiting Francie Brady on some kind of midwifery errand that Jedediah knew better than to ask about: his Aunt Pell had been as responsible for bringing him up as either of his parents, and minding his own business about women's doings was one of the first lessons he'd taken in. Janet's chatter could wear on his patience if he heard too much of it at once, but he found himself regretting the lack of it sometimes; she was a good woman at heart, even if she lost her common sense as often as John lost scarves and mittens.

Better still, Jedediah spotted his friend Franklin Thorpe crossing the square, and hailed him.

'Mister Smith!' Franklin exclaimed. His tracking dog Soots followed at his heels and little Thomas bounced on his back. He and his daughter Francie had always been close, and his son-in-law Anthony was positively devoted to him. Franklin was delighted with his grandson and stole him away for company as often as he could.

'Well, now, Franklin Thorpe,' Jedediah said, pleased, giving

Soots a familiar scratch behind the ears. 'How's my friend Thomas today?'

'The best of boys,' Franklin said, seating himself and swinging Thomas onto his lap. 'Molly, my dear, I'm glad to see you're well. You must be hard at work with Clementing due.'

'I am,' Molly said, a little bleakly. 'Celdie says I'm better at cooking and the village will want the best.'

Jedediah snorted. He loved Celdie and Vevie too, of course, but their cheek was less amusing when Molly had to bear the weight of it. 'Want me to get after them?' he said.

Molly looked more comforted by the support than by any expectation that it would work; Celdie and Vevie could charm their way round Jedediah pretty nimbly, and everyone knew that she'd get the cooking done with or without their help. That was the trouble with being reliable: it made folks rely on you.

'Perhaps you could get Mama after them,' she said. Janet was as often a participant in the twins' mischief as she was a guard against it, but she was also the only member of the family who was any good at shouting. 'Still,' she added with a respectful sigh, 'I don't suppose you came by to hear this, Mister Thorpe.'

'Ah, it's a hard life for a good girl,' Franklin said with sympathy, if a little muffled. 'Thomas, darling, not Grandpa's nose, if you please.'

Since Franklin was a grandpa devoid of sternness, Thomas continued to chew. Soots regarded him with disapproval for making so free with the master, but Franklin had trained her impeccably and she was resigned to the fact that this small insurgent was not to be scolded by the likes of her.

Jedediah permitted himself a grin of fellow-feeling – he'd found it hard to resist the attentions of his infant grandchildren too – and would have said something else if, at that moment, there hadn't been a burst of running feet and a shrill voice yelling, 'Grandpa! Grandpa! Grandpa, you can't think what's happened!'

Soots jumped away from Jedediah's caresses, entirely ready to defend the company, until she recognised that it was the master's wayward little friend. Jedediah himself dusted off his hands. John had been an adorable baby, but he had not grown up to be restful company. 'Take a breath, lad,' he said, not much alarmed. John had his own notions of what was exciting: Jedediah's first assumption was that the boy had found an apple wormed with hissing spitfires, or something equally ordinary.

'That's all as may be,' John said, gasping a little, 'but you can't think what's befallen the Clementing day feast.'

'What?' said Molly, looking up with quick foreboding.

'Oh, dear.' John was struck with compunction. 'Oh, Molly, it will be hard on you, for I reckon it's you will have to find a way to cook things. I am sorry, dear.' He patted her on the shoulder with more condolence than clarity; John was very fond of Molly. She had often looked after him when they were both little; he lived by the assumption that she approved of him, and never ceased to be surprised that he sometimes annoyed her.

'Perhaps you might come to the point, John,' Jedediah said; there was nothing that made him feel so young as a mild skirmish with his grandson.

'Oh, and Dada said to fetch you as well, Mister Thorpe. Good day, by the by,' John said, bowing, 'and I hope you find yourself very well.'

Jedediah met Franklin's eye with rising concern: if Matthew thought it worth their attention, that was more serious.

'All right, John,' he said, standing. 'Since it seems you've come to talk in circles, you must explain as we ride to meet Matthew. Let's go, Franklin Thorpe.'

'You don't mind, I hope, Molly dear?' Franklin said, putting Thomas into Molly's slightly parsnippy hands and sending Soots over to her with a snap of the fingers. 'I'll look for you here or at Francie's house. Thank you very much, it's most kind of you.'

The equable Thomas, who was as content to chew his Cousin Molly's hair as his grandpa's nose, didn't object to the change, and Soots was used to being sent to wait for the master: dogs and the People do not tend to get along. As Grandpa and Franklin hurried to fetch their own horses, John said to Molly in helpful explanation, 'You see, the pig we were to roast has taken to revolt, and in truth, I'm on the pig's side.'

Molly gave a sigh deeper than ever. Her menfolk lived lives of danger and chaos, and she wasn't sure she'd like to live that way, but her life of good sense was starting to wear a little thin as well.

Anthony Brady had hesitated a little as the pig begged him to open the gate into the woods between Pell's land and the Lendens'; he wasn't very experienced with fey things, but he did know that the People loved the forests.

But then, young Cousin John had asked Mistress Pell only today whether the woods contained child-stealers, troubled trees, or an Ab-tree, whatever that was, as she had said no to all three. And the pig was a good beast who had saved him from something. Anthony had been isolated from his neighbours most of his life, and didn't feel able to refuse anyone's friendship.

Thus he found himself following a bristling beast through the gates of the Lenden woods up to a great cloven chestnut tree half-smothered in fog.

The tree was deep-set and heavy-armed, reaching around itself in every direction. Anthony, exhausted as he was, had the vague sense that it was broken-hearted: the cleft in the middle of it was almost as tall as a man, with a chain hanging limp across it. He could see that the pig had been gnawing at the bark: gouges, damp and weeping, sat either side of the split, and trotter-marks scored themselves up and down like tallies on a wall. There was just one nail left that was too high for a pig, even a pig on its hind feet. It held the chain loose in place; Anthony thought hazily of how uncomfortable it felt to slip about in a boot coming unlaced.

'*Free me, friend! Let me fly away safe!*

'*Pull out the pin! Unpeg this poor pig!*'

Anthony had a moment of wondering whether he should ask the pig exactly how it had learned to talk and what that had to do with this tree, but at that moment, there was a little tap on his head. It shouldn't have stunned him – it was just a chestnut, tumbling loose from a twig above. It didn't even hurt, just a flick of sensation. He couldn't have said why it staggered him so badly, knocking from his head every thought he had, so that the only thing he could think to do was the last thing he had heard.

Anthony Brady, meaning no harm to anyone in the world, reached up and pulled the nail from what he would later learn was called the Ab-tree. The bark was old and soft, and the nail came loose with almost no effort at all.

'I hope we are going the right way,' Matthew said. It hadn't taken the others long to find him: John had a precise sense of how far any horse could carry anybody, with no apparent calculation except the assumption that interplay between the horse's strength and rider's weight should be obvious to all. Now Matthew and Jedediah rode side by side, John sitting behind Jedediah, with Franklin bringing up the rear.

John craned his neck to make sure everyone could hear his opinions. 'Oh, I'm sure of it,' he said now, with a confident gesture at the Lenden woods. 'Wouldn't you like to go this way if you were a fey-struck pig?'

This was a scenario Matthew did not find as easy to picture as John evidently did, but it was at that moment that they heard the crack.

It wasn't loud. The sound of breaking wood; not dry, but a quick, neat *pop*, like the splitting of a sodden old branch. There was no reason to be deafened by it.

It was far off – it must have been – and yet in the moment it snapped, it drowned out every other noise in the world – the thudding of hoofbeats, the wind through the leaves, even the sound of their own breaths in their chests. There was nothing, for that long, deep instant, but the sound of wood, gentle and neat, breaking open.

'Dada?' said John. His voice was very quiet.

'Stay by me, Johnny, we'll—' Matthew began. Johnny was far too fearless for the most part, but in this instant he had a white-faced alertness, almost a look of fright, that was so unlike him that Matthew was halfway through reaching out to his boy when the trees shattered.

The forest burst from deep within. The sound was a deep, resounding *puff*, like a clay pot struck with a toadstool, soft, almost sweet, and thick enough to drown your ears. From within the canopy, jagged grey and scurfed with dying brown leaves, there fountained billow after billow of sawdust, tumbling skywards in a tumbling tower of gold.

It came from the middle of the Lenden woods: not the collapse of just one tree, but many: high and ancient beings, once armoured with bark, transfigured all in an instant to roiling curls of powder.

The men and boy stared for a moment – and from within the depths, there burst forth a screaming creature. It was flying, almost, its wings spread wider than an eagle's, but there was nothing right with it: it thrashed like a wounded pigeon, and they could hear, from the soft, emptied silence of the woods, a terrible, deep-throated screaming.

'It's coming this way, Dada,' John said, almost matter-of-fact, his eyes trained on the floundering thing that was staggering, air-bound, towards them.

Matthew craned his head, trying urgently to make out the

monster that had arisen from the wooden clouds. It couldn't be a bird; its body was too hefty and the colours were all wrong; it was green-backed and shaggy, red-winged beneath, and its head was thick, lopped off somehow, as if the beak had been snapped at the root.

As he shielded his eyes, he felt a patter on the back of his hand. It wasn't rain; it was warm, and sticky. When he drew his hand back to look at it, he saw he was spattered with blood.

'Left-Lop!' John yelled, 'Left-Lop, get down here!'

There was another shriek, and then with a thump that set both horses dancing back, the thing landed at their feet. It had the head of a pig, that much was true, and the back of a mossy log.

What had once been front trotters were wrenched outwards, jagged flaps of hide stretched across them. The skin of its back had been flayed by something sharper than any mortal knife, paring a bat-wing of flesh off the pig's heaving flank. The muscles, exposed, pulsed like flinching slugs.

Matthew managed not to be sick. His first thought was that something had crucified the animal – and then, afraid of the blasphemy, that it had been jointed alive like a chicken. He kept hold of Johnny, who patted his hand, almost distractedly, staring at the pig with a concentration too deep for horror or pity.

'Mister Smith,' said Franklin with deferential resolve, 'I can put it out of its pain this moment if you bid me.'

Jedediah opened his mouth to say yes – Franklin had a huntsman's skill that would probably give the quickest death – but John held up his hand with a shrill, imperious, 'Wait!'

Franklin, already dismounted, hesitated.

'What has happened to you, Left-Lop?' John demanded.

'*So sore! Sliced and unseamed!*' came the squeal.

'*Pity the poor peeled pig!*'

John leaned forwards, pulling back on his mare's reins in a firm refusal to let her bolt as common sense would suggest. 'I gather something did this to you,' he said. 'Tell me what, then.'

'*Help, help! I hurt! I hurt!*

'*The liar ripped me red and raw!*'

'No doubt,' John said, with a kind of fascinated calm. 'But who by?'

'*Called me friend, said I'd fly to freedom!*

'*Cheated poor poor me, charmed me with chestnuts.*

'*I snouted for supper and snapped them up swift,*

'*And then heard the heartless whisper for help.*

'*Told me to fetch a fellow to free it*

'*And said it'd show me a skyful of safety.*

'*Forlorn,*' it added with a grunting sob, '*I find it didn't mean feathers.*

'*Cruel as cooks are all creatures in Creation.*'

'There, there,' Matthew said, distracted from the ghastliness by the pig's despair. 'Never lose hope, there's a good lad. I'm sure we can . . . er . . . well, we'll do our best for you.'

'We can't just kill it, you know,' John said, 'That'd be more or less murder. Here, let's wrap you for now.' He stripped off his jacket and, before Franklin could catch him, knelt down beside the pig. 'Let's see. This is a neat job; if we stitch it you should be quite tidy, though as to the bones . . . no, they're just out of joint. Really, it's a fine job, in its way.'

The pig gave a horrendous shriek as John took one of its legs and, with a grunt of effort, snapped it back into its socket.

'Never you mind,' he said a little absent-mindedly as he tucked the flesh back into place, neat as a tailor. 'I'm sure it's a troubled life being a pig, but we do the same to folks when their limbs go askew, and I reckon it hurts them just as much. Nothing against you as a pig, you know. And I've been practising.'

'Johnny, steady now,' Matthew said, a little thickly. It was true, setting bones was a farrier skill – proverbially, you weren't a smith till you'd broken at least three of your own fingers, and putting them back in place yourself saved time and money – and if John was to perfect the knack, then in fact a pig was a better thing to practise on than a suffering man or woman. But you wouldn't handle a man or woman so rough. Out of pure habit, Matthew said, 'There's no need for hard and hasty. That's not a small finger-joint; slow and steady is kinder.'

'With a man, I do think so,' John said. His tone was full of interest, and he didn't look up from the pig; instead, he flexed its mended leg with precise hands. Matthew had always felt it would be better not to suffer so much pity for your patient that it unsteadied your hand, and he worked hard to manage it. It was a little disturbing to see his son, not yet thirteen, do just that. 'But a man knows to hold still,' John observed, 'and I reckon that's too much to ask here.'

The pig shrieked again as John snapped the other limb into place. 'No wonder you flew poorly,' he said. 'You can't make a pinion with no bones to attach it to. Or did they pull out of joint when you flew? I wouldn't wonder; you've far more weight to you than a bat. I don't know what notion of bats or birds this thing did have, but . . . oh, Cousin Anthony. There you are again.'

So absorbed in the beast had they been that none of them had noticed Anthony Brady until that moment. He stood shuddering before them, gilded in every pore with fine sawdust, gaping with horror at what, unquestionably, was a real animal and not some dreadful nightmare that had ripped itself apart and flown away from him.

'M-Matthew?' Anthony said, starting to cry. 'Can I speak to you?'

'Speak to Matthew, by all means,' said Jedediah, his voice a little hoarse. 'But I reckon it's something we need all hear.'

Anthony's account of what he had seen, stripped of the self-recrimination, was fairly simple. After the chain had fallen, there had been a murmuring, a creak, and then the world had burst into stinging gold and his eyes were full of motes. He had heard some things: a tearing sound and some shrieks, followed by the sound of laughter – not spiteful, he thought, but self-delighted, the piping little cackle of a voice that felt it had done very well indeed. After that, there was the flap of wings, too many wings, he thought, and he'd heard someone running, or some creature. Something had run by him, but he didn't know what, and by the time he'd been able to rub his eyes clear, there had been nothing left but a clearing where there used to be a wood, and something dreadful lolloping through the skies overhead.

It was all his fault, but what had he done? What was the tree in there?

*

During the recitation, Matthew stood dumbstruck with dismay.

'I . . . I'm sorry to tell you, Cousin Anthony,' he said eventually, 'that this is bad news. There was in that tree a fey that we . . . well, we would very much have preferred to keep it there. But . . . but never mind that now. By the sounds of it, your wits were somewhat blasted. It happens. It's . . . it's unlucky, but it happens. Blame never mended bone.'

This was a saying of Smith origin; it hadn't been used much in the days after Ab first attached itself to Clem, but Jedediah had revived it when Matthew was little and Matthew held to it now, unable to find words of his own to encompass the situation.

'I've done that, Dada,' John said, taking the proverb entirely on his own terms; he'd bound up the pig in his own shirt and stood bare-chested, rubbing his blood-smudged hands on some damp leaves. 'But what do you mean by a fey?'

'Johnny,' Matthew said, a little wildly, 'put on your jacket, do. It's a cold day.'

'I'm fine,' John said; he didn't mind cold weather and resisted all attempts to bundle him in heavy layers. 'And the jacket itches with no shirt under it. What do you mean by a fey? Aunt Pell said the trees weren't troubled in there. I asked her particularly just today; Anthony heard me. And she said they weren't.'

'Did she now?' Jedediah said. His mouth was growing dry.

'Oh dear,' Matthew said, putting his arm around John's shoulders. 'Well, love, I'm sorry to say this, but – I don't go to blame you, Cousin Anthony, but it's a pity she said it before you. She – well, I reckon she didn't trust Johnny with the truth. A white lie, I'm sure, and I'm sure she meant no harm by it, but – oh, Cousin, please don't cry.'

Franklin put his arm around Anthony. The pig, bandaged up, had been squealing quietly to itself, but as the men fell silent, it looked up at John, regarding him with wet black eyes.

'*None of them like to name it now,*' it confided in him miserably. '*I know the name, but the meaning, I know not.*

'*All I can ask is – what's an Ab-tree?*'

'Franklin,' Jedediah said, very quietly, 'do you take Anthony Brady home. Never you mind, Anthony Brady. Matthew's right: blame never mended bone. But we've things to do.'

Matthew's arm stayed around John's shoulder, but it tightened. 'What's to do first, Dada?' The question was asked almost steady, and Jedediah looked at his son, this tall man he'd once carried on his hip, standing still and braced for the storm that was about to sweep down across them all.

'We'll warn folks first,' Jedediah said. 'Warn everyone. We'll want talismans, and we'll have to speak to the parson and ask him to call folks to church so we can—'

'Oh.' John was still leaning against Matthew. As he straightened, Matthew almost reached to shield him – except that they didn't know where the danger would come from, and he didn't know how to protect his children from this.

'Oh dear,' John said. 'Oh dear. I think we should hurry, don't you?'

Jedediah drew breath, almost relieved that John was being tiresome; that was familiar, comfortable. The worst hadn't come as long as young Johnny could make a pest of himself. 'If you'd share your notions with the rest of us,' he said, almost in his usual tone, 'perhaps we might.'

'Oh dear,' John said again. 'Well, Ab had ideas about Clem, didn't it? First that it was his friend, then that he was a crow-killer. You know, if you'd been in a tree for decades and decades, you'd be pretty angry when you got out, I reckon. And if Grandpa Corbie Mackem wore a mask to lock Ab in, then it wouldn't know who to be angry with. But it'd remember the last man it was angry with, and that was Grandpa Clem.'

'That's true, Johnny,' Matthew said. He didn't know where his son was headed with this, but he felt a sinking in the pit of his stomach.

'Well, then,' John said, sounding only a little concerned, 'hadn't we better haste to the graveyard? Or you and I could go, and perhaps Grandpa and Mister Thorpe should ride around warning folks and bring poor Left-Lop back to the smithy to care for. But Grandpa always says how thin you make the Clementing wreaths, Dada, and we haven't put the new ones on yet. It'll only be the old ones, and they're rusted away. There's no iron over the grave. Clem's grave is unguarded. Don't you think we'd better go there before Ab gets after his bones?'

As they hurried towards Gyrford, John and Matthew passed a fox, dead at a crossroads. Something had sucked the gold out of its coat. Your eyes slid off the soft heaps of fur, unable to find any tint to it, and the moment you looked away, you couldn't remember what colour it had been.

There was a bat, lost and panicked in the daylight, struggling to rise. As Matthew slowed Dobbs, just for a moment, thinking he'd better put the injured little creature out of its pain, it suddenly got the knack of its new self and rose into the air, flying a kim-kam, drunken path through the air on wings that had been shredded into dark, meaty feathers.

There was a nest of rats, trying to flee in different directions on paws as skeletal as a sucked chicken bone, but they weren't getting anywhere; something had locked their tails together in a true-love knot, binding each to each in miserable unity. A rat in the house should expect no more sympathy than any other burglar, but John just hadn't the heart to stamp the nuisance out of these ones. He did the best he could, which was to sever their tail-tips from the knot with quick chops of his pocket knife; he got himself bitten a few times in the process, but he could hardly blame them.

Following the small corpses and the crawling wounded, John and Matthew raced home.

Matthew was hot with sweat and had forgotten his jacket; he'd only had time to run into the smithy and out again. The new wreath, a pretty circlet of black petals, was light in his hands, ready to cast upon the grave, if only they could reach it before anything else.

Clem Smith's last resting place was a simple one. He had died under Corbie Mackem's rule, quietly and politely, apologising to the nursing woman for putting her to trouble. Jedediah had told Matthew once that he'd wondered about getting a finer headstone after he himself became elder, but he'd thought better of it in the end; let Clem lie in peace.

So Clem Smith lay on the east of the church under a plain stone bearing his name. Jedediah hadn't mentioned it, but Matthew knew from his friend Gilbert Liddiard, whose clan had been stonemasons for generations, that Corbie Mackem had paid for nothing more than the headstone and Clem's name. Still, it bore the Smith emblem, a simple pentangle under a hammer and tongs, the five points of endless knot indicating that if you didn't make continuous use of the five wits God gave you then your forefathers had the right to be disappointed. Gilbert had privately told Matthew that Grandfather George had carved that as a gift, shocked at the notion of a Smith being buried without it. Corbie took exception, but in the end declined the cost of changing anything, and made a new habit of flirting with George's wife even though she didn't like it.

So Clem's grave was a respectable one. Or it had been.

There upon the mud-hatched winter grass stood a man, tall and tattered and gasping. He was bare to the waist, his britches torn as if he'd clambered through something jagged. His back and chest were muscled like an ironworker's, and in the dim evening, his hair shone gaudy red without a streak of grey. While he dragged earth from the ground, his fists held no tool for digging; he was scooping up the soil bare-hand, driving his fingers down hard and then flipping up palmfuls of dirt as if from a shovel blade. The red cracks through his fingernails showed even through the mud.

Across his arms there wound a twist of something, dark and feathered, but not really a bird. It was like wings half-formed, all wire-tight muscle and crushed dander, gripping the man's flesh tight as talons.

Dig, my friend! it exclaimed. It wasn't a man's voice, nor quite a bird's caw, but a voice without species; there was no mouth anywhere, just the words thrumming from its twining pinions like a chirp arising from the legs of a cricket. The man was stooped in exhaustion, but unable to free himself from the implacable helpfulness of the wings that grasped and wielded his bare arms.

Dig, my friend! The voice rang out, forcing the man's hands into the soil again. *They shall take us back – we will give them the crow-killer so they do not flee. Make them take us back.* It was almost a wail, but still it wrangled the man's bleeding hands into the soil like a mother shoving a child's arm into a sleeve.

John had been staring at this spectacle, entirely forgetting that he should have been struck with compassion. He'd felt it for the mauled little beasts he'd passed on the road, but the sight of this flexing pillory pleading to be reconciled with the crows had a sound to it that drowned out everything in him but curiosity. It wasn't a bird or a man or any other kind of creature; it was absolutely and entirely fey.

Matthew made an attempt to shield his son, but, realising the lad was rooted to the spot, stepped forward. What caught his eye was not the wild tangle of sinew and yearning, but the bloody-handed man, being forced to drive his hands again and again into the unforgiving soil.

'Kind friend!' he shouted to the fey, lifting the wreath high, 'here is iron! Loose the man or it will close around you!'

The man was whipped around by his captor to face them. The thing had no eyes, but it saw Matthew Smith.

You shall not sorrow, friend, it keened. *He friends us not. Break not your heart. You shall not know your kin.*

Matthew wasn't sure what this meant, but there was a man

bleeding and nothing to do but make a dash to free him before the thrashing thing broke his bones.

'Dada, you might not wish to—' John said in a voice too quiet to register, and Matthew ran, holding the wreath like a shield until he reached the red-haired man and dropped it around his neck.

There was a blink. The world blinked; everything was wrong for a second, without colour and depth, as if cut from shadows. Then it was clear again and the man dropped to his knees, exhausted, glaring up at them in utter confusion.

'Dear oh dear,' said Matthew, crouching down beside him and taking off his own shirt to cover the ragged survivor. 'You poor man, what a dreadful thing to happen. Here, take this – it's big for you, but at least it'll cover you for now. You poor fellow. Never you mind, we've salves at the smithy, I'm sure we can put your hands to rights. There, there.'

John was creeping forward, not in shyness, but like a sheep-dog flowing over the ground towards a flock.

'What's your name?' he asked, with an intent curiosity that prompted Matthew to say, 'Gently, John, he's had a bad time of it. And he's "Mister" to you, love.'

John didn't take this in; instead, he asked again, 'What's your name?'

'Caleb,' the man said, shaking his head as if trying to clear it of something that was bothering him. His answer had the brusqueness of a man who'd been asked the question twenty times over, which John felt somewhat unreasonable.

'Who are you, then?' John asked.

'Johnny, manners,' Matthew said, helping the man to his feet.

John was quite unable to explain why 'Mister'ing this man felt premature. 'Is that right?' he said.

The man stared at John. He had blue eyes – not the deep blue John had inherited from his mother, but a bright, light shade, his irises shot through with streaks so pale they were almost white. It gave him a sharp look, fiercely alert.

'Magpie,' he said, nodding at the boy who stood so inquisitive before him.

'Caleb?' Matthew said, ducking down to look closer at the man's face and see if he showed any signs of concussion. 'What did you say, my friend?'

The man grunted at Matthew. 'Dove,' he said.

Nursing isn't a farrier's primary duty, but you must have at least a little basic skill with the injured and the overset. 'My name's Matthew Smith,' that farrier now said patiently. 'I'll take you back home with me, get you clean and dressed, get you something to eat. We'll have you feeling better soon, never fear. Can you say my name? Matthew Smith?'

The man's eyes didn't exactly cross; they focused just a little away from Matthew as if he couldn't find him in the space. 'Dove,' he said, impatiently, as if annoyed at being forced to repeat himself.

'Can you say "Matthew"?' Matthew took the man's head carefully in his hands, looking to see if the pupils of his eyes were too large. For that bit of ministry, he got himself swatted away.

'I'm not sure he can, Dada,' John counselled his father. 'You remember my name, Mister?'

'Chatter, chatter, Magpie,' the man snapped. 'If we're to get a decent meal in my poor old belly, let's be about it.'

'I don't think you're old,' John objected, 'or if you are, then so's Dada, and he doesn't like it when I say so.' This was true – Matthew and this man did seem to be much of an age, which was to say, in their late thirties. This not being the moment to discuss it, Matthew ignored John and proffered this Caleb an arm.

'Well, glad to meet a courteous bird in this world,' the man Caleb said distractedly, and took it, walking alongside Matthew with a fair spring in his step. His hands were bloody and his whole body smeared with mud and – yes, John thought, looking closer, there was sawdust all over him where the mud hadn't covered it up. Amidst the dirt, the white-blue eyes glinted like stars.

They hadn't gone far before the air twisted: feathers, pearl-grey and soft as snow, snapping themselves into existence, a roiling twist of dove-sweet plumage that wound itself round Matthew's arms, grappling him to the ground.

Caleb screamed, then started running; it was only because John tripped him that he didn't escape into the woods. John had moved out of pure instinct: this man had been the fey's previous host and he had no business dashing off and leaving Dada to be mauled.

Already, John could see his father's face whitening. His arms were lifted upwards, pulling him to his feet as if the thing were shaking a doll it hadn't quite understood the point of.

'Kind friend, stop that at once!' John yelled, grabbing his iron knife from this pocket and tossing aside the leather sheath. 'Dada, can you hold it still? I can cut it off if I don't cut you, but . . .'

Dada. The word pulsed through John's body, an echo of his tone that shook the word as it had been shaking Matthew, searching it for meaning. *Dada. Dada.*

There was a dull bubble of sound, and then another: the wet thud of a butcher jointing a cow.

Matthew was a brave man. He didn't scream, but he choked and gasped out, 'Johnny, run!'

'I will not!' John exclaimed, in the moment weeping more with fury than distress, and hurled himself at his father. Matthew gave a groan of pain as the dense little body landed upon his – but John had to cling on tight, for Matthew's arms were loose in their sockets now, held a-dangle by the feathering fey like laundry on a line.

'Kind friend, *off* my father!' John yelled, and slashed. Why he struck with the flat of the blade rather than the edge wasn't something he could have explained, even afterwards; he slapped hard at the fizzing tumble of white down, and then the feathers burst away, unpeeling themselves from Matthew's maimed arms.

The thing cracked in the air like a snapped rope. There was a shuddering wail, John's word *Dada* crushing everything under the sound, and then there was nothing left of the thing but a few specks melting away into nothing but a glint of light as they drifted down.

Matthew was on his knees, breath scraping into him, out; his face was grey. It was with a horrible smile he said, 'Thank you, John darling. You're a good lad. But don't risk yourself again, eh?'

'"Run" indeed,' John said crossly. 'I like that. You, Mister – he addressed Caleb, who hadn't quite run out of sight before the fey thing vanished and was now picking a wary way back, 'come and help me up, will you? You've been about as much use as a pig in a pulpit.'

'Now, now, Johnny,' Matthew said through his teeth, just about managing to get to his feet unaided; his arms dangled heavy by his sides, giving him the look of a broken scarecrow. 'That was a fearsome thing. Let's not judge a man for being afraid.'

'That's all very Christian,' John said, taking firm hold of the man Caleb's arm before he could run off again, 'but I don't think you should set such a standard for me. I'm not about to forgive him for leaving you to be hurt like that, however scared he was, and if you set me a better example, you'll only tempt me to the sin of despair, and then you'll be a party to the sin yourself.'

'Consider the ravens, which have neither storehouse nor barn,' Caleb said, with a bark of laughter and little apparent theology.

'I – I fear,' Matthew said, struggling to consider the holy laws ahead of the blazing pain in his shoulders, 'you both of you have things a little mixed up.'

The three of them staggered down the path to Gyrford, each in his own way failing to consider the lilies.

Franklin was standing at the church door, giving out warnings – or he was trying to, but folks from everywhere were busy trying to tell the men news of their own: birds had been seen around the neighbourhood fleeing to far woodlands, burying themselves in holes, and in the case of one particular magpie, curling up with a mew that sounded as if she'd learned it from a cat, making a very fair attempt to tuck her wings and beak away and pass for a sleeping kitten. Jedediah had taken the bag in which its finder had trapped it and was out in the Smith garden, making an attempt to reason with it – without success, for the creature was determined to be a cat and unresponsive to any iron. He'd managed to confine Left-Lop the pig in one of the cages they kept out back, but the beast refused to have its wounds stitched by anyone but John; it shivered behind the iron bars, grunting with pain.

The skies were empty and the lanes were silent. Somewhere, there was a terrible gulf.

It was Janet who saw John trying to support her staggering husband, with a bewildered-looking red-headed man trailing along beside them. She had been pruning the strawberry plants beside the house, but at the sight of them, she dropped her shears and ran, her eyes already full of tears before she reached them.

'Matthew!' she exclaimed. 'Oh, my darling, what's befallen you? What's happened to your arms? Matthew, darling, can you speak to me?'

'Of course he can,' John said, attempting to be reassuring.

'Let your father speak!' Janet exclaimed. 'How is he to tell me how he is if you don't let him have a breath of time to answer me? Let him speak!'

'I—It's all right, Janie,' Matthew said, with some difficulty, both because he was trying not to be sick from the pain, and because neither his wife nor his son were giving him much of a chance to get a word in. 'We found this man here afflicted, and between us we drove the fey off. I – I fear it's pulled my arms out of joint, but – but never mind, love, a disjoint heals quicker than a break . . . Do you think Dada's about? I'd be glad of some help with . . .'

'I'll fetch him,' Janet said tearfully.

'I'll go,' John said, and took off.

'Now, don't cry, love,' Matthew managed. 'Don't worry yourself. It'll . . . it be all right in good time . . .'

At this, his lost his footing and fell against the red-haired Caleb, who had been regarding Janet with hard eyes.

'What were you about at the house there?' he asked. He said it with a grunt, shouldering Matthew back onto his feet with little apparent notice of his injuries.

'Oh,' Janet said, wiping her eyes and feeling rather conscience-stricken: Matthew was being very strong – well, of course he was, her Matthew was the finest man ever to walk the earth – but crying over him and making him comfort her was not measuring up to his heroic example. 'I beg your pardon. I see you're the worse for wear too, sir. I'm Janet Smith, I'm the farrier's lady in these parts. If you've a need to have your cuts dressed, I can—'

'You're *what*?'

Even through his pain, Matthew heard the sharpness. The man spoke with a snap, an edge of real hostility that made no sense at all. Matthew gathered all his resolve and said, 'I'm the farrier's son here, sir, and this is my wife. Do you understand me? I see you understand my Janet; do you hear what I say?'

Matthew's words did not seem to make an impression on the man. Instead, he stared at Janet, looking her up and down with open assessment and no warmth at all.

'Louise Smith, is it?' he demanded. 'Louise, you must be.'

'Er – no, sir.' Janet prided herself on being up to any crisis, but not with Matthew so hurt. 'Janet Smith is my name, sir.'

'God help us, when did he marry you?' The man Caleb shook his head. 'And a woman twice his age, by the look of you, or near enough. What do you with a husband of not long past twenty, Madam? You must have powers indeed.'

'Sir,' Janet said, feeling more desperate by the minute, 'I believe you are thinking of Mistress Louise Smith, my mother-in-law, sir, or she would have been, God rest her. She was married to Jedediah Smith, Mister – wait, how old did you say you thought him?'

It was at that point that Franklin Thorpe, tugged along by John, came into view. 'Matt!' he exclaimed. 'Oh, God bless you. Come on, lean on me if you like, we'll get you out to the garden, that's where your father is.'

'Will you come, Janie?' Matthew asked, trying not to sound too pathetic, and so it was the entire group that entered the garden gate.

'Matthew, good God . . .' Jedediah said, rising to his feet – but then he stopped. The magpie-puss leaped from his hands, raced under the bushes and was away, but Jedediah was still, his mouth half-open, emptied of words.

Franklin, whose attention had been on Matthew, turned to look, and when he saw the red-headed man, he too froze.

'What's the matter with you?' Janet exclaimed. 'Father, Matthew's arms need setting!'

Jedediah couldn't speak. The man wasn't so big as he remembered, but it was him, every line and shade of him.

'Heal me, help me, hide me from horrors!' the pig contributed from its cage.

'The elder and master of men and metal

'Is struck silent at this sight!

'Sirs, am I safe? Is it safe here, sirs?'

Jedediah cleared his throat. 'Well, now,' he said. Then, almost as if something spoke through him, 'It's all right, Mattie. Sit yourself on the bench, we'll have a look at you. Never fret, son, we'll get you to rights.'

'Dada?' Matthew would have been grateful to sit, but his father's tone stopped him. Jedediah hadn't called him Mattie in decades.

The man squinted at Jedediah. 'Rook,' he said. Then, gesturing to Franklin, he added, 'Treecreeper.' He frowned, as if trying to get something straight in his head, and said, sounding louder but not much less confused, 'Well, for God's sake, if we're to have a to-do about my house with hopping every which way, at least give a man a drink.'

There was a long, tight silence.

'Mister Mackem?' Franklin said, very softly. 'Do you remember me, sir? The years have changed me, I'm sure. Franklin Thorpe. I was only a boy when you saw me last.'

Corbie Mackem shook his head. 'Treecreeper!' he shouted, sounding very sure he was making sense.

'Dada?' Matthew said, his voice shaking. 'What's to do?'

Jedediah drew a deep breath. It was hard; his chest was stiffening, muscles locking around his ribs as if an old fist had come back to clench them. 'Good evening, Father,' he said. 'I reckon you've been away somewhere. You haven't aged a day.'

'[illegible] say we hide [illegible]? The [illegible] continued [illegible].

'[illegible] make a [illegible] and [illegible]

[illegible]

[illegible]

Ichabod [illegible] around. [illegible] something [illegible] through [illegible] it all [illegible]. [illegible] on the [illegible] well [illegible] we'll get you [illegible].'

[illegible] Matthew would have [illegible] that [illegible] open [illegible] Matthew [illegible].

[illegible] he said. [illegible] Frankly,' he added. [illegible] the [illegible] something [illegible] his head and [illegible] not much [illegible] which way [illegible] have a [illegible].

[illegible].

[illegible] he said [illegible]. 'Do you [illegible] [illegible] were a boy [illegible] you [illegible] last.'

[illegible] shook [illegible] he shouted [illegible].

'[illegible],' Matthew said, his voice shaking. 'What [illegible]?'

Ichabod [illegible] a breath [illegible] looking [illegible] [illegible] you [illegible] somewhere. You [illegible] dead.'

BOOK THREE

JEDEDIAH

In his earliest memories, Jedediah Smith had two mothers, the silver and the brown.

The silver mother was Mama, his own mother, Constance Smith, who was beautiful as an angel and always a little baffled. She was fun, Mama, enchanted with the cleverness of 'little one' and endlessly pleased with his games; his favourites were hers and she delighted in them. It was some years before he understood that Mama had trouble telling whose feelings were her own and whose were someone else's, and that they didn't really share the same tastes at all. It was years more before he understood that this didn't cheapen her love, and that within her confusion was a woman who truly did rejoice to see him happy. All he knew at the time was that Mama had gentle hands and a face like nothing on earth, and she liked to stroke his hair, and he wished he could keep her attention on him better than he could.

Jedediah loved his mother with a furious, protective passion that upset her if he showed it too fiercely, for she could never understand anything if folks grew too stormy around her. She should have been able to, for she was alert to everything, but it took so little for her to become agitated – and when that happened, she got lost. She would sit and shake, turn from him and call for Agnes; she would pick up a stone or a frayed old shift and nurse it, crooning reassurance, without even a glance at the child standing beside her.

It was because of Agnes, his brown mother, that Jedediah was fed, clothed, clean and sensible, because while Agnes had trouble with things like pulling weeds and killing chickens, and could never so much as rap his knuckles no matter how stubbornly he behaved, she also was the one who remembered that boys must eat at regular times, that cold wind makes for cold skin, and that he was her kin and must be safe and able to give account of himself. She called him 'my dear'; only his father bothered to wrap his tongue around Jedediah's long name. Agnes was towering, almost the width of his father, although not so tall, and her mighty arms were always good for giving him a swing through the air, or picking him up if he tumbled.

Agnes worked beside Constance with a harmony Jedediah would later associate with life-long partners in skilled trades, but at the time he just assumed they were both his mother, or part of her, and if Agnes often comforted Constance as well as himself if he grew upset, well, that was the nature of mothers.

His father, in those years, was mostly a voice. He was tall and bulky with a spray of reddish hair and a redder beard he liked to scratch against Jedediah's bare chin, but more than anything, he was a voice: a shout from the smithy, a boom across the supper table, a call across the yard to fetch him this, find him that, for the love of God spare him having to listen to anyone's complaints about the other.

Jedediah was aware that his mother went quiet when his father was in the room, and he supposed she was afraid of him. Why wouldn't she be? It was his father who wielded the belt on Jedediah when out of temper, and then his mother cried too, for hours, craning her neck to search for bruises on her own back, searching her pillow, her clothes, the dented apples in the stores, frantic that she was unable to mend the marks of damage on every item in the world. Jedediah learned young that if Corbie Mackem was out of humour, it was best to stay very quiet, very grave, and give no spark of spirit back to kindle his father's ever-present frustration. It was his mother who would bear the brunt of it, though in his opinion Mama was very good except when she was mixed up. She wasn't stupid either, whatever Father said about her: even as a child, Jedediah could see a kind of frustrated intelligence in her silver eyes, as if she had the wish to understand the world but simply couldn't sort out the jumble it presented her. Feelings, to her, came from unknown directions; ask her to talk to anyone and she was unable to make sense of things. She would struggle, then give up, directing whatever comfort she could in hit-and-miss guesses. Agnes she trusted, and Jedediah she petted when she could keep calm enough to remember who he was, but her words wouldn't come out straight and most of her guesses were wrong.

But that wasn't what angered Corbie. When Corbie was in the room, Constance would get up without a word and swathe herself in clothing: her shawl; Agnes' shawl, even if she had to pluck it from her sister's shoulders; horse blankets; cleaning rags. Corbie would see her bundle herself and snap, 'Oh, for God's sake, woman.' Then he'd stalk out.

But if he was angry with Agnes, he'd come in all sweet and tender to Constance, putting an arm around her shoulder, kissing her cheek. Then Constance would forget everything; she'd sink to her knees and retch, gasping and clutching her throat and hiding her faultless face within her silver hair, and Agnes would say, 'No, stop it – please – look you, I take your point. Please, take it up with me, Mister Smith. *Please.*'

And after that, Corbie would usually have his way over whatever it was.

So Jedediah was afraid of his father. It wasn't so uncommon in Gyrford to be a little cautious around fathers, who were usually the ones tasked with disciplining their sons, but Jedediah could see that mothers weren't usually so frightened. Most women smiled if their husbands kissed their cheek. But then, most mothers talked like Auntie, in full sentences with their words all in a row, and they had her air of exhausted sense. It might have been better if someone had married Auntie instead, for no one kissed Agnes and she might have liked it better.

But by the time he was old enough to 'prentice, certain things had been made clear to him.

The explanations came from his Auntie Pell, who Corbie wouldn't have in the house. God had given him two Smith women under his roof and that was enough for any man; three, Corbie declaimed, would be the straw to break the camel and they must have mercy upon a poor fellow hard at his work with no more sins on his soul than any other fellow, if that fellow was rather put upon, heaven help him.

When he started to go on like this Constance would run

and hide, so Pell didn't press the point. They went for walks instead: she would take Jedediah by the hand and march him down the lanes, making no concession for his smaller legs, and as they marched, she would give him information like one speaking such unalterable law that there was very little more to be said.

'They won't tell you what's what,' she'd say to him, 'for Constance doesn't know it and Agnes can't say it, for she reckons it'd hurt your feelings and that ties her tongue. And maybe it will, but it's no world for a weak man, my boy. You'll have to stand on your own feet, that's all there is to it.'

Jedediah, hurrying after her on feet not quite up to her speed, was too breathless to argue the point.

'I was there when you were born, lad,' Pell informed him, 'for you need one able to cut a cord as well as hold a hand at such times, and Agnes does what she can. No fey touch on you, that's for sure. We'll have none of that any more, God willing. But your mother, she took it hard. There's been harder births in this world, for Constance always was well-made in every limb, God help her, but she had no notion of what had befell her for the last nine-odd months, and she thought the whole world was sick – that the trees' joints were aching and the river's stomach was queased and the rain was the clouds being sick and I don't know what-all. She thought the world was ending when you came, my lad, and that's the truth. She was sure it was the time of hail and fire and blood – and why anyone let her stay and listen to that sermon I'll never know – and the world was all to burn up and the seas to boil and suchlike. Poor lass. Can't blame her; it was a fair guess given the stirring-up her mind got. When out you came, my lad, away Agnes took you and wrapped you up warm and gave you a wash, and I gave your mother willow bark in cider, plenty of it, till she was – well, I won't say quite drunk, but not of the mind she'd been an hour before, let me tell you that. Then Agnes gave you back to her and she thought you were a gift from someone. Always took to you, she did, but she didn't put you together with all the carrying and the bearing, and that's as well for you, lad. But she did put it together with how she got that way. That's why she won't have your father too near now. Wasn't made to bear, that one. Nor me; never could fancy a man enough to put up with his nonsense. You're all I'll have for son or sprig, my lad, so you'd better be a good boy. I'd have you myself, if His Majesty would have it. But you'd need your wits about you in that house, Jedediah, so mind you do. Keep up, will you, and don't dawdle, we've miles to go before we're home yet.'

When he was seven, Jedediah was officially apprenticed to his father. Corbie showed him how to feed the forge, how to judge the heat of the coals, how to heft a hammer so his calluses would build in the right places, and told him that from now on he had to finish his dinner whether he liked it or not, or he'd get a boxed ear. Jedediah wasn't quite sure of the connection, so he asked Auntie Pell.

'Could take the trouble to explain, that man,' Auntie Pell said, walking faster than ever; Jedediah's breaks from work were shorter now, and she was clearly determined to cover as much ground as possible.

'There's nothing to it, lad,' Pell said, giving the sky a

suspicious glance. 'Boy hammers iron, he burns up food. You burn up more food that you've ate, you grow thin, and a smith needs brawn on his back. And most like, His Majesty's noticed you haven't the Mackem heft to your bones. Never you fret: there's many a slight body with strong sinews, so don't you listen if he cavils at the build of you. You'll be a finer-looking man than him come the day, and that's plain to see. And don't break yourself working to prove yourself strong, either: you rest when you have to. Just don't miss your supper; you've seen underfed horses. God made your body proper. You feed it.'

So while Jedediah did indeed hear comments about sparrow-boned idlers, he finished his dinners and Pell felt over his arms and back with firm, suspicious hands whenever she saw him, and poulticed or massaged any muscle she didn't approve the state of. But he'd started to think it wasn't right, the way his mother only ever licked at her spoon, taking proper bites when Corbie looked and then, when his back was turned, picking over her pottage with light fingertips, shaking her head and shaping the silent words with her perfect lips, 'Not hungry. Not hungry.'

It became clear, as Jedediah's apprenticeship wore on, that Corbie was a man who liked to enjoy life. He wanted his son to enjoy it too, and would have been glad to share with him any good bread he was given on his rounds, any sip of ale or perry or, if he could get it, strong mead from when the monastery near Kidderminster found its bells infested with wayward shapes that sang like brass and writhed like women, giving Corbie many jokes to tell upon the subject of monkish virtues and their unsuitability for the life of man.

The drinks made Jedediah cough, and if he did swallow them, they made him sleepy. This didn't stop Corbie offering them, or finding it a flaw in his character if they didn't give him the sense of defiant delight he felt they ought. Agnes worried about strong drink being pressed on so young a lad, but she never dared say anything to Corbie; Jedediah could see her trying hard to hide her concerns for fear of tempting Corbie to force him to drink more just on principle.

'My dear,' Agnes called him; 'my lad,' said Pell. Even Corbie would 'my boy' him often enough, though he liked to say his full name too; he'd chosen 'Jedediah' as a joke that would never wear old, saying that as marriage had shorn a syllable off his own surname, he'd better give his son a few extra syllables just in case. Never did Constance call Jedediah anything but 'little one'. She had never spoken a phrase to him that carried within it the notion of 'mine'.

By the time Jedediah was twelve, he was strong-backed and had his own ideas of farrier work. He'd broken his fingers four times, swinging the hammer in his stubborn moods; better to miss his stroke than show himself a weakling before his father. You were supposed to be a proper smith after three breaks, but Corbie had stopped joking about that after the second finger; he would say only, 'Well, your arm's getting better, but your aim needs work,' as Jedediah stared at his side-skewed hands and tried to breathe rather than shriek.

Corbie showed him how to set bones and by the third time, he'd decided he'd rather set his own. His father, finding this amusing, said, 'That's the man,' and after the fourth break, left him to it without offering help, saying, 'Well, you'll settle that yourself, then. On you go.'

There might have been boys in his position who would still be devoted to their fathers. Corbie knew that Jedediah wasn't, even when he said nothing to provoke – or at least, he tried, but he didn't succeed, because Corbie could be provoked by anything if it struck him at the wrong moment. But Corbie could see the lack in Jedediah, and by the time he was thirteen, Jedediah had stopped trying to hide it. He could keep his face still as stone, but he seemed to have transparent skin. For Corbie, at least, it was easy to see through to the unfilial heart beneath.

The one thing he couldn't accept, however, was that he was wrong-headed. Corbie wasn't in the habit of shielding him from the bloodier cases, and Jedediah was starting to form his own opinions – more certain, in some cases, than his father's, although it was better not to say so.

Corbie disliked the land around these parts. The scent of the may didn't please him, and the cider, for all that he could drink it by the jug, tasted wrong on his tongue; the customs and ways of talking all struck him as foolish. Jedediah called him Father, for a start; the local word, Dada, was in Corbie's opinion babyish, and there were only so many times a boy could call for his dada and get mimicked for it before he took the point. Back in Tinsdowne folks said 'Pa', but Jedediah stuck to 'Father' and was regarded by casual visitors as an unusually respectful young man.

But he couldn't respect everything about his father's ways of farriership; in particular, he couldn't feel right about approaching the fey of the land as a conqueror. It had been a fine feat to lock up Ab, no doubt about it, and customers liked a man who flexed his arms and roared in their defence, but Jedediah loved the countryside around Gyrford and didn't feel equipped to conquer it. He wasn't an arriving gallant; he was *from* here – it would be like conquering his own feet.

And that was getting harder to hide, and it was harder still when certain customers were beginning to prefer him to Corbie. It was a minority opinion, of course: Jedediah was a skinny boy with a plain way of speaking and no flourish to his presence, and set beside his father, he was easy to ignore.

But the case of the stone wolves, and the troubles that followed it, formed a definite rift between them: a fine thread of difference running through the bedrock of father and son that might one day split open.

The stone wolves sat at the crest of Hawton Down. By day they were nothing more than sarsens, great sharp-tipped rocks pointing skywards that kept a perfect circle around the plateau's top – although which order they stood in might vary from day to day. Possibly they'd been placed there in the time before history, when men were giants and could carry about sarsen blocks like hay bales, which was all very well if you were a giant, Jedediah reckoned, but folks these days weren't of the size or strength to swat the People away. These days you needed iron and good sense, and there was neither in the stone wolves of Hawton Down.

By night, they lowered their pointed snouts and crept, hunting in a slow, dragging creep over the churning earth, and the sound of grinding rock against soil was enough to set your teeth shuddering – or, in the case of that little girl Maisie Dawes, who had far too much imagination, creeping all the way out of her mouth. The poor lass got lost one evening and had to pass them, and by the time she reached her home, every last molar had fled her mouth and studded itself across her cheeks from ear to ear like buttons in a blood-caked coat. That was the point they'd come to beg Corbie for help.

Corbie had managed to set the girl's face back to rights thanks to a heavy drowse of sleeping-draught, a pair of pliers, and a complicated mesh of notes to set against the vibration of the stones that was still echoing around the girl. Jedediah played them on the fiddle – Corbie was only a good enough musician to entertain his neighbours, which by farrier standards made him a bad musician, while Jedediah was excellent: within a perfect geometry of sound, he could create some peace and order in the world. Mama and Aunt Agnes loved music, but if he presumed to play just for them, Corbie chased him out to practise cold-fingered in the open air, telling him to stop annoying everyone.

Any job requiring Jedediah's playing put Corbie out of temper. 'Well, we'll have the fee of them for her pretty face,' he said sourly. 'They'll have all their girls sweet lures on a hook to land some poor man into a bed he can't escape.'

Jedediah couldn't agree that a girl's face was nothing more than a trap to bait men, but he said nothing; if he irritated Corbie mid-work, he might just leave Maisie half-finished. In the end she was left with a smile as gummy as a babe, but the scars on her skin were no worse than pock-marks. She was sent to live with an affectionate auntie far from the sarsens, who could dress hair so fine that a little marring on the cheeks didn't matter so much.

But the stones still crawled at night. Folks gossiped that Maisie had got her face turned inside out because the People caught her staring, or worse, that she'd wandered inside the stone circle and the People had sent back a monster. Corbie found the whole thing entertaining and refused to correct anyone, only roaring with laughter and saying he looked forward to the next time he heard the story, for he could watch its growth as tenderly as a proud father. Jedediah, who had never known his father proud of him, tried to correct the story behind Corbie's back and got his ears boxed for it.

But then there was the day that Winifred Lenden and her little sister went out to play, and came back full of tales.

Jack Lenden, looking pale and frantic, stalked into the smithy, swearing that he'd pay Corbie any amount of money if he'd only settle matters. Jack – whose grandson Ralph would one day find himself treed by a righteous pig – was a neighbour of the Dawes family, and unlucky enough to live even nearer the stone wolves. The Lendens had three children surviving, Winifred, Cissie and baby Amos, who was kept particularly close because the People had a habit of taking boys.

Corbie reckoned it was only natural, for a boy was worth more – or at least, he believed this in principle, even though his own boy didn't delight him all that much. Jedediah wasn't so sure – the People could be male or female, both or neither, and sometimes changed their sex with less concern than a man changing his shirt; to his mind, it was more likely that the People drew their notions of a child's value from how folks around them behaved, so they favoured boys because that was what families usually did. (He felt confirmed in this theory decades later, when Sairey Baker's best chicken was stolen away by the People: Sairey had seven fine children and took almost no interest in any of them, spending as much of her day as possible in the chicken-coop, *chuck-chuck-chuck*ing away. He'd got the chicken back by means of an iron trap, told Sairey that he'd traded her children for it and sent them to live with their granny, an arrangement that suited everyone. But that was much later, when he was old enough to feel sure in his opinions.) Be that as it may, the infant Amos Lenden was cossetted and kept close, while his older sisters were allowed to wander, and on this day, they wandered back out of joint with themselves.

Cissie was quite speechless, tripping over her feet as if she couldn't quite work out how many legs she was supposed to have. Jack had shaken Winifred, demanding to know what they had been about, and Winifred, insisting that they hadn't been naughty and shouldn't be shaken, said they had only gone to visit the sheep, but the People had taken them to a place that looked just like the fields but wasn't, for the grass was full of faces and the bark on the trees was full of birds, little woody birds with crumpled wings and knot-hole eyes, and the sky overhead ran like a stream. Winifred had prayed and prayed to come home, and she'd walked them both out of it in the end, and she'd been very brave and wanted her mama and shouldn't be punished.

Winifred was a good girl, but she was only six and you

couldn't trust a six-year-old to know whether she had brought home the false or the true sister home. That was what was shuddering Jack Lenden's heart, and why he swore he'd do anything to get his daughter back.

Corbie stood by the old methods, and the old method here was clear: you set the child out on an iron shovel, and there it stayed overnight. The iron would hurt any fey thing's feet, and a night and day without sleep would torment it worse. Before long, the People would collect their suffering hostage and return you yours.

The first night, Cissie cried and cried – not the fey shriek of a lost thing, but a raw, droning keen, the wail of a child out in the night when the skies were cloudless and any heat of the day had long vanished into the black.

Corbie sat his watch, smoked his pipe and waited. Nothing came to get the changeling.

But when Jedediah sat his watch, he couldn't do it. He didn't know if this crying creature before him was fey or mortal, but he couldn't sit for hours in the cold watching a three-year-old girl standing weeping in her shift.

When Corbie came round in the morning, he found Jedediah asleep on his leather pallet, which had been tanned and waxed for such watches. His blankets were heaped atop him, and nestled against him, her back tucked close to his chest and her head on his arm, was the creature that either was or wasn't Cissie Lenden.

His father whipped him for that, which was what Jedediah had expected; he'd learned years ago to set his teeth and knot his voice deep in his throat so his mother heard nothing.

Corbie always preferred to return to joking and jollity straight afterwards, seeing his belt less as a weapon than as a good-natured argument, driving the plain fact of his greater standing deep into Jedediah's skin. In Corbie's view, once everyone was back in his rightful place there was no call to sulk about it, and Jedediah was used to pretending it hadn't happened so that his father wouldn't decide to re-emphasise his authority over Agnes or Constance.

But just this once, he ran away for the day. Corbie might be angry if he couldn't find a way to laugh it off, but Jedediah urgently wanted to trace the Lenden girls' path. There was another night on the shovel coming up for little Cissie.

It took most of the morning searching, but he found it towards the middle of the afternoon. There, at the edges of the field near the Lenden farm, where the sheep were white-faced and pink-eared and irresistible, were clumps of mushrooms, stems fine as thread and caps sharp-tipped and brown and dainty as a little girl's thumbnail.

Jedediah took the caps to his best friend. Tom Attic's father had come over to cook pastry for his master, a Moorish ambassador in the city, and eventually left for greener places, saying that life in this country was cold and wet, and that if God's will had placed him here, he'd like to spend his time amongst its flowers. Mister Attic had converted to Christianity for the sake of peace and taken the baptismal name Paul, which nobody used; he had married a local girl and dedicated himself to a study of kitchen gardening and the many delicacies you could flavour with the local greenery.

Jedediah and Tom had taken to each other from the first,

and Tom had worked out early in life that seasoning food was all very well, but useful salves and brews which kept for weeks or months could be sold to packmen. Over their years of friendship the boys had spent many a cheerful day making themselves usefully sick, giddily drunk or occasionally well in their search for the best combinations of medicinal herbs. Mister Attic said Jedediah was a good influence, so Jedediah was welcome to spend as much of his time as he could at the Attics' home, where Mister Attic was always kind to his wife and children.

'Tom,' Jedediah said now, 'we'll need to try these and quick.'

'Well, good morning to you too, dear lad,' said Tom, grinning at his friend's serious face. 'Are those what I think?'

'I don't know what they are,' Jedediah said, sitting down a little clumsily; his back was stiff from his father's attentions. He'd been planning to keep it quiet, but Tom was sharp-eyed.

'You need some salve?' he said.

They'd had fights about this in the past; Jedediah didn't like to talk about it, not even with Tom, whose father left punishment to his soft-hearted and soft-handed wife. Most families in Gyrford backed up their parenting with the occasional resort to stick or belt, and among those folks, Corbie's fathering was easy to brush off. But Jedediah kept quieter about it than most: all lads were eager to avoid a whipping, but others didn't seem to struggle with the killing rage it provoked in him, deep down where he kept things locked that might hurt everyone if he let them out. And even if they were punished, other lads were able to love their fathers still. Jedediah, however, resented the beatings and slaps, even the casual little shoves that didn't hurt all that much, which only went to back up his father's opinion of him as hard-willed and stubborn. And probably he was.

Tom, on the other hand, didn't blame him for being angry, and was annoyed with him if he wouldn't accept any help. It was a consolation to know Tom was there when they were apart; Jedediah often sustained himself with thoughts of Tom's partisan outrage, of Mister Attic's sweet cakes and patient eyes and his deep voice telling him he was a fine lad, of Mistress Attic's warm exclamation of, '*There* you are, love!' when she saw him coming. But when they were together, Jedediah didn't want to think about Corbie and his quick-swung belt, and found it hard not to snap at Tom, who didn't understand that.

Yes, Jedediah thought bitterly, no doubt he was hard-willed. And it wasn't the time to lash out. If the mushrooms were what he suspected, it would be very stupid indeed to eat them while in unnecessary pain. What was in them could make a bad mood a great deal worse, and he'd had enough upsetting experiences for one day.

'He spares not the rod,' he said, with his best attempt at carelessness, 'so he hates not his son. So yes, if we don't talk about it, I'll take the salve, but we need to test these mushrooms, and it must be today.'

'Well,' said Tom, who was gentle-spirited even if he did like a joke, 'never say I lack the spirit of brotherhood. If these turn my guts inside out again, let it be known my dignity died in the name of knowledge.'

Jedediah smiled for the first time in what felt like weeks. 'I'll buy it a headstone,' he said. 'I can't eat too many, though. I'll need to be sober by tonight.'

By the time Jedediah reached the Lenden property that night, he had a stomach ache, a bright idea for a new design of hoof-pick, a lingering sense that everything at the corners of his eyes was flowing like water, and an answer to what had happened.

It was the farmhand Rob Johnson who stood watch over little Cissie that night; Corbie must have decided to make new arrangements since he couldn't find his stubborn son, and perhaps Jack Lenden couldn't bear to. Or perhaps Jack would be on watch later, tearfully implacable against the creature he thought had stolen away his daughter.

Jedediah pulled himself together. He could see, even in the soft moonlight, how scarlet Cissie's bare, frozen feet were beginning to turn; he could hear her crying.

'Evening, Rob,' he said, sounding as deep and sure as he could. His voice was starting to change, and it was the Mackem voice, unfortunately; exercise could make it tuneful and true, but nothing could make it sweet. Still, he practised singing with patient care – Agnes trained him behind Corbie's back and her voice was beautiful – and he managed now to keep it from cracking. 'My father sends me, says to bring the lass to the smithy. He's thought of something.'

For a day so frantic, the actual rescuing of Cissie Lenden was undramatic. Rob wasn't sorry to have a chance of getting to bed, and Corbie was known to be a changeable man. Rob yawned, touched his forelock and left Jedediah to it.

As Jedediah approached the little girl, she burst into louder tears than before, holding up her chubby arms and howling.

Jedediah felt awkward with such a small creature, and a little cross at his own awkwardness, and couldn't think of anything to say except, 'All right, dear, up you come.' He put her on his saddle and rode behind her to Gyrford.

He didn't go into the house; there was Corbie to avoid, and also his mother and aunt, and he couldn't face any of them until the edges of his eyes had stopped wavering. He laid down the pallet in the smithy in front of the warm forge and buried himself and Cissie under the blankets.

The next morning, of course, there were explanations, and it wasn't a difficult story once Jedediah had it worked out. The Lenden girls had found some mushrooms and, not yet knowing the difference between those to eat and those to treat with caution, made a morning snack of them. But these were the mushrooms Tom had christened 'seer caps' because they made your eyes drunk: you saw things that weren't there. Jedediah had been pretty sure of that the moment he'd found them, having tested them with Tom before, and eating them confirmed it beyond all doubt: he and Tom spent the entire afternoon fascinated with a square foot of scrub grass. The mushrooms were good fun if you knew tipsy dreams from fairyland – but if the world had started wavering around two little girls, what else were they to think?

The effects would wear off; all Cissie needed now was some extra watching until she felt better. More than that, though, she needed not to be placed out at night, feet freezing on an iron shovel, and dragged through days of wakefulness until she broke altogether.

Corbie was a man of tradition, but he wasn't stupid; he barked with laughter when Jedediah laid the explanation before him and declared that was a joke on mankind, even if Jedediah must snatch away small children against his father's orders like some kind of fey being himself. He whipped Jedediah again anyway, for the sake of form, but he did send Cissie Lenden back to her family with the instruction that she was quite all right now. He didn't bother to dispute the issue of whether she'd been a changeling or not; he regarded that as farrier business. Jedediah quietly asked Tom to send over some salve for her cold-flayed feet.

After that, Corbie decreed that Hawton Down needed settling because it was causing nothing but trouble, making his son rebellious and trying a poor old man's patience and breaking his spirit before his time. (Corbie was just past thirty then, and had been claiming himself old and infirm ever since Jedediah learned to talk well enough to answer back.)

The folks around Hawton Down had no sense at all, Corbie said. He set Jedediah beside him in the cart and drove across the countryside, all the way to Wesselham Hill, where a white chalk horse galloped, cut in the ancient days when the giant men must have had big tools to sketch such pictures across the land. The horse was curve-limbed and gleaming, for the Wesselham folks considered it good luck and made a point of weeding it every year. Corbie pointed at it and said, 'That's the idea. You're the penman, Jedediah, my boy. Time to put your scholarship to use, eh?' (Jedediah had learned to write from his grandfather, Clem Smith, who petted him timidly as long as Corbie wasn't there; Corbie had still not forgiven either of them.) 'Let's see you draw something like that – only a wolf, of course. Good and fierce. Tail and ears up, mind, like a dog showing who's strongest.'

Jedediah blinked at his father and Corbie gave him a clump on the head that wasn't quite gentle. 'Wake up, my lad,' he said. 'We'll be about it when we get home.'

As they drove back, Corbie told stories of the chalk men on the hills of his own home further north, great-armed fellows with spears a-flourish and, in one case, with a standing prick so large a man could lie with his head on the tip and his feet on the bags. 'There're couples up there every summer night,' he said, with a reminiscent frown. 'I'd say one in five children in the nearest few villages were got on that lad's cock. On the long nights we'd go up there with torches and ale and dance every which way, and if you couldn't get a girl to lie on the grass then you weren't trying. Even the married ones would play in the dark, bless them. They don't sing those songs down here, though. I like a good horse, but it's nothing to have a festival over.'

'Wasn't that rash?' Jedediah asked, trying to sound less uncomfortable than he felt. 'Wouldn't the People there be tempted in?'

Corbie woke from his reverie and gave Jedediah a look of annoyance. 'Nay, boy,' he said, 'why would they? It was men made the thing. The People get themselves in other ways, most of them. There's no harm in a good dance if you do it within the chalk lines.'

Jedediah said nothing, and Corbie's mood darkened. 'There's that slate you like so much in the cart,' he said. 'Packed it, I did, and some of your bits of chalk. Get them and start your sketch. Sooner the better.'

No one had taught Jedediah how to draw, or at least, not to draw for beauty rather precision. He could map out the measurements of a case, but the wolf he produced was a rather jagged affair. Corbie, though, regarded it with some satisfaction.

'Just about crude enough to work on 'em,' he said, and he made every able man and woman in the village of Hawton dig it into the slope, picking off clods and scraping through to the white underneath until there was a spike-backed wolf with stick lines for fangs, an eye the size of a cooking pot and hunched white claws cut into the upper slopes of Hawton Down, glowering opposite the stone circle.

That night, Jedediah and Corbie watched from the cart, their ears stuffed with rags soaked in iron-stored oil, just in case. The moon rose and the stones shimmered, the shadows of clouds rippling across them like a bristle of fur. Then, slow as a cold frog, they lowered their muzzles and sniffed the air.

Across the valley, the white of the wolf shone, the naked chalk exposed to any nose that could smell the scent of stone.

The sarsens froze. They regarded the chalk wolf, which bared its fangs and did not move.

Slowly, slowly, the stones shrank back, retreated to themselves, setting their crags back into place, sitting a little squatter than they had done, in a crouch of grey-edged, petrified submission.

In the dark, Jedediah could see the glint of Corbie's grin.

'Well,' he said, 'that showed 'em who's master.' The grin dropped a little and his brooding expression returned. 'You'd think some Smith would have thought of it generations back,' he said. 'Stupid. Well, there's the wolf for you all now. You could have put a cock on it, though, Jedediah. Wouldn't have killed you. Just for sentiment's sake.'

That was that, then. Corbie Mackem had put his mark on the landscape, all across the hill. The Lendens, who could see it from their farm, were supposed to feel it was keeping them safe; Jedediah was aware they felt it more as a dreadful reminder of bad days, but they weren't the sort of folks to say this to Corbie.

Cissie Lenden was bewildered for three months and clumsy for nine, and she grew up with a near-religious adoration for Jedediah that just about stayed him from asking how she could forgive her father for what he'd done to her. But the Lendens were fearful folks before the mushroom incident, and more so after it, and all three of their children grew up on tales of the People and of how narrowly Cissie had escaped.

Some folks called Corbie the Sarsen Shepherd after that. No one much remembered that it was Jedediah's design, and Jedediah didn't contest the issue; within a month or two he could see that Corbie himself didn't think that an important fact, and if Jedediah was going to be whipped or laughed at, he'd rather it be over something that mattered. Besides, Corbie was the elder farrier, and it had been his idea. Everyone outside his family loved Corbie, at least if he hadn't seduced their wives, and in a world where only a bad son blamed his father if he was punished for disobedience, there was nothing left for Jedediah to say.

Jedediah spent as much time with Tom as he could; he had other friends too, but the Attics lived a little away from Gyrford. The Attic place was safe, and some Sundays Jedediah was able to borrow the cart and drive there after church, taking his mama and Auntie Agnes with him.

'Drive my cart all over the country, is it?' Corbie demanded the first time Jedediah asked, and Jedediah kept his face bland and said, 'I thought you might like to visit with friends of your own, Father. You might have the house to yourself.'

It tied a knot in his stomach to make that suggestion. He knew full well that his father had other women – not one woman who he loved, but a changing scatter of them, as a matter of habit. Corbie wasn't even discreet about it; a man was a man, as Auntie Pell said with some disapproval, and his wife cried when he went near her, so what, Corbie's irritable jollity seemed to say, was he supposed to do? He didn't force his wife; he was a civil husband, given what he had to live with, but if he wasn't a brute, he wasn't a eunuch either. Corbie might not speak of this openly, but it was plain enough in his jokes, his comments, his views on the marriages of his neighbours and the hard life he declared was the natural lot of any husband.

And what were any of them to do about it? If there wasn't crying under their roof, that was as good as life was likely to get.

Agnes felt very much indebted to the Attics. They were kind to her beloved nephew, and to her sister, and sometimes when she visited and Constance was happy out in the garden, she was able to sit and talk with Bet about something other than Jedediah and Constance, which brought a little brightness into her eyes. She was so deeply obliged for this that she felt the need to give a great deal of help; although digging was beyond her abilities, the earth being so dangerously full of beetles and grubs and lithe, easily hurt worms, she performed quite a lot of heavy labour around the place, and felt herself done a great kindness by the Attics that they allowed her to do this without giving her any of the looks she'd had so often in her life: that doubtful, half-angry watching, as if she might go on the rampage at any second. Lifting stones and carting water was no trouble at all to Agnes, but being looked at like that was enough to sap all the strength from her spine, so she built walls and stacked bales with a will, requiring only one of the smaller Attic children with her to watch out for mice and earwigs to make sure she didn't crush any on her way.

And Constance – well, she *unfurled.* She didn't become an ordinary woman; her beauty was as mask-like as ever, she still got things mixed up, and her speech held some of the muddle of a woman who had to learn in a welter of confused distraction. But the Attics all liked each other and were safe in each other's company in a way that made for an easy overlay of feelings. You didn't have a room filled with bursting outrage and smothered anger and abject fear all at the same time: if one of them was put out and another triumphant, one exasperated and another amused, there was a fellow-feeling beneath, like notes all struck in the same key.

Constance loved music; all the Smiths did. Jedediah, watching her alert as a guard-dog, saw how her head rocked softly while the Attics joked and teased and thanked and wheedled each other, finding a kind of rhythm to their interplay. She didn't say very much – she'd never quite been at ease with words, which other things drowned out for her – but when little Lily Attic brought her a flower, she said, 'This is pretty, it scents very most sweet!'

'Can I comb your hair?' Lily asked.

And Constance let Lily climb up onto her knee and said, 'Let's be soft together, pretty-face.' She smiled in delight, not only from the pleasure of an amiable child on her lap, or the peace of their mutual hair-plaiting, but with the relieved pride of a woman who'd found herself able to hold a whole conversation in clarity.

So they went more and more; away from Corbie, they took to calling the place 'Happily'. 'Do we go happily?' Constance would ask, letting fall her shawl as they settled into the cart, and when Jedediah said, 'Yes, Mama,' she'd stare at him until he smiled for her. Then she'd smile herself. It could be difficult to force a smile for her on days when Corbie had been in one of his tempers, but it had to be done. Once she started smiling, away from the house, she'd keep smiling until the moment she was told it was time to go home.

Then, when he was near fourteen, Jedediah became able to think about money, and that started to change things.

It began simply enough: he and Corbie couldn't agree on something. In later years, Jedediah couldn't even remember what it was; he'd been finding it harder and harder to bite his tongue as he got older. Corbie had started sending him on cases by himself when he was thirteen, and while some of them were difficult, he didn't feel incapable of dealing with them. Despite the freedom to use his own judgement this brought, though, he was getting angrier. Agnes had noticed enough to say that he shouldn't worry, it was just his age, and she warned him that if he had something to say, perhaps he might bring it to her instead of his father; she was just thinking of his mama, dear. That made Jedediah angry both with Agnes and for her, and such things tend to build up.

And one day, he and Corbie couldn't agree on a simple case, and he grew a bit too stubborn, and Corbie started to unbuckle his belt with the air of a man who bears no hard feelings, but can't miss the opportunity to make an obvious point.

Jedediah wasn't at his full height yet – and it wasn't a decision; there was no strategy in it. He felt his fists rising, and he let them rise. His voice flat, he said: 'I'll fight back. And maybe you'll beat me still, but I reckon I can make my fists tell.'

Corbie had glared back for a frozen moment. Then he must have made a decision, because he threw back his head and laughed hard, and said, 'Well, well. Now there's a day I've lived to see. You instruct me, my lad.'

He clapped Jedediah on the shoulder, hard enough that it was still a blow, and went out. He was gone for hours.

He returned hours later, somewhat ruffled and a little the worse for drink. Jedediah braced himself for a fight: on his warning, Aunt Agnes had taken Mama out for a walk in the direction of the Attics'. He'd lose, that was sure, but he could still put a cost on his skin.

His father regarded him for long enough that Jedediah could feel the tension locking up his arms; regarded the tightening look on his face. Then he sat down and picked up his strongbox.

'Since you're such a man,' he said, 'I suppose I must give of my share, son of mine. A tenth a month to you for now, and you live at your own cost and pay for your own follies. We'll call that bit of temper your journeyman piece. I shall consider my long descent into dotage, my own son, and let's see if you prosper.'

He handed over a stack of coins with a look of satisfaction that might break into anger or laughter at any moment.

It took Jedediah a few seconds to unlock his muscles, take in what had happened. When he was able to loosen his tongue, he said as quietly as he could, 'Thank you, Father, I shall strive to do you justice.'

'Oh, spare me that, at least, boy,' snapped Corbie. 'Have some mercy on a poor old man.'

And for a time, things went on. Corbie didn't recant his whim; he gave Jedediah his tenth every week, and Jedediah paid for his share of the food and charcoal and all the rest of a smithy's needs, and locked away as much as he could. He bought a pot of honey for his mother, and she curled around it and licked at the sweetness.

He practised as hard as he could, often sitting up well into the night, which caused Agnes to whisper to him tentative little worries about hurting his eyes labouring by coal-light, and

Corbie to joke often about the sober and celibate life he was leading; a smithy full of pounding hammers and hot pokers gives a man plenty of scope for a pun. Jedediah put his arm around Agnes' shoulders, which were still bigger than his, and told her not to worry, that it was a good skill for a farrier to work by touch, and Corbie overheard him, and entertained himself upon the theme for the next three months.

It wasn't a desire for chastity that moved him. Tom and Jedediah went to dances when they could. They kissed girls when the girls would let them. But Jedediah worked every minute he had.

He was a journeyman now, despite never having made a proper journeyman's piece, and he meant to prove himself up to the task. That was how you were supposed to earn the position: you created something that showed your skill, and your master – usually your father – granted you the rank. By Smith tradition, it was a document signed and witnessed; by Mackem tradition, it was a small, ornate brand stamped on your wrist.

Corbie had taken the opportunity to stamp one on Jedediah's arm the day after granting him a wage. Jedediah would have stood still for it, but Corbie found it funnier to brand him by surprise, mid-morning when he was absorbed in polishing up the decorative head of a poker. The brand was, as a result, a bit smudged and askew; it's hard not to flinch when burned without warning, however braced against your father you are by habit, and Corbie seemed to find this obscurely satisfying, as a mark, perhaps, of his inexplicable and ill-made son.

Jedediah fretted at the scar until he got used to it, but there was nothing to do that would make it tidier. He made his work tidy instead, shaping geometry and sheen late into the night.

One day, he suggested that Constance and Agnes might like to spend the night with the Attics. Mister Attic refused Jedediah's offer to pay for their board, so Jedediah made a gift of some of the Lendens' best dried beans to Bet Attic. He would have brought them Lenden pork as well, but Mister Attic didn't eat that. He always claimed that pork gave him the stomach ache, just as he claimed that strong drink gave him the headache – or at least, that was what he told most of his neighbours, and if he said in private that he could swallow a new name comfortably enough but not a *haram* meal, that was something Jedediah didn't feel called upon to repeat. He just confirmed that the beanfields never came into contact with the pigs and made sure Bet knew the food was all right. Tom and his siblings had never bothered about *najis* things, but Mister Attic had a quiet reliance on Jedediah's advice: folks were used to farriers asking inexplicable questions, and young Jedediah Smith's interest in which fields were wandered by dogs and swine had long been shrugged off as just one of those things. Thanks to his advice, there were several farms in the neighbourhood that were surprisingly *halal* in their habits, had they but known it.

Bet Attic prepared a bed for them and cooked for everyone. Constance sat supping at the Attics' kitchen table with the rest. Nobody taxed her with tangles of words or found fault with her many shawls; nobody demanded she swallow more than she could bear. Bet set out a cushion for her with a smile and a caress, and set a bowl and spoon before her saying, 'Eat what you like and leave what you don't, dear.' Constance looked around with anxious eyes, but as the Attics ate their own food and chatted amongst themselves, giving her smiles when their glance caught hers, she began to settle. Allowed to eat slowly, she actually fed herself – not a big meal, perhaps, but more than Jedediah had ever seen her take without suffering. Uncommented upon, her body relaxed, and after a while, Constance let one of the shawls slip. She sat quietly, watching the rushlight. The little scrap of flame held itself in steady grace, filling her eyes with gold.

It could work. Corbie wouldn't be sorry to have Constance out of the house, nor Agnes either. Mister Attic could do with Agnes' help around the place. Mama wouldn't be frightened all the time – she could rest by the river or by the fire, watching the Attics laugh and tease each other and quarrel and make peace again, and nobody would threaten to kiss her.

But the only way to do it was with money. Jedediah couldn't just drop two women on his friends without paying for their keep. It wasn't fair to the Attics, and besides, Corbie would have to be managed. A pair of lodgers, paid for and looked after, would be understood; it was one way to accept that a marriage was over. Farriers married in church, that was the tradition, and it wasn't quite doctrinal to set aside a wife you were tired of, but if you paid for her keep somewhere, nobody thought much the less of you – indeed, if you were known to be paying for her to be kept well, you might be thought magnanimous; certainly Corbie could pass off that story if nobody knew his son was responsible. And while Jedediah didn't feel any the warmer to his neighbours for the thought, the reality was that folks who didn't know the Attics might even think of it as sending Constance off to be waited upon: Mister Attic was foreign, and folks found foreigners easier to swallow if they were supposed in the service of some good Christian. In fact, it would be only right, thought Jedediah, to pay more for such an insult. It would be a tremendous favour taking in Constance, even though Agnes would certainly care for her and work hard. Jedediah wanted his mother out of hurt's way, but he was damned if he would make his best friends pay for it.

So he needed money. A tenth of the smithy's take wasn't bad for a worker owing no one rent – fairy-smithies always prospered, and Corbie was popular – but it wouldn't be enough. Jedediah had his own keep to pay for. He wore his clothes patched and repaired to the point that Corbie made remarks about having begotten a scarecrow instead of a son of flesh; he drank little; he kept things as light as he could with any girl he walked out with. Everything he could, he saved – but it wasn't enough.

Corbie only ever spoke of marriage as a yoke, a shackle, a spider's trap; he particularly liked the latter comparison because Jedediah wasn't very fond of spiders. Corbie loved all animals with the expansive enthusiasm of a man prepared to lavish great affection on anything that couldn't answer back, and this included the creeping beasts of the earth. He tended to befriend any beast that came their way with such possessive bonhomie that there wasn't much left for Jedediah to do; even though Jedediah liked most creatures as well. But when it came to spiders, Jedediah simply couldn't bear them. It was bad luck to kill them, and he knew better than to try, but that meant removing them from the smithy just in case, and Corbie liked to make sure that was Jedediah's job.

'Go on, my boy,' he'd say, 'time for a heroic quest against a fearsome monster. We should call in some damsels to witness your courage, eh? Win yourself some lady's favour.'

He hadn't yet followed through on the idea and called in a Gyrford girl to watch Jedediah's set face and reluctant hands as he guided the boiling scrape of legginess into a pot, ready to be shaken out the door, but by the time he was fourteen, Jedediah was interested enough in girls for this to be a serious threat.

His interest wasn't yet mature enough to turn into love, not least because his exposure to the facts of life had come largely from accompanying Aunt Pell on midwifery visits. Pell was of the view that a man should know what was what, a phrase that covered things in quite intricate detail.

'You don't know it all,' Jedediah had tried telling her when she first used that phrase with him, speeding up his step to challenge her, for all he was not entirely sure what she was getting at.

'Of course not,' Pell said, matching him pace for pace. 'Good for you, my lad. The sooner you realise no one does, the better. You'll be a grown man when you work out that it applies to you as well.'

'I didn't say I did,' said Jedediah, near a jog, 'but that's a cheap point. Just because I don't know it all doesn't mean you do.'

'Excellent,' said Pell, not to be outrun, regarding him with unfussed satisfaction. 'You always were a clever lad. You hold your ground, my boy.'

It's hard to remain irritated with someone who scores your performance in quarrelling with them, especially when they rank you high. So he accepted that he was to be lectured, and later, when passing on the information to Tom – some of it quite surprising – they both agreed that it was probably good he had held his tongue. Pell was a source of information about matters Constance couldn't cope with and Agnes probably didn't know about. (Corbie would have been only too delighted to share his expertise, and was alternatively amused and offended that Jedediah was so passionate in his insistence that he didn't want to hear it.) Pell, though, was so devoid of embarrassment herself that you forgot to feel it in her company, and she proved remarkably enlightening for an unmarried woman. She mixed her lessons in anatomy with a great deal of commentary about how a man should treat women well or he was no man at all, but Jedediah didn't find himself in disagreement about that, and it was good to have some knowledge about girls, even if he hadn't quite got to the point of getting his hands on one.

'You'll be a well-looking man,' Pell said, with nothing in her voice to indicate a compliment, 'so don't you fret, lad. Hold up your head and speak kind, and for pity's sake don't look guilty or she'll think you have bad intentions. And if she does like you, don't just jump on her. Take time and pay attention, lad. You wouldn't jump on a horse without greeting it first, would you? Same thing. Horses talk with their bodies and so do folks. Pay heed, and you'll be fine.'

Sometimes she asked Jedediah to bring plants from Mister Attic's garden. She had little patience with the trade in aphrodisiacs, or 'notions and potions', as she called them – if you thought a brew was the way to heat your lover's blood for you, she'd say, then you were doing something wrong in the bedroom, and if manners wouldn't get you someone's heart, then there was no point witching for it. Her interest was in herbs for pain, and for stopping things before they came to the point of needing a midwife.

'There's no sure herb,' she told Jedediah, watching his progress with a critical eye as he dug her garden, 'not to prevent. To get a girl right again once she's caught, yes, but it's a messy business and full of chance. It's all very well for me to tell the girls to play other games or have the lad pull out in time, but someone needs to tell the lads, that's what.'

'Well, don't look to me,' said Jedediah, giving the spade a particularly energetic swing by way of excusing his flushed face. 'I won't do it.'

'Get you married first,' Pell conceded. 'Someone should tell your father, though I expect he knows. Trouble enough with village girls, he is. But for God's sake, lad, use the head on your shoulders when it comes to girls. That's been a house of unhappy marriage long enough.'

During all this time, there wasn't much communication with Jedediah's uncles in Tinsdowne. Farrier clans kept in touch as best they could; there were Gowan cousins to the east who he rather liked, though Corbie didn't arrange visits as often as he might have done, and there were Faber cousins southwards too. All of them were literate, more or less, and Jedediah exchanged letters with them, though he didn't tell Corbie about this. The letters were sent to the Attics' house, and Jedediah read them there, and asked Mister Attic what he could to do make amends for the trouble.

'Never a trouble, dear lad,' said Mister Attic, who had treated him with a kind of grave respect since he was far too young to deserve it, and Tom, who was less earnest, told him, 'Look at all the ironwork you fix every time you come, you fool. Mama says you visit like a tenant trying to work board. Now just sit down and eat some of Dada's cake or he'll think you don't like it.'

It was true, Jedediah did work around the place whenever he visited. He loved it there, but not being used to considering himself a welcome sight, he wasn't quite sure how much it took to guard against being a burden.

Exchanging letters with most of his cousins wasn't the same as having their company; the missives were mostly to do with sharing new discoveries and passing along general good will; he never felt it worth the while to mention that he didn't send along their respects to the resolutely illiterate Corbie. He didn't want the argument, or the sideways punishment that might fall on some head other than his own.

To stay in touch with the unlettered Mackems, though, could be done only in the flesh, and he seldom met them. Corbie had two brothers, Dunstan, the eldest, and Asher, known as Sweep. That was the Mackem way: the oldest boy must be a Dunstan, and then after that it was catch-as-catch-could, with a fondness for whimsical names. They liked nicknames too: Corbie's name was Caleb if you went by what had been said at the font, though Jedediah was well into his teens before he found that out. Corbie had an uncle Balthazar who everyone called Ballock, and apparently Ballock didn't mind – although Jedediah wasn't sure he could trust Corbie's word on that. It wasn't a custom Jedediah cared for, having fallen prey to the whimsy without the nickname. Perhaps he should be thankful; 'Jedediah' was ridiculous, and he was sure Corbie meant it to be, but it could have been worse, and it wasn't beyond Corbie to make it worse now, if irritated enough, and what play might be made out of 'Jedediah', he didn't like to think.

Names aside, his memory of his uncles was pretty vague; he remembered big, hearty men with hair as red as Corbie's own and voices as loud. The first time he could remember meeting them, he was fifteen; there had been a case of a fey creature on the border between them, a long-legged, velvet-furred blackit of a thing that sang in the night and kept folks awake. Jedediah thought that it was a case for negotiation, but by the time he and Corbie reached the border, Dunstan and Sweep were boisterously happy to announce that they'd already settled the matter: they'd dug a pitfall between the hedge, baited with night-light wyrms they'd trapped the previous month, and the creature had been so enticed by what struck it as an edible glow that it had fallen right into the trap before it knew what was what, and was buried alive with a turnabout sigil laid over the earth so it would be confused back underground if it tried to retrace its steps.

'Never mind, little brother,' Sweep told them cheerfully, slapping Corbie on the arm. 'Farrier work's not for the slow, eh?'

Corbie's face reddened, but before he could say anything Dunstan had gone over to greet his nephew. Jedediah was getting ready to bow when Dunstan hugged him, pounding him on the back and then holding him at arm's length, saying, 'By God, Jedediah, you make me feel old, grown as you are. I suppose that's the Smith face you have. Beloved of God, you must be, to be spared this old visage of ours.' Indeed, the three brothers did resemble each other, but while Jedediah looked for the sting in Dunstan's remark, he wasn't sure he could see it.

Sweep gave Dunstan a playful jab on the jaw and said, 'Could be that he's less of a sinner than you, Dun my lad, and was spared the curse passing down unto the next generation. Glad to see you, nephew, and I hope you practise Christian forgiveness.' He hugged Jedediah as well, saying, 'What do they call you, son?'

'Er – Jedediah.' He tried not to sound disrespectful, glancing at Corbie, who was still scowling. It was hard to know what to make of the question.

'What, the full measure?' Sweep said. 'By God, you must be a serious man. Well then, Caleb, sir,' and he gave a flourishing bow to Corbie, 'let's at least drink to our success. There's a fine inn over our way, let's along to it.'

'I know.' Corbie's voice was curter than usual. 'I do remember.'

The alehouse had clean tables and a married woman serving behind the bar to whom all the Mackem men gave the same grin; then Dunstan turned back and said, 'Come now, Corbie, what's your trouble? Haven't you the fairest wife in the world?'

Corbie's face, for just an instant, held a look of absolute bitterness. Then he bared his teeth and said, 'I do, by God, and no brother to bother me neither. Swallow that down with your ale.'

'We'll drink to your good mother, lad,' said Dunstan, and handed Jedediah a cup. Jedediah looked at it with some reluctance. He didn't like to unsteady his head in this company, and he would be expected to pay his share. And drinking to his mother, here, sat ill with him.

'Oh, he's a stiff-necked man, this one,' Corbie said, seeing Jedediah's caution. 'Can hardly bend it to tip back a drink.'

'Temperate, is it?' Dunstan said, and gave Jedediah a convivial punch; it didn't hurt much. 'Well, you've a farrier's arm, right enough, so maybe that's how they make 'em in Gyrford. Clean living and moral thoughts and the world go hang, eh?'

Jedediah had the sense that Dunstan wanted him to play; he knew there were men like that, who didn't feel safe with you until you'd roughed around a bit. He was uncomfortably aware that, while Corbie could manage this superbly, he himself wasn't good at it, growing stiffer and less likeable every second when someone tried.

'No,' he said, eyes on his drink, 'I have a poor head for it, that's all.'

'Ah, no such,' said Corbie, draining his own mug. 'You wouldn't know, my boy. You never put it to the test.'

This wasn't entirely true – Jedediah didn't mind drinking with friends, and could carry as much as most – but he was careful not to test how a hazed head might mix with Corbie, so he kept quiet.

'Boy's busy being a man,' Sweep put in. 'Good for him, eh? Can't stay little forever, eh, little brother?'

The joke sounded fairly amiable, but Corbie picked up the jug and poured himself a drink with such force that some of it slopped onto the table.

'Tell you what,' said Dunstan, leaning forward with a portentous look somewhat magnified by ale, 'you should send the boy back with us. We could have him a month or so, show him our tricks, he could show us his. Spend time with his cousins awhile. Like that, Jedediah?'

Both Corbie and Jedediah went still. For Jedediah, it was a matter of worry: how was he to leave his mother alone, with only Agnes' great, halted arms between her and Corbie's humour?

Corbie, meanwhile, glared at both his brothers. 'Oh, by all means,' he said. 'Leave me to work alone, why don't you, while he goes off on the trot. Heap my anvil, load my back. Oh, I'll camel along, won't I just?'

'Now, Corbie,' said Dunstan merrily, 'don't tell me you can't manage yourself for a few weeks? I thought you were a farrier.'

The brothers drank into the evening, and Jedediah sat quiet. It was like watching a joust, invisible weapons driving towards each other. The heat between them rose and fell, broke out in snaps, cooled to merriment, spat sparks again. Jedediah drank as slow as he could and paid his share of the tally with as small a flinch as he could manage.

Corbie was hung-over the following morning, which was his stated cause for being out of temper with everything. The sun had risen to dazzle his eyes, the wind to pound his eardrums, the birds to shriek at him, and the road below his cartwheels was a massy enemy shaking him for the delight of turning his stomach. Jedediah, who was apparently being young and healthy out of sheer spite, offered to take the reins after Corbie grew offended with their blameless horse – a cob-boned, unintelligent sumpter of mild disposition, unfortunately bearing the name Sir Magnificent, thanks to Corbie. After the second time Corbie struck out with the driving-whip, Jedediah said, as kindly as he could tone it, 'Father, we're well on our way. Why not let me drive while you rest a while? Do you hand me the reins and lie back.'

'Lie back and let this malefactor run your unblemished skull over every rock in Christendom,' said Corbie, but he tossed Jedediah the reins.

'Never you mind,' said Jedediah – mostly to the patient beast he called Mag whenever Corbie wasn't around, but Corbie slumped down a bit at the sound. 'We'll be home soon enough.'

'Aye, indeed,' Corbie muttered, his cap drawn down over his eyes. '*You* will.'

And for a long time after that, it was the last Jedediah saw of his Mackem kin.

When he was eighteen, Corbie raised Jedediah's share from one tenth to two and told him to spend it on drink and women, for it wearied his heart to see a young man sober.

Jedediah saved every penny of the extra tenth. He kept the accounts – Corbie could sum well enough, even if he couldn't read, but he referred to Jedediah's notes and calculations as 'money-witching' and amused himself discoursing on how it failed to magic any further funds out of the strongbox,

Jedediah living as ragged and monkish as he apparently did. But Jedediah gnawed his knuckles over the books, trying to think what else he could do. He needed more money, especially as he had, somehow, acquired a kind of fosterling.

He'd managed to avoid it with Cissie Lenden, who still worshipped him; whenever he ran across her, he'd ask her if she'd been a good girl, and when she nodded earnestly, he'd say, 'Good,' with an air of judging someone's workmanship, and then get away as quickly as he could. But Franklin Thorpe, he had on his conscience.

Franklin was a small boy, thirteen years his junior, whose father Joe scraped by on whatever work he could find season to season and drank as much of the profits as he could. Franklin was not at home in the world the way a boy his age should be. He wandered from place to place, starting back like a squirrel if an adult crossed his path, picking leaves from the hawthorn and chewing them with the furtive air of a thief. He was thin, his shoulder blades stark points through his worn shirt, and Jedediah had seen him with a black eye a few too many times.

Jedediah hadn't known what to do until the day he found Franklin crouched over the scrap-bucket, picking out left-overs intended for the pig. Corbie approved of pigs; having traded work for pork often enough, he had decided one day to build a small sty and trade for a weaner, a pink-snouted, fox-haired barrow hog he named Flitch, since the beast was destined to hang in slabs and might as well have time to resign himself to his fate. He took a certain pleasure in chatting with the beast and calling it by name, and fed it with something near tenderness every day.

Jedediah had nothing against the animal personally, but he was afraid that Constance would grow fond of it and make certain connections between the food in her bowl and the absence in her yard, something which, to date, had always been avoided. Agnes and Jedediah created between them an explanation that the creature was afraid of women, had a horror of them as deep as a unicorn's love for maidens, and as Constance was not clear that there was no such thing as a unicorn outside of children's tales, she accepted that and lived with only some of her days given over to misery, for the smell of the sty was clear when the wind changed and she couldn't lose the fear that the pig must smell her and Agnes and be suffering dreadful horrors.

There was no point saying any of this to Corbie, as he regarded Flitch as a friend and ally; he was sometimes heard to tell it that perhaps a gelded life would be better, or so you'd think if this was your kith and kin. But the smell could be kept down if its pen was cleaned frequently, and as Corbie was more assiduous in feeding than in mucking out, Jedediah had a habit of stopping by whenever he had a moment and doing some quick work with a shovel.

That was what he'd been doing when he heard the scuffling. It was so quiet that his first fear, that Flitch had used his clever snout to unlatch the door and get into the scrap-bucket, possibly in sight of Constance, lasted only an instant. Then he thought of rats. He didn't expect to find a thin-armed, dirty-haired child rooting through the bucket, pulling out burned porridge skins with hasty, delicate fingers.

He only said, 'Hey, there.' It wasn't a shout, or any kind of scolding. But as the child whipped round, arms clutched to himself and eyes like scorch marks in his face, Jedediah felt something familiar: the matter-of-fact weight of another soul settling itself upon his tired back. It was plain before him: there was a starving child eating pig-fodder in his garden, and there was no other course of action but to take the boy in and feed him.

Franklin sat in the smithy and shivered. It took Jedediah a moment to realise that he needed to explain something.

'Look you,' he said, 'I haven't brought you in to hit you. I won't, all right? I don't care if you took some scraps, except they're not so clean and could sicken you. We've some bread and cheese in here – have that instead. Do you like apples?'

The child looked exhausted, so unsteady on the stool that Jedediah felt the need to prop him up. As he ate – first of all taking slow nibbles, desperately polite little bites that came faster and faster as Jedediah didn't tell him to stop – Jedediah sat and held him by the arm just to keep him from falling. The arm through the worn shirt was all bone.

'You eat up,' Jedediah said. He really wasn't sure what to do; there were men who weren't good fathers, he could have told anyone that, but this underfed little scrap looked more afraid than he knew how to handle. He'd seen horses in this condition bought for next to nothing at a market by poor farmers who'd risk trying to feed up a skeletal beast; he'd felt them flinch as he shod them, and sometimes they'd snap and kick in the utter certainty that he'd land a whip on them any moment. Most of them became good workhorses if they were kept by a patient man.

But a child in this state was something else, and what, he felt with frustration, was he supposed to do about it? He was nobody's father; he was eighteen years old with no wife and all the care he knew how to give was for balky horses and old ladies with their wits askew.

What would he want, if this was him? 'Don't worry,' he tried, 'I'll tell no one you were here. Your Dada needn't know.' At that, he felt the child relax, just a little bit, against his steadying hand.

'Chew your food,' he said. 'You'll have the belly-ache if you swallow it down too fast.'

It was odd, sitting with this tiny boy. Jedediah knew what it was to be afraid of your father at this age, but Franklin didn't seem to know how to be stubborn, for he obeyed every instruction with eerie alacrity.

The cheese was gone, so Jedediah fetched an apple, and as Franklin reached to take it, Jedediah saw the sleeve fall back. Beneath its ravelled hem was a deep red bruise, cracked down the edge.

It shouldn't have been a shock; most fathers in Gyrford took to the strap from time to time, and Joe Thorpe wasn't the man to try anything else. But this looked bad – and what was worse was the way that Franklin froze, dark-eyed and white-faced, when he saw where Jedediah's eyes had come to a stop.

Jedediah swallowed. He'd lanced boils on horses before now, and picked maggots out of cuts; there was no reason to feel sick.

'Wait you,' he said, and reached for a pot on the shelf.

'I fell down,' Franklin volunteered as Jedediah came back with it. It was the first thing he'd said.

'You can say that if you like,' Jedediah said, dabbing as gently as he could. 'I know nothing, and will say nothing. But if you don't like to lie, well, I won't make you. I can mind my own business.'

Franklin's arm shook, and Jedediah didn't know what to do except keep salving.

'I know nothing,' he said, 'and won't unless you tell me, but if you'd like salve for the other bruises, there's plenty in the jar.'

At that, Franklin snatched his arm back, rising off the stool and looking frantically about.

'You can go if you like,' Jedediah said, stepping back. 'Come again; I've more bread. And if you'd like more salve, I have some. Like I said, I know nothing.'

Franklin covered his mouth. His small fingers parted over his face, meshing it across, and the words came out in a terrified whisper: 'What do you mean, sir?'

'Let's say,' Jedediah said, keeping his tone carefully calm, 'that I know a belt-mark when I see one. If it's on your arm, you had your head covered. And if you had to cover your head, well, that's not a beating you deserved, whatever you did. I won't ask if you don't want me to. Let me put some salve in a pot and you can take it home with you. And you can come again if you need something. Only don't let my mother see your bruises, there's a good lad, such things upset her.'

Franklin lowered his hands, just a bit, peeped over the top of them. He didn't seem ready to let go of his face, so Jedediah pressed some salve into a small pot and slipped it into Franklin's pocket.

'I reckon,' he said, sitting down, 'you're not sure what to say.

Never mind, eh? I hear a deal of talk all day. Tires my ears. You just sit by the fire, get warm. Stay a while. No need to talk if you don't like to.'

And, because he couldn't think what else to do, Jedediah went back to work. The two of them sat there in a silence that was quite companionable; Franklin was no trouble.

Of course, once Corbie came in, that was the end of that. Franklin was hunched on a stool beside the forge, chewing his nail in what Jedediah suspected was a compromise in the struggle not to suck his thumb, while Jedediah himself sat on another, grinding away at a grate.

'What's this?' Corbie demanded. It wasn't anything more than his usual explosive bonhomie when faced with anything unexpected, but Franklin jumped up like a cricket. 'I see my stool's kept warm in my absence, if there's any warmth at all in those little gaskins. Hired yourself out as a cushion, have you, lad?'

'I – I beg your pardon, sir.' Franklin's voice was barely a whisper.

'It's all right, Franklin,' Jedediah said. He was surprised how angry he found himself. Maybe it was just that a moment ago things had been quite snug, and now there was uproar for no reason at all. 'I don't suppose we live to begrudge a neighbour a seat.'

'Far from it, far from it,' said Corbie, settling his own haunches down onto the stool Franklin had abandoned. 'Come one, come all, that's what I say. I just had it in mind that we should open an almshouse.'

Franklin whispered, 'Excuse me, sir,' and ran, and that was

that for the day. But next time Corbie was absent from the smithy, Jedediah saw Franklin hovering and called him in.

By way of excuse, he gave the child a message to run, and Franklin ran it smartly and came back with an answer memorised word-for-word. Franklin appeared another day, saying, 'Good morning, Mister Smith,' with the kind of shivering courtesy children use when they're frightened to ask for an invitation, and when Jedediah gave him an errand Franklin collected the package and brought it in right-side-up, saying he hoped he'd done as he should because he'd heard it clink, and it occurred to Jedediah, with a sinking sense of responsibility, that the boy was clever.

The day Jedediah saw Franklin's buckle-cut back, he felt a rage that he had to fight to hold in. He knew immediately he was angry with Franklin Thorpe for hurting the boy; it took him a while to shake out the thought that beside Joe Thorpe, Jedediah Smith had nothing in the world to complain of. But being angry and confused wasn't about to help little Franklin, who needed salves and food and a fire to sit beside when the day was cold, and in the longer view, money. If he could be trained for something, he might get away from the mess he'd been born to.

If he'd had a home of his own, Jedediah might have cared for the boy there. You couldn't go around stealing children, of course, but there were nights when Franklin was afraid to go home and all Jedediah had to offer was a blind eye if the boy crept into one of the cages in the garden built to house stubborn members of the People. Jedediah found him sleeping there even when the cage next door was occupied by a furious nixie, which streamed out an endless spattering whisper to the effect of,

'Pretty lad, pretty lad, lift the lid, pretty lad . . .' in its attempts to get Franklin to release it from the washtub imprisoning it. Franklin was clearly afraid of the leeching, silver-bubbled fingers the thing was trying to wind towards him, but he must have been more afraid to go out into the cold morning, either to drag his feet home or wander around a village empty of places to take him in.

If Jedediah had had a house with a spare pallet somewhere, he could have given Franklin a key, but he couldn't do that: it was Corbie's house, and Corbie was irritable about acts of charity cluttering up the place.

'Haven't been up to what you shouldn't, have you, boy?' he demanded, with a conspiratorial laugh not entirely merry. 'I can't say he features you, lucky for him, but you're eager enough to amend poor old Joe's fathering.'

That was the moment that it dawned on Jedediah that he did want a home and family of his own. His life was a lot less monkish than he would have Corbie believe, but the kind of girl who just wanted a bit of fun was the only kind of girl he had anything to offer. He was even mildly popular with girls looking to play for the sake of practice: he'd been taught the facts of life by a midwife, could pass an evening with a lass without telling the world about it and had no intention of doing anything to beget a child he couldn't feed. It was a life of discreet and casual company leading nowhere that Corbie would have thoroughly approved, and that was a truly depressing thought. This wasn't how he wanted to live, not really; he wanted a girl he could confide in, who might touch him more in passion for himself than in rehearsal for some other man, but he couldn't have that, and he was careful not to trifle with any girl he might come to like too much. He wanted children whose love he could accept, not have to hold at arm's length for fear of encouraging false hopes.

Very possibly, he thought, he was practising fatherhood on Franklin. That wasn't fair to the child, who wasn't a piece of iron to be hammered about and set aside dented. Jedediah realised, along with his own wishes, that he'd made a promise to the boy, in deeds if not in words, and now he was going to have to keep it. He needed to earn more, because nobody would set aside money to train that boy if he didn't. He needed a home, and he didn't have one here.

There was nothing to do for the moment but deflect, so he said, as flat as he could, 'Father, my voice wasn't broke when that lad got started. If you think me that much of a man, I wish you'd tell the girls.'

Corbie roared with laughter and retold the tale with embellishments to every attractive woman who came into the smithy for the next two weeks, and in those moments, he was almost pleased with his son. Agnes, who Corbie liked to have around as a witness to the story, sighed as she heard it, for she'd enjoyed doting on her nephew when he was small, but now he was growing tall and able to talk about fathering children, and Agnes' very limited experience of men was mostly that once they started getting interested in women that way, it didn't turn out for the best.

When the word came that Corbie's father had died, Corbie said almost nothing to anyone for several days. He slammed around the house, stroked Constance's neck whenever he came near her, and the one time Tom came by, shouted at Jedediah to get his heathen friend out of his sight.

Corbie's father hadn't died a splendid death, but a painful one, of a leg wound that went bad. A hob had bitten him when he wasn't quick enough stepping past its kitchen corner, and while you wouldn't get the rot just from a fey bite – if the People mean to poison you, they did it thorough – Jedediah thought, quietly, to himself, that the leg might not have mortified if he'd had the right salves on hand, and Tom might have known what was needed. He didn't say that, though. He'd barely known the man.

This meant that now his Uncle Dunstan was elder farrier in Tinsdowne. He remembered a man hard-handed and playful, not unlike his father, except more inclined to like Jedediah. Jedediah had hoped he might see his uncles again; though his grandfather was laid in the ground before the news reached Gyrford – it was summer, and they couldn't leave him to rot worse than he had in life – there was a service to be held for the old man.

Corbie went to visit for a week or two, at least, but Jedediah was told sharply that he wasn't invited. 'God help us if we let the smithy stand empty,' Corbie informed him. His eye was less steady these days; it glanced more or less everywhere, except at Jedediah's face. 'Why you should come, I can't think. There's no inheritance for either of us, lad; it all goes to your dear Uncle Dunstan, may he hold the forge in peace or whatever else he likes. And besides, I thought you were a Gyrford man. You'll stay home. This is your home, isn't it? Fine thing, to have a home. Now don't let me see you ungrateful, my fine fellow.'

So it was no great shock when a message came, asking Jedediah to look to a case just over the border while the Mackems were mourning their fallen elder.

Jedediah sat on a stool, polishing his favourite set of pliers, experiencing the odd peace that went with Corbie not being around carrying his own storm-clouds with him. And in the quiet, it wasn't a difficult decision: Mackem or Smith, he should go. If he borrowed the Attics' horse he could be there before day's end, and helping folks troubled by the People was the right thing to do. If he was lucky, he might avoid Corbie altogether.

The message had said that a herd of prize pigs, possessed of silken back-fat as smooth-tasting as cream, had suffered a sudden disaster. One of the sows – only a sow, mercifully, not the breeding boar – had disappeared, and at first the owners, the Palmer family, had thought in terms of thieves – until a week later they were greeted by the dreadful sight, there, in their own farmyard, of the corpse of the sow herself, withered down to an empty sack of bones, black skin leathered over her stark skull, where her hardened lips leered at the Palmers in a grin of ghastly anguish, as if she had died of pain so dreadful that there was nothing left to do but laugh at a world that could contain it.

(Such was the enthusiastic account of Tim Scranton, the packman who had been paid to carry the news; he had added the philosophy for free. A man who affords his supper based on the ability to talk up his wares would be remiss if he didn't take such an opportunity to practise his powers.)

Before he set out, Jedediah knocked on Joe Thorpe's door, offering him sixpence if he could borrow young Franklin as an assistant for a few days.

Joe Thorpe had a severe headache, as did his wife, both because of Joe, and neither were sorry to be spared the trouble of a child, while Franklin was so happy that Jedediah felt embarrassed. The two of them set off on the horse Mister Attic had lent them – and yes, he'd pay them for the hire, or find some gift to make amends for it; really, the smithy needed another horse, which he couldn't afford. Jedediah brooded for a short while, but Franklin grew more and more relaxed as they headed across country until the trip felt positively cheerful.

Alone, he could have reached the place in a few hours, but Franklin was new to riding and Jedediah was enjoying himself more than he had in months, so he took a lazy pace. They rode till nightfall and set up camp near the farm. On learning that one could sleep outside in comfort with a leather pallet to keep you off the cold ground and sheets pitched above you to keep away the cold wind, Franklin was as delighted as the discoverer of a new continent. Jedediah reminded himself to find a place to store a bit of gear so that the boy could camp out by himself if he had to. He showed Franklin how to make a fire safely, and made him a gift of his steel and flint – easy enough to forge himself another once he got home – and the two of them, sharing bread and sausage, agreed that they'd start the job early next day.

They slept out the dark, and when they woke the day was fine and clear. Franklin was up like a lark, his blankets carefully packed, the birds were loud in their song, and Jedediah resolved that at least for the day, he would not worry about money.

The Palmer property was extensive and brown: pigs dotted the furrows, their fanned ears drooping as they nestled their snouts against the rich earth. Franklin, who was sat in front of Jedediah on the saddle, perked up tremendously, looking around in something like wonder.

'Do they not fight, Mister Smith?' he asked.

'Haven't you seen pigs in a field before?' Jedediah knew the lad didn't have much of a life, but he surely must have been out of the village at some point?

Franklin hung his head a bit. 'I might have, Mister Smith,' he said in a small voice. 'It might be I just forgot.'

'Well, never mind it,' said Jedediah, feeling as if he'd kicked a puppy. 'A pig kept in a back pen might have at you if it's nasty-tempered, but out in a field they have to get along, I reckon.'

Franklin regarded the world around him. 'Maybe they're happier with more room,' he said.

'Couldn't blame them for that,' Jedediah said. 'So, here's the gate; wait you just a moment.' He dismounted, lifted Franklin off and took his sack of tools out of the saddle-bag. Most likely he wouldn't be able to do anything more than survey today, but if he could give a decent report to his Uncle Dunstan, then the Mackems could take it from there.

'Can I carry your sack, Mister Smith?' Franklin ventured as they headed up to the house, ready to brave any weight if it made him useful enough to deserve this trip.

'No,' Jedediah said judiciously, 'I don't reckon you can, so don't trouble yourself with it.' He meant to say something more – but then he saw the girl, and that was that.

She bent from the waist, stacking logs in a basket with a smooth, easy grace, laying each atop the next in a pattern so apt and neat that they sat quite steady. She wasn't fast in her work, but there was no dawdle to her either; it was a patient rhythm, as if setting the logs together in a well-thought array was her way to find some interest in the performance of a dullish task. And the look of her: tall, with the wide shoulders and strong arms of a girl who lifts logs, but with a pretty waist and a neck so long and smooth that her head sat atop it like a nested wren. He couldn't see the colour of her hair or the features of her face, but she leaned to and fro between the basket and the log-bin so quiet and natural in her movements that it didn't feel, just then, like ogling a girl without her knowledge. It was like watching a blackbird take a wander across the grass, a sight to rest your eyes on and be at ease. It was like watching a river sparkle in the sunlight.

The thought came to him, though, that he *was* ogling a girl without her leave and he ought to stop. 'Morning, Miss,' he said, and as she turned, took off his cap.

It wasn't long, really, that they looked at each other. Her eyes were green and flecked, her mouth pink, and cracked across the lips as if she could never drink enough water. 'Sir,' she said, making a half-bob, and of course, she must be the maidservant here because her dress was worn and her hands red and she was out here fetching wood, which folks like the Palmers didn't do for themselves. He'd never liked being called 'sir' – it was a name for the gentry, a breed of folk he hadn't much use for – but it shouldn't have felt so wrong, coming from this girl. You couldn't expect a girl not to be mannerly just because she was – he wasn't getting as far as thinking of a word for her. Was she handsome? Lovely? Yes, perhaps. He couldn't describe her to himself. She was there before him: white-grained skin and dark brows, a black curlicue of hair falling down from her cap, a girl he didn't want to stop looking at.

'I hope I find you well this morning,' he said, bobbing his head.

She looked at him, a little cautious; evidently, when she deferred to folks, they didn't usually defer back. 'Thank you.'

'You're welcome,' he said. 'Would you be the one to ask where to find Mister Palmer?'

Franklin, beside him, made an anxious attempt at a bow, and at that, the girl smiled. 'You'll be the farrier?' she said to Jedediah.

He found himself grinning. There was nothing particular in her words that made a joke, but there was a friendliness, and her voice was low and pleasant, a wood-pigeon's chuckle. 'It's the sack, isn't it?' He hefted the tools on his back.

For just a moment her eyes flickered, and as they did, he felt the air clarify around her a little; she came sharper into focus, the lines of her body picked out by the morning sun. He wasn't especially bulky as smiths went, but you don't hammer iron for hours a day without putting some muscle on your arms and chest, and sometimes that meant girls watched you while you set about your work. He'd never taken it very personally; he looked at girls when they went about their work too, if he could do it without obvious staring. But she glanced at him, then looked away, and then met his eyes.

'You're expected,' she said, and her cheeks flushed, just a little. She gestured towards Franklin, baring the tender flesh of her wrist. 'Have you brought your son?'

The boy looked so pleased, so red-faced and hopeful, that it was almost cruel to deny it. 'My friend,' Jedediah compromised, much relieved when Franklin's smile didn't die. It felt important to add, 'I'm not married.'

At that, the girl smiled herself. Perhaps he'd said it awkwardly; no doubt he wasn't a subtle fellow – at least, he spent a lot of time having it noticed in the smithy that he'd said something comical. But with the smile, her whole face became vivid, alight, endearing. Then she was back to her tucked-back self. 'You're awaited in the back yard,' she said, and he followed her smooth, long-legged stride around the house. He wished now that he hadn't brought Franklin, but perhaps the boy's presence would keep him from saying anything truly ridiculous. He'd met fine-looking girls before. It was just that this girl, he wanted to keep looking at him. Her eyes were ferned with black lashes, with a warm tilt to them, as if they smiled even when her face was grave.

They dropped, though, when confronted with her master, a short, ruddy-faced man pacing to and fro and occasionally tugging at his hair as if his energetic fists were agreeing with his boiling brain that things were appalling. He was so absorbed in enacting his feelings – which, it had to be admitted, were justified, considering the juiceless, blackened pig lying before him on the cobbles – that it was a moment before he noticed Jedediah.

'Oh, dear me,' he said. 'No, I sent for the farrier, Mister Mackem. This won't do. I sent for the farrier.'

He sounded so wild at the horrors of the world that Franklin edged a little closer to Jedediah.

'And I came,' said Jedediah, taking off his cap again, and shifting just a little to shield Franklin. 'That's Smith, though, Mister Palmer. Dunstan Mackem's my uncle. I'm here on his word.'

'Oh, worse and worse!' lamented Mister Palmer. 'No, I sent for the *farrier*, young sir! How old are you, even?'

Jedediah cleared his throat. 'Old enough,' he said. Technically he was still a journeyman: while farriers usually made a master-piece around the age of eighteen, Corbie had never quite got around to suggesting that he make his. Jedediah was confident that he could make something good enough; Corbie liked to challenge him to make this or that difficult thing when he was going off for a few days of unspecified 'business' and leaving Jedediah to mind the place, and Jedediah had yet to give his father the satisfaction of welcoming him home with a piece not up to standard.

But Corbie also liked to lament, in regard to nothing in particular, that he felt much over-mastered by his many misfortunes. Jedediah knew with dreary certainty that if he asked to be set a master-work, it would somehow end up with Constance crying in a corner. He was waiting for Corbie to be struck by the right whim; God knew how he'd inflict the second brand, which was supposed to be placed in a cross-hatched pattern on top of the first, but burns healed and master status lasted.

None of this was news to reassure a nervous customer, though, so Jedediah passed it by, hoping the man wouldn't ask to see his brand. 'My . . . grandfather's died this week past,

Mister Palmer, and those who knew him best are at home to mourn him. My uncle sent me.'

'Oh dear, oh dear,' Mister Palmer exclaimed, evidently seeing the old man's death from a personal perspective. 'Now look you, here's my poor sow and none to help me, and must my whole herd be killed dry like this? I'll tell you, young sir, once we had a mouse dead in the kitchen and we couldn't find it for all the stink, till one day we found it under a bucket and it was flat dead and dried out like this. You lift it, young Mister, it weighs not a bit. And you, Louise,' turning upon the lovely girl, who had stood quiet beside them, holding her head carefully lowered. It was respectful, at least in show, but the way she raised it, with slow, silent poise, made Jedediah feel he'd been seeing something else, a gravity at the centre of her, like some deep well into which she could gaze when there was too much fluster around her. 'Louise, what do you here, idled about?' Mister Palmer demanded. 'And this boy . . .' he gestured at Franklin, a wordless flap of the hand as if no amount of speech could convey the hopeless chaos of a world that sent strange boys traipsing in upon your troubles.

'Shall I show Mister Smith the rounds, sir?' Louise said.

Louise was her name. *Louise.*

Her quiet voice must have done something, because Mister Palmer said, 'Yes, yes,' as if he'd been pleading for someone to show that much sense all this time, and then wandered away, apparently deep in silent conversation with himself.

There was a moment of peace. No one felt much like breaking it.

Louise's smile was soft as she turned to Jedediah. 'I can show you the place,' she said. 'Will you like to come with me too, young man?' She held out a hand to Franklin; it was reddened from work, callused around the palm, graceful as a leaf. Jedediah resisted the urge to take it himself. 'By the by,' she said, turning to him with a gleam of amusement, 'how old are you?'

Jedediah found himself grinning, despite the pig; for once, somehow, he could think of a joke to tell. 'I was nineteen when I woke this morning,' he said. 'I fear I may leave this place feeling much older.'

She laughed, and something in him, a voice that didn't answer to his common sense, said: *You*. Her face was troubled, he could see that. She looked tired; her skin, so bright and smooth against black, neat eyebrows, had a dusty cast to it, as if she didn't get enough to eat, to drink, enough time to rest. But she laughed, and Franklin took her hand in docile confidence, and Jedediah Smith, who truly could not afford a sweetheart, had already begun to fall in love.

The pig was scab-dark and husked empty; even its bones were just brittle nothings. Jedediah cut it open with his Clem-knife, the light, narrow, sharp-toothed blade that his grandfather had designed. This was a favourite tool of Jedediah's; it was a good device and comforting to wield, knowing that the grandfather who had thought you a good lad had at least been skilled at some things.

Ordinarily he would have worked by himself, but today he was surrounded, and strangely, he liked it that way. Louise sat on a stool near him, ready to hand him tools, and he could feel the warmth of her skin through her clothes from two feet away – or at least, his mind was unable to stop imagining it. Franklin held the pig's body steady, very serious-faced about the task, while Jedediah carefully sawed through the crumbling flesh of the belly. A lifetime of farrier work strengthens even the weakest of stomachs, and Jedediah wasn't easily disgusted, so as he pulled at the cuts and the carcass ratcheted open with a dry crack, sending puffs of flesh-dust up into the air, he was mostly feeling contented rather than dismayed – even if the carcass itself was a puzzler.

Jedediah had seen pigs butchered; Corbie had taken him to every throat-slitting possible from as early as he could remember. Inside should be wet white bones and rich red muscle and glossy baubles of offal, but this dry pouch was empty. Only some ribs and backbone pieces remained embedded in the hide, half-dissolved to a honeycomb of dry bubbles; traceries of flesh and dried strings of organ stuck to its dark insides like the burned scrapings of an overcooked stew inside a pot. Something had hollowed it out.

'Thanks, Franklin,' he said, sitting back on his heels and rubbing his hands with the watered-down vinegar he kept for cleaning up after dirty jobs. Louise passed him a cloth to dry them, easily, without being asked, and he said, 'Thank you,' and waited a longer moment after her quiet, 'You're welcome,' than was really necessary.

'Well,' he went on. He might be able to think out loud here without drawing any sudden roars or hearty slaps. 'It's an odd thing; I haven't seen the like. This isn't my holding, though. Do you know, Miss Louise' – he would be polite, he would show respect – 'any tales here of draugs or guls?'

Louise frowned a little at the words, just a quick moment of thought, before she said, 'I don't know those words, Mister Smith. I'm not from these parts, you see.'

'Oh. Where are you from?'

She looked down. 'Here and there. My folks follow the work. I've been here since last Michaelmas, but I was over the county border before then, down south.'

'That's my county,' Jedediah said, too interested to think about pigs. 'How did you like it there?' If her folks 'followed the work', that meant they had no home of their own, nor much money to rely upon. A girl without portion, working for her bread – she must be weary, living that way; it was a hard life, at the beck of folks who could replace you next Michaelmas if they didn't like you. The quiet with which she held herself started to make sense: if she didn't carry some peace within her, she'd get none, for the outside world had none held in trust for her. Though very few folks had the strength to reason that way.

'Well enough,' she said, with a slight quirk of her mouth. 'I must like where I am.'

'Mister Smith, what's a – a drag?' Franklin interposed, and Jedediah reminded himself that the boy was only asking a polite question.

'Oh.' Jedediah pushed his hair out of his face. 'A draug's a beast that drinks blood. Never saw one, but there's tales. And a gul – well, I don't reckon we'd have them here, it's just something Mister Attic told me of – you know Mister Attic? It's a kind of affright that eats bodies. Don't be afraid,' he added, seeing Franklin's face whiten and cursing himself, 'you're with me.

And I don't reckon we have those here. Too cold and wet for guls, at least. It's just, something ate the inside of this pig.'

'Y-yes, Mister Smith,' Franklin said, trying very hard to be brave.

'Nothing to fear there,' Louise said, and stroked Franklin's head. 'After all, we eat pigs ourselves. If you worry over beings that eat pigs, you'll find one stood in your boots.'

She gave Jedediah a long glance. It was almost tranquil, and he wanted to keep her eyes on him, but there was something there, a question he didn't know how to answer.

'She has the right of it,' Jedediah told Franklin. He stopped himself, because it wasn't right to haul a small child into your attempts to please a girl, but Franklin looked a little reassured and took Louise's hand again as she stood and said, 'I reckon you'll like to see around, Mister Smith.'

'No need to Mister me,' he said, a little awkwardly. 'My name's Jedediah. Take you a while to say, I'm afraid, but there it is.'

Surely he couldn't be this much of a fool. She was fine-looking and pleasant, but there were other girls in the world, even girls with black hair and long necks and kind, bright eyes. The feeling she gave him, as if she carried a layer of clean air around herself, was just that, a feeling. She wasn't even perfectly clean; there was soot on her apron, and close to, she had a scent, like fresh dough, soft and edible . . . No, he was being stupid. He'd never thought himself imaginative, but his imagination was evidently playing trick on him, trying to justify the fact that she was a girl with a pretty face and swaying hips by somehow convincing him that in her presence, the storm-clouds some folks brought with them calmed and the weather grew gentle.

Except that by the time they'd surveyed the farm, which took some hours longer than it strictly needed to, he hadn't been able to change his mind. All he'd done was gather some information:

That the Palmer lands were extensive, that they provided a pig for the yearly Clementing celebration in Tinsdowne, and that they were held in high regard.

That Louise was clever, though she'd had no teaching, and wished she could read and write so she could send letters to her family.

That the fields were edged in well-wrought iron fence-posts, styled in a design Jedediah recognised as similar to his father's.

That Louise's surname was Ditton, that she'd been named for a French great-grandmother, that she was the same age as himself, that she was fond of animals and had hidden a litter of barn-kittens from the mistress to save them from drowning.

That Franklin enjoyed seeing kittens with a delight that spoke of a lad who must be desperately bored as well as frightened at home, and that he had a touch with them remarkably light and deft for his age.

That Louise wasn't used to horses up close, but once she'd gathered herself, she stroked its nose and gazed at it with glowing eyes.

That the Palmers wintered their pigs in a well-made barn, which showed no signs of fey inhabitants.

That Louise liked to laugh: resignedly, at herself, but at him, a low, teasing chuckle that seemed to draw him out rather than set him back.

That Mister Dunstan Mackem, the new elder farrier that was, was a regular to the farm, finding Mister Palmer's company amusing.

That Louise took to saying 'Jedediah' easily, and that his name was a lighter burden when shaped smooth by her soft tongue.

That the Palmers had built a new barn lately, the old one being so teeming with rats that neither barn-cats nor a ferreting man could keep them down. The old barn was a wreck, and time would soon spare Mister Palmer the trouble of dismantling it, so it was left to the rats, Mister Palmer apparently feeling that going inside it as if it were still a used building might somehow discourage time from getting on with the job.

That Louise could wait patiently, no matter how long you inspected a place, either chatting to Franklin or, if Franklin's extra hands were needed, humming to herself in a sweet, velvety alto that did nothing to shake Jedediah's ideas about her carrying calm weather about with her.

That the pigs were fat as chestnuts, but still approached the fence whenever they saw you pass, grunting in greedy hope.

That Louise walked them out of the path of the old barn, and didn't suggest they visit it.

He didn't want to do this. He truly didn't. What he wanted was to send Franklin on an errand, talk more to Louise, tell her the truth, which was that if he put his mind to it and lied to his father, if he started early and returned late, he could visit here every week or so. That he wanted to see her again. Just to be there with her eyes on him would be enough. That wasn't all he wanted to do, but he was just about retaining sense enough to remember that you didn't say that to a girl you'd only just met.

Instead, he drew a breath. He couldn't neglect his work. That was how Abs got out into the world.

'Look you, Miss Louise,' he said, 'if there's a thing you feed in the barn, I must look at it. I needn't hurt it, if it's a good fey and you care for it. And I dare say the Palmers were easier to fool, if they're rich enough to afford your eyes to notice what needs cleaning for them. But I—' He cleared his throat. 'I think you're clever,' he said, 'and a good woman. I'd like to think so still. Just let me see what's hid there and I'll hear you out.'

The question that Louise had been holding back all day flared in her eyes. He saw it now: *Can I trust you?*

'You don't know me,' he said. 'The Mackems don't either, not much, if I'm honest. My father and they aren't – they aren't common visitors to each other. But I won't lose you your place. I can lie my tongue black if it spares someone.' He expected amusement at that, but she looked at him startled – startled, but with a glimmer. Moved? Stirred? Thrilled? He had to stop asking himself before his heart beat so hard it knocked his shirt open. 'I can,' he said. Evidently he'd quite lost his wits. 'Not to harm, but there's folks don't need to know things, and things folks don't need to know, and it could be there's both here, and—' He stopped himself before he dropped his entire history at her feet like a cat inflicting the gift of a half-gnawed mouse. 'As to the barn,' he rallied, 'well, I'd rather not be cruel if I can help it. That's all I can ask you to believe.'

'He isn't.' A small voice came from behind him. Franklin,

when Jedediah turned to look at him, was flushed crimson, almost stammering, his fists clenched as if outfacing some desperate ordeal. 'He's a very kind man, Miss Ditton.'

No one had called Jedediah kind in all his life. He didn't know what to do with it.

Louise looked at him. The smile she'd carried like a shield all day dropped for a moment and she looked tired, vulnerable, endlessly bruisable. 'I don't court trouble as a rule,' she said. 'I'm far from my kin here, and it's lonely.'

Jedediah could take and give back flirtation, if there was time, and he could let insults blow themselves out around his head. At this moment in his life he discovered that what he couldn't withstand was being trusted. A small crack appeared in his heart, and it never really went away again.

'Come on,' he said. 'Let's go.'

The barn was quieter than he'd expected. He'd thought there'd be some scrape and scrabble; a rat could thump about so loud you'd think there were dogs under the boards. But as his feet crunched the straw, everything went still.

Then above, in the hayloft, there was a rustle, a dry, swift-footed patter. It sounded hard as a horse's hooves, but not so heavy, and more than that, it was a complex drum of foot on board. There were too many feet up there.

'Good day, kind friend,' he said. 'Be you up there?'

There was a crackle, not straw, but the rattle of something spitless and quick.

'I've iron below, and it needn't come above,' Jedediah said. He didn't like the sound of this. 'Be you up there, kind friend?'

'No.' It was a throatless voice, not toned and warm like a man's, but a whistle of a thing, like the sound of air sighing over the lip of a jug. Some feet scraped, as if huddling themselves up, and then some more feet, and some more.

Jedediah braced himself. The back of his neck was creeping, which was not how a farrier was supposed to feel, nor a young man next to a girl he wholeheartedly wished to please.

'Glad not to meet you,' he said. 'Good thing there's none to harm up there. I wouldn't like to do ill by mistake.'

There was a chittering sound, sharp as flint on flint.

With immense reluctance, Jedediah started to climb the ladder. Louise was here, and so was Franklin, and Franklin thought he was impressive. Folks impressed with you, he was discovering, were a great deal harder to defy than those who found you ludicrous.

'Risk not tender feets on the hard rungs,' came the echoing rush of air. 'Waste not pinions when no one is not here nor to be found. Talk then to Louise. Louise is fond of no one. Louise is good to no one. Talk then to Louise.'

Jedediah turned. Louise, with the still face of one whose fate has been sealed, gave a deep sigh.

'Oh dear,' she said. 'No One, dear, I think he means you no harm. Perhaps you'll come down.'

Jedediah swallowed. He'd been prepared to be brave, but this was enough to make a man sit down and beat his head on his knees. He was about to make an absolute fool of himself.

'Cannot come down,' came the voice. 'No one can come down when no one is here.'

'But if No One came down, there'd be No One down here

for us to see,' Louise pointed out. She still looked dismayed, but as she spoke to the unwonted thing, a little warmth crept into her voice, the amused air of a woman bargaining with a beloved child. 'Riddle me that.'

There was a silence. Then the air *stretched*: there was a splitting sound, a sticky tearing that went on and on, and as the long gleam unspooled from the creature that lowered itself, Jedediah managed not to hide behind Louise. He'd faced down a great bear made of thorn and candlelight before now, and the wildest stallion didn't trouble him much, but he simply couldn't like spiders.

The thing wasn't all spider, mind. It had a scattering of eyes, shaped like the eyes of a man, but more of them on each cheek than most beasts need on their entire head. They blinked clear, lashless lids at him with an air of wistful sorrow. Around its mouth were many curved and hinging claws; it grubbled them together like a woman wringing her hands, but somehow Jedediah couldn't sympathise. The beast was as big as a badger and fanged at every tip.

He swallowed. He couldn't quite make his voice sound as firm as he'd have liked. 'I see No One.'

'Gentle ways bring under shade and shadow,' the spider wheedled. It had no lips to shape the words, but its mouth parts flickered to and fro, quick as a harpist's fingers. 'Hurt not the feeling tips of many toes or the weak waist that joins body to notions, or what shall the air do for pretty thoughts?'

It sounded genuinely heartbroken at that last comment, though Jedediah couldn't fully agree that a world without fey spiders would be all that impoverished.

'Louise says you're her friend,' he managed.

'Here now, the girl of salt and clinker and dry bread.' It was an airless elegy. 'The bright taste of Louise-skin, No One smells with every knee. Rub rub rub Louise-hands go upon the stone. Put one toe to the ground, free the sole of that blindfold of pickled skin. Hear then the rub of brush on the stone.'

Jedediah swallowed again. He himself was not immune to thoughts of how Louise might taste, but they didn't feel quite so erotic when uttered by a giant spider.

'No meat to drink,' came the mournful gust of sound. 'Dry down to the poor gullet, so No One hears the click of meat on meat.'

The thing had appallingly intimate hearing as well as a welter of legs, it seemed. 'Franklin,' Jedediah said, since he couldn't save himself from this conversation, 'stay behind me. Don't go near.'

Franklin had been gazing wide-eyed, but there was no order of Jedediah's that he wouldn't obey on the instant. 'Yes, Mister Smith,' he said, and turned.

A scratchy sigh filled the barn, soft and inescapable as silk. Jedediah instinctively grabbed Franklin's shoulder, prepared to swear on the rack that he did it to reassure Franklin, not himself.

'Break the heart-web of thirsty longing, for No One is poor,' it whispered. 'Rats of grime and bone and cats of hair and rat-blood, and No One drinks sip by sip. A butterless back on so small a beast, but no more pigs come, and when out walks the boy of bread and scented bruise, goes with it poor No One's hope of damp and dinner. What shall the silk do for rainbows of light when No One hungers?'

'Now, behave yourself, Miss,' Louise said, sounding gently firm. 'This boy is not for you to eat, and if it was you ate the pig, I'm very disappointed in you, for you know I promised to keep you quiet here if you kept down the rats and left the rest alone. The cats were sad enough. The pigs are not for you.'

'Trotter and pleat and moist whiffle of blood-rich nose,' No One husked, sounding a bit defensive. 'When the silk is there and the cream of flesh, what shall dinner-melt do for dinner?'

'Spider,' Jedediah said, 'if you take one bite of this boy, I will pull off your legs.'

This proposition was greeted with a flurry of sighs, insinuating enough that the very slats shivered. 'What shall be done with poor shell and shelter if the beauty of hinge and scent shall be—'

'Furthermore,' Jedediah said, interrupting what he suspected would be another burst of aesthetic grieving, 'you cannot stay here. You ate a pig, and I don't trust you not to eat another one if it comes in here looking for the old feed-bins.'

No One snatched itself into a bristling ball, crossing four pairs of hooked feet over each other in a prayful clasp, like a martyr laid out after death. 'Wrongful and murder to the spirit,' it murmured. 'Struck from the air is the joy of pretty thoughts, and how is No One to reweave? Such is the blow of stick to truth, that snaps the silk and makes pattern to dangle and dust to coat the living strand of—'

'There, there, dear,' said Louise. 'I'm sure he doesn't mean to be unfair. He's fond of the boy, that's all. I'll tell you what. Franklin, dear?

Franklin was somewhat confounded by No One's latest burst

of melancholia, but it was turning out to be a day of new experiences, and Miss Louise had been nothing but kind to him. 'Yes, Miss?' he asked.

'Why don't you and No One play together a while? I'm sure you can trust each other. I'll talk to Mister Smith of justice to spiders and the wrongfulness of accusation' – she glanced at Jedediah, green eyes in the shade, and his heart began to pound – 'and you and No One can make friends and talk of the plans you can make.'

'A-are you sure,' Jedediah said, wondering if this was one of those trials of temptation that the parson made so many trenchant comments about, 'that it's – quite wise to leave the spider here with a boy it wishes to eat? I don't go to call you foolish, but I own I cannot see your reasoning.' He was sounding more like Corbie the more tense he got, and he was wrestling with the urge to shake himself.

'Oh, indeed,' Louise said. 'I think it the safest, in fact. I'd like Franklin to be well protected, you see, for he's a very good boy. And No One doesn't eat friends.'

Franklin, bewilderingly, did not seem to find spiders any more alarming than he had the kittens earlier. He reached out and gave No One's stretched-out claw a careful poke, and No One swung too and fro like an appalling pendulum.

'Would you like to play?' he asked. 'I think you look very fine.'

'Another nature of man in size and temper,' No One considered, polishing its fangs one against the other in a nervous shimmy. 'Cruelty to legs and feet perhaps is not in fresh blood, and if No One is not shielded by friends of the man of iron and tearing, what shall become of the skeins?'

'Oh no,' Franklin said, 'I don't wish to hurt your legs. I dare say they matter very much.'

'Boy of eyes and scentless nose. Taste is locked within the tongue and only eyes to scent the world,' No One told Franklin, as if offering to help a lame man up a set of steps.

'All right,' Jedediah said, 'but mind, I'll be in earshot, Franklin. You just call. And Spider, if you hurt a hair of him, I'll set you afire.'

'Tasteless and blind are the hairs, and man of iron burns sorrowing flight for manling carried not on any back nor wrapped in any silk of flame.'

'I like your web,' Franklin said. 'Can I touch it? I promise not to break it.'

They didn't go far; there was space to be alone round the back of the barn. It was quiet; fields stretched beyond them, shadowing down in the sunset. The sky ran with liquid fire, every cloud alight.

They stood, looking at each other.

Louise spoke first. 'I like your little friend,' she said.

Jedediah shrugged. 'Glad of his company,' he said. 'You sure he's safe in there?'

'Oh yes.' She brushed the lock of hair from her face; it dropped back down at once, glossy and full of weight. 'No One just wants to play. She'll take to anyone if they're left alone and keep talking to her. Well, I don't know if "she" is right, but I took a guess and she didn't mind. Perhaps only because I'm a woman; I reckon she wished for some fellow feeling.'

'It'll – she'll have to go,' he said. That needed to be got over with. 'I don't know what my uncle makes of such things, but I know my father'd want it killed. I don't want to do that if you'd grieve for it, but it – she can't stay here. Not around livestock.'

Louise sighed, but she looked relieved as well. At least, he supposed, he wasn't threatening to tell her employers.

'There's places friendly to the fey,' he said. 'There's the Bellame woods, though it's a long way from here, and if Lord Robert got himself spidered we'd never hear the end of it. There's a smallish place closer, though, in my own holding. The Lendens, they're the folks who own it – they keep pigs, but I can make iron leashes for them. They won't ask too deep into the whys and wherefores, not if I ask them not to. Can you make the spider go there?'

'I think so,' Louise said. 'I – I beg your pardon if I've caused you trouble.' It wasn't exactly an apology; it was more like a recognition, a word or two that spoke of the trouble he'd be going to, telling him she'd seen it.

Jedediah was pretty quick at spotting when a girl liked the look of him; you had to be, when all your life had room for was a bit of snatched pleasure here and there. Louise was slower than that, though. She wasn't flashing her eyes at him, or giving him a fluttering grin. She looked at him to see if she could *risk* liking the look of him. That was what he'd been seeing, he thought, or he hoped. Along with whether he'd lose her a place she needed, there were other things he could do against her: toy with her virtue, or her feelings, or her good name.

And he didn't want to do any of them. Or rather, he had many thoughts about what he would like to do with her, and only some of them were virtuous, but he didn't want to toy with her feelings. He wanted to hold them; he wanted them to be for him. The fact was that he'd had the sweetest day he could remember having in years, just working, and talking to this girl. He hadn't felt tired or lonely, and the knots in his shoulders were come loose.

He'd have to go home tomorrow, so it was now or never.

'I'm not sorry,' he said. 'Meant I could spend the day with you.'

She just looked at him: freckled eyes, cracked red lips, almost level with his own. She wasn't turning aside.

'Look you.' His voice came out rough; he meant to speak soft to her, but he hadn't enough spit in his throat. 'I've a family to keep, and not enough to keep it on. My mother's touched in her wits and my aunt cares for her, and my father doesn't like either of them. And there's the boy, too. He's not mine, nor kin to me, but I made him trust me, and his own father won't do a thing for him but knock his head off walls. I work for my father, and he's not over-fond of me. It's a mess, that's the truth, and I can't offer more than a mess that I need to pay for and don't know how. But I'd like to see you again.'

As his words sank in, the softest of smiles traced the edges of her lips – held back, but there, and then he couldn't keep from watching her mouth. 'I barely see my kin one year to the next. I work for my bread, and it doesn't pay enough to save a dowry.' It was a recitation, matching him truth for truth; there was just a shadow of anxiety in her eyes. 'I've neither home nor name. And I never learned a trade, except to scrub floors and carry pots. I'm not anybody. I'm not even from anywhere.'

He didn't quite dare smile back. 'I mean it honest,' he said. 'I know I've asked you just as I learned a secret that could cause you trouble. I won't tell the Palmers if you say me no, I mean. That's not what I want. Not to – see you against your will, I mean.'

At that, she relaxed enough to laugh. 'I should hope not,' she said. 'It would be a shame if you lost me my place. I'd have to walk the roads with nothing to tell the world but that the farrier is afraid of spiders.'

He had to grin, then, all at once. Of course she'd seen. What a thing it was: to be held in the gaze of a clever woman.

'I beg you not to,' he said. The birds were calling to each other, note to note across the fields.

'Is it the farrier way to beg?' she said. There was just a glimmer of wickedness in her face now, and he couldn't look away any more. 'Or is it yours, Jed Smith?'

For a moment, he was too startled at hearing himself so named. It was like being touched, her voice reaching across the space between them.

He drew breath himself, not quite sure that he remembered how. 'Mine,' he said. He meant to add something, he wasn't sure what, but her eyebrows raised, just a line, and the low afternoon light was gilding her face, and the reality of her rang in the bird-stricken air.

So instead he said the only thing he was thinking, which was, 'I'd like to kiss you. May I?'

The smile dusked, her lips coming soft in her face. She didn't reply, but she put her arms around his neck, and her mouth, when he reached it, was chapped as ash, and warm as a sun-dazed plum.

*

'It doesn't hurt,' Franklin said, rather muzzily.

Louise's shriek had sent No One into a knotted bundle of joints. All its eyes were wide with confused sorrow, like a dog scolded for an offence it doesn't understand.

And to be fair to the creature, Franklin himself didn't appear to feel that anything was wrong. He was dangling upside-down from a rope of glinting silk, and his limbs weren't where they had been. His arms and hands had been attached to his waist; his mouth was fringed with a flexing spray of fingers and toes. But when they'd returned to the barn – which neither had really wanted to do, but Jedediah's conscience eventually interposed itself between himself and Louise's soft lips – all Franklin had said was, 'Look, Mister Smith, I'm a spider!'

'Play with boy of pretty thoughts says the man and Louise of the blinking eyes,' No One said now in a voice of hopeless self-defence. 'Pretty thoughts are of the little one.'

'Franklin, are you all right?' Jedediah was at the boy's side, so aghast he couldn't even hear the fury in his voice. 'What in God's name happened here?'

Franklin, under the foggy impression that Mister Smith was angry with him, began to cry. 'I'm very sorry,' he said. 'Please don't say I can't visit you again.'

Jedediah reached out, tried to put a steadying hand on the boy, but it was difficult to know where to start. The gesture sent him twirling round in a bobbing circle.

'I don't blame you, lad,' Jedediah said, though Franklin could have been forgiven for doubting him: his voice was so angry you could have struck flints off it. 'You. Spider. Mend this at once, or before God I'll come back here with iron stakes and fix you to the wall limb by Godforsaken limb.'

It wasn't the right approach: No One, who had been crouched on the floor, rolled over on its back and folded up its legs. 'No One lives not to do harm,' it whispered. 'No One dies and none can blame a dead thing.'

'I'll maul your corpse,' Jedediah told it.

Louise, who had been trying without success to loose Franklin from the thread, looked back and said, 'Now, No One dear, let's . . . let's not be silly.' She didn't sound entirely steady; there were tears gathered in her eyes. 'If you did this, you must undo it. The boy needs his limbs where they were. I swear,' she said, turning to Jedediah, 'I didn't know she could do this.'

'It's my fault,' Jedediah snapped, 'mine and this thing's. You two stop blaming yourselves this minute. You're neither of you farriers and I'm the one should hang for this. Let me set this right and then you can both rail at me. You, Spider. Get yourself back to life and fix this lad, or you'll wish you had died.'

No One might have spent longer in wistful self-excuse, but Jedediah's voice was so sharp that it flicked itself upright – a long-taloned stretch of so many legs that he felt a genuine desire to be sick – and swarmed up Franklin, sharp toes suddenly busy. The spider itself held steady, except for an outbreak of skilful feet; it was Franklin who spun, so fast that it was hard to see quite what was being done to him. There was just the deep, notching click of limb unsocketed from joint, and a slight ripping sound, softer than tearing cloth, as skin unpeeled.

'Franklin?' Jedediah called. 'Are you all right?'

'Ye-es, tha-ank you,' came a little voice from the centre of the whirl. 'Just a lit-tle dizzy.'

There was a plash of jaw and the threads holding Franklin parted. He landed with a thump, limbs re-ordered and face very flushed.

'I'm so sorry, Mister Smith,' he said, head hanging. 'We only meant to play. P-please don't say—'

'Oh, never mind that,' Jedediah said in haste. 'I told you, you're my friend; visit whenever you like. Just – just use your common sense another time, eh? Don't let the People put you about, it's not always to be mended, and' – the boy's face was still white with dismay, so he tried to find something reassuring to say – 'and you're very well the way you are. And you, Spider,' he added, 'you've been in the wrong here, and you'll make amends. There's a place I'll let you live, but you'll stay there, or I'll—' He hesitated. With the boy back together and the first horror past, it was a bit more difficult to make a credible threat. 'Or I'll know of it,' he ended.

'Mar not No One with ugly.' Jedediah had never heard anyone whimper without a proper voice before, but this spider accomplished it. 'Only for the asking of Louise the friend would No One have done this turn. Hurt not the pretty of limb on limb, or what shall be of the scent of unsweet blood?'

It wasn't the vow most likely to settle Jedediah's stomach, but it sounded sincere, and that would have to do. For relief, he looked at Franklin, who was beginning to stagger. 'What is it, lad? Did it bite you? Are you hurt?'

Louise wiped a tear from her eye, and managed a very small

laugh. 'No One, dear,' she said, 'you've left him dizzy. You need to set his eyes back the right way up.'

By the time Dunstan Mackem, new elder farrier of Tinsdowne, arrived on the Palmer farm with his son Stan, the old barn was ablaze. The Palmers hadn't been present to witness an angular bundle scuttling its way out of the building to hide in the bushes near their gate; what they knew was that the trouble had come from an infestation in the barn, which was in the process of being destroyed with burning brands and prevented from coming back by driving nails into the scorched earth in the pattern of a Gowan star. (Or rather, an eight-pointed star, rather than the more traditional Gowan seven, Jedediah having views about multiple legs that he felt the need to express in ironwork.)

He stood listening to the bluster of the flames and watching the air above the barn melt into writhing trickles of heat. Louise sat on a stool nearby with Franklin on her lap, officially to make sure he didn't go too near the fire, but also because she'd offered and he'd climbed on with the willingness of a boy currently inhabiting a world containing so many dream-like apparitions, such as dismantling spiders and sufficient food, that he might as well take whatever benisons it offers.

Mister Palmer, who appeared unable to calm down no matter what his circumstances, was pacing before the blaze, exclaiming that it was one thing to have an old barn falling apart and another to have an inferno, and what a dire shock it would be to the pigs to hear such noise from their paddock, and was there no hope in this world of a quiet life?

'Well, you should have one after this,' Jedediah said, feeling a bit unappreciated.

'To think, a haunting on our very farm!' Mister Palmer exclaimed.

'Now then, Thomas,' came a voice from behind them. They hadn't heard footsteps over the roar of the fire and Jedediah turned, a little startled. 'Farrier work's no exorcism. Would you make a parson of my nephew? Are you feeling Godly today, Jedediah?'

There he stood: Uncle Dunstan Mackem, a few years older, just as hearty-voiced and sturdy-limbed, rough-bearded and red-haired like Corbie, but with a bit of a pleased look on his face at the sight of his nephew. He wore a black rope around his neck with a scrap of what looked like horseshoe knotted into it; his son Stan (short for Dunstan, of course; he was this Dunstan's firstborn) wore something similar. That must be their mourning sign, Jedediah thought; most likely, you took the last shoe the dead man forged, or something similar, and broke it into pieces for those left behind. It wasn't a Smith custom, but it made sense.

'Good day, Uncle,' he said politely. 'I was sorry to hear of your elder.' Perhaps he should have said 'your father', he realised once the words were out of his mouth; Dunstan looked tired under his smile, genuinely bereaved.

'Not sorry enough to join us, though?' That was Stan, only a year older than Jedediah and approved of by everyone in the Mackem clan. The two young men barely knew each other; the last time they'd met they'd been children and expected to like each other because they were much of an age. It hadn't been a success, though: Stan had had little to say except to tell Jedediah it made no sense to be called Smith when his father was Mackem, and to be annoyed at the illogic when Jedediah replied that he was sure he knew his own name.

Jedediah stiffened. It wasn't his fault he hadn't been invited. 'My father bade me mind the smithy,' he said, addressing Dunstan more than Stan; that was the courtesy due to an elder and also, conveniently, talking to the friendlier figure. 'I hope I've been of use to you here, though.'

'Ach, this place, it's lost this or that bit of livestock once in a while since before my time,' Uncle Dunstan said, waving his hand in dismissal. 'If it's not the People after your pigs it'll be the foxes after your chickens, haven't I told you that often enough, Thomas Palmer? We aren't put on this world to live untroubled, eh?' He said the words 'Thomas Palmer' with a slight self-consciousness; it was an elder farrier's privilege to call everyone from a beggar to a lord by their full name, but he evidently hadn't been at it very long.

'Well,' Jedediah said, a little encouraged by this unblaming attitude, 'I'm sorry if I've given cause to doubt my work and pulled you from your business.'

'Ah, you're a mannerly one, aren't you?' Uncle Dunstan said, with something like a conspiratorial grin. 'Nay, lad, we came to ask you to join us. We drink my father's name thrice by thrice tonight. Come and mourn your grandfather.'

The barn-sparks flew around them. Jedediah tried, for a long moment, to work out why he felt so certain that he couldn't go.

'I've left the smithy unmanned,' he said.

'Oh, I know you're a weighty lad,' Uncle Dunstan said, 'but

one more day? Come now.' He handed Jedediah a rope, black and iron-spangled like the ones he and Stan wore.

Jedediah tied it round his neck, slowly, playing for time. His uncles had always been friendly, and Gyrford could probably spare him another day. But there was Franklin. He couldn't leave the boy behind – and while the Mackems might not object, they'd be raising their cups thrice by thrice. If he joined them, he'd put Franklin in company with Corbie when Corbie was drinking.

Stan glared at him. 'Too Smith to join us?' he said. He was a tall lad and would no doubt be burly as his father in due time, but at twenty years old his features were still a little too big for his face. 'Reckon you could write and send your condolences?'

Jedediah wasn't about to get into an argument about whether writing was or wasn't a fit skill for a farrier. He looked at Louise, who was stroking Franklin's dirty hair with a light, rough-skinned hand.

'I've another job to do on the way back,' he told Stan. 'I don't mean disrespect. Only my father bid me mind the smithy. I'm sorry. I am.' He was sorry, in a way. He'd loved his own Grandpa Clem; if Stan felt that way about the late elder, it was hard to blame him for being angry. 'What you get for calling in a journeyman, I fear.'

At that, Uncle Dunstan's look sharpened and he suddenly looked more like Corbie. 'What's that?' he said. 'You're what, near twenty? Still a journeyman?'

Jedediah nodded, as bland as he could. Journeymen his age weren't uncommon in other trades; some lived and died journeymen, never gaining the right to call themselves master craftsmen unless they headed up a workshop of their own. But farriers apprenticed young; in a way you were 'prenticed at birth, for you began learning an ear for pitch with your cradle-songs. A master farrier's workshop was as much the fields and forests of his holding as it was the forge at its centre, and if you weren't able to manage that by the time you were seventeen or so, then you weren't much use.

Jedediah had been obliged to use his own judgement for years – Corbie was not a patient supervisor – but he hadn't the right to call himself a master: Corbie hadn't granted it. It was one thing to pay him a tenth or two to show that a boy too old to be beaten was too old to be kept, but it was another thing to bring him up too close to Corbie's rank. Or, indeed, to pay him accordingly. Master and elder farriers usually split the profits equally. Even three-tenths might get Mama and Aunt Agnes out of the house.

Uncle Dunstan looked him up and down. 'So the rags aren't just to keep the girls from throwing their hearts at your handsome feet?' he said. 'What does my brother pay you, lad?'

Jedediah shook his head. He'd have liked to talk about a lot of things to do with Corbie if there was someone who'd see his point, but he wasn't close to his uncle. It might be comforting if he was: the man appeared to wish him well. But if Dunstan respected a man who blurted out all his business on so little acquaintance, then perhaps he wasn't a man safe to be close to. 'That's not my place to tell you, Uncle,' he said. 'I don't complain.'

'The clothes on your back do, loud enough,' Uncle Dunstan said. 'Your face, too.' He gestured, and Jedediah felt a flicker of resentful shame: it was true, he couldn't afford a barber. Agnes cut his hair as best she could, but the risks of a razor were beyond her. The Attics had a marvellous device he sometimes used when he visited, a small looking-glass of Moorish workmanship that reflected your face without a ripple, but such things weren't to be had from English artificers: most of the time he had to work by feel and shave himself, and he knew it was a rough job. Mackem men grew splendid thick beards – were born with them, probably – but Pell said the Smiths weren't so hairy and it'd be a few years before his own face could manage such a money-saving grace. Better a ragged shave than stupid straggles, and he'd thought he looked all right. Evidently not. And the man had to point it out in front of Louise.

'I hope you'll forgive me, Uncle,' he said, trying to sound calm. The beams in the burning barn were cracking now. 'If Mister Palmer likes to pay me for my day's work, I'll be the richer, but I won't presume on your holding. I am sorry – truly – that I can't come to mourn Grandfather.' The word felt unnatural in his mouth, but what else was he to call the man? His name had been Dunstan Mackem, and everyone around here was Dunstan Mackem. 'But I made a promise to call in on my way back, not expecting you to invite me, and I wouldn't break my word.'

'And why in the name of hell's teeth wouldn't you expect it?' Uncle Dunstan had been fairly cheerful, but this offended him. Jedediah glanced around. Mister Palmer was tugging his own hair again, family disagreements evidently being yet another sign of a cosmos in chaos. Franklin was pointing to them and whispering, and Louise was soothing him; he could see her shake her head – *Not to worry* – and he wanted to step away from this too-hot bonfire, take both of them and go – to somewhere else, some other place where he wouldn't be followed by all his worries. Except that no such place existed in the world.

Uncle Dunstan was glaring at him, but his eyes were shrewd and Jedediah wished he knew the man well enough to know whether he was angry with him or with Corbie.

'Excuse me,' he said, withdrawing into himself the way he did when Corbie was in one of his dark moods. 'My father bade me mind the smithy.'

Neither of them was shouting, exactly; with the flames rushing and snapping like sheets in a gale, they might just be raising their voice to be heard. And if Jedediah had been less drawn to Louise, less smitten with her kind voice and downy neck and parched, warm mouth, he might have been less aware of her behind him. Neither Dunstan nor Stan nor Mister Palmer turned their heads as she made a soft hissing sound, too quiet to cover the unmistakable patter of too many legs.

He couldn't turn his head; that would draw attention. He kept looking at Uncle Dunstan, who was now staring at him sharper than ever.

'Your father's in my house this minute, Nephew,' he said, 'and under my roof, where I'm elder farrier, God help the holding, and head of our clan. Think he'll put you over his knee if I ask you home and you mind me? Come on, you're a big strong lad.'

Jedediah managed not to flinch. He liked invitations to stay with folks: it was fun sitting in a different kitchen, having food set before you by women you didn't have to guard; he always slept best in an unfamiliar bed. If things had been different, he would have been glad to go.

'Jedediah, my lad,' Uncle Dunstan's voice was getting a little hard as Jedediah still hesitated, 'come along. Don't keep your elder waiting.'

Down the years, Jedediah often wondered what Uncle Dunstan had truly wished to offer him. Other cousins always got along well with Uncle Dunstan; the word was that he was open-handed and liked to make gifts, of goods and of money. Stan's cousin Judy was got pregnant a few years later, and while she should have known better than to believe her lover's promises that he'd set aside his wife for her, Uncle Dunstan made his opinion public that if no girl ever closed with a fool or a knave the men of the world would have a dry time of it, and no one was to reproach the girl, for he had always liked babies. Before old age wore out his wits, Uncle Dunstan was a generous man – at least, to those he felt part of him and his. Jedediah knew, even at that moment, that if he didn't go home with him that day, he would be putting himself for ever outside that circle.

But Uncle Dunstan wasn't his elder. Corbie held the Gyrford forge; he had bought it with his name. He might have regretted the bargain, but he had taken it. One day Jedediah Smith would be an elder farrier, and he would not live as if he and his didn't pay their debts. Stan Mackem could say what he liked. Jedediah had been right, back when he was a child: he knew his own name.

And yes, he would have liked to do otherwise. He couldn't even fault Uncle Dunstan for being offended; nobody liked an ingrate, and it would be cosy sitting with company, breaking bread and sharing chat, and letting the world outside grow dark. But it was growing dark here and now, and the flames burned gold at their heart and red at their hems, and he'd had enough of being pushed. He wouldn't leave Franklin with strangers at nightfall.

'I'll mourn him in Gyrford,' he said. 'You'll have to forgive me, Uncle. I've promises to keep. I must mourn him in Gyrford, as a Gyrford man.'

There was a rush of heat and the barn collapsed entirely; something snapped, some prop or stay, and the blackened beams spilled sideways like a dropped sheaf. There was only a heap of flame and char, crackling away like a Clementing festival.

When Jedediah looked back, a quick glance away that Uncle Dunstan didn't catch, he saw that Franklin Thorpe looked a lot less skinny than he had this morning. Under his shirt, something bulged. Jedediah's throat twisted – dear God, who of sense let even a common spider onto their chest, never mind hiding that great thing like a smuggled puppy? But the creature must have been gripping him pretty tight, for if you didn't look hard, all you'd see was a boy with a peaked face and a plump belly.

He must feed Franklin up some more, he thought, distracted. How thin must a boy be that he could hide a whole fey spider under his shirt?

When he looked back, Stan Mackem was scowling at him and Uncle Dunstan was regarding him with a face as stiff as if a tanner had been at work upon it.

'Well,' Uncle Dunstan said, and his voice had a flat finality to it, as if pronouncing sentence, 'God by you then, Nephew.

We'll be off. I reckon we've each of us got our way to get along.'

Mister Palmer had expected to put Jedediah up for the night, but after that, it wouldn't have been right. All he could do was set off for home, then make camp with Franklin not too far from the gate.

The spider was, indeed, hugging the boy's chest with an anxious grip. 'Are you scraped or squeezed?' Jedediah asked, looking at the awful thing, tick-like in its hold on the unperturbed boy.

'I don't think so, Mister Smith,' Franklin said. His answer was quick, obedient, as eager to please as ever. Jedediah supposed that at his age, the conversation of grown folks was mostly one incomprehensible blur, and the lines between what could and couldn't be were not defined enough to make a day like today any stranger than most.

'Well, Spider,' Jedediah said, 'we've camp to set. You can – can find yourself a tree, catch birds or what-have-you. Tomorrow I'll take you somewhere you can stay that won't catch afire. No need to thank me.'

'No One is no grateless maw,' came the whisper. 'Fires and uncles are a day of falling, and how shall the limbs hold when the beams split and the men cannot but bite?'

Franklin gave the carapace a thoughtful pat, apparently recognising the despondent tone, but Jedediah felt the need to make something clear.

'What's between my uncle and me is not your business,' he said, as firm as he could. The creature didn't have any fewer legs than it had had this morning, and there was a set of bristles around the tips of its toes that could not have been more revolting if they had been the master-work of some malicious craftsman.

'Ah, for the sorrow of two on one web, for one must drink the other,' No One condoled in a breathless hush.

'My father and I do not drink each other,' Jedediah said, firming his voice up still more. 'That's spider business, not man's business.'

Franklin was almost asleep. During the daytime he was careful not to cause offence, but here under the shelter of a pegged-out canvas and with the stars clear above him was a world away from trouble and terror, and it was with a slightly dreamlike honesty that he said, 'I'm a little afraid of your father, Mister Smith. I don't mean to be rude.'

'Nay, nay, I don't blame you,' Jedediah said, putting the thickest blanket on him. Probably the boy was just naturally clever and well-behaved, for taking care of him had turned out to be a great deal easier than Jedediah had expected. 'You're right there. You just step wide around him, and if you need something, it's me you come to, yes?'

'Mm,' Franklin said. 'Thank you, Mister Smith, you've been so good . . .' He yawned.

'Go to sleep,' Jedediah said, feeling uncomfortable; he'd got the child taken apart by a giant spider, set him in the path of what looked like it might have been a rift between two clans, and couldn't offer him anything more than some bread and cheese for supper and a bed on the ground. The boy himself might be comfortable, but that was entirely to his own credit. 'I may step off for a little while in the night, all right? Don't be afraid if you wake and I'm gone, I'll be back soon. Just stay here. Spider, you'll watch the boy, all right? I'll have you if I come back and find him any the worse.'

'Drinkless man of veins poison, hurt not the feelings or pinions of poor unpresent No One,' the whisper pleaded. 'Fang not No One with nail and gnarl. Louise of the brush will have her mate and hurt will come not near pretty limbs.'

'All right then,' said Jedediah, hoping that Franklin hadn't picked up the comment about mating Louise. He sat up for a while, watching the flames dip and chatter within the circle of stones he'd set up, a tiny imp of warmth compared to the massive wall of scarlet he'd seen collapse earlier that day. When he was very sure Franklin was asleep, he left as quietly as he could, pointing a stern finger towards No One as he went. The spider clutched its legs to its body and looked at him with multitudinous, defensive eyes.

Louise slept in the kitchen, away from the Palmer family. It was a draughty, dingy spot, and her pallet, tucked away in the corner, had nothing like enough straw in it. But it had Louise upon it, and there was no other place in the world he wished to be that night.

There wasn't time to do all that much, or to talk all that much either. The Palmers weren't to be shocked at the morals of their maidservant, and Franklin shouldn't be left for too long. He knew already anyway that one night, however long, would never be enough of her.

It was time enough to learn that she had Sundays to herself;

that there were quiet copses within walking distance where none but she ever went; that she would meet him even if they had to lie on the ground.

It would need to be a secret for now: if Corbie knew his son had a girl he'd tell everyone he could, and Louise had little enough name without Corbie clarioning it all over the county. But Corbie's visits to other women – or to sample the preaching of another church, as he usually called it – occupied enough of his Sundays that if his son was gone before he woke, he wouldn't notice, or care to ask why. Jedediah could borrow Tom's horse, journey to that far-off copse and find her.

There was time enough settle that, at least. Time enough to find that her hair was smooth and slipped in waves through his fingers, that she rubbed her neck with rosemary, leaving a faint, wild taste; that her legs were long and her hands deft and her breath could stop in her throat; that he'd thought himself young and strong and used to his body answering him, but was still capable of shaking.

It was the last thing he needed, more complications, another soul he loved and couldn't pay to keep, but he couldn't help it. He'd needed her all his life.

Franklin was well rested the next morning, if quietly unhappy about returning to Gyrford. He didn't complain, but the brightness of his face was dimming and Jedediah didn't know how to console him. What could he do for the boy? He couldn't keep him. He wouldn't know what to do with him even if he could; having a child to watch all the time was exhausting, and the minute you turned your back to kiss a girl, they got themselves spidered. Jedediah stepped on that thought as fast as he could – he was damned if he'd sustain any opinion that put him in company with Corbie, and 'small boys are tiresome' was definitely one of them – but there was nothing for either of them to do but go home, for what 'home' was worth.

'Look you,' he said, putting Franklin up on the saddle, 'I know it's not such a joy to go back. I'll bring you out with me again, any time you like, if it's safe. And you come by if you need anything, all right? There's only so much I can do; it's not my house and I haven't much money, but I'll do what I can. I'm not sorry to have your company.'

No One suddenly dropped down from the tree, landing on the horse's tail and giving the poor undeserving gelding a moment of utter terror that took all Jedediah's patience to calm. 'No One's company is shadow and air and the peace of absence,' it whispered, seeming flattered – at least, its many mouth-parts were cupped together like a girl holding her blushing cheeks. 'What shall man do but be glad, for who can hate what is not there?'

'I wasn't—' Jedediah began, but there was no point saying he hadn't been talking to the spider; at least the awful thing was acting compliant. 'Well, you,' he said, 'if you'd make me glad, I know a place for you to live. It's a little forest, with trees to nest in and birds to eat and such, and there's People there too, so folks don't go in it so much. If I take you there, will you stay?'

'Scent of Louise-skin and saviour of pretty knees from burning barn,' No One said. Jedediah held himself rigid as the creature reached up a pointed, flint-hard toe and gave him a dry pat. He hadn't wanted to befriend the thing at all, but if it had the confused idea that he was a rescuer – which he supposed he was, in a way; Corbie would have done something much worse than relocating the thing – then that was all to the good. And if they could get off the subject of whether it could scent on him the shadow of Louise's work-rough hands and soft arms, especially in front of Franklin, then all the better. He did not want to associate any memories of last night with the opinions of a hinge-limbed scuttler.

'How can No One move from where iron and spit and beating heart would place, when No One disobeys the cloth-muffled skin and voice of ringing meat?' the spider declared, apparently in favour of Louise having some romance in her life.

If his family history had taught Jedediah anything, it was that promises with the People needed to be carefully worded. He could tell the spider not to leave the grove without his permission, but that could go horribly in the long run: he wouldn't live for ever and No One might, and if some day a hundred years from now the woods were cleared and a house built, then the poor inhabitants would never get the spider out.

'All right,' he said, mounting up behind Franklin, and trying to ignore the sensation of No One flattening itself over the horse's croup. It was a brisk morning, but he took off his jacket and tied it loose around his waist so he could drape it over the clinging arachnid; it wouldn't fool anyone who took the time to study them, but they could go by quiet lanes and look nothing strange at a distance. 'We're off, and Spider, you – you will do no harm nor cause no mischief, and stay put until I tell you otherwise.'

'No One hides upon the horse. Stirrup of poison and nail and bolt of metal cruel are near, but courage is the gift of No One and stillness shall be to the man of Louise and shelter.' The appeasing whisper crawled all the way up his neck, tickling his nerves with icy fingers, and Jedediah just managed to stop himself from kicking the horse harder than was fair.

Franklin took some happiness in the ride, but Jedediah, who usually liked peace and quiet in the open air and enjoyed having Franklin around when there weren't beautiful girls to distract him, found himself shivering along the cool lanes. It was, he told the concerned boy, just that he'd taken off his jacket.

When they reached the Lenden property, he was able to get in without any of the adults knowing. Winifred and Cissie were engaged in the earnest business of training the Lenden's half-grown pup; Wag was a scruffy brown scrap of a thing with bright eyes and a tail quivering to please any and all. Jedediah liked dogs very well, and had been known to stop and play with Wag; farriers don't keep their own dogs, it being unkind to subject such a creature to the thousand shocks and slights to reality that the People inflict, so he was glad to take the chance to exchange courtesies with anyone else's. Franklin shrank back, clearly unused to dogs, as Wag, scenting something wrong with the whole jacketed-horse arrangement, began to bark at them. Still, he sat up as bravely as he could when Jedediah said, 'Never fear, Franklin, that dog's all bark and no bite. Get you down, now; hold out your fist, like so, to greet him, and let him sniff, and he'll know you have manners. Down you get, lad.'

Jedediah dared not dismount, not with No One to mind, but Franklin managed to slither off and stood on rather shaky legs, holding out his fist as steady as he could. Wag continued to bark at the horse until Jedediah rapped out, 'Enough!' – at which Wag sat right back down on his haunches. Years of dealing with the People had given Jedediah plenty of practice in sounding stern.

Franklin tried again, and this time Wag gave a tentative huff at the little fingers, then licked them. Franklin's face burst into smiles.

'Very well,' Jedediah told the girls, 'I've something to check in your woods. Nothing to fret over, just some business I need to see is in good repair. This is my friend Franklin; play with him for a little while, will you? I'll be back for him soon.'

'Yes, Mister Smith,' Cissie Lenden said, gazing up at him with a kind of soldierly devotion, apparently ready to entertain a whole battalion of visitors if so commanded. It made it easier to say, 'Good girl,' and ride off briskly. At least this time he was leaving Franklin with nothing worse than some children and a puppy. And the boy needed to learn how to be around a pup. There would be odd jobs for a quick lad when Franklin was a year or two older, and if he could command a dog, there'd be more of them.

Louise would like to hear that thought, Jedediah said to himself as he rode off to the forest. She'd said she liked Franklin, and any sensible girl would favour a man who was kind to children. Perhaps he could bring her flowers next Sunday – or no, one of Tom's salves, something for her chafed hands. He'd bring her a gift, and tell her of his good deeds, and maybe she'd know he was trying to impress her, and laugh. He'd see her soon; in a week, God willing. In the privacy of his own mind, he repeated the words: *My girl. In a week, I see my girl.*

The forest itself was shaded, the trees fringed with shimmering ivy; little spots of sunlight reflected off their dark leaves. Jedediah dismounted, hung the horse's bridle on a branch and said, 'Get you down, Spider. You're here.'

'No One is to dismount for the beast of earth and judder and the creak and ache of pretty legs is to storm the crushing air . . .' It was a somewhat wavering stream of words.

'Well, I can't help it if you're travel-sick,' Jedediah said. 'Off you get, then you can find yourself a spot and rest. Now, if you please.'

With Louise's quiet voice in his ears he'd found it easier to speak gently, but his throat was tightening back to what he had just noticed was its usual position, the words coming out crisp and authoritative. Under such a goad, the spider leaped from the horse's back, flinging off the covering jacket. The jump happened too fast for Jedediah to see; one moment it was gathering up its back legs with dainty, tippy-toe precision, and the next thing it was in a tree, clinging on with its sharp knees hinged high above its head, quivering its abdomen with an air of tentative satisfaction that made Jedediah feel pretty travel-sick himself.

'Many are the gaps in air and nowheres to be found and fed,' it husked. 'No One is here, and within the rainbow innards of web and weft shall still and melt the tasty innards of bird and blood for No One's delight.'

'Very well,' said Jedediah. He'd been thinking hard, and this was the most careful phrasing he could come up with. 'I lay command on you, Spider: you are to start no quarrel, and to neither hurt nor kill any man, woman or child, nor any creature belonging to any man, woman or child. Your prey may be only the wild things neither mortal nor fey will miss. For this, I have found you a home away from the flames, and will spare you the iron. Do you understand?'

'Deep are the secrets and No One understands that is not privy,' No One hushed, rather unhelpfully. Jedediah picked up his jacket, shook it with a snap; he was indeed cold, but he couldn't make himself put it on until he was sure no spiderly hair remained.

'Say me yes or say me no, Else away I shall not go.' Jedediah spoke a bit slowly, as if to one of the stupider People; they sometimes needed rhymes to keep their attention on the subject.

'No One's cleverness is known to the pretty air,' came the slightly insulted scrape of sound, 'and true to pretty deeds is the flex of joint and shell. Yes.' It guddled its front legs around, scooping up a sudden, glimmering ream of liquid from the tip of its abdomen, and pasted the shining, visceral fluid around the tree in the form of a ladder. It happened fast, and then, with a horrible ripple of legs, it was up, into the branches and out of sight. Only the wind through the trees remained, still whispering, 'Yes, yes, yes . . .'

By the time Corbie Mackem returned home, tired, irritable and displeased to see his wife cowering behind her sister when he slammed into the house, the smithy was cleaned, Franklin Thorpe was somehow known in the village to be a useful errand-boy, and Jedediah was making himself a new strike-light, having apparently sold his old one. It was all maddeningly blameless, and Corbie, who had a headache, took exception to the mourning band still knotted around his son's neck.

'What's that for, eh?' he demanded. 'Come on, son of mine, tell me what you've got tied there all dainty and fine?'

'Uncle Dunstan gave it to me,' Jedediah said, keeping his voice as mild as he could and his attention on the strike-light. 'To show my respects to Grandfather.'

'Ah, you have been on the gad, haven't you, lad?' Corbie said. 'One holding to the next, free as a bird. From what I heard, you've been playing quite the fire-raiser, burning barns here and bridges there and giving God-knows-what all round. Why in the devil's way didn't you come when you were bid? Must you make a fool of me, boy? Answer me! What in the name of all things damnable did you think you were about?'

This was the kind of voice that had presaged a beating when Jedediah was younger, and while Corbie had never yet turned to a fist-fight, his tone was rising and rising. When things went this way, Corbie could talk himself into a red haze, chasing his own feelings up into rage, and Jedediah knew if he didn't break this quickly, either into a better mood or else a blast falling upon himself, Corbie would go into the house. Mama had been so relieved when Jedediah came through the door that it was 'little one' and not her husband who'd come home.

Tom, if he'd been here, might have thought of a joke to turn the fury aside, but Jedediah had never been funny. He was just going to say the wrong thing, again, because that was all he knew how to say, and then maybe Corbie would stay home out of spite so he wouldn't be able to see Louise next Sunday – or he could, but he'd have to go to her with a bruised face, and then she'd have to know why she should save her heart for someone less trouble than him. For a moment, Jedediah felt something he normally never allowed himself to consider: the utter misery of his life.

'I reckoned,' he said, 'that while you were from home, there'd be women for you to eye up, and maybe more. I won't say I'd have been sorry to spoil your pleasures, for you wouldn't believe me, but you do your best to keep it from our own door, I'll give you that, and I didn't want to see it.'

Corbie didn't hit him. His hand came up, fast, and Jedediah stood very still. He tried not to screw up his eyes; all he did was grit his teeth together so that if Corbie did land a blow, they wouldn't crack against each other.

It was a long time before Corbie moved. The forge, stoked and burning, ground together its shifting coals. When he did, his gesture was soft, almost delicate. He lifted the scrap of metal around Jedediah's throat, gave it a slight twist. The rope was tied snug, and the movement tightened it around him like a noose.

'What we do,' Corbie said, his voice shaking, but almost gentle, 'is save the first shoe a man forges. It hangs on the smithy wall all his life, by its own hook. When the man goes, we take it down, break it into pieces. His mourners wear it for as many days as he lived years. Then we throw it into the forge and let it burn the rope and melt the iron. And so it goes, son of mine.'

Jedediah waited, drew a deep breath. He wanted to say, *Tup who you like, I don't care, if it keeps you from Mama.* Or, *Mend your own roads if you want them.* Corbie's father had arranged the marriage to Constance, but his brothers weren't to blame; if Corbie wanted more of his old life than he got, stuck in this village so far from where he'd been born, with his frightened women and his bitter son and his anger never quite joked away, he could have visited Tinsdowne long before his father died there. *Or, We do our best, Mama and Auntie and me. I do my best. I was born who I am. Why don't you love me?*

None of it was worth saying.

'Thank you, Father,' he said. 'I shall look to you to know the day we burn them.'

'Oh, no doubt you will,' Corbie said. He turned aside, picked up a door-knocker he'd been working on before he left. It was coiled in the shape of a snail-shell, strong in its lines and full of wit, but it didn't appear to please him now. He set it on the forge, gazed at it, saying nothing more. The iron sat black against the red, showing no signs of the heat growing within it.

And that was life in Gyrford: Corbie worked at the forge, his designs growing ever more lavish and handsome, and he settled the People with a ferocious gamesomeness that kept farms quiet and the neighbours in admiration. He charmed female customers when they came in; he disappeared on long trips.

Every Sunday Jedediah rose early, visited the church to pray – and also to allay any comments from the parson – and then rode for hours. As far as the farrier house knew, there was nothing afoot.

Or at least, Corbie didn't, which was what mattered. Agnes noticed Jedediah's new habits with secret relief, for while folks tended not to include her in Gyrford's sexual gossip, she'd overheard the odd whisper that had made her worry her innocent little boy was growing to be a man like his father. If he was going to this much trouble, though, some girl must be important to him, and that meant he had a good heart after all. For that, she would hold her tongue as long as he needed. Agnes' own life had always been at the behest of others, but if her nephew had a chance of something of his own, it was a comfort, of sorts.

Constance, meanwhile, was nervous for a few weeks, for it was unlike 'little one' to be absent on the days when the bells rang. She was able to work out in due course, though, that this new confusion wasn't a threatening one. Agnes' face conveyed no alarm, and he always came back. He even smiled more these days.

At home, he worked with passionate care, learning and labouring to be the best man he possibly could. He didn't ask to be set a master-work: Corbie wasn't in the mood. He hadn't ever been in the mood.

But Jedediah was happy; amazingly, newly, he was happy. It was like stepping from a sweltering hot day into a cool stream. It was like honey.

Tom was willing enough to lend his horse; Jedediah had walked out with this or that girl here and there, but to travel this far for the sake of a few hours together was positively chivalric. Jedediah accepted being teased, and brought Tom back all the herbs he could find, and sold his salves along the road as best he could; Louise had loved the stuff for her hands, and word spread slowly that there was a fine salve-maker whose pots of physic would cure any ill you claimed to own, and possibly make girls think you the handsomer as well.

And Louise did find him handsome, which was extraordinary. His face had mostly just been a thing to hide his thoughts behind, but now there was someone to lay her hand against it. They met in the summer, and as the weather grew colder, they wrapped such clothes as they had around themselves, and travelled to meet each other still more.

Months passed from Sunday to Sunday. When Louise's contract with the Palmers ended, she travelled south for the next Michaelmas fair and got herself hired to scrub and cook for the Berretts, a sour old couple who lived on baffled fury at the six children who never visited, and ruled the two who remained with implacable bile. Louise didn't complain, saying that a farrier must know how to dodge a horse's kick and a maidservant when to clean the other side of the house, and Jedediah promised himself that one day, he would have a place for the two of them where they could close the door and lock it behind them.

Later, she would tease him that he proposed because he was cold. And she wasn't wrong, not entirely. He just understood one day that his visions of being warm no longer included a world without her.

They'd got good at finding places to meet unseen: Jedediah had always lived by the rule that he'd do nothing to get a girl with child, and they held to this as best they could. It was frustrating and lovely, and he lived the summer in a sensual haze; the very sun kissed his skin with warmth. But the seasons turned: autumn added bite to the air, and they shivered in each others' arms.

Close to Clementing, he asked her, 'Are you tired of sitting out in the chill?' He couldn't quite bring himself to ask, *Do you care for me enough to put up with this?*

Her eyes flickered, taking in the tension of his face, which Corbie saw as sullenness and most folks read as severe. She usually greeted that look with reassurance, but this time she looked nervous. 'Are you?' she said.

'No,' he answered swiftly; had he made her think he was leading up to ending things? He was bad at this; a quick dalliance was one thing, but perhaps he couldn't keep from saying the wrong thing when it was a girl he really wanted. 'No, I'll sit under a waterfall if you like. I just don't . . .' He didn't know how to put it.

Louise laughed. 'That's a rash promise, my lad,' she said. 'You might tempt me to take you up on it, just to see if you're a man of your word.'

'Winter's coming on,' he said. 'It'll get worse than this.'

'And,' Louise said with a sigh, 'it'll be too cold to shed a stitch. We'll have to sit here in icy chastity. Will you still like to meet then?'

He put his arm around her. 'I'll try not to be dull.'

She wasn't wrong: it was too cold. Winter was dry that year, for a mercy, but as November shifted into December, snow feathered down from the sky and the frozen earth crackled under their feet and it was all they could do to huddle together, both, for the sake of the other, making no complaints. Jedediah dug a small firepit in the best-sheltered copse, and Louise stacked up the wood. He liked to watch her mittened hands laying twig on twig with delicate precision, ready for him to strike a spark.

'My father calls me a dry stick,' he said one day, watching the flames wrap themselves around the little branches.

'Well,' Louise said, pulling the blanket closer around both of them, 'they say dry sticks kindle the best.'

He'd taken to smoking a pipe, mostly to have a little warmth within to keep his mind off the cold without, and at that, he laughed, choking on a mouthful of smoke. 'Do not,' he said, not quite finished coughing, 'ever say that to him. I will be forced to murder you and bury you under a stone that reads, *Here lies the joke my father will never let me live down*.'

'You don't scare me, Jed Smith.' She was resting close to him.

'No,' he said, stroking her hooded head with his thick-mittened hands. He could feel almost nothing of her but the solid fact that she was there. 'No, grim creatures don't scare you.'

'Silly.' She said it gently, and it was that word, more than anything she could have said, that sealed him to her. He lived his life between a master who never missed a chance to make him ridiculous and neighbours who demanded wisdom of him and insisted on believing he possessed it. Bitter flakes stung his face and the cold pinched with vicious fingers, and after he'd kissed her, he said, 'Marry me?'

Louise looked at him, a long, clear-eyed gaze. 'Yes,' she said, soft as the snow.

'I don't know when we can,' he said. 'I can't make you live with my father. You mustn't. He'll . . . We'll have to wait. I'll work something out. We'll have a room with a fireplace. We can winter indoors.'

She gave him a half-amused pout, a little moue of red lips and affection that he knew he'd hold in his mind for the rest of the week. 'Nothing like bad weather to make up a fellow's mind,' she said, and kissed the tip of his icy nose.

He should have felt the urge to defend himself; that was how he would have been with anyone else. But he didn't; something had relaxed within him. 'You may be right,' he said, pulling her into as close a hug as their baffle of clothes would allow. 'Or at least, to force him to get his courage up. I've known about you all along.'

Louise didn't make a joke; she rested her head against him and breathed out, a long, billowing cloud of steam like a fanfare tumbling through the cold. Jedediah watched it rise, the warmth inside her made visible in the winter air.

Corbie's women came and went. Jedediah could deduce their ebb and flow: there were Sundays where he left Gyrford to the west, and Sundays when he left to the south. The times when he complained most cheerfully about being overborne with a world of cares were the times he had more than one woman at once; the times he was most bitter in his sarcasm against marriage and most likely to lose his temper with the women in his house were the times when he'd only had one and she'd lost patience with him and returned to her husband, or her widowhood, or whatever else made it certain she could never expect Corbie to marry her. Jedediah said nothing about having his own girl; it was the quiet place in his life, and as long as they couldn't actually marry, there was no need to break it open.

Jedediah was saving every penny, and so was Louise. She was bound to her contract for the year in any case: the Berretts resented that she was to be lifted from humble servitude to respectable wifehood, and felt it their duty to help her earn her good fortune by paying a good tax of endurance towards them beforehand. Letting her go before they absolutely had to was out of the question.

Then one day a mist blew in upon the Lenden property.

Corbie had gone to install a new window-latch for a handsome young widow by the name of Jill Parker, who had been troubled by small fingers prising open the pane and small voices whispering that she should have a dress of golden primrose if she'd only come out through the window and play with them – an offer that might not have seemed so menacing if Jill's bedroom hadn't been two floors up. He had jumped at the job, and was gone a great deal longer than strictly required. So it was Jedediah minding the smithy that Thursday when Jack Lenden hastened in, his face as agitated as ever. He had Cissie with him, but not Winifred.

'Well now, Mister Lenden,' Jedediah said, resolving to be as courteous as ever he could. Living near the stone wolves was enough to make anyone a little nervous; Corbie's wolf had kept the sarsens from wandering, but there were still echoes under the ground; if you stepped on the wrong patch of earth on your way past them, your footfall echoed with the sound of a bark. And besides that, Jedediah had made rather free with their little patch of woodland, depositing No One within it. He didn't want the creature to make any more trouble than the place always did – you were all right if you walked it in iron shoes, and the rest of the time it was occupied by People of a mostly mild and disinterested temper – but still, he was a little relieved Corbie wasn't there to hear Jack Lenden's latest worry. Just in case. 'How do you today?' he asked.

'Mister Jedediah . . .' Lenden began. He almost wailed it,

which eased Jedediah's nerves, although his conscience still pricked him; whatever the man had to say, it wasn't going to be an accusation. 'Sir, you've done kindly by us in the past, indeed you have, but what are we to do? I'd thought Cissie might be on her ways again, but here she stands, and now it's Winifred. I can't find her, sir, and the place is misted over and I swear I don't know what to do.'

'I'm a good girl,' Cissie said, rather earnestly. She was about twelve now and had never quite lost her notion of Jedediah as a kind of knight-errant, saving the innocent from confusing horrors. 'I wouldn't trifle with anything unkenned, Mister Jedediah. You wouldn't counsel that, would you?'

The sooner he could get married, Jedediah thought, the better; he had no idea how to turn aside a girl too young to understand how much younger than him she was, not without hurting her feelings. But how to achieve 'sooner' was an endless stone in his boot these days, so rather than dwelling on its chafe, he said, as brisk as he could, 'No one with sense would, Cissie Lenden. Mister Lenden, as to Winifred: when did you see her last?'

'This morning,' Mister Lenden said, 'but then, sir, she went off into the mist, and I went after her, but I couldn't find her. Sir, if she's been changed, how am I to—?'

Jedediah stood up, grabbed his sack with as loud a clatter as he could contrive. The Lendens had a maggot in their heads about changelings; better to head them off before Winifred wandered back out of the mist and Jack started beating her just in case she was the wrong Winifred. He had some private doubts as to whether Jack Lenden was quite all right in his mind: he was a man prone to ideas, and when one seized hold of him he forgot certain things, such as the importance of treating his children with care. But between those ideas he was an earnest and dutiful fellow, and Jedediah didn't feel qualified to do much more than keep things as calm as he could.

'Let's see to it now,' he said. 'Quickest is best when it comes to your children, eh?'

Luckily the Lendens lived within a short walk of Gyrford, so the fact that Corbie had the horse wasn't a problem. Along the way Jack Lenden had a great deal to say about the speed with which the mist had come in, running on white feet; in another man Jedediah might have taken this literally, but Mister Lenden was an excitable fellow and prone to a little trouble telling what he witnessed from what he feared.

It was quite a surprise, therefore, to see the man had not been wrong: the mist hung over the northernmost field, which was scrubby and steep, and for that reason kept for sheep. The fact that the stone wolves were also to the north must have been an added worry for the Lendens, but this didn't look like a wolf-mist. It was fringed all around with little white twists, thin enough to see through, but coiled into a pattern of unmistakable, delicate paws. They weren't vulpine; they were soft-looking, with claws of pallid light. Seen individually they had a prettiness to them, like the foot of a cat or a stoat, but as they carried on around the entire blinding cloud, the whole thing had rather more the look of a woodlouse, a great hump of white carried along on infinite shifting toes.

Jedediah was torn between compunction for doubting the

man, who definitely had something unkenned on his land, and a sinking heart, knowing that this would only make Jack Lenden more excitable than ever. 'You did well to come to us, Mister Lenden,' he said. 'Try not to fret now; I'll take it in hand.'

Cissie nodded with disquieting faith while her father sat down in despair, whispering to himself about his swallowed-up Winifred.

At least they wouldn't interfere. Jedediah's boots were already hobnailed and he always wore his iron ring; he fitted an iron torc around his neck for extra protection, and took out of his bag the bullroarer he kept for explorations. The bullroarer was a thin, narrow slat, carved to a point at both ends, made from treated oak into which was sunk a small iron charm; while the patterns varied from clan to clan, it was such an old instrument that no family could say who had created the first of them. You swung it from the end of a long cord – the cord varied too, though Jedediah suspected that it didn't make much difference as long as it worked – and the wide circle it cut through the air made a low drone not unlike the complaint of an irritable bumblebee. Jedediah wasn't especially fond of the sound, but it could create a circle of protection around you and send a general message in uncertain surroundings. Mostly it was used to avert fey thunderstorms, but he reckoned that if it helped in one weather condition, it might help in another.

He walked forwards, and as he swung the bullroarer the mists unlatched themselves, startled twists of white ravelling backwards away from the hostile sound. There was a figure within them, but it was difficult to make out, except it wasn't

Winifred. It was slim and graceful, or else possibly broad and hefty; its hair melted away into the whiteness around it, but it couldn't keep its colour; it kept silvering over, then returning to a brown that washed away into silver again.

Jedediah did not like the look of this at all. There were People that enjoyed shaping their forms to fit their moods, and those moods could change quickly, but they didn't usually try to be two things at one and the same time. He felt a kind of ache in his heart, too; it hurt to look at the creature. He felt thirsty and sad, marooned all of a sudden, entirely alone, though the field wasn't vast.

There were sheep huddled around the figure, he saw now, butting their heads: grown creatures, trying to suckle the mist.

'Winifred!' he called.

At that, the figure – you couldn't say it changed; it hadn't been stable enough to have anything to change from – but it sharpened itself somehow; the sheep butted each other in confusion and started to run away from it. It was looking at him, its eyes gleaming silver, and they held a kind of hollow beauty, a lost hunger that tightened his ribs until it was hard to draw breath.

'Kind friend,' he said, still swinging the bullroarer, 'there's a girl here needs to get home.'

It was only when the last of the sheep stumbled away that he saw Winifred, curled at the apparition's feet, her head nested on a pile of sheep droppings. The mist's paws, a great battalion of them, dandled her hair, stroking it upwards into braided loops. They were still at their work, he saw, with a dryness in his throat that the wet air did nothing to loosen, weaving delicate plaits thin as twine, twisting each into a crown around the girl's head. But it didn't end at her forehead; it was being woven further and further down, over her eyes, cutting her off from the light so she'd find nothing in this world except the cold caress of this shifting mist.

Jedediah swallowed again. He'd been too busy staring before now to notice the scent of this dampness that baffled sight. It was sweet, thin; it tasted of milk.

Words came, not shaped by a mouth but heard from above, soft as a cradle song. *Little one wants me, little one. Leave little one to rest.*

Silver eyes. Little one. Silver hair, brown hair.

It wasn't wise to swear around the People, so Jedediah managed to keep his mouth shut, but behind his teeth, the words were roiling: *God damn it. Damn it to hell. God damn the beast*—It *was* a child-stealer. No wonder he couldn't see its face clearly. The People tempted children out with gifts, with games and sometimes, with the illusion that it was nothing fey that called you but only your own mama.

Silver, brown. He'd never been entirely clear on whether it was Constance or Agnes, or even Pell, who he should look to as his true mother.

There was nothing for it now: he was here, and it was reaching out a hand to him and weeping, pointing to the iron. It rubbed a patch of light that was suddenly its stomach, like Constance after a meal, like after Corbie kissed her. 'Don't,' it said in Agnes' voice. 'Please, Mister Smith, don't. Don't hurt her, Mister Smith. Please.'

And at that, Jedediah ran forwards. He'd never liked harming the People, not when he could avoid it, and if it hadn't said that, if it hadn't begged Mister Smith not to hurt it, he might have stopped and thought about it. He did not believe in acting on blind fury; he had never supposed a man couldn't control a killing rage.

The bullroarer dropped from his hand as he reached up to tear the torc off his neck, leaving him ironless but for his boots.

The arms of the mist reached round him now, cool as a woman's skin; with each racing step, he felt himself rocked, cradled; his throat was full of milk and he didn't need to see, not with the mist watching over him and someone above his head loving him. He was safe. He could sleep. It was all all right, little one. It was all all right. Someone held him; someone loved him.

And with something like a shriek, he reached forward and snapped the torc around the slim neck of the mist-mother.

There was a boiling; for a moment, the cold, damp mist was black and hot and he was burning with a fever that would surely kill; he had been left to die and nobody would come and save him. And then he stood in a ragged green field, sheep-shit on his boots and his clothes quite dry. Before him on the ground sat Winifred Lenden, sitting up and rubbing her eyes, which were covered in an ugly tangle of clumped hair.

Next to her, writhing and whining, was a smallish creature with the dull white skin of a grub and a face more or less womanish, but so plain and unmemorable of feature that the second you glanced away, it was hard to recall how it looked. Its head and neck were more or less man-sized, but that must be the influence of the collar; beneath, it had shrunk to about a foot in height, skinny legs thrashing and hands grappling the torc in utter outrage.

'Change and change and talk of change!' it yelled at him. 'Feed the girl on milk and change!'

'No man or woman wants their child stolen,' Jedediah said. His voice came out flat. Inside, it felt as if someone had stirred him with a filthy stick; he wanted to scrub himself clean, to drink boiling water and vomit out the silver and brown and the words he'd heard. He recognised the feeling: violation. The People liked to tell you what they could see of your mind – and for that matter, Corbie liked to do the same, with barely more fellow-feeling than a sprite. You didn't get used to it.

'Talk and change and change and . . .' The thing was furious, implacable: there was nothing in its face but hunger.

Sometimes it was bad luck to kill the People, and sometimes it wasn't necessary. He had no taste for cruelty. But this thing had stolen a child.

The most dramatic method would be to bear it home in triumph and throw it into the forge. Some of the neighbours would be comforted at the display, as long as Constance didn't have to see it. Corbie would be delighted at such a dramatic spectacle; he respected strength.

'Would you be free of the collar?' Jedediah asked. His voice was still toneless. He needed the creature to agree – at least, the kind of agreement other People wouldn't quarrel with.

'Yes, little one, yes!' the creature howled.

Little one. His last flicker of compunction guttered and flamed out.

'So shall you be,' he said. 'Winifred Lenden, wake yourself, girl.'

Winifred was still rubbing her eyes, her skin, bewildered. 'Mama?' she said.

'You'll be back to your mama in a moment,' he told her. 'I'll take you to her. Just one thing first. My sack is at the corner of the field. Go and get it. It'll help if you take a part in this.'

'Mama,' Winifred said, starting to cry. The girl was near fourteen, he thought. What must it be, to have a mother you could go to for comfort at that age?

'Be a good girl,' he said, gentle as he could. 'Get my sack, then we'll get you to Mama.'

Winifred stumbled to her feet. Her hair was smeared with sheep droppings and she fretted at it with confused hands as she crossed the field.

'Thank you,' he said, when she clanked the sack down at his feet. 'I know it was heavy. Now, go you to that corner, where your dada waits you. Tell him I sent you, there's a good girl, and you've come to no harm.'

Winifred blinked. Her mouth shaped the words, *sent you* and *come to no harm*, mumbling them a little, like a toddler trying to teach her own tongue. She did not look like a girl quite ready to convince her father that she wasn't a changeling.

'Tell him,' Jedediah added, 'that if he lays a hand on you before he speaks to me, I'll kick his backside from here to Kidderminster. And then I won't help him any more.' The latter was a hollow threat, and probably the former as well, but Jedediah didn't feel entirely unwilling to kick someone just at that minute.

Winifred giggled, a puzzled sound, but something like the return of her wits, and turned around.

Jedediah looked back at the creature, which was still thrashing on the ground, trying to get out of the collar. It couldn't shrink its head small enough to slip free.

'Little one, bad boy!' it hissed. 'Tell your father, get the belt!'

'Well,' Jedediah said, keeping his voice almost steady, 'we are agreed. You wish to be free of the collar.'

'Yes, yes, bad son, yes!'

His hand on its chest felt nothing but cool skin, slightly damp, like yesterday's catch of fish. There was no bone in it, nothing to resist the knife he drew from the bag.

It was only the work of a moment to slice its head from its body.

The collar fell on the smeared earth, unquestionably removed from the creature.

There was no need to bury or burn it; the People's bodies don't last long once you put an end to them. Jedediah sprinkled forge-ash over the ground to make sure, washed his hands, splashed his face. Once the thing was gone, he felt a lot better.

He had to get Mama and Agnes out of the house. The thought pressed down on him harder than ever. He had felt safe with them once – he must have done for the fey thing to have affected him so – but even when he was a baby, they couldn't have felt safe themselves. The People and Corbie together had swallowed up their lives.

He had to get out too: he couldn't suffer Louise to live with Corbie.

Jedediah stood, brushed himself off, looked around. The Lenden farm had never been properly ironed; it would have been foolish to iron the little forest, for that was where the truffles grew, and who knew what harm such a rich crop might come to if you fiddled around with the earth? And as to the rest – well, Jack Lenden was a man of moods. If he felt it was a crisis, it needed dealing with at once; if he didn't, it didn't need dealing with at all. He'd tormented one girl in childhood, thinking her a changeling when she wasn't, and now he'd come very close to having the other stolen away by a real fey. The man needed to pull himself together – but if telling folks to do that was enough to make them do it, then they wouldn't need telling in the first place.

There was a small stone barn in the next field, Jedediah noticed, or rather, the walls of one. It was well-made, except that it lacked a roof. It could have been a useful place if Jack Lenden had ever caught the mood to sort it out.

He was thinking about that, the lack of roofs on the Lenden farm, both literal and figurative, when he reached the edge of the field. Cissie was fussing over her sister, but both of them turned and looked to him with embarrassingly worshipful gazes.

Jack Lenden, too, looked dazed. 'Sir,' he said, 'how did you do it? My Winifred says she was snatched, that she thought her own darling mother was in the middle of the field, and then she was all lost – and look at the state of her clothes and her poor hair . . . If you feel the need to kick me,' he added, apparently swept up in admiration, 'I will stand still for you, sir. I will let you kick me, if it thanks you for the return, first of one daughter, then of the other! You may kick me, sir.'

He looked like he was actually about to turn around and proffer himself, and Jedediah forestalled him with a hasty, 'No, thank you. Just mind your girls, yes?'

'My darling girls,' Jack Lenden said. The two of them were looking at him, not entirely relieved; he was getting over-excited again. 'My jewels, sir, that the fey cannot keep from!'

'On that note,' Jedediah said, a bit more sternly, 'I've something to say to you, Mister Lenden. You are to talk no more of the fey, and no more of changelings. From what that thing said, I've a notion that it was your talk that got its attention. The People hear when we speak, sir: talk of changelings all day without you know your iron and it could be they'll hear you. You need more sense, Jack Lenden,' he couldn't help adding.

It would have been a rash thing to say if Jack Lenden hadn't been so overwhelmed with gratitude, but as it was, he nodded emphatically. 'I shall say not a word, sir,' he said. 'Not a word.'

'We'll go up to the house now,' Jedediah said, 'for I want your hand on a Bible for that.' It wouldn't make Jack Lenden a steady man, but if he could be kept off one subject at least, that would surely be one less problem for his children.

As the four of them turned, Jedediah glanced back; the field was quite ordinary-looking now. The sheep were nuzzling the grass again. They weren't grazing the spot where the child-stealer had fallen, but no doubt they would in a few days. A bit of honest sheep-shit would be the best thing for it.

'I do not know how I can repay you,' Jack Lenden said. 'It's a world of troubles and that's no error. I only wish I could have the benefit of your wisdom in these trying times.'

Jedediah was half-listening; it wasn't too long a walk back to

Gyrford from this troubled spot. He didn't entirely like Jack Lenden, but you couldn't go around refusing the company of everyone you didn't like. If anything, the man needed a closer eye kept on him.

He was tired, and he had beaten his brains for more than a year now trying to think of solutions. He never again wanted to hear his Aunt Agnes beg his father not to hurt Constance.

He stopped, gazed at the field. The barn needed a roof. It would be freezing in winter; they'd have nowhere to cook except a fire outside. Or perhaps a fire-pit in the middle of the floor, if they could build a chimney in the right place; he'd seen such arrangements in some of the more remote homes, and he was pretty good friends with Mark Brown, the roofer's son, who was well skilled by now. Mark was courting Tom Attic's sister Lily and could understand the need for a home.

It would be cramped, poor, a lot to put up with. He thought of Louise's battered hands, resting over his heart. The carping of the Berretts. The fine house in Gyrford, with Corbie in it.

'Mister Lenden,' he said, 'I've a proposition for you. If I could put a roof on that old barn of yours, would you let me live there? I'd put down any troubles, work for my keep.'

Jack Lenden stopped, gazed at him astonished. 'Sir?' he said. 'Why – what could you mean? I don't think it's given in this world, to have such help as we need. Do you not have a better home in Gyrford?'

'Does that mean you'd agree to it?' Jedediah asked.

'Of course, sir, of course,' Jack Lenden said, apparently transported, 'but I cannot, sir, see why you would wish to leave your good home.'

'I mean to set up my own house,' Jedediah confined himself to saying. 'I'm to be married, you see.'

He said nothing about it that evening. Corbie came home late; Agnes had hurried Constance to bed before her husband's return.

Jedediah sat up with a rushlight, making calculations. Most likely Corbie wouldn't let him take any furniture, so there'd be that to manage; they could get by with a straw pallet and he could knock together some kind of bed to keep them off the ground where the rats and weasels might come for them. He could make cooking gear in his own time. He didn't own much and Louise owned less; they could keep their things in a chest or two. Then there'd be the keep for Agnes and Constance, which monthly should come to . . .

At this point in his reckoning, Corbie, returned from whatever adventures he'd been up to, banged on the door, commenting a little hoarsely on the presence of his rushlight and his undoubted intention to burn the house down.

'No, Father,' said Jedediah, looking at his figures. He could manage it. They could actually leave. Michaelmas, when Louise's contract ended, was in three months. They could have the place roofed by then if they worked hard, and especially if Tom could get his sister Lily to honey Mark Brown into helping out. Which she would; she was a sweet girl. She'd like Louise. The two of them could be friends. He could speak to the parson tomorrow, set a date. Three months from now.

'Well, it's either you're a fire-raiser with plans to torch the place to the ground and live a wandering philosopher's life, or else you've got a girl in there without the manners to show herself and bid her poor old host good even like a Christian,' Corbie said. He sounded pleased; this kind of badgering was the overflow of cheerful spirits.

'No, Father,' said Jedediah, snuffing the rushlight. 'That's not what I have in mind.'

Mister Attic was a little surprised at Jedediah's proposal – not because he was sorry for the good women's company, he added, but because he couldn't think it needful to charge a guest. Had he made Jedediah feel unwelcome? He was sorry if so.

'Not a guest, Mister Attic,' Jedediah said. 'Tenants. I'd like to see you a landlord, wouldn't you? We could tell the world how well provided for they are, and everyone would think us fine.'

Mister Attic was silent for a moment, looking from Jedediah to Tom, who had no objections to the plan and had come along to keep Jedediah company. Mister Attic's face was grave and thoughtful. Then he laid a hand on Jedediah's shoulder. He'd always liked the earnest, fierce-eyed boy Tom had brought home one summer morning, and while he was too careful to make any comment to his neighbours on how Corbie Mackem treated his wives – well, his wife, but Mister Mackem was not a man inclined to any single woman and had multiples both in the home and out of it – he had not liked it. His own wife Bet's cheerfulness and warmth were the hearth fire of his life in this wet, chilly country; if young Jedediah had a woman who meant that much to him then it was out of the question not to help him along. And Atiq – or Paul Attic, as they said it here – wouldn't want any daughter of his living under Corbie Mackem's roof. The man was admired, he knew, but Atiq had seen enough of court life before he lost his taste for it to know that a fine manner didn't make a fine man. While he had always counselled Tom to bear with patience any gibes about paynims and Saracens and all the rest of it, that didn't mean he admired the folks who made them.

'I won't spurn your coin, my lad,' he said. 'I can't deny it'll help, and I know you wouldn't see your mother live on charity. That's a right feeling; a man should respect his mother. I tell you, I'll be glad to have your aunt's willing hands about the place, and your mother's a dear woman. We'll be happy to, Jedediah.'

Jedediah swallowed. He'd never been good at thanking folks, and certainly not for favours too great for mere gratitude. Mister Attic had been kinder to him than any man he'd known, and here he was again. However much money Jedediah paid, it wouldn't be a recompense.

'I can't match you in kindness,' he said in the end. 'I don't think I ever will. But – but you'll have tenants who love you, Mister Attic, that I can swear. And if I can ever do you any favour, any you name, it's yours.'

'Well,' said Tom, seeing embarrassed tears glint in the eyes of both and feeling the need to bring things back to a more comfortable footing, 'that's a settled thing, then. The more the merrier, I say, especially when one of them can carry a carthorse for us, bless the good woman. Now, am I to truly meet Louise? I swear, I've been a patient soul.'

It was true, Jedediah hadn't introduced her to any of his

friends, not when the hours they could snatch alone together were so few. 'Only if you promise not to tell tales of my young and foolish days,' he said, finding his grin again.

'Can't be done, I fear,' Tom said, grinning back. 'Come along, let's have the girl at our table. She could sup with us next week, if she likes. Get your mama and auntie settled first, perhaps, then bring her along. I suppose she does eat, this swan of yours?' Jedediah hadn't quite known how to describe Louise, except to say that she was tall, dark-haired, long-necked.

'I'll tell Bet,' Mister Attic said, tactfully removing himself; no doubt the young folks wished to talk more frankly. 'She'll be glad of the company, never fear.'

'Yes, Tom, she eats,' Jedediah said, relaxing now the most important part of things was settled. 'Though I doubt we'll dine on goose and veal. We'll do well enough, though.'

Tom had felt a need to be a little delicate about things as long as Louise was a distant maiden, but if she was going to be a new friend, it was only fair to know what was what. 'You'll live in a shack with her? Love and scraps out in the wilderness? You want her that much?'

From anyone else Jedediah would have resented the question, but he was starting to feel happy. 'I do,' he said. 'You'll just have to meet her. You might not see it. She's just right, is all. Makes me laugh. I don't know, Tom. There's only her. It just feels good to be with her.'

'Ah,' said Tom, with a bit of a smile.

'Don't,' said Jedediah, feeling embarrassed again. 'That's my wife.' The word was premature, but he wanted to say it.

'Dear lad,' said Tom, 'you really are in love.'

'Well, I told you I'd marry her, didn't I?' said Jedediah. 'Stand up with me at the wedding, will you? I'll need a best man.'

'Charmed. When do I meet her? There's a dance at Beresmere next week, will you bring her to that? She could dance with you and tell the other girls what a fine fellow I am. Maybe one of them will marry me.'

He couldn't see her face, didn't need to. Her breath slowed against his forehead and her hair was over his face and the dark shape of her filled his sight.

'Are we fools?' she said. It was a whisper, breathless and shaken.

'I don't care. I don't care.' He couldn't let her go, couldn't lose the idea that if he took his arms from her waist, she'd stand up and leave him and he couldn't bear it. 'Don't be sorry, don't.'

She didn't answer, but shook her head. If he didn't meet her gaze soon it was going to be a barrier between them, but he couldn't let her lean back from him. She only had a few minutes before she'd have to hurry back to the Berretts, but the finding of a home was such news that they'd both forgotten practicalities for a while. Forgotten caution and patience, forgotten that they had to be sensible because they couldn't afford to be free. But he couldn't let her go.

'It's all right,' he said, to himself as much as to her. He didn't know anything any more.

'I love you,' she said into his hair, and at that he took her face in his hands, held it back so he could see her eyes, flecked and beautiful and looking back at him.

'I love you,' he said. They were words, they couldn't contain what he was feeling. She was there, resting against him, a weight of life holding him to the earth.

'I'm not sorry,' she said. The shape her lips as she spoke was all he could see. 'Three months.'

'Three months,' he said. 'We'll have a bed and a roof and a door we can close.'

She was growing calmer; she laughed a little. 'I meant to be good,' she said, but her voice was still soft. 'You're too fine.'

He shook his head, cupped her cheek. 'You.'

It had been two years since he'd first seen her. It was a long time to be careful, to remember over and over that it wouldn't be wise to start a baby, to be content with what Pell had instructively described to him, during the course of his education, under the heading of 'fooling around'. Now her kisses were cooling on his lips he was remembering that it had all been good advice, but it wasn't very real when set against soft skin and supple warmth and glad caresses that turned serious. His body was calmer than he could ever remember, but it wasn't making him sober; his heart was too caught up with Louise, with the sight of her, the scent, the unbearable tenderness of her face. There was a burr in her hair, which was black and beautiful and should have had fine combs in it instead of the debris of the rough earth.

'Here,' he said, picking it out with slow, lingering care for each strand. 'Some day I'll give you a featherbed, I swear it.'

Louise kissed him, a light brush. 'Some day we'll be old and burdened, and we shall miss the days when we could roll around in the fields.'

His back was scratched with twigs – well, manners were manners, and there was a certain drama in the thought of interposing himself between the scrapes and scuffs of the world – and he thought of the cold stone walls, the little he could give her. 'Are you sure?' he said. Now he'd started, he seemed to be begging for reassurance. 'Why would you live in a field?'

'I need a man to dress my hair,' Louise said, her voice turning sweet and wry. She drew back, started to arrange her clothes; the sun was slipping down the sky with careless ease.

'Don't go,' he said, knowing she had to.

'Three months,' she said. Her smile in the dim, and then she was gone.

Agnes cleaned house that Monday, tirelessly, for two days. In the course of cleaning, she packed her box, and Constance's, and when Corbie complained she was putting him out of every seat and perch with her everlasting flap and swipe, she told him that she and Constance were to spend a night or two with the Attics and she wouldn't have him troubled while they were gone; there was plenty of pottage, and everything had been made right.

'Heaven help us, that's a grand promise,' Corbie said. 'I hadn't known I was housed with one of God's living saints, setting all aright with her sanctified broom. I'll have to tell the parson. And for God's sake, let me have a moment's peace, woman. Get out. Go and clean something else.'

So the next day, they got out, and went to clean somewhere else.

★

That left the last thing: to tell Corbie what was about to happen.

He chose Saturday evening, four days after Agnes and Constance had gone. Corbie hadn't made much comment on their absence, and as the evidence suggested he had at least two different women on the go, it was as good a time as any, which wasn't saying much.

Jedediah had tried to enjoy that Saturday as much as he could. The roofing was going well; Mark Brown had taken to it with a will, saying that it was an interesting puzzle to make a roof in a style so old, and Lily Attic was so pleased with him that it was well worth the labour. Jedediah had visited the Attics to see Agnes and Constance settled comfortably into their shared room, and while neither of them had quite lost their cowed look – it was early days – they both looked happier.

Best of all, he'd brought Louise along – a heady start, introducing her to so many folks he loved at once, but she'd carried herself with the same warm grace she did everywhere, and afterwards, when he'd fretted, she'd teased him that if she'd known he was loved by so many fine folks, she'd have made him marry her the sooner. She wasn't even troubled by Mama. She'd sat beside her, held out her hand and Mama had taken it, let herself be stroked.

'I love Jedediah,' she said, and Tom, to his credit, managed to keep his younger siblings from giggling, 'and I'm happy to meet you.'

Mama examined Louise's hand, which was still red raw from

all the scrubbing, and grew a little anxious. 'Sore hands are no good,' she said.

'Oh, these aren't sore,' Louise said, quick and warm. 'You are kind, but I feel well. Jedediah gives me salves. His friend Tom makes them, clever man. They make me quite well again. And look how comfortable you are in this nice chair.'

'I like my cushion,' Mama told her. In Corbie's house she'd sat on hard chairs, but the Attics kept a particular cushion just for her. It was blue, with a pattern of stars stitched on.

'Oh, how cosy!' Louise said, her voice very soft. 'Look, it's such a pretty blue.'

'It is blue,' Mama agreed. She was stroking Louise's hand now. They were talking about something she knew how to describe; her earnest tone and caressing fingers told more than her words. 'Look, blue here, and other blue here.'

'You know, you're right,' Louise agreed. 'And here, it's blue here too.'

So it had been a day of balm, and by the time he reached home – no, by the time he reached the house in Gyrford – he wasn't tired. He rested on the bench outside the smithy, but it was hard to think he'd ever feel tired again. He wanted just another moment of peace, watching the gold soak out of the sky, before he had to turn his mind from Louise to Corbie.

He was watching the trees shade to black when his father poked his head out of the smithy.

'Jedediah, my boy,' he said. It was a genial roar, loud enough that probably all the neighbours heard. 'I see your wanderings have brought you home at last. Are you planning to stargaze and improve your understanding of the heavens, or might you join your poor old forebear in here?'

Well, he thought, standing up without a word, that was that. The afternoon was over and now it was time to have the necessary conversation. He followed his father into the forge; the door stood open to the world, as always. If they spoke at common volume, folks wouldn't hear the details of their conversation, but the presence of a potential audience usually spurred Corbie to act his best self. This was the safest place to try it. If Jedediah's luck held, Corbie might choose to play the open-hearted man.

'Father,' he said, 'I need to ask you for some time away. Two days, perhaps three. I think the work is in hand enough that I could go tomorrow, but I could wait till Tuesday if there's anything you want finished first.'

'Are you off on the gad?' demanded Corbie. 'What's all this racing about Creation? Why do you need three days away?'

'Because I'm to be married,' Jedediah told his father, 'and I should speak to her parents. They're a day's walk from here, and you'll need the horse.'

'What!' exclaimed Corbie, regarding his son, who stood in the smithy like a visitor, straight-backed and expressionless. 'Married, my eye! Who do you marry?'

'Louise Ditton,' said Jedediah. 'I don't think you know her.'

'Ditton, Ditton.' Corbie mulled in a loud rumble. 'I know no Dittons around here.'

'Her folks live in Loddeston, for now,' said Jedediah. 'They follow the work. Louise maids for the Berretts until Michaelmas. We'll wed after that. I've spoken to the parson; the banns will be read next week.'

'Well, well,' said Corbie. These details carried quite a lot of information, particularly that Jedediah was marrying a girl with neither dowry nor connections, but the mass of organisation behind his back had Corbie at a temporary loss. 'Tell me of this woman you have, then,' he said, falling back on heartiness. 'I suppose she takes your eye for some reason beyond her fine floor-sweeping, unless you're even more of a practical man than I thought. Come now, did you say to her, "Louise, my flower, I saw how you cleared the dust from that sill and you gathered up my heart in your rags; I pray you, come live with me and be my own and I will give you soot to sweep as well as my troth? You have no gold in the pockets of your worn skirt, but come be my treasure in useful housekeeping?" Come, lad, what about her?'

Jedediah showed nothing much on his face as he said, with careful politeness, 'You shall meet her, if you wish. Come with me next Thursday, if you like.'

'Jedediah, Jedediah,' said Corbie, opening his hands with an expansive gesture of helplessness, 'my boy, I'm to gain a daughter and you stand there tight-lipped as the back end of a dog. At least cut a caper for joy, or tell me something of this lass.'

'Well,' said Jedediah, giving a small nod, 'I thank you for your blessing. I suppose I may leave on Monday, then?'

'You exist to sport with my endurance,' Corbie said, as if complimenting a worthy opponent, 'as well as to be my son and heir, of course. I must bite my nails and wait for the revelation, I see.'

'Is that a yes?' This was important, Jedediah told himself, and snapping would not get him where he needed to be.

'Oh, I wouldn't stop you,' said Corbie, his sportive manner

cooling to a moody imperiousness. 'Mind, if you come back late, you're not to slam the door and wake me up. You come back drunk, you sleep in the smithy rather than clatter into the house.'

Jedediah, who hadn't wasted money on drink in years, said, 'Yes, Father.'

'Well, well,' said Corbie. 'Louise Ditton. Another one taking on the Smith name. Don't tell me you're as cool about her as you pretend, my boy. I'd not have thought you one for sudden fancies, but I suppose you're flesh and blood like the rest of us.'

'I never said otherwise,' said Jedediah. This was a discussion he very much did not want to have, especially after recent days. It wasn't many more weeks till the wedding, and they should have thought. And there was nothing at all to say in his defence, except that some vows had to be made with your body, and in the moment, nothing had mattered more. Corbie had always implied that it was unnatural to expect a man to withstand the temptations of women, and Jedediah didn't at all want to find himself in a conversation where he'd have to concede that point.

'Indeed,' said Corbie, with a ferocious grin, 'or you wouldn't have come home with your shirt inside out.'

Jedediah's hand flew to his chest and he looked down to check before he heard Corbie's shout of laughter. No, his shirt was fine. It couldn't have been otherwise; Louise, today, had done nothing more than kiss him goodbye. He felt more angry with himself for falling for the joke than he did with Corbie for making it.

'Well, well, my boy,' said Corbie, his humour restored, and gave his son a clap on the back; Jedediah wasn't quite braced for it, so it knocked him forward half a step. 'We must take our joy where we can in this life, and I see you agree with me. Bring this lass of yours round when you can and let me get a look at her. And your mother too, whenever she deigns to rejoin us in Christendom.'

Here it came. Jedediah braced himself, said as lightly as he could, 'As to that, you needn't trouble yourself. Mama and Aunt Agnes are settled at the Attics.'

'God help us, you needn't tell me that,' Corbie said, looking around the smithy for a drink. There was food in the stores and the house was still in some kind of order; Corbie spread crumbs across the table in a violent spatter across the kitchen table every day, and Jedediah cleaned them up.

'I mean to say,' Jedediah persisted, 'that they won't be back. Since I'm to marry, we thought it time for some—'

'What's this?' The words burst out of Corbie loud enough that Jedediah's ears buzzed.

'Time for some changes,' Jedediah said. Sometimes, if you appeared not to have noticed Corbie's crotchets, he was quicker to move on from them. 'I've taken a small house on the Lenden farm; I should be at work same times as always. And I thought you might find it tiresome to have Mama and Auntie there without my help. The Attics have taken them – it's at my cost, but we can say it's yours if you like, I won't contradict you.'

Corbie had been clattering around with his usual loud movements; he was unable to open a drawer or close a door without announcing his presence to the hearers. But he grew still, watching his son through narrowed eyes. At this last, his voice boomed, 'Won't contradict me, is it, my man?' he demanded. 'Won't contradict me, God's truth! A fine man now, aren't we, to clear out my house behind my back and come to me like a king with your pronouncements. Who do you think you are, Jedediah Smith? Just who, pray tell, do you take yourself for?'

Jedediah quietly braced his feet into a wrestling stance, but kept his hands loose at his sides and his voice very bland. 'You don't care for their company,' he said. 'I know that. Let the world know you've set them aside generous and you'll be thought well of. I know you can make a speech on it: your only son gone to marry, heaven help him, and as long as Providence sees fit to sweep the chicks from your nest, you felt it only pious to sweep alongside . . .'

The slap was a backhanded one, hard-knuckled and painful. Since Corbie didn't acknowledge that he'd hit his son, Jedediah didn't either, but carried on, his voice only a little duller than before, 'I don't go to mock you,' he said. 'You'd be happier, if you choose to be. You could bring a mistress into the house. You could take another wife, if you'd a mind to, and brave it out, or have as many women as you liked and tell them you weren't free to marry them. It'd be the better for you too.'

'Oh, indeed, Your Majesty,' Corbie said, 'and thank you for your gracious descent to mortal matters. I beg to know what business is it of yours to arrange my life for me, eh? Am I a dotard, Jedediah? Am I racked in wits and ready for my grave? Prepare me a coffin to lie in, I reckon, while you take out the furniture to set yourself up some other place, though God knows how you plan to do it on a journeyman's tenths. You'll have no higher wage from me, my man, do you hear me? And not a stick from this place, so you can forget it entirely. You'll have no more from me than you've ever had, and see how you like to marry and keep women on that.'

'I didn't expect it,' Jedediah said quietly. 'We will live within our means.'

'A fine reckoning!' Corbie yelled. 'Don't tell me what you *expect*, Jedediah Smith!'

By this point several folks, passing by the smithy on their way home to dinner, had stopped to stare.

'Father,' Jedediah said, even softer than before, 'there's neighbours can hear you. May we take this in the house?'

'Take this in your own house, my fine man!' Corbie shouted, and flung out his arm, as if to cast something against the walls to shatter. 'Mind you this, Jedediah: you'll have no increase from me so long as you defy me, not a farthing. I'll view no master-work from you, nor pay you a penny more for your labours, not if you make the gates of Heaven itself. You defy me, you'll be a journeyman all your life so long as I live, and I mean to live a long life, my man. I'm not twoscore yet, and I'll outlive you if I have to, Jedediah Smith, you mark me. See how you like a wife and brats on a journeyman's life!'

Jedediah stood very quiet for a moment. He'd known this was a revenge Corbie might take. He'd hoped not, but he must have botched the discussion somehow. He had never quite grasped the knack of handling Corbie. The threat might not be followed through, not if he played it carefully – Corbie was prone to threats just for the effect, and likewise, to hurting his family without bothering to threaten first – but Jedediah was tired, and not good at this, and he didn't know what the right move would be.

'I'll honour your authority, Father, and you must choose as you see fit,' he said. 'I'll be off as you order me, then, and back to work tomorrow as usual.'

'You be off!' Corbie shouted, as Jedediah trudged through the square. He passed Numps Peggot, who was gaping at the confrontation with slightly addled dismay, and Moll Dinnan, who was never going to miss the chance to spread the word about this to every cousin she had, and two of the Thomason brothers murmuring together, and after that he lost the heart to count. What caught his eye, shadowing the very edge of the square, was little Franklin Thorpe, his hands pressed over his mouth.

'Never mind, Franklin,' Jedediah said, going up to him. 'Things pass. Come along, I'll set up out of doors tonight; would you like to join me? I should show you the way in any case. I've a house half-roofed over at the Lendens.'

Franklin was shivering, but followed him at heel, hanging close to him without quite daring to reach up a hand. 'Good lad,' Jedediah said. 'You must be tired. Get you up on my back.'

He crouched down and lifted the boy; it was something to do other than look at the crowd around the smithy. He could hear his father declaiming something to them, but he didn't want to know what it was. Jedediah hefted the child, who clung tight. 'I've some news for you, Franklin,' he said. 'You remember Louise Ditton, that kind girl who liked you so much?'

Jedediah tried to keep talk over the next couple of weeks on practical matters.

The Dittons themselves were welcoming. Robert Ditton was

shy and pleasant, Mary Ditton was warm and quiet, and the prospect of their daughter wed to a settled man was better luck than they'd ever expected. Any home of her own would be an improvement, even a stone shack, and once they realised Jedediah's careful respect wasn't sarcastic they were entirely pleased, and Mary Ditton briefly tongue-tied him by telling him he had kind eyes. Jedediah thought, with regret, that he could understand why Louise missed them so much, and no doubt her brothers and sisters too if they were stamped in the same mould. If he had more money he could have made it easier for them to live nearby, but there was nothing to do but be glad for what he had.

He introduced Louise to Pell. The holding had had no farrier's lady, not a proper one, since his grandmother's time, so Louise would have to learn the ways of it, and Jedediah was not surprised to find she was eager to do so. Louise didn't believe in repining, but the closer they'd grown the more he understood how deep ran her frustration at her lack of schooling, for she had a quick curiosity about the world that a life of obedient toil did nothing to sate, and an admiration for the skilled that made her laugh at her own ignorance for fear she might despair of it. At first he'd hesitated to offer to teach her reading – he didn't want to set himself above her – but as soon as he mentioned the possibility she'd begged him show her and practised in her every spare moment. The prospect of understanding bodies and herbs and all that went with midwifery made her hug herself in delight, and Pell, who could recognise a girl with something more between her ears than sheep's wool, approved of her.

'Well, my lad,' she told Jedediah after their first meeting, 'you're a deep one, keeping a girl tucked away two years without anyone the wiser. Heaven help her if you take a mistress, though mind, if you do, I'll not look aside as I do for your father. I slapped you the minute you were born, and I can do it again if I have to. You be good to that girl. You made a right choice; now it's to you to be a good man to her.'

'I mean nothing else,' Jedediah said. There was praise hidden somewhere in amid the scolding, so he took it for what it was.

'Ah, well,' said Pell, bending a cynical eye on him, 'I'm sure Adam told the trees the same thing. She'll make a midwife, that girl, never fear. She has the hands for it, and the way about her.'

'I know,' Jedediah said, and Pell threw up her own hands in exasperation at the unshakeable contentment in his voice and told him she'd be giving them a box-bed as their wedding gift, for she wouldn't have it on her soul that they'd froze to death in that hut of theirs.

'Thank you, Auntie,' Jedediah said, truly struck with the generosity: Pell wasn't rich, and a bed they could shut themselves away in at nights would make an immense difference in the winter.

'Never you mind that,' Pell said. 'You don't see a horde of sons and daughters around me, do you? Just you be a good husband, lad. The world has need of them. And for pity's sake, pat your father down if you can. He's not in the habit of having folks decide his life for him. The last time they did it, they married him to your mother, and two-and-twenty years haven't got him over that grudge yet.'

★

Corbie had not yet said whether he'd come to the wedding. The two of them worked the smithy side by side, saying almost nothing unless a customer came in.

There were many small jobs to be done in those months, and Jedediah grew entirely sick of being asked how his father was taking the news.

Tim Morris, the wheelwright, who had prospered beyond his greatest hopes since Corbie had started working with him on his wheel-bands, asked Jedediah quietly if his father might be sorry to lose his company, and with Mister Mackem being such a fine man, might it not be quite pleasant for his bride to live with her father-in-law in the house? A man must have a fondness for his family, after all?

Bob Morey, who had a mouth on him bigger than Corbie's, said he'd heard Jedediah's mother had run off, and was it truly the time to ask Mister Mackem to put up with another woman? Women were a trial to man, after all, and who wouldn't want a rest from their mischief?

Jack Lenden wouldn't hear a word against Jedediah coming to live on his property, but did tie himself in some knots about whether Mister Mackem might have some objection to the marriage, and was Mister Jedediah sure there was nothing against the girl? Nothing to say against Mister Jedediah, of course, and no doubt his saintly nature wouldn't lead him to a wanton, but to marry a girl from far away was something of a risk, for who knew what kind of folks she might come from?

Liz Martin, the weaver's wife, drew Jedediah on one side and whispered that she'd heard Mister Mackem was out of temper about the wedding, bless him, and while of course young folks were young folks and she wasn't put on this earth to judge, no doubt Mister Mackem cared for his name, and if Jedediah was marrying in haste for the oldest reason then of course he was a good man to stand by his girl, but she knew his Aunt Pell might have some ideas for how to get her to rights again. Then they could marry when Mister Mackem had no reason to object, and have children after, and everything would be peaceful.

Numps Peggot said it was a world of trouble, and he supposed a man of the forge had to be a man of fiery temper; he'd seen what he'd seen and wished folks would stop asking him about it.

And Moll Dinnan said her cousin Peggy knew a man over by Bambermere who delivered eggs to a farm in Tamwell, and the cousin of the farmer was a river-man on the Byde, and he had his hull to repair in Tinsdowne, and the word was that word had reached Tinsdowne that Elder Mackem's nephew was to be wed and there was some trouble about the business, and Elder Mackem said it was time he paid his brother a visit.

Gossip travels faster than men. It was three weeks before the wedding when Dunstan Mackem came to Gyrford, and by that time, Jedediah was gnawing his nails.

Mama was all right; she and Aunt Agnes were very comfortable at the Attics, and as no one ever suggested it was time for her to go home, she had become relaxed, upset only if someone stepped on a snail or stubbed their toe. Mister Attic said that Miss Agnes was the finest help a man could ask for; he'd more repairs done in two months than he'd expected in two years, and come the winter, they would all be snug as eggs in a nest.

The house in the Lenden field was all right. Mark Brown had told his father that he felt ready for a master-work, and by his leave, he'd like it to be the roof of his friend's new house. Mister Jonathan Brown, an amicable man who had found his son a satisfying fellow since babyhood, said that was fine by him, and as long as Mark was still there in the workshop to help out with any rush jobs, well, why not? It was about time Mark had his chance, and no doubt he'd do it well. So now the house had a fine roof, and Mark Brown could call himself a master craftsman whenever he took over his father's workshop, which God willing, wouldn't be for many years – and while the place was sparsely furnished, Jedediah could sleep there on difficult nights, and Franklin Thorpe had a key to the door.

The wedding was in a couple of weeks, and Louise looked beautiful. Her eyes were tired and shadowed, but her cheeks glowed like a daisy at noon; as Jedediah met her that day, he thought of how she'd look holding a bride's posy, and also how she'd look in the shadows of a box-bed, bare as a petal and just as silken.

She still hadn't met Corbie. His anger towards Jedediah filled the smithy from corner to corner.

'I've news for you,' he said, taking her hand and walking out of the Berretts' view as quick as possible; the fact that she was marrying the young farrier provoked them, as it spoke of ideas above herself. 'Lily Attic met with a packman last week who sold her a dress, near new. She says it's for you, that it'll become you very well. She said something about hems I didn't follow, but she says if you come over they can fit it to the last seam.'

Louise made an effort to smile, but it didn't hold up. He was puzzled, for he'd expected this to please her; she didn't complain about either of them being ragged, but surely a girl would like a pretty dress to marry in?

'I – I have to tell you something, Jed,' she said.

She looked nervous, and he took both her hands, feeling himself brace. If Corbie had done something, he'd – he didn't know what, but if Corbie had done something . . .

'I'm not sure,' she said, 'but I think . . . I think we may have started a child. I – it's too early to be sure, but . . . I think I may be carrying, Jed.'

Everything froze; the world narrowed in on a single point, which was that if he didn't say the right thing at this moment, it would be between them for the rest of his life. He wanted to be happy, to throw his arms around her, and not to worry about the enormous fact that he had no idea how to look after a baby – or even about the selfish fact that this meant a shorter time when they'd have a bed just for the two of them. He wanted to feel thrilled, or even proud.

But he couldn't, because it meant something else, too: Corbie would have to know his first grandchild was grass-gotten.

That was how folks put it in Gyrford: a child not strictly illegitimate, but a little on the borders: born in wedlock but probably conceived in some grassy spot by a couple who hadn't quite waited until they had a marriage bed. It wasn't usually important; if the couple lived as husband and wife and brought up their children properly, then after a while all but the most vicious gossips forgot how many months after the marriage the children had come along. If Corbie wasn't so furious with

Jedediah, he might even have been delighted; he found piety irritating and felt a hearty kinship with anybody who fell short of it. Probably he'd have made a favourite of the grass-gotten child over its more impeccable siblings.

But he was angry, and he wasn't a man to make much scruple over the causes of his anger. Sons were less likely to be cast out for fornication than daughters, but it wouldn't be beyond Corbie's talents to whip up a sudden fit of propriety. The Mackems, at least, believed that the People enjoyed stealing bastard children. Jedediah didn't: he agreed with Pell that this was the kind of tale young girls told when their kin wouldn't help them and they could think of nothing to do with their fatherless babes except abandon them and blame it on the fey. But that wouldn't stop Corbie declaring that he would have no ill-conceived heirs to his smithy, and as a man of iron, he'd no choice but to send away his sinful son and begin anew.

Corbie wasn't too old to beget more children, not by decades, and he was more or less free to take a new wife. Jedediah himself had cleared the path for him.

Louise would need her husband. This child, if it existed, would need its father. And if Corbie took the whim, Jedediah could find himself out in the world without a forge, only a journeyman fairy-smith with no holding, no welcome in Gyrford or in Tinsdowne, or any other farrier's shop, not without causing a feud between the clans. Could he work as a common blacksmith? He had the skill, but what blacksmith would want a young journeyman with ideas above his station? He'd be out in the world with a wife and a child to support, as well as an aunt and mother. Some years, the Dittons had to take jobs so many miles apart they never saw each other from one month to the next.

Louise's grip on his hands was soft, but her face was pale. For once, there was no glance of amusement about her. She was shaking.

'Well,' he said, and laid his hand against her cheek. 'I always thought you were a good woman.'

She blinked, and he saw the tips of her eyelashes were wet. All he could do was put his arms around her. 'Louise, love,' he said, gently, 'this is not bad news. If you aren't, well enough, no harm done. And if you are, I can tell you all that will happen: in three weeks we'll marry, and six or seven months from now we'll have a babe, and we'll say it came early. Our neighbours will pretend to our faces they believe us while the worst of the gossips talk it up for a week, then find some other cause for their prate. And you and I will be safe at home with our son or daughter.' He stroked her hair. 'You can choose the name. Just not Jedediah. Anything but that.'

He tried to believe in this vision of the future. If it wasn't for Corbie, that would be all they had to face.

'I – I don't think your father will take it well,' she said.

Jedediah wanted to say, *It's not his business*, but he couldn't frame the lie. The word was that Uncle Dunstan Mackem, who hadn't spoken to him in years, would be in Gyrford in a few days, to seek an explanation for the rift. Things would soon come to a crisis.

'Well, it might shock him to hear a farrier lay with his own woman,' was what he found himself saying.

Louise's giggle, muffled against his shoulder, was half a sob.

He put his hand on the back of her neck, rested his cheek against hers. 'It doesn't change anything,' he said. It didn't change what he'd promised her; it only raised the cost.

'Don't be sorry,' he said. 'I'm not sorry. When my uncle comes,' he said, 'I'll do what I can. We'll . . . we'll get by. Promise me, love. Promise me you won't be sorry.'

Dunstan Mackem arrived in Gyrford at a tactful moment, three days before his nephew's wedding. Anyone who wanted to gossip could speculate about what side he might take in the dispute, for it was evident to all that Corbie Mackem hadn't accepted his son's marriage. Uncle Dunstan, though, replied to every enquiry, 'I'm here to see my nephew wed, of course.'

Jedediah was a little concerned that Uncle Dunstan had also brought Stan. Later, he realised it shouldn't have been a surprise; in the years to follow, he liked to bring his own son when he went travelling. But at the time, the idea of a man enjoying his son's company didn't occur to him, so he regarded Stan Mackem with suspicion: was he brought here to witness the dire consequences of disrespect? Was Jedediah to be made an exhibit? He regarded his cousin balefully as Corbie looked up from the anvil and saw his brother, hands on hips, filling the doorway of the Gyrford smithy.

'Well now, brother mine,' Uncle Dunstan announced, 'here's a neat old place you have here. I wouldn't have thought it of you. Have you learned tidy ways at last?'

Since it was Jedediah who tidied the place and Corbie, in his darkest moods, who resented it as a silent criticism, it was an unfortunate beginning. He scowled – then he smiled and said,

'Dunstan, my boy. I see you've come at least to eat of my ale and drink of my bread. You honour this poor castaway.'

'Aye,' said Uncle Dunstan, giving a sharp look at Jedediah, who had merely bowed, not feeling it wise to talk until Corbie decided which way he was going to jump. 'I hear there's family feelings every which way.'

'Indeed,' Corbie said, with an edge to his voice. 'And why, I beg you, need it trouble your ancient and admired line? I would have thought you'd household enough to manage of your own.'

'So would I,' Dunstan snapped, 'but when I can't turn around without someone asks me what of my brother and nephew and whether there'll be a feud, I do take it as my business. Last week I had a man in my smithy who put up a whole wall of sarsen pieces between his land and Gyrford, in case the People came over from your holding – but the damned fool broke them off a standing stone where folks had left wine every full moon for centuries past. Every bluestone in the county bled and we had drywalls so far from dry they slipped down to rubble, and arguments up to the sheriff over whose wandered sheep were whose. We had to drive iron rings through the fool's ears, him who chopped the stone, and bid him wear them the rest of his life, and as to appeasing the People whose rock he'd chopped, Sweep's still at it with every brew and blessing he can find, and if he's not an old man by the time I get home, my fellows, it won't be you we have to thank. Next man does something that stupid, I might have to let the People eat him just to make it clear to the holding how daft they're being – and God help us if you drive us to that.'

Corbie laughed, a harsh bark, at the story of the earrings, but his face darkened again as Dunstan's blame continued. 'I was given to know,' he said, 'that it's not my holding any more. If you can't keep folks from foolery there, you needn't thank me for that, either.'

Jedediah made some rapid calculations. If his father quarrelled enough with Uncle Dunstan, he might decide to forgive Jedediah just by way of choosing the lesser of two offenders. On the other hand, he might decide to cast Jedediah out in proof that he wouldn't be dictated to.

'It sounds to me like a tale grown in the telling,' he chanced. 'Father and I aren't in any feud. I got ahead of myself in some arrangements and he took my manners amiss, that's all.'

'Oh, you have a tongue, do you?' Uncle Dunstan turned to Jedediah. 'What I have to say to you, Mister Smith, is who is this girl of yours? We've heard no message from you, nor invitation, and if I'm to bless my nephew's wedding, I'd like to know who it's to.'

'He can look to his own elder farrier for that,' Corbie said, his voice rising. 'And that man stands before you, Dunstan.'

Jedediah felt a moment of hope that Corbie's whim might be turning in his favour, but Dunstan greeted this pronouncement with such a look of cynicism that his heart sank.

Corbie's face reddened like a blown coal.

'By your leave, Uncle,' Jedediah said as fast as you could, 'if you'd care to meet my betrothed, Father hasn't met her yet either. I mean no disrespect to either of you, only she has a contract to serve out and her employers aren't easy folks. And if you'd like to come to the wedding, I'm sure I'd be glad to see you; I only didn't wish to trouble you when I know you must be busy. By the by, Father, do you remember the wolf stones you settled with the chalk beast? Perhaps you might like to bring Uncle Dunstan to view it? It's held this while, and those wolf stones are sarsen too. You might like to see the case, Uncle, and think over whether it'd please you to try something the same or not.'

'God help us, you've a courtier's tongue on you when you need one,' Corbie said angrily. 'Court a girl behind my back, sneak away your mother and your aunt and set yourself up a new home out in the fields, and then dance back in to lord it over, that's your way. God knows where you got it from, for I've tried hard enough to teach you plain talk, and it wasn't from your idiot mother, that's for sure.'

Jedediah clenched his fists behind his back and scraped a bitten nail along the edge of his thumb to distract himself, but Dunstan, to his surprise, said, 'Corbie, what now? Call the woman a whore if she ran to another man, but don't revile a man's mother before his face. You never did know how to keep folks in order.'

Corbie's face wasn't red any more but almost grey around the eyes with rage.

Jedediah closed his eyes for a moment; thought, *Oh Louise, Louise*. How had he come to this? He was acting the courtier; this wasn't about the trade, or the common good, or about anything but money. But he loved the holding. He loved his aunt and mother, who had struggled all these years afraid; he loved the Attics, who'd always told him, when the elder farrier joked at their brown skin and 'paynim' name, that he shouldn't argue back for their sake when it only got him a beating; he loved little Franklin Thorpe, who he could afford to feed only on scraps, while the boy insisted on thanking him for them as if they were a grand feast. Their courage was a life-debt upon him; he owed them greater amends than he might ever contrive. And with his hands empty, all he could do was stand by and watch the world wear all of them down to nothing.

And he had a baby to think of, perhaps, a son or daughter. He felt, for the first time, the stirring of a flat, implacable, iron-hard knowledge that if there was a child in the world that was his, there was nothing to do but do anything, anything at all, to keep that child away from a life of picking scraps from other folks' waste.

'In strict regard for truth, Uncle,' he said, his voice coming out dead and toneless, 'we must say that Mama is . . . not in the common way. You know, I reckon, that there was some fey trouble to her father before she was born, she and her sisters, but for my Aunt Pell. My mother . . . is something puzzled.'

Dunstan looked at him with a face Jedediah recognised, all at once, of real shock, and Corbie turned to him too. His hands were clenched, jerking up and down at his sides, as if he had to restrain them over and over again from lashing out, and there was such bitterness in his look that Jedediah heard, in his mind, a word he'd never thought to apply to Corbie, not as a word he'd feel instead of inflict: *humiliation*.

Dear God, Jedediah thought, *they didn't know. All these years, his brothers, while he was married to Mama: they didn't know.*

The tale of Ab was not one quickly told. It was Jedediah who had to tell it, for Uncle Dunstan insisted; he had decided that it was his nephew's responsibility, having been one to break the silence Jedediah had never known was there. He told it as plain as he could, everything he remembered from Pell's accounts and the odd, submissive, uncomplaining remark of Grandpa Clem. It was a harsh story, the way it came out; there was little in it to redeem anyone.

'Having told all that,' Jedediah concluded, his throat dry from the long recitation, 'I'd like an answer of my own.' Corbie, who sat in the corner of the smithy and snarled at intervals, gave a quiet growl, but said nothing. 'What is it you were told about Mama?'

Uncle Dunstan's face was stony. 'That she was beautiful, and not quick of mind,' he said.

'That isn't quite so.' He hadn't meant to dispute, but he couldn't stop himself. 'She's no fool – only the world comes to her disordered. No one could make sense of it if they were her.' Uncle Dunstan did not look overly concerned with the subtleties of a mind afflicted, so Jedediah returned to surer ground. 'Did your father not go to meet her?' His stomach braced itself as he asked this; Corbie would not have tolerated such prying.

'He did,' Dunstan said, the lines of his face unbending. 'He'd been on the watch for a wife for Corbie. Couldn't keep him off the girls, and he wasn't one to take a command at home. Always leaving jobs half-done because he wouldn't be told. A wife and his own forge to command – Pa reckoned it'd do him good.'

'I must visit his grave and thank him,' Corbie said. His voice was harsh, unresigned.

Jedediah could hear, somewhere in his father's sarcasm, a note of real pain. How would it be, to marry a girl who—? But no, he couldn't forgive. Corbie could have done other things. He could have accepted his lot, lived for the forge he'd bought with it. He could have treated Mama kindly while he took his comfort in other beds. God help her, she'd been barely eighteen; what might she be now if she'd had two decades of patience and peace? Corbie could even have brought a mistress into the house if he'd wanted a true lover, called her his housekeeper, brazened out the gossip until the world recognised her for his real wife; Jedediah wouldn't have minded bastard brothers and sisters, not in a family that treated each other well. If she'd been a good woman – if she'd been a woman worth marrying – Mama might even have loved her. Propriety meant nothing to her; she just wanted folks to be kind.

Mama never had a chance to think straight until she went to live with the Attics. Corbie blew a tempest of fear through her being and whirled every impression she had into chaos, and he did it on purpose.

All at once, Jedediah felt obstinate, stiff-necked, all the things his father had called him. If his grandfather Dunstan had lied to his sons, it shouldn't be Mama who paid for it.

'I'm sorry, Uncle,' he said, a flat challenge, 'if this is news that your father wasn't the man you thought. It's a hard thing, to have a father not the man you wish him. But as to the business here, it's only that Father is out of temper that I sent Mama away to folks who'd care for her gladder than he does. He can live as he likes now. If he wishes to feud with me over it, it's a feud with one side, for I say I did him a favour.'

Stan Mackem had hung by his father's side all this time, watching the proceedings with defensive eyes. Now he spoke up. 'You carry it with a high hand, Cousin. You should watch your manners. If it's not Pa who's your elder, it's Uncle Corbie, and you've no business to elder it about as you do.'

Jedediah had many years of practice in not lashing out. He took in his cousin, a big, gangling young man with the Mackem redness of hair and bluntness of face, angry in a simpler way than Jedediah was used to. It wasn't knotted bitterness; he was just on his father's side. He and Stan hadn't got on as children, but then, they hadn't had much occasion to try. Possibly he was a straightforward lad.

'If your father's a man worth the following, Cuz, then I'm glad for you,' he said. 'You'll forgive me if I'm fond of my mother and feel I'm the only man in this forge who is.'

'Well, as to that,' Uncle Dunstan said, stepping into the tension with a brisk authority, 'we'll have to see about her. If she's fairy-struck . . . yes, yes, Corbie' – this to the hiss from his brother – 'a man might quail to treat his own wife, and besides, you weren't long a master when you married and I don't reckon Pa had much time to teach it you. But we'll overlook her. If we can set her to rights, she can come home and put an end to this nonsense. Work it good and hard and she'll be in her senses before the wedding, God willing.'

Jedediah froze. 'Overlook?' he said. It wasn't a term they used in Gyrford, or at least, not in that way. Some folks might describe a victim of the People as being 'overlooked' if they meant they'd been cursed with the glance of a particularly nasty eye, but this didn't sound like that. And what it did sound like, he didn't like.

'Aye, overlook,' Uncle Dunstan said. 'I'll teach you as well as your Pa. Set her on iron, watch her wake a few nights, then have her sneeze the trouble out. Or cough, or – well, there's purges and purges, but we'll try what we can. Your auntie – Agnes, yes – her we may as well leave, for there's no harm in a strong woman that can't use her strength for naughtiness. But it was spoken, the blight put on your Mama? It'll have gone in at her ears, then. We'll work on those. We've three days before you marry; that ought to be enough.'

'You'll do no such thing.' Jedediah's heart was racing. 'You lay a hand on her and I'll kill you.'

'Now lad,' Uncle Dunstan said, not unkindly, 'you have feeling for your ma, that's right enough. And I see now why you wouldn't leave the smithy unmanned, even for a funeral. Wouldn't you like a rest from her care? It's for her good, lad.'

'She's cared for.' Jedediah could hardly speak; he'd learned, over many years, the perils of raising his voice, and now he wasn't sure how to – but getting the words out without shouting them now almost choked him. 'She's been cared for all these years, and she's better cared for now. She is who she is, and if you maul her about, you'll break her. You'll break her, Uncle. She'll die of fear. You lay a hand on her, and—'

'Now then, son of mine.' Corbie rose like a swelling tide. 'That's my wife you speak of – *mine*, Jedediah. I should know, carrying her all these years.'

'You carried not an ounce of her.' Jedediah's throat twisted; he was coughing now, his tongue itching and raw.

'My dear brother,' Corbie said, slapping Dunstan on the back, 'I regret very much that I never knew such methods. I don't reckon any woman ever died of fear,' he went on. His face was almost blank, but there was a wildness under the mask, an edge of hysteria as of a man taking a leap off a cliff into the hard, tumbling waves below, a lake that might drown him, or cradle him and set him safe and free ashore. 'Besides, there's much to cure about that woman. Don't pay any mind to my son; he was born rebellious, and always was something skirt-led. The Attics, is it, she stays with? Well, they're heathen folk, Brother, and can't help it if they don't understand the laws of marriage, but we can settle them quick enough if they go against them. You needn't come if you're tender-stomached, Jedediah. Man the smithy, there's the boy.'

Jedediah couldn't talk. There was nothing to do but stand in the doorway, his fists raised. He was ready to fight; he'd been ready to fight for years.

'Now then, Nephew,' Uncle Dunstan said, in a tone of reasoning, but Corbie brushed him aside. He strode up to Jedediah, and Jedediah drew his arm back, readied himself. *I told him I'd fight back.* The thought was wild in his head, instantaneous, unmoored as a leaf in a gale. *You're too old to whip. Stop him. You aren't afraid of your father. You don't love your father. You can hit your father.*

Afterwards, Jedediah told himself that these thoughts were true, that he could have done it; it was only that Corbie was quicker. Before Jedediah could strike, there was a fist under his ribs; it staggered him, knocked his lungs empty, and then his cousin Stan was beside him, a hold on his arm – to stop him fighting, to stop him falling – and Corbie had him dragged across the smithy. He struck him again, on the back of his skull this time, and before Jedediah's head had stopped reeling he felt the cold scrape of iron around his neck, heard the click of a lock.

It was a tree-shackle, he knew, an iron band designed to go around the trunk of a sapling that had been lifting the skirts of passing maidens with its groping branch-tips. He'd made it himself; it was nearly finished.

He'd chained it up against the smithy wall for safekeeping.

'We'll be back, never fear,' Corbie said, his voice cheerful and his eyes blazing as he swept the various files, cutters and lock-picks out of Jedediah's reach. 'This looks to be work we'd do in shifts, eh, Dunstan? You'll be safe enough. Reckon you can work, even, though you might need to piss in the corner; I hope you went lately, my boy. We'll come and undo you soon enough. Only a few hours, eh? Just enough to take Constance out of the Attic house, bring her somewhere else. Then you can't get in the way, and we'll all have happy clear consciences to present on Doomsday.'

Stan, who had let Jedediah go as soon as Corbie laid hold of him, looked at his father a little doubtfully and Dunstan said, 'Bit harsh? I'm sure the lad will see sense.'

'You won't talk that one round if you chatter your tongue black,' Corbie said merrily. 'He'll be fine. Come on, let's go and put an end to the nonsense of my wife, eh, Brother?'

Over the next hours – but was hours? Jedediah heard the church bell not long after the hoofbeats died away. He listened, listened again, listened again and it didn't ring. Time must surely have passed; every second weighed upon him, drawing out the scrape of the iron around his neck, the queasy warmth it gathered from his skin, and every moment he listened out again, looked, and time didn't pass. It dripped by in slow, melting seconds, each one as stubborn and unyielding as an icicle.

The key to the shackle was on the other side of the smithy, where he couldn't reach it. He shuffled forward, strained: neither his feet nor his hands could reach any tool. And he couldn't see the lock; Corbie – Corbie, his father – had placed around him a collar, and he would sit here, collared like a dog, in full view of Gyrford, while they did to his mother . . .

What would they do? Jedediah remembered little Cissie Lenden, weeping on the shovel, cold flaying her feet.

Mama, he thought. He couldn't bear to add more words. *Mama.*

Jedediah was never able to say how long passed while he sat there. Somewhere, his mother was being taken away to be tested and teased and broken into pieces.

I don't reckon any woman ever died of fear, Corbie said. God damn the beast.

It wouldn't take long to destroy Mama – with horror, with anguish, even just a slip of the tool: a death really believed to be an accident by Dunstan Mackem, at least. A great, final joke against his son and heir: to marry in mourning, bringing to the forge a new farrier's lady under the shadow of the old one's gravestone. Here lies Constance Smith, who never knew she was beautiful.

He didn't know how to cry. Somewhere in his early years, knowing that his mama could hear him weep when his father raised the belt, he'd lost the knack of it.

He was working at the collar, his fingers raw, fumbling

hopelessly, when he heard a small voice from the very door of the smithy, timid, quiet, not sure if it could hope for an invitation in.

'Mister Smith?' whispered Franklin Thorpe. 'A-are you all right?'

Jedediah looked up. His voice dragged through his throat, hoarse, slow, but he could make it work again. 'Franklin,' he said. 'Thank God for you. Fetch me the key from that table there, will you?'

He didn't know where they'd gone. They wouldn't do it at the Attics; Agnes couldn't stop them, but Tom and Mister Attic would try. Corbie was right: if it came to a fight, any magistrate would take the word of two elder farriers over a Moorish convert and his children . . . but no, it would be easier to just take Constance away somewhere.

Franklin looked up at him. The boy was shaking, but he stood firm on his feet. 'Can I help you?' he asked. 'I – I don't know what's the to-do, but if I can help you, Mister Smith, I – I'd like to.'

Some day, Jedediah promised himself, *I'll do something for that boy*. He'd had too much time to think, and while he was shackled, he hadn't been able to sort his ideas; they'd frassed over each other, disparate and useless. But now he was free and there was somebody with him, even if it was only a bruised boy of eight. Franklin was his friend, and things started to snap together.

He couldn't take a knife or an axe. *I'll kill you*, he'd said, but that had to be put away: he hadn't even been able to punch his father, and while he could spar if he had to, he wasn't a murderer. If he went to kill anyone, he wouldn't get anywhere at all: the thought would stop his hand mid-air.

He needed something else, and he had an idea. An appalling one, but he could do it if it kept Mama from the overlooking.

'You're a good boy, Franklin,' he said, already hurrying them along. 'I'm beholden to you for your help. You remember your riding?' He'd been teaching the boy how to sit a horse this last year; Franklin was developing a good seat and had the friendliness with beasts that children afraid of men sometimes show. An unfamiliar horse might be difficult, but of all the folks within his reach, Franklin Thorpe was the only soul Jedediah knew who would, without question, help him act against his father. 'Good. We head to my friend Mark Brown just now, to borrow his horse – you remember, he put the roof on my house? We'll ride it together to the Lendens, and then we'll borrow theirs, which you'll ride to the Berretts. Go round to the back door and fetch my Louise.' If anyone could sneak somewhere undetected, Jedediah thought, it was this skinny child, but he added, 'Bring her to me yourself without you tell the Berretts, if you can. If you have to speak to them, tell them Midwife Pell Smith sends for them, for there's a woman dying in childbed and she won't be denied.

'Fetch Louise,' Jedediah told Franklin again as they reached the Browns' door and Jedediah hammered on it, 'and bring her to me, in the little forest on the Lenden land. Can you do that, Franklin?'

'Yes, Mister Smith.' Franklin was panting, determinedly keeping pace with his rapid stride. 'What shall I tell Mistress Louise about why you need her?'

'Tell her—' What could he say? He couldn't accuse his uncle of murder, or explain to a boy this young the deathly complications of an overlook. But Franklin was used to being chased away from doorsteps, and needed to understand that this time, he mustn't let that happen. 'Tell her that my father goes to hurt my mother, worse than he has before, and if I can't stop him, this time she may stay hurt. You understand?'

'Yes, Mister Smith.' The words were too heavy for such a small tongue. Franklin stood, dogged and exhausted beside him.

'Good lad,' he said. 'You've been brave many times; I – I think much of you.' There was nothing that excused dragging Franklin into this, except that if his mother was to be tortured, he had to do all he could to stop it. 'Good lad. Ah, Mark,' he added, as the door opened, 'can't say how glad I am it's you. Look you, I need to borrow your horse.'

Above the Lenden woods the sky was smeared with cloud, as if a great thumb had rubbed across it. Jedediah tethered Mark Brown's horse besides them, not wanting to subject the innocent mare to the woods; since the introduction of No One, the whole place had the feel of somewhere given over. This forest needed iron around it, and one day, when he wasn't in fear for his mother's life, some time in the future, he'd live here in the tiny house with his wife and his children and he'd put a fence around it to keep the People in. One day.

He took the bullroarer from his sack, swung it around his head, once, twice, thrice. Mist sliced across it, rolling back from its blade, until he stood in a patch of clear air.

'I'll do no harm to any here. Spider friend, pray draw you

near,' he said. He hated reciting these little doggerels; they were effective in getting the People's attention, but they made him feel foolish. For most of his life, it occurred to him, he'd lived with a father eager to make him ridiculous. Perhaps if he'd grown up like Tom, in a family who laughed at each other in delight, he'd be less stiff a man.

The wind muttered through the trees. Up above, Jedediah saw a flicker of wings, feathered like a jay, but fast as a dragonfly. Just wings, with no body attached. It was there, then gone, offering him no help at all.

He waited. He recited the lines again. He waited some more.

Beyond him – many miles beyond, except that he could hear it clear as a chime – rang a tiny choir of laughter, bright and thin as the edge of a blade.

Beneath his feet, the earth was damp and littered over. It was clean, the scent around him: crisp soil and old moss and the faint, distant tang of rain. There was much in this place that was natural, he told himself, and what wasn't, he had no reason to fear.

Which tree had he left No One at? It was covered over with ivy, he remembered, holding a soft clatter of leaves. That wasn't these trees here; these were hornbeams, bursting up from the ground in multiple sprays like a gathered bouquet, and holly, fanged and innocent in the white swirls. It should be further in; there was a green haze beyond that looked promising. Jedediah took a rag from his pocket, tied it to a hornbeam branch and set off.

He'd passed the same rag seven times when he heard a crunch of rapid feet. For a moment he raised his bullroarer, ready to swing and keep whatever he had to at a distance – then he saw the shapes, two of them hand-in-hand, and a soft voice called out, 'Jed? Jed, is that you?' There was another figure beside them, he saw, small and upright and impatient and safe: somehow, they'd found Pell and brought her with them.

At the sight of Louise, relief rushed over him so deep that for a moment, nothing else mattered. Absurdly, the first thought that came to his mind was, *You shouldn't be here, putting yourself in danger in your condition* – but she'd come at his call, and there was no way he could find the spider without her. It had succumbed to him, thinking him a deliverer from flames, but he'd never been its friend, and much of him – his crawling nape and chilled belly and revolted skin – never wanted to see the thing again. While the People's notion of who was their friend and who their enemy could be eccentric, it mostly rested on whether the man or woman showed them courtesy, and he'd not been able to say the words 'Spider friend' with any kind of conviction.

He put his arms around Louise and kissed her neck before he remembered that Franklin was there. Well, let the lad see a man who liked his woman, for a change. 'Louise,' he said, 'we've a need to find that No One of yours. It won't come at my call, but it'll come at yours, I'm sure of it.'

'Well, my boy,' Pell said, a little acrid at being ignored, 'if you mean to conjure up the People, I hope you've a good reason for it. This girl shouldn't be dragged about.'

'Are you well?' Jedediah asked Louise, distracted.

'Healthy as can be asked,' Pell said, dryly. 'Though I should box your ears, lad, after all I've taught you. Well, your child will have a better father than you did, and that's all there is to say about that.'

The ground unsteadied itself beneath Jedediah's feet for a moment and he had to pull himself together so he didn't lean his weight onto Louise. It was one thing to have it suspected by the girl herself; having it confirmed by a midwife was another. He felt entirely unfit to be anybody's father; he couldn't make a world fit to bring anybody into.

'P-please don't box Mister Smith's ears,' Franklin said – very bravely, Jedediah thought, considering that he'd wasn't very familiar with Pell and she was, if you didn't know her, a little formidable.

That thought rallied him; he kissed Louise's cheek, stroked her hair and straightened himself. If the child could be bold, so could he.

'She won't, Franklin,' he said. 'This is my auntie, she's all bark and no bite. Louise, love, can you call No One? I have to stop my father hurting my mother, and—' He swallowed. 'If it's just me against him, I'll need help.'

'We have to find them,' Jedediah said to Pell, as Louise sat within a grove of ivied trees and coaxed, calling, 'No One, dear? Come on, come on, come on . . .' as if offering meat to a kitten. 'We'll start at the Attics,' Jedediah went on. 'They'll at least know which direction they headed . . .'

'You'd take a child to this?' Pell demanded. She had Franklin in her lap, more in the manner of a man shoeing a horse than an auntie cuddling a child; she was not one of those God made to sit still, so she was combing his hair with her fingers for something to do.

'I can help,' Franklin said resolutely.

'I know, Franklin,' Jedediah said. 'But I wouldn't wish you hurt. And if my father carries it back to yours . . .' He didn't go on. If Franklin had crept out to the forge to find him this late in the afternoon, it most likely meant Joe Thorpe had been drinking during the day. And if Joe knew Franklin had been running about counter to the elder farrier's wishes, the boy would be lucky to escape broken bones. Jedediah hadn't mentioned to anyone – not Franklin, not Pell, not even Louise – that he was taking on his uncle and cousin as well as his father; if he was going to start a war between the clans, he should leave its bystanders as innocent as possible. He could very well lose; most likely, the best ending would be Constance rescued and himself cast out. He'd manage somehow; they could go far away. Louise would come with him; she was used to rootlessness – and maybe Franklin could run away with them; he was too old to pass off as a son, but men following the work did sometimes have young brothers under their care.

But Pell was midwife here; she shouldn't be placed where the Mackems could blame her. If you have to take a whipping, you lock your teeth and stay silent so you don't inflict the pain on others.

'Pell,' Jedediah said, 'can you take the child back with you? Let him stay the night in your house?'

'Can't be done,' Pell said, which made Jedediah forget for just a moment that he loved her. 'I could have a woman groaning at my door any moment. You want to keep him secret, mine's not the house for it.'

'All right then,' Jedediah said, too upset to argue, 'leave him at my house on the Lenden farm, will you? There's not much to eat there, but you can have what there is, Franklin. You stay safe there so I don't have to fret over you, all right?'

'No One?' Louise called up the tree. 'Is that your pretty foot I see, dear? Come along down to Louise. Come on, come on . . .'

'Just mind what you do, lad,' Pell told Jedediah. Her hands around Franklin were almost gentle, and her voice was as close as Jedediah had ever heard it to tears. 'Don't be a fool above the neck as well as below it. We'll need you for elder farrier one day.'

'Mister Smith is clever,' Franklin dared to say.

'Head full of tangles,' Pell said, turning back to Franklin and the blessed opportunity to scold without sorrow. 'I don't know who cares for you, lad, but they should think better of it. Lucky for you you've a handsome face, or you wouldn't be fit to be seen . . . Ah, Jedediah, I think your wife has something for you.'

Jedediah tried to answer, but he had to turn his head and acknowledge what he'd been feeling up and down his spine for some time: No One had shimmied down from the tree, thick rope scratching in the air, and now sat hunched on the ground by Louise with the air of a very good dog.

The spider was bigger than it had been before: grotesquely big, the size of a goat, with legs as thick as Franklin's and a collection of eyes gleaming brilliant in the soft-misted woods. As Jedediah approached it, it wobbled its abdomen in the air, a horrible cocking of the glimmer-furred, sharp-tipped bulb, though Jedediah could not take it as the hopeful greeting No One seemed to intend.

'Harm to no man nor beast of man has been the way of pretty spin and twining wind,' came the familiar, unwelcome voice.

The mist, which still rolled away in curling spirals from Jedediah's iron-nailed boots, sat soft and comfortable between No One's many hairs. 'Glad should be the man of flame and fire and beloved of the beloved Louise, for No One has been good as empty air and feasted upon the bubbling flesh of squirrel and fox alone, sweet and rich beyond barn rat, and too, the man of flame has set within the egg-sac of flesh that is Louise of the blooming veins, and see, he has stepped away undrunk and lived on, perhaps to see the hatch of his own eggs in slow-sighted glory.'

'Don't you start,' Jedediah said; he'd still not quite got used to the idea of having children, but whoever he discussed it with, it wasn't going to be this thing.

No One's abdomen dropped; evidently it had expected to be praised for confining its diet to wild animals. 'Words are skeins that cannot be eaten, and if flesh blames No One for the flies that fall in them, what are pretty thoughts to do with the air so teemed with life for which No One is blamed?' it mourned.

'Well,' Pell said, with the crisp decision of one who didn't like spiders any more than Jedediah, 'that's as much as I like to see. I'll take this boy back to your house and feed him, for it's not a fit business for a boy this little, my man. You need flesh on your bones, young what's-your-name.'

'Franklin Thorpe, Miss Smith,' the child said in a polite whisper. He looked at Jedediah, waiting for instructions, and Jedediah nodded. The boy didn't need to see any of what lay ahead; God knows, he'd seen his own mother hurt enough in his short life. And he didn't need to see how afraid of spiders Jedediah was either, come to that.

'Off you go, Franklin,' he said. 'Don't fear Aunt Pell, just talk back to her if she pushes you too hard; she'll like you the better for it. Louise . . .' He turned to his girl. 'Stay with me until you need to hide. We'll take both horses, but you ride with me; just hold the other's reins, will you? I'll keep you safe as well as I can. And you, Spider,' he added, 'you sit atop the black horse's saddle, you hear? Hunch down flat as you can, hold the saddle, not the skin, and don't fright it. And if you bite it, I'll . . . *Don't* bite it.'

'No One of the fang and flex is bold in the beloved of righteousness,' the spider declared, leaping on to the saddle with a truly disgusting flick of its legs, 'and with no tree to store a great horse, and only stoat and owl to pierce and pry within, truly perfect is the stick of friend to friend.'

Jedediah was too frightened for his mother to object to this definition of the two of them. Somewhere, they were beginning to overlook her.

If he could have ridden fast, he would have; he would have flown down the paths, striking aside any branch that leaned in his way. But he rode with Louise, who was not to be shaken, and the horse would drop under the weight of them both if he pushed too hard. As the day greyed into dusk and rain began to spit against their faces, there was nothing to do but press forward: walk, trot, canter, slow to a walk again. He'd known the path to the Attics all his life, but never as it was now, every blind turn and looming tree standing like sentinels, rough jags of chalk lurking like goblins, the very weather pushing against him.

'What is to be of tender breathing leaf and water-blocked knee?' No One complained atop its mount; the balls of water gathering between its hairs were round and bright as stars.

'Be quiet,' Jedediah told it, tightening his arms around Louise, then for her sake added, 'so please you.' Here he was, dragging her across the country with a fey spider, a child in her belly – when he'd promised her a featherbed, not this life.

'I'm sorry,' he whispered. Most likely the spider could hear them; he wished they were alone, for it was hard to say out loud, but needed to be said. 'If you want to be out of this, I won't blame you – bringing No One to me, you've already done so much. You can dismount at the next road . . .'

She half turned, gave him a glance that was almost fiery. 'You think I'd sit still while they pull your mother apart?' she said. 'If you'd want children out of a woman of that kind, Jed Smith, you're not the man I think you.'

Constance had been taken from the garden, Mister Attic said. He was so distraught that he kept forgetting words in English, and Jedediah had to scrape together as much Arabic as Tom had taught him to be able to follow the story.

Constance had been watching the stream, the little fish there that she liked to feed. Mister Attic had been at work in his kitchen, then Agnes had come to him, and she'd said – no, she hadn't said, she'd been too – Mister Attic couldn't find the word in English, and Jedediah didn't understand it in Arabic, but he recognised the gesture: the knotted arms and twitching face, the way Auntie Agnes got when she could neither speak nor stay silent without risking hurt to someone. Corbie sometimes teased her into such a state when he was in a particularly sour mood.

Mister Attic had gone into the garden looking for Constance, and her cushion was there, and her shawl, but she was gone. He was so sorry – he was *so* sorry . . .

Jedediah would have liked to put his arms around the man who'd been so good to him all his life, but he didn't quite know how. Louise, who had been weeping tears of mingled fear and fury, went up to Mister Attic and hugged him herself, and Jedediah wanted to kill someone, probably Corbie, for hurting the two of them like this.

'It's all right, Mister Attic, sir,' he said. He'd very seldom 'sirred' the man, but this seemed the moment. *Well, they're heathen folk, Brother,* Corbie had said. 'I know – I do know you aren't to blame. All I need to ask is, did anyone see which way they went? That's all I need.'

'I'm so sorry, my boy,' Mister Attic said, 'but when I came out – by the time I came out – they were gone, my boy. They were all gone.'

'It's all right,' Jedediah said. 'That's what I thought likely. Mister Attic, by your courtesy, I must ask you to go in the house. I wouldn't drag you in. If there's trouble, you deserve none of it. I think it best if you go in and take care of Auntie Agnes, if you would do me that kindness.'

Mister Attic gave him a look, haunted, almost lost. He reached out, patted Jedediah on the shoulder. 'You're a good son,' he said. 'When they let you, you're a good son.' And he went back into the house. Jedediah looked to see if he could spot Agnes through any of the windows, but no, the rooms were dark. Tomorrow he'd come back to her, he'd say something to help her, if he could. Tomorrow.

'Spider,' he said.

There was a quiet shuffle. Jedediah had tethered the horse behind a tree, where Mister Attic couldn't see it. He wasn't about to give the man a secret like that to worry about.

'No One waits man of fire and tasteless hairs, for how shall the pretty scent be ranked in wet and questing feet?'

'That's what I thought,' Jedediah said. 'I remember once, you said something about scenting and tasting with the hairs on your legs.'

'Prison-tongued is man,' No One conceded. 'What is to be of a skin-blind bag of flesh that cannot the world ensnare and enscent with the wisps of nothing that grow on arm and head?'

'And you must be pretty good at it if you could smell Louise is with child,' Jedediah said. 'So you see this cushion, here, the blue one?'

'Skies of scent and flowers of scent and cloth with feathers of many birds,' No One lamented, evidently confused by the concept of colour.

'All right, but this cushion? You put your feet on it, or your hairs, or what you have. There's a woman sits upon this we need to find. You get the scent or the taste of her, and then, Spider, you track for us where she went. I don't keep a dog, but you and I will go on the hunt.'

Around them the sun set and the sky was silver-pale and starless. Louise rested against him as No One scuttled ahead, stopping every now and again to grovel its sharp feet in the earth before catching the scent again.

And after a day of horror and confusion, it came clear to him, as they wound their way along, something he should have guessed. They were going back the way they'd come – by different paths; these were roads flat enough for a cart, while Jedediah had ridden the narrow shortcuts, and if he hadn't, damn the bad luck, he might even have met them halfway. But they were racing back towards the very woods where they'd found No One. The spider itself didn't comment on this; it was following the path with the ravening eagerness of a predator thinking of nothing but the quest.

'God help us,' Jedediah muttered.

No One was too hot in pursuit to take any notice, but Louise said quietly, 'What?'

'I know where to go now,' he said. 'I see their thinking.'

A farrier's lady needed to be an intelligent woman; she'd have known when to slip a word to her man and when to keep her lips shut. Louise gave him a long moment, before saying, with a soft prompt, 'Jed?'

'They'll sound out the tree,' he said. 'The Ab-tree – where Corbie trapped the fey that blighted her. They'll take her to the tree and whatever they do to her, they'll do with wood from it. They're taking her back to what did this to her.'

No One scuttled on as Louise said, her voice a little shaky from the motion, 'Is that bad?'

'It won't work,' Jedediah said. 'Ab never took back a gift in all its days. And they daren't let it out of the tree; it was the worst blight we've ever known. They'll just take her there to the fey woods, and . . .' He thought of Cissie Lenden, feet freezing on the shovel, waiting to see if the People would come and rescue their poor, mistreated hostage.

'They'll put her where they know the People are,' he said, 'and they'll hurt her till the People come to take away what they put in her. But you can't take out what's been made of someone. You can't take out what someone is.' From the fields around, he heard a sound that wasn't a woman, wasn't a reason to stop and weep; it was just the scream of a crow. 'So they'll hurt her and they won't stop. They'll have no reason to stop.'

There were those who said you could feel it when a fey place was disturbed. It wasn't Jedediah's greatest strength, but he needed no special talent here: it was loud in these woods. The mists were clotting thick as cream between tree and tree and he could hear too many things: the screech of crows and the clank of iron, and closer than they should have been, the voices of men, and underneath them, the raw sob of a woman, a droning misery of words that were only, 'Agnes. Agnes . . .'

Jedediah pulled up the horse and leaped off. He stopped himself just long enough to help Louise down and whispered to her, 'Stay here. Hold the reins, but if she bolts, let go, don't be dragged along. Just – just stay here. Be ready to take Mama, if I can bring her to you.' He tried to swallow, but in this congealing mist, his throat stuck dry. 'Better she be taken to a woman.'

And he stepped forward into the muffling white.

*

He'd never seen the Ab-tree. Aunt Pell had told him plain that he wasn't to go near, and that if he did, she'd tell his father – a threat she'd never made on any other subject, which meant she was in dire earnest. He knew only the tale: a chestnut tree with a hollow inside, trapping a brace of crows that his father had trained to his service and then abandoned to the company of an imprisoned fey, a being so stormy in its friendship that it could plant bird-voices in the throat of a baby, or twine a future into her muscles, or break her understanding.

Grandpa Clem had always spoken of Ab as a persistent giver, something touchy and prone to misunderstanding, which made it sound small. Father, when he spoke of it at all, spoke of the iron chain he'd sewn up the tree with, laughing unhappily at his first attempt at the female arts that had bound him into a life beset with women.

What neither of them said was that Ab was *powerful.* Ab brought on weather and whipped up waves; Ab carried fruit from the Africs and dust from the moon. Ab could take any form - and yes, the People liked to change themselves, but Ab had changed the bodies of mortals as well. And it did all this without conditions: it didn't even know that there was anything outlandish about such feats. Ab was a wild mad thing that should never have been touched; the best you could hope from it was that it never knew you walked upon this earth.

Well, he was walking towards the tree now. All he could see in the curdled fog was a spreading beast of trunk and leaf; it stood alone, as if the earth around it had been sucked dry of life. There was nothing growing from the soil by the Ab-tree: no saplings, no ferns, no straggle of green at all for a full three paces; nothing but an empty shuffle of leaf litter. Across the tree's bark, like an ill-stitched wound, hung a dark iron chain festering into rust.

Mama was there. One of her arms had been shackled to a branch, one of her legs bound to the trunk. She drooped as if the hangman had been at work, weeping in steady, hopeless sobs, no plea or appeal in them, but just a soft, empty rhythm of despair. *Agnes. Agnes.* Her sister; her touchstone, with whom the world almost made sense.

Jedediah had expected a shovel, but no, she stood barefoot within an iron grille, the better to trap her within its spiky bars. He could smell vomit. There were two bulky men holding Constance, and another watching behind them, the red gleam of their hair just showing through the white murk. One man gripped her head while the other tugged at her ear, extending into it something long and iron and sharp.

Constance screamed, and Dunstan's voice said, 'Hold her steady, damn it. Now look what you've done.'

'Dear oh dear.' That was Corbie, coaxing and concerned as he'd never spoken to Constance in all of Jedediah's life. 'Hold still, Connie dear, we wouldn't like to hurt you. Beg your pardon, Brother; she does fight against her good sometimes.'

Jedediah wanted to yell, *Stop!* His whole body was full of the cry. But when had any word of his ever held Corbie back from anything?

'No One,' he whispered, 'that woman on the tree: that's my mother. She loves Louise, and these men don't, and they'll hurt my mother. They're to be stopped. Do you remember when you took apart Franklin Thorpe?'

'Hard of throat was man of flame and mauled in cruel thought the unsinning carcass,' No One whispered back, in evident reproach at his having been harsh about it at the time.

'My father spoke through me,' Jedediah said. It was a lie, but it occurred to him now that his was not a gentle nature, and for that, it wasn't Constance or Grandpa Clem he had to thank. Perhaps Ab could have taken it out of him, or No One set it end on end. But you couldn't trust the People to understand your words, so there was nothing to do but keep your own bad nature in iron chains. And if you wouldn't . . .

His mother sobbed from the tree.

'I want none killed,' he said, 'but I want my mother saved, and for that, we'll stop them. Go you in. Go to Dunstan Mackem; he's the man holding the iron. Place – place his eyes back to front, so he can't see what I do. Don't trouble Stan unless he troubles you. And my father—'

He drew a breath, a lungful of blindness. So many murders flitted through his head. On the Day of Judgement, he'd have to carry these before the throne on his back like a sack of rocks.

'Bind him,' he said, 'for now. Get his hands off my mother and bind him in silk so he can't move, then I'll tell you more. If you do that, Louise will – will love you gladly, and I'll bring you a whole pig to eat. I'll ask Jack Lenden for one of his. You can have it all.'

'Drinker of play and gladness within the unsilked air is No One,' the spider fluted, which appeared to be something like a battle cry, for the next moment it scuttled off, all joint and knee-tip and flickering speed, and the dark lines of its many legs were the clearest thing he could see in the empty blankness.

Jedediah stared into the white darkness. His mother still wept, and one of them reached for her again . . .

And there was a burst of motion—

One of the men was down on the ground, clutching at his face; there was a whir of limbs around it and he wasn't screaming, but gasping in a kind of frenzied confusion. The other man rushed towards him – his hand touched the tree—

It was a grab for support, nothing more, but he held, for a moment, the chain, the blood-black rusted zigzag that had held Ab bound for so many years. There was a clatter; truly quite quiet, nothing you'd hear unless you had your attention upon it – then it slid down, link by link, dropping to the ground and falling from the trunk

—and the tree burst apart.

There were too many figures in the grove, men and women, and wings, black wings starker than midnight cutting through the mist. Feathers flew, a storm of dark snow, and he was dazzled with nothingness; all he could see was slashing whirls of black and white, and all he could hear were screams and sobs and the crack of wood.

When his sight cleared, there was a figure beside Mama, a woman, lifting her foot from the grate to set her safe upon the earth. Then something black swooped up: crows, dark crows bigger than eagles, and – *Two decades?* Jedediah thought wildly. *How could crows live two decades trapped in a tree with a fey?*

And then he was running forward and he'd lifted the iron

chain and something snapped together in his mind, saying, *Stupid question. Ab kept them alive. God help Corbie, who trapped them within. What did Ab say, all those years ago? There is justice in the crows of the air.*

'Father!' he yelled, 'the chain's broke and the crows know you – cover your face! Cover your face, Ab's crows are loose!'

He couldn't see very well, but he saw the crows swarming his father. There were only two or three of them, but fury scattered from their wings like dander. He'd made a woman train them to be her allies; he'd trapped them in the tree with a mad fey, and now they were out and lunging at him arrow-beaked; slashes of blood flew gleaming through the air.

There was a woman beside Constance, or two women, or maybe fifty for all Jedediah could count; there were too many birds in motion. He could see Stan Mackem crouched, appalled, over Dunstan, who was holding his hands over his blinded face. Everything was in chaos, and he needed to find Ab.

Jedediah, frantic, turned around, losing sight of everything else. He had seconds, maybe, before Ab set upon them, in friendship or in justice; he had seconds to find the creature that could take any shape, it could be a man, a bird, a monstrous thing—

—and there, there was a figure, tall and bulky like a man, naked and strong, but with a mask of feathers gleaming upon its face, all rough-traced features and soft, shimmering barbs: a crow-man, staggering towards him with its hands clawed out.

Jedediah raised the chain in his hands. It was old and rusted and he was no cunning trickster like Corbie; he could only swing the iron and drive the creature backwards, shouting, 'Back! Back! Go you back!'

The figure staggered, and Jedediah, too crazed with panic to think of anything more subtle, punched at it with the iron chain in his fist.

It was enough. The creature fell back within the tree, and he yelled, 'No One!'

Earth chittered; leaves scattered. A hideous collection of legs crouched itself beside him.

'Weave around the tree,' Jedediah said, 'fast as you can. Keep the thing within it.'

'Faster than No One, no one can be!' whispered the spider, and with the dainty viciousness of a victor, it set about pinning shimmer to shimmer across the broken trunk. There was a cry from within, an animal roar, smothered as the silk was laid on thicker and thicker, thick as cloth, thick as snow.

The silk wasn't iron, but it was fey, and it was made for traps. A silence fell. Within the tree, no sound could be heard.

Jedediah stood back, gasping for breath. The mist was clearing. He looked about, trying desperately to see what was what.

Uncle Dunstan was lying on the ground, clutching his face. Stan was beside him, shaking his shoulder, calling, 'Pa? Pa, what is it?'

'Stan,' Jedediah said, 'Stan, give me what iron you have about you – nails, chains, anything. I need it fast.'

Stan, too upset to say anything, emptied his pockets. Nails, yes, the nails would do it, and there were rocks on the ground that would serve as hammers. Jedediah hastened to the tree, where the web No One had cast across the re-imprisoned Ab was dulling to a mushroom-white, opaque and plain as if it had always been there.

Jedediah raised the chain and looped it back through the

holes in the trunk. It would hold if he nailed it right; there was just one link that had broken in the middle. Everyone was crying and calling around him, but he leaned over his work in fierce concentration: nail into trunk, chain-link beside nail, nail hammered over it to form a hook. One link, then another, then another, until Ab was bound within by silk and by iron.

The tree was closed.

He turned to see Dunstan sitting up, leaning on his son. His eyes were striped with thin skeins of red, unseeing and shocked. Corbie sat beside him, looking almost equally shocked; he kept rubbing his face, shaking his head, for once in his life utterly wordless.

'Mama,' Jedediah said, and turned to see her, still chained and whimpering. Her head was nestled against Louise, who was holding her in comforting arms, whispering, 'We're all well. There, now. We're all well.'

Beside her stood Pell. Where the devil had she come from? But he found he wasn't surprised: it wasn't in Pell's nature to flee a catastrophe.

'Well,' she said without any excuse for her presence, 'I see you tracked your way here. Glad you managed it.'

'Why?' he asked. 'If you knew they'd bring her here, why didn't you say?'

'I knew no such thing, lad,' Pell said. 'I heard a racket in my woods. Do you think I'd let my big strong nephew run off and leave me here to fight them off alone? I'm glad you think me fine, lad, but if you think me that mighty, you've confused me with my sister.'

'What – when did you hear it?' Jedediah demanded. A dreadful suspicion was dawning on him.

Pell placed her hands on her hips as Louise kept soothing Mama: 'It's all right, dearest, it's all right . . .'

'Do you not think,' she said, 'you'd do better to free your mother than question your auntie?'

'Stan,' Jedediah said. Corbie was still sitting on the earth, his head in his hands. He'd penned Ab in once before; the sight of it emerging from the tree again, crow-attended and feather-faced and powerful enough to twist him into an acorn, must have shaken him. 'Stan, whoever has the key to these shackles, give them to me now.'

'What have you done to my father?' Stan demanded, his voice near hysteria.

It was a fair point, but Jedediah wasn't about to concede it. 'Saved him from a thing that could suck the life out of him,' he said. 'That fey I drove into the tree – that kind friend – that's the one did this to my mother. And my Aunt Agnes – and God only knows who else down the decades. I drove it back, Stan Mackem, and I locked it up, and if you'll give me a minute, I can set your father right. But give me the keys, right this instant, or I swear to God and before this tree, I'll leave him blind the rest of his life.'

Stan's face was white, expressionless. There was a little vomit on his boots, Jedediah noticed; his own or Mama's.

He didn't move right that instant; he stopped; thought about it – then he held out the keys in a shaking hand, and Jedediah unlocked his mother from her chains.

She blinked at him, saying, 'Little one? Little one, your

ear . . .' There was a dark snake of blood running down her neck; the prong Dunstan Mackem had held had pierced deep and her whole lobe was dripping red. How close to her brain had it gone? An inch? Half an inch? Only a little further would have stabbed her to death.

'We'll go home to Mister Attic,' Jedediah said to her. 'Tom has a drink that can make you sleep and take the hurt away. Never fret, Mama. I'll take you home.'

'Will you now?' Stan said. Both of their fathers were still sat in confusion; he stared at Jedediah, still struggling to hold on to his challenge.

Jedediah stood his ground. He could put iron into his eyes when he had to. 'One day,' he said, 'we'll elder it together, Cousin. You and me. Don't fight me now. I wouldn't counsel it. You're in my holding, on my earth. I was born here. I'll set your father right, and send your aunt where they'll care for her. Leave it be, and come drink at my wedding. It'll be a small feast, but you'll be welcome to your share and it'll be good food. My friend Mister Attic will cook the pastries.

'And *you*, Franklin Thorpe,' he added, turning his voice a little stern, 'step out from behind that tree. Don't think I don't see you.'

He could not, in fact, see Franklin; the boy was a master of hiding. But he must have believed Jedediah, for he emerged, a little shaky and a little shame-faced, and crept up as far as Louise, putting his arms around her waist. It was something of a balance for her to keep petting Constance and him at the same time, but she managed it.

'I'm sorry, Mister Smith,' said Franklin, sounding a great deal less harrowed than Jedediah had expected. 'I heard the noise too, and I thought you might be at risk, or Mistress Louise.'

'And you watched all these fey sights?' Jedediah demanded. How was a boy untrained in the fey arts to live after seeing the explosion of crows and silk and whirling black snow?

'Well,' Franklin said, a little shaky, 'it was very bad what they did to Mistress Smith. They stabbed her ear. So I'm not sorry you knocked them about.' His voice was hard for a second, and Jedediah saw, in his clear, dark eyes, the ache of trouble that would follow you for a lifetime. 'I'm not. But I wasn't afraid of the People because I saw you coming.'

Jedediah experienced, for a silent and unsteadying moment, the appalling shock to reality that is a child's belief you can protect them. Fatherhood suddenly stared him in the face. It wasn't a good world, but if he could act out a tiny good space within it, enough to cover a few children – well, he had to do it, that was all. It was a new thing among the many that, like it or not, he'd better start getting stubborn about.

'All right,' he said to Franklin, 'but don't be sure I always can. Ask me another time. And Stan, I'll set your father right, but if I were you, I wouldn't watch. Aunt Pell, can you set him up for this?'

'Here,' Pell said, hauling the blinded man to his feet and pushing a twig between his teeth without any tenderness. 'Bite you down on this. Helps with the pain.'

No One's ministrations wouldn't hurt, not by Franklin's account, but Jedediah wasn't in the mood to dispute it.

'I've another thought,' he said. 'You hear me, Uncle?'

'What in the name of Heaven did you do, boy?' Setting him

upright had rallied Uncle Dunstan somewhat; he'd stopped swiping at his blind eyes, although their vein-branched appearance was not very comforting, and he spat out the twig.

'What I said,' Jedediah told him. 'I saved you. Father knocked open the Ab-tree. He's the one who shackled it, and I was never allowed to visit. If he didn't keep the chains from rust, well, he's a thoughtless man. But on that score: when he locked the kind friend in the tree the first time around, he locked in some crows as well, and they lived out the decades there. I suppose the kind friend liked their company. But they're something grown now, and crows hold grudges – can hold them for generations, my Aunt Mabbie used to say, and that being so, I don't reckon this holding's a safe place for him.'

'What?' Corbie croaked. His face was a mesh of red trickles and his head lolled as if his brain had been rattled within it.

'The crows,' Jedediah said. 'They'll blame him now. And there wasn't time to catch them, so I reckon they'll be off to make some friends.'

Uncle Dunstan was a brave man, Jedediah had to give him that. Blinded, he stood firm on his feet and said, 'Well, what of it? Go and iron them. We'll do it together if you don't think you can manage.'

'Every crow in the county?' Jedediah said. He found, now things were beginning to settle back into the plain, common world, that his voice was matter-of-fact. The crows from the tree must be pretty well touched by now, but the crows they'd find to share their outrage would be ordinary flesh and blood. Ironing them would do nothing at all. Uncle Dunstan would remember that, when he calmed down.

'I had no idea this would come about, Uncle,' he said. 'You're the ones who brought your folly to this tree. I barely remembered there were crows trapped in it, and if I'd thought of them, I'd have supposed them dead of hunger decades ago. But if you'd told me you meant to come here, I could have told you it was stupid. Father never did know when to hold back. The crows will be against him now, and I don't reckon he'll be safe. He could go masked every time he steps outside, but they'll know his face. If I were you, I'd take him home for a while. Give them a generation or so to forget.'

'And you'll hold the forge, is it?' Dunstan said. 'I might be blinded, lad, but I'm not struck foolish.'

Jedediah shrugged, then realised that was a pointless gesture just at this moment. 'I can set your eyes right,' he said. 'This is advice for my father's good. Crows live – how long, a decade-odd? I'll send him his share of the smithy, never fear. I'm not out to cheat any man. But he wouldn't like a life within doors, and I'll tell you plain enough that I don't think he ever liked this county. Take him back with you, and if he decides otherwise, well, he's a free man. Believe me, if I wished ill-gotten gains out of this, I'd not be giving this counsel. I'd take him home in an open cart and let the crows peck him apart.'

Dunstan stood and stared unseeing for a long while. Stan came and stood beside him, but he didn't pay much attention to Corbie; his care was all for his father, his streaked white eyes.

'Well,' Dunstan said in the end, 'he's welcome enough to come home, if he likes. You send him his half fair and honest, mind you.'

'Fair and honest,' Jedediah said, and after a very rapid struggle with himself, 'his share of the smithy up until today has been eight-tenths.'

'Well, for God's sake,' Dunstan said, sounding more himself. 'That's just foolery. Send him five. You'll have a wife to keep, won't you? And God help you if you have sons of your own kind.'

Jedediah bit back the urge to say, *It'd be better for their mother, though*. Instead, he gestured to No One, who had been clinging to the Ab-tree ever since the binding. 'Kind friend,' he said, trying to sound like a man used to commanding horrors, 'this man would have his eyes restored.'

'Set a-straight and fang to fang and spread a web across the whole of wishing,' came a whisper.

'What?' Corbie said dazedly, but Jedediah had nothing to say to him. *Now look what you've done*, Dunstan had said as Corbie jerked Mama's head down onto an iron spike.

He could prove nothing; he could never convince the world Corbie had tried for Mama's life. But he could keep her from him. She could live gazing at candle-gold and water-silver, surrounded by folks who smiled at her.

And if he felt he might choke on anger, well, that wasn't useful. He turned to Franklin instead, put a hand on his shoulder and said, 'Looks like I might be living in the smithy house, then. More room for guests, at least. Remind me to give you a key when we get back to Gyrford.'

The wounds around Corbie's face didn't heal well over the next few days; they kept growing tiny feathers at their edges and his skin was fever-hot to the touch. Never a man to suffer patiently, he lay in bed, silent and brooding, and when anyone brought him food he snatched it without a word and turned his face to the wall.

The house being big enough, Uncle Dunstan and Stan stayed the next couple of days in anticipation of the wedding. Corbie was abed, of course, but he was such a surly patient that Dunstan didn't press for many visits; he was, after all, well used to his brother's absence. And between Jedediah's stubbornness and his farriership, both of which Jedediah was quite prepared to demonstrate within the smithy, Dunstan was losing his interest in the conflict between father and son. The lad Jedediah had a neat hand, he was starting to say, and looking at such folks as the Lendens and the Attics and that little Thorpe boy, it couldn't be denied that his neighbours liked him. Not all easy cases either; that Jack Lenden was a headache customer if ever Dunstan had seen one, and yet Jedediah had kept all his children unharmed down the years, and didn't even complain that he'd had to promise to visit him weekly in lieu of living on his land. The more Gyrford folks Dunstan met, the more he took to saying that the holding was in better order than he'd have thought, and the lad must have been working like a mule with an eel up its arse.

As to the business with Corbie and the blinding and all the rest of it, well, it was queer work, but as the lad Jedediah said, that was a fey place all right, and if the land answered better to him than to strangers, that was nothing uncommon. In any case, it was true that Corbie couldn't live crow-plagued in Gyrford, and Jedediah was grown up a strong man. To quarrel him out of his place with things as they now stood would be plain foolish.

It wasn't quite the recognition of a master-work, but Jedediah wasn't pushing his luck. The peace would hold till the wedding, and then Uncle Dunstan would leave.

Pell came to visit Corbie. Dunstan was far from sure that this Smith woman should be allowed to nurse him, as it appeared that she had never been fond of the man, but he did share with Corbie the appreciation of a good opponent.

'I'm here at the asking of my nephew, Dunstan Mackem, and if you don't think him the man of the house, he's more that man than you are,' Pell declared standing in the doorway, her bag of herbs resting over her shoulder like a cudgel. 'And as to physic, I've no time for the opinions of a man who thinks he can cure a woman with an iron prong in her ear. Constance will be deaf in that ear till Doomsday if I'm any judge. And I am. If you'd care to set your physic against mine, I suggest we each take the last cure we tried on some poor soul, and see which of us feels better at the end of it.'

At that, Dunstan actually laughed. 'You're a fierce woman,' he said. 'Pity no man had the courage for you. Pity Corbie didn't, I reckon; you'd have been well able for him.'

'No, thank you,' Pell said. 'I prefer the company of those with sense, and the sons of Adam never did strike me that way. Now, do you mean to stand aside and let me nurse your brother, or must we have words, Dunstan Mackem?'

And up the stairs she went, spent some time with the patient, and returned downstairs with the brusque diagnosis that he needed time to himself, and nobody would regret his company while he was taking it, for she'd seen women torn from one end to the other who sulked less than His Majesty upstairs. And if young Stan here had nothing better to do than stand about and gawp, perhaps he'd draw some water for a thirsty woman.

'High time there was a farrier's lady in this house again,' she said, sitting down at the kitchen table. 'I feel my age, these days.'

'Pell,' Jedediah said, 'you're not five-and-thirty.'

'My lad,' Pell told him, 'between one man's foolery and the next, it's quite enough to make a woman tired.'

It was true, Constance's ear would never recover. On her left side she could hear nothing at all, and her balance was somewhat thrown. She grew prone to falls, and was more than ever glad to stay near Agnes or the Attic children, whose steadiness on their feet helped her keep a sense of which way was up. But though the pain of her wounds distressed her enough that Pell ordered Tom Attic to mix up his best draughts and keep her asleep a few days, the deafness didn't. The world was full of hurtful noises, cries of pain and snaps of conflict, and though Constance felt much safer at the Attics', it proved a comfort to her that she could turn one side towards upsetting things, close her eyes and not have to hear more than she could bear. Quite soon the Attics started talking about her 'shield ear' rather than her 'deaf ear', and Constance began to sleep on her right side, with a silent world, empty of trouble, covering her like a soft, warm blanket.

*

The bells rang the wedding of Jedediah Smith and Louise Ditton, startling the crows from their trees, and nothing swooped down upon anybody's face. Corbie was not at the church, but it was understood that he was too sick, so the best-meaning of the parish thought it a sad pity. The worst-meaning might have had more suspicions, but these were hard to stand to when, on returning to the smithy house to witness the parson bless the bed, the door to what had been Corbie's bedroom was standing open, his possessions gone and a letter on the sheets that read as follows:

Not being a man of letters, I, Caleb Smith, known as Corbie Mackem, will have it known that I mean to travel. Until such time as I return, I expect the forge to be held by my son Jedediah Smith. A settled life has been uneasy for me and I present this to him as my wedding gift, for what good it may do him. Perhaps I may stop in time to time at my home in Tinsdowne, but I am not best pleased with my kin for how they did me in marriage, and do not mean to stay in one place. My wife may remarry if she likes, and any man may marry her if he dares. I shall take no shares from my son as I mean to keep myself and not live by charity. This has been written at my word by one who knows the pen, but none need expect any further letter, for it has never been my way, nor that of those of my name.

Jedediah, who was a little edgy already because he really didn't want the parson messing around with his marriage-bed and had had quite enough cheerful jokes over the past couple of days about keeping the coals hot and so forth, read the letter, astonished. It was like Corbie, he thought, to make his generosities as ungracious as possible. Resist a whipping and get a journeyman's wages; defend your mother and get a smithy – but don't think I like you any the better for it.

Louise, flowers in her hair, sitting on the bed surrounded by Gyrford girls with whom she had started to make friends, looked to him for an explanation. She'd made much of his lessons, but the Berretts had allowed her little time to practise and she was still slow at reading. He could teach her more now; he'd been teaching Franklin behind Corbie's back, and all of a sudden there was no one around to shout at them.

'Well,' Jedediah said, handing the letter to the parson to read to everyone, 'I reckon he can do as he pleases. We'll have more money than we planned for, mind.'

Louise gave the slightest shrug, not looking inclined to question a gift. Bless the girl, she kept her hands folded on her lap, knowing that however much he wanted her touch, he didn't want it before the parson and his congregation. Tom was doing his best to deflect some of the ribaldry – any neighbour who can resist the chance to joke about how well a literate bridegroom knows the pen must be a strong soul indeed – but he was distracted by Tippit Jennings, a friend of Louise, who had red-gold hair and sparkling eyes and a beautiful laugh he was trying to set off as much as possible, and no young man wants to look an entire prude before such a girl. And perhaps it was for the best: some folks looked sorry Corbie was gone, but to was hard to stay regretful amidst raucous merrymaking.

'I didn't marry you for money,' Louise said softly, But if anyone can put it to good use, it'll be my own man.'

He gazed at her, her green eyes full of light, her slow, sweet smile. He'd had enough of strife and all he wanted to think about, just in that moment, was when all his good, kind neighbours would be so good and kind as to go away, so he could kiss his wife.

He sent letters to Tinsdowne over the years; if Corbie stopped in, Uncle Dunstan could find someone to read them to him. The first was simple:

Dear Father,

I hope this letter will find you in good health and that you will have no trouble to find someone who can read it to you.

I write to tell you that you have a grandson. Louise and he are well. The boy is strong and full of health and most fine in body and temper, and we have baptised him Matthew. The name is his mother's choice and I think it a good one. He looks much like her and it suits him.

The work is in hand and you need not worry. I wish you joy of your travels.

Your respectful son,

JS

He waited anxiously – he did not want his father anywhere near his new little son – but Corbie didn't come. Neither did he write back. Jedediah wrote now and again, always adding that the work was in hand and there was no need to help. He didn't admire his father's lack of interest, especially when it came to Matthew, who was exceptionally interesting, but it did make life easier.

Dunstan Mackem and Jedediah did not keep much in touch. There was family news in the letters Jedediah sent: Matthew had learned to walk and talk, and gave the world many proofs of a good disposition; the lad Franklin Thorpe had been apprenticed to a forester and was doing them credit, and Corbie need not fear, for Jedediah had paid the indenture from his own savings; Matthew learned music and tuning most quick, and had been given by Providence a sweeter voice than had been heard in the smithy for some generations, and it would be a fine tool in his work as well as a pleasure to hear. If Dunstan had cared to comment on such matters – which were of great moment to Jedediah, at least – then Dunstan could have done so.

But he didn't, so that was that. Every now and again a traveller through Gyrford would mention the doings at Tinsdowne smithy, and a couple of times carried gifts to Matthew from young Stan Mackem, who appeared to enjoy making whirligigs and spinning tops in his spare time. And that was all.

It was clear that the Mackems did not consider him close kin, not after all that had happened. Jedediah had made himself entirely a Gyrford man and a Smith, and he was to be left to carry on that way. And if that was their conclusion, and it kept Corbie away from Matthew, and Constance, and Franklin, and Louise, and Jedediah, well, why quarrel with a blessing?

Then, one day, he was twenty-seven and Matthew was five, and she died. Louise died.

It was nothing fey. It wasn't even childbirth. It was a winter fever; one day she was herself and happily playing apple-peel with Matthew, and the next day she didn't feel very well, and then a week later, there was a body in the bed, cold and stiff and in need of burial, and Louise wasn't in its eyes. They weren't green any more, but milked over, and her warm, wry smile lolled open, and Jedediah didn't know how to step out of that room and walk out into a vast, dizzying world that didn't contain Louise in any corner of it.

He had to write to Tinsdowne. He watched his hand form the words *Louise is dead*. Corbie didn't reply, but Dunstan's wife Mary Bea, farrier's lady of her own holding, came to visit for a while. She hadn't seen Corbie, it turned out – nobody had; wherever he was, he wasn't interested in the doings of his son – but that didn't stop her taking an authoritative tone with him. She made a lot of observations about how he should let the motherless boy stay with a woman for a while, until Matthew had a chance to 'get used to things'. She wasn't the only one; his Gowan cousins made a similar offer, proposing that a motherless boy might enjoy some time with a bigger family. And Agnes, who was the only one he forgave for it, said that he looked worn-out and if he wanted a rest she'd be glad to take darling Mattie for a little while, bless the sweet lad.

Jedediah felt the words 'motherless boy' like a fist in his gut every time, and every time he drew himself tighter and said that no, he thought the boy should stay with him.

It wasn't that he didn't feel the temptation. If he had been asked – not that anyone was going to ask him what was in his heart any more, or no one he wanted to tell – he would have insisted that it was wrong, that Matthew needed his home; he needed a father who would make it *be* a home for him, even if it was just the two of them left. And it was true. Jedediah would have to do that, every day; he would have to lock up his grief so the boy could stand on his strength without having to wonder if it ever might crack.

Jedediah was exhausted with loss, and if Matthew wasn't there, he could give in to it. He could close the smithy doors and let folks find their own shifts if the People bothered them. He could hitch up his horse and travel somewhere else, somewhere with no memories; he could find an inn or a house and go inside and fix the latch behind him. He could rest. He could lie down and sleep for years, and maybe someday wake up on a morning where he was older and he'd forgotten Louise and wasn't so lost without her.

Or he could get up every day and look after the boy and serve his craft and bear down the condolences, and take every blow and stay on his feet.

It was the harder option, except for Matthew. He couldn't put him with folks who'd make of Matthew a motherless boy. Matthew must be a boy with a father.

Sending his son away would be a betrayal he'd deserve Hell for. He didn't even think it with passion, but with a blank certainty he couldn't find feelings for. If he let Matthew go, it would be so he himself could lie down and die, and he didn't get to do that. This was his life now, and there was no point saying he could bear it, because you could tell the whole cosmos you couldn't bear something and nothing would relent.

There was some talk of Corbie's absence, and the fact that no one had seen him in years, but Jedediah didn't have the space in his heart to worry about it. As long as Corbie wasn't here frightening Matthew, it didn't matter where he was. In some strange woman's bed, most likely, and as long as he didn't bring her to

Gyrford, he was welcome to her. Jedediah was afraid all the time that someone would take Matthew from him. By the time he'd turned away every offer and demand, the gossip about Corbie had lost its freshness.

There was only Matthew, and if Jedediah didn't know how to be the father of a motherless boy, he had to trust that Matthew knew how to be a son. Jedediah got by on asking simple questions they could both understand. *Are you tired? Are you hungry? Does your head ache? Would you like an apple? Did you have a bad dream?* There were answers to those, and answers he could give back: *go to bed; here, eat this; come here, lie down with me for a while.* Other questions, he didn't know how to put: *Can you bear your life? Am I enough for you? You were born good and I'm not what you deserve: what can I do so you'll forgive me?*

It held him together in the end. When Louise was alive, when he'd been happy without even having to work at it, Jedediah had cherished Matthew with an ease that surprised him; other babies were well enough, but Matthew was perfect, and he only worried that the child had so imperfect a father. Now it was different. Matthew was his North, the direction he had to keep himself towards.

He could not think, *Louise*. He had, instead, to say to himself over and over who he was, so he wouldn't stop being who he had to be. *I carry the name Jedediah Smith. I am seven-and-twenty, eight-and-twenty, nine-and-twenty years old. I am a Gyrford man. I am the master of my trade. I live with my son.* When he said it all together like that, when he did not say, *I am widowed*, but, *I live with my son, my son who is my apprentice*, it didn't sound impossible. If he was the same man every day, a man unblurred by complications, Matthew would feel safe, and Jedediah could get through each of the days one at a time until he'd worn a path to walk along.

Corbie wasn't there for any of this, and in those years, Jedediah didn't think of him very much at all. He was tired. Matthew had nightmares, so he took the boy into the bed with him for the first few months; he lay awake, Matthew's small head resting on his arm, and tried to think sensible thoughts. After the nightmares passed, he moved Matthew's things into the master bedroom and moved himself back into the small chamber he'd once slept in as a bachelor. It suited them both: the son got to curl up in a bed that held memories of Louise, and the father didn't have to. The boy would marry one day, was all Jedediah was willing to say to himself, so he might as well have the room now and save trouble later. He gave away the old bed to Franklin, who could do with some property of his own, and set up the box-bed Pell had given. He lay within the wedding gift that had never been a marriage-couch and closed its doors against the silent house. And unless Matthew woke and came knocking, he could lie in the dark, with nothing unbearable to gaze on.

It didn't occur to him that he might re-marry, or not as a real choice. True marriages didn't happen so often in this world that you could expect to find one twice, or not without being a lot easier to love than he was.

He worked through the day until he was so tired he had no choice but to sleep, and that was how he lived until he was used to it.

He wouldn't live like his own father had done. And he was done with being a son; the son of the forge now was Matthew Smith, and Matthew Smith, whatever the cost, would grow to be a happy man.

Old men know their fathers have passed beyond their reach. And before he was thirty, Jed Smith had made himself old.

BOOK FOUR

JOHN

He sat up into the night to write it, and when it was finished, the letter said this:

To Elder Dunstan Mackem, known as Stan Mackem, at the smithy in Tinsdowne. To be read to him by one who can read.

Dear Cousin,

It being that you are now elder and your respected father is in your care, I write to you. Do you give him my respects if you think it good.

I reckon you remember when we were young men that we bore witness to the escape of the fey known as Ab from its chained tree. Also that not long after, my father and your Uncle Caleb Mackem, known as Corbie Mackem, did go to travel and was not seen since.

By unseen mischance, the fey is loose again and the tree broken. I would not trouble you with the haps of my holding, except that from the tree did also come your Uncle Corbie Mackem. It seems he has been pent these twoscore years, and has grown no older in body.

In mind he is something touched, as he sees me and mine as birds, all but Matthew's Janet. This we have as yet found no cure for. It is the work of the fey Ab, which is mighty.

We shall see to the fey. But Corbie is your kin and I would not so fail in respect as to let the news reach you by gossip and not let you hear it from me.

If you wish for his company at Tinsdowne forge, as was once planned when we were young, you may have it.

My respects to you and yours.

Your cousin,

Elder Jedediah Smith

He sat up, the dim glow of his rushlight illuminating the page. Matthew might have phrased it better, and would certainly have written in a finer hand – or he could have, if he hadn't been so hurt.

When Jedediah closed his eyes, he saw again the terrible business of setting Matthew's arms. Strong cider had been needed to loosen the muscles before setting to with the method Jedediah learned from Grandpa Clem: you laid the man face-down, tugged slowly at the disjointed limb, pulled and waited, pulled and waited, moving the shoulder blade as gentle as you could from time to time, until, with a grisly thud, the arm snapped to. If he could have gone for Pell or Tom, they might have had something better than cider for the pain, but he couldn't leave Matthew. Even with men he didn't think were injured doves, Corbie had always planted his foot on the patient and snapped joints back together fast and hard; he'd never had the patience for anything else. He'd tried as much with Matthew, whose proper shape he understood with his hands even if his eyes were sure they saw a dove, and when Franklin, ashen-faced, pulled him away, he'd swatted around himself with hard, random swipes.

Now Franklin had a black eye – another bruise after a lifetime of too many. Jedediah hadn't been in time to protect him, and Franklin was too old now to be comforted by a few kind words and some bread and cheese in the smithy.

So Jedediah wrote the letter. He didn't mention Matthew, arms strapped to his chest, facing bandages for weeks and months unable to hammer – or at least, Jedediah was damned if he'd let Matthew overstrain himself until he was properly healed. That was how you crippled folks.

God help him. His beautiful son.

But he couldn't say that. He couldn't say, *My father would have overlooked my mother to death, and if he doesn't recognise me, he hasn't forgiven me. And my mother is yet alive. I have granddaughters. I have children. My family are not afraid of each other. I made myself the man Corbie wasn't to protect them.*

Take him away, because if he hurts me and mine, I'll have to stop him. And I'm no longer young. I've seen Death take those I love and it can come again to guard those I love; I can bring it about. I never was a killer, Stan, not before now. But I have children, and I know how easily bodies can break.

Corbie came uninvited into the smithy the next day, but it wasn't long before he grew restless. He'd made loud complaints against Janet's cooking, and further complaints about nesting in a rookery with birds every which way and nothing where it should be.

'Hey now!' he roared, when he spotted a young boy waiting near the smithy, staying clear until there were no customers. 'You there, come in here!'

Jack Edmonds was one of a large and threadbare family who had followed the work into Gyrford. All the Edmonds children were on the watch to earn extra pennies, and Jedediah and Franklin often employed them for errands. At the prospect of a job, Jack brightened – only to look a little confused at finding himself under the orders of a stranger.

'That's right, you, lad. I don't see another boy in the square, do you? Just a host of pretty women,' Corbie added, with a wave at the various matrons who'd gathered to gossip, 'and if I gazed too hard at them, so much beauty might blind me.' This raised a laugh from the gathered women, who knew when a man was laying on the butter. 'Now, lad: you know where those pagans live, do you not? Attics by name?'

'Er – I don't know any pagans, sir,' said Jack, tugging his forelock. 'I know Mister Tom Attic and his kin, I do jobs for him sometimes, but—'

'So,' Corbie interrupted, 'have they with them a great lump of a woman, Agnes Smith?'

'Hey now,' Matthew said; he could see where this was going. Jedediah looked frozen in discomfort, which was alarming in itself, and while he didn't like conflict, someone needed to say something. 'Agnes is family to the Attics, sir.' He hadn't quite worked out what to call Corbie yet, not helped by the fact that Corbie never looked him in the face and only half-perceived anything he said. 'She's settled and they rely on her, and it'd be no kindness to any of them to—'

'I,' Corbie cut across him, 'am a man of flesh and blood, and flesh and blood shall not live on the offerings of a woman who can burn and undercook the same bowl of pottage. This place needs a housekeeper, young lad, and I'll have you go and tell Agnes she's to come back.'

'Jack Edmonds, you do and I'll clout you,' said John.

The Smiths all had firm views on threatening those weaker than yourself, which, if you hammered iron, was pretty much everyone your own age, but to John's discomfiture, Jedediah did not chastise. He stood still, staring at Corbie, rubbing his beard with a tense hand.

'Jack,' Matthew said in some haste, 'would you run to – to Anthony Brady's house and carry any message they have there to Franklin Thorpe, there's a good boy? I'll give you ha'pence, only – only you'll have to ask my wife for it, my arms are – well, as you see.'

Jack set off with the alacrity of a lad who saw a better dinner for his family in prospect, but when Matthew met his father's eyes, he saw what they both knew: they'd only delayed the inevitable. Half a dozen women in the square had heard that Corbie wanted Agnes back, and soon enough the news would reach Agnes herself.

'Sir, as to housekeeping,' Matthew attempted, 'I'm sure we can improve. Mostly it's my Molly does the cooking, only she's been busy with Clementing. I'm sure that—'

'Ah, good day, sir!' Corbie boomed. Heading up to the smithy on a fine roan mare came a customer whose appearance made Matthew and Jedediah look at each again.

Piers Gresley was, if you asked John, a good rider who knew how to handle a soft-mouthed horse, but lost a little credit for that because some dry amusement of his own had led him to name his horse Joan. Anyone who chose a horse name because it rhymed with this horse's coat colour was either very stupid or quite tiresome, in John's view, and it was difficult to persuade him to be properly deferential to the man.

Which was unfortunate, because Joan the Roan's owner was, in fact, a magistrate. Franklin testified before him all the time, watching out for poachers being part of his job. Franklin had a natural sympathy for those who must get their food where they could, and it was one of the more wearing aspects of his life to keep up the pretence that he was near-sighted and couldn't say for sure that the shivering wretch before the bench was the man seen committing a capital crime in his Lordship's woods.

Franklin, in short, was not Piers Gresley's favourite forester, and towards Jedediah and Matthew, both of whom also testified from time to time when an inquest had to deal with incidents by 'means mysterious', Piers felt nothing more than grudging respect. Jedediah as an expert witness was short-spoken, resistant to cross-examination and only as courteous to the magistrate as he was to anyone else, while Matthew was so earnest in his efforts to speak the whole and unadulterated truth, so help him God, that he could equivocate past anyone's patience – especially when he too was reluctant to see a man hang. Piers Gresley bought his cold iron from the Smiths because their work was beyond question, but theirs was, at best, a relationship of mutual tolerance.

Confronted with Corbie, Piers Gresley turned to Jedediah with a certain twist to his lips. 'Farrier business, Elder Smith?' he said.

'That's Elder Mackem, good sir,' Corbie said, his voice raising in aggressive cheer, 'though you may Smith me if you like, for I did marry to the name, may God forgive me. If you've a liking to hearing your questions answered quick, though, I'd commend you to Mackem it, for I never did quite break in to that harness.'

'How's that?' Gresley's wry look changed to the kind of bland imperturbability that a magistrate tends to adopt when he doesn't wish his subordinates to think that events are getting ahead of him.

'Corbie Mackem, sir, at your service,' Corbie said, with a flourish of his hand. 'The world may be out of joint, but Corbie Mackem I am, and that's for sure.'

'Is it shoeing you need today, Piers Gresley, or have you need of more?' Jedediah cut in, as civil as he could; he did not need the magistrate deciding they were all mad. Fairy-smithing was an old and honoured trade, and both church and state distinguished it from malefic work and other witcheries, but Piers Gresley was book-learned and of good estate, and such men tended to be out of touch with the earth from which the need for fairy-smithing sprang. Nobody had taken a farrier for a witch in recent memory, but it was best not to antagonise the men of law.

'She's cast a shoe,' Gresley said – but he said it to both of them. 'And I don't like the knots on the leg that cast it, so look her over, so please you. Elder Smith, some cousin of yours?'

Jedediah sighed, and tried to restrain his anger that Matthew had been standing in Piers Gresley's sight for the entire conversation, bandaged like a parcel, and Gresley had not bothered to ask how he was. 'My father,' he said, just keeping this side of peremptory. 'He went down some fey path when he went a-journeying, and now he's back. Can't take in what I say, though, nor Matthew, nor Matthew's young ones. Got some touch on him and thinks us birds.'

'Well, glory be to God,' Piers Gresley said, with something close to real warmth. 'I congratulate you, Mister Smith. You must be most glad at this reunion. I wish you quick fortune in putting to flight the troubles of his mind.'

That was high folks for you: always assuming it was no strain to untangle the impossible. Jedediah concentrated on that thought so he didn't have to consider how to answer the assumption that he'd be pleased to see his father. Or to notice that Piers Gresley had addressed him as 'Mister' Smith, not 'Elder'.

'Hop you down, sir, you can pray as well on your feet as on your saddle,' Corbie said. It was a rash way to speak to a magistrate, but he said it with a kind of easiness that Jedediah had never been able to manage, and Piers Gresley took it for pleasant village manners.

'Come along, my beauty,' Corbie told Joan, taking the reins. His voice was firm but warm; there was a kind of joyfulness in the way he spoke to animals that he'd never shown at home, and he reached, with timeworn precision, to the exact spot on her withers that every horse wishes a man to scratch. In no time, Joan was putting her nose to his, exchanging breaths and showing every sign of a mare thoroughly courted.

'Well,' Piers Gresley told Jedediah, 'there's a pair of hands you'll be glad to have in your smithy and no mistake. I'll be back for her in an hour. I suppose you'll leave your new contract to the parish church's keeping and not mine?'

'Sir?' said Matthew. He didn't mind being ignored – being

trussed up this way felt rather ridiculous – but he saw Jedediah's face go dead and someone needed to ask the question.

'Well, your grandfather never resigned his eldership, did he?' Piers Gresley said. He had the unfortunate habit of looking up the official records of every man who regularly testified before him. 'Not formally; from what I understand it was only left to your father *pro tem*. It'll be Elder Mackem's smithy by law. Sorry to see the hazards of your trade have worked you about so, Mister Matthew, by the by. And no doubt an elder who can't hear his underlings will make life interesting for you, but then, an underling who can't hear his elder is worse.'

'What!' John burst in. 'It's not his smithy, it's – it's everyone's.' He gestured towards his family. Of course the forge was *held* by Grandpa, but that was just a question of who got to order who around. *Owning* the place was like trying to own a slice of sky.

'Another Smith who's no lawyer,' Piers Gresley remarked. 'I'll see you in a – hey now, mind your manners, man!' He'd been turning to go, but he'd bumped into Bill Morey, who was regarding the business with jolly curiosity.

Bill was supposed to be a cobbler's journeyman, and he could patch a shoe pretty well, but he was also of a lively disposition and enjoyed testing his sole-work by wandering around and bothering folks. His workshop was, in his view, primarily a place to gather gossip and make jokes that distinguished the little hammer he worked with from the bigger hammer his female customers might like to play with. The smithy, which contained many customers to chat with, and even more opportunities to compare hammer sizes, was one of his favourite haunts, and while he wasn't especially beloved there – the Smiths didn't care for men who pestered women the way Bill did – he was a cousin-in-law of Franklin Thorpe's, and could not be dissuaded from assuming himself welcome.

'Oh my,' Bill said, bowing with a happy lack of regret. 'No insult meant, sir, no insult meant. Can hardly see my nose in front of my face, some days. Now then, Matthew, what's all the wrappings?' He indicated both Matthew's bandaged shoulders. 'Giving the wife something more of a challenge to get you undressed? Good, good, never will do to let a woman stop working to please a fellow.'

Matthew felt stung. For a start, it was unfair to Janet, who could never be accused of sexual laziness, but today he was also depressed about his love life. He and Janet had always agreed very well and she was eager to comfort him for his wounds, but last night he had been far too sore to enjoy her attempts. It was dawning on him that the smithy was not the only place he'd have to spend months being careful, and for an active man this was a truly sad prospect.

Corbie, however, called back with enthusiasm, 'Let 'em remember what they were made for, eh?' A couple of women in the square looked a little put out at this, but others laughed with the amused forbearance that comes from accepting that men are men.

While he spoke, Corbie was running his hand down Joan's shoeless leg with casual ease; Joan, so pleased with his company that she didn't even twitch when he shouted, gave a little snort of relief. 'Aha!' Corbie exclaimed, reaching back for a pair of pincers. 'Well, our fine and high man was right about you, wasn't he, my lass? Look what we have here.'

'Have you business here, Bill Morey?' Jedediah asked, not feeling strong enough for this. Piers Gresley was right: Corbie never had formally resigned the smithy. At best, he'd left it in Jedediah's keeping. As Gresley had mentioned it so calmly, Jedediah had felt his blood run so cold that his teeth ached.

'Ach, I don't suppose you mind me greeting a new friend,' Bill said, while John ducked under his arm, crouching beside Corbie and staring at his work with intent eyes.

Corbie had discovered an elf-knot just above Joan's fetlock. It was small, barely the size of a bean; whatever had nested there hadn't had much length of hair to work with. John was a little surprised the man had found it so quickly; of course, he'd trained Grandpa and Grandpa would have found it just as fast, but nothing about this new Corbie reminded him of either Grandpa or Dada.

'Now, what have we here?' Corbie said, working the pincers through the knot with a neat touch. 'Tell you what, friend of mine,' he added to Bill Morey, 'here's a lass who keeps her secrets well beneath her coat. Send your wife to her and tell her to take lessons.'

Bill laughed hard, less because the joke was funny than because he was pleased to find such jokes within the smithy at all. None of the Smith men minded a little bawdy commentary, but Jedediah was very stern with men who traduced women and Bill felt it could get rather too pious in there.

'Great-Grandpa,' John said, tugging at his sleeve, then stopped. 'No, that takes too long to say, I'll call you Uncle Corbie. Uncle Corbie, listen.' There was definitely something within the lock, something huddled and anxious. It didn't feel malevolent to him, and as Corbie drew it forth – a narrow wisp of a spirit, rather bigger than the knot it had hidden within, with multiple little arms and a face rather like a crumpled owl – it thrashed like a worm on a hook.

'Less of the peck, Magpie,' Corbie said, shouldering him off. 'Now, then, here's mischief.'

'It's not mischief.' John felt rather breathless; Grandpa might scold him, but at least he listened. Corbie might not quite understand that John was talking to him, but he showed some awareness of the things said in his presence. It was just that John's defence of the fey didn't interest him. 'I don't think it's wicked, Uncle Corbie,' he persisted. 'I've seen fey like this before – they mostly nest in teasel-heads.'

'Have you, Johnny?' Matthew asked, interested.

John, who investigated fey things any time folks took their eyes off him, nodded quickly for the sake of manners, though it felt more urgent to talk to Corbie. 'I reckon Joan must have stepped on one and got it caught on her like a burr,' he said. 'If we find it a teasel, or just a field where they grow, I reckon we can—'

The crack made everyone jump. Corbie, without any indication he'd heard John, dropped the spirit on the anvil, where it thrashed like a salted slug until he slammed a punch, flat end downwards, onto the thing's shrieking face.

There was a small burst of light and the fey's body scattered into sparks. The scream echoed, a dissonant chord within the slam of metal on metal, but the smithy walls were lined with tools and the sound soon withered against them.

'Well, *that's* something like!' Bill Morey exclaimed. 'Never saw a quicker job, nor a brighter. Tell me I'm wrong about *this*, eh, Ida?' From among the women in the square he singled out Ida Pearce, one of Gyrford's more censorious matrons, who directed her smile of approval to the despatchful Mister Mackem rather than waste it on Bill.

'Tell you what, mister,' Bill went on, 'there's been a something in my thatch for a while; chatters away about butter-churns whenever I knock the ceiling. Your fine fellow here' – he indicated Jedediah, who was standing very still – 'told me not to waste my time on it as long as it didn't do any harm, but I tell you what: a man can hear enough about butter-churns, and I say it's harming my temper. What say you come out and see to it? Never mind what Brother Matthew says here.'

'He – he's not my brother,' Matthew said, trying to get past; John was standing there ready to overspill with tears, and Matthew didn't know what to do – he couldn't hug his son, and he couldn't tell him not to be upset, not when he was upset too. The creature in the elflock hadn't looked wicked to him either.

'He's my father.' Jedediah spoke with something like rawness in his voice, but then he stopped, made it flat again. 'Might as well know, Bill Morey, Ida Pearce, all of you; the world will hear it soon enough, and sooner still if you give it tongue left and right. He got lost with the People for a while, but now he's back. Corbie Mackem: that's who he is.'

'Well, *there's* a wonder!' Bill exclaimed, overjoyed. 'I'm glad to welcome you back to Gyrford – some time you must tell me about the ladies of fairyland, sir. Hey there, Sir Manners!' Piers Gresley was passing through the square again; evidently he was taking the chance to make business calls while he was here. 'You'll never guess how fast Elder Mackem here settled the Good Neighbour plaguing your horse, sir!'

John didn't want Corbie to see him cry, so he went for a long walk. He didn't even bother to make an excuse; Corbie was only half taking in what they said, and only acknowledging anything when he cared to.

The skies were pale and empty; the swallows and swifts had already fled the coming winter. Folks said they buried themselves in the mud under ponds to sleep the cold months out, but John had his doubts on that: he'd watched the local ponds all his life, but never a bird had obliged him. On the contrary, Godfa Tom Attic said his dada used to see them in the Africs come December, so perhaps there was some fairy-way up in the sky that helped them travel so impossible a distance. John truly wished to know, and he felt that it must be possible to ask the birds, but he hadn't contrived a way yet, and anyway, autumn wasn't the season for it.

The trouble was, it didn't appear to be the season for other birds either. There should be robins, bramblings, black-capped tits and round little dunnocks chirping, but no matter how starey he got, he couldn't see a bird anywhere.

John walked, thinking he might drop some bread at a fox-hole he'd found lately; he knew foxes were pests and chicken-killers, but he still had a wish to make friends. As he found the place, though, things were queer: there was a scraping around the edges, more finely scored than a fox-claw would produce, and within the earth was a rustling. John crouched, tossed the crust he'd saved and waited in silence. He was good at that; too good for comfort, if you asked some folks, for if things got intriguing he could stay still for a moment without time, only realising his legs were cramped and he needed to piss when someone disturbed him.

Gazing into the brown shadows, he waited.

There was no saying how long it was before the creature inside decided to take the risk. There was a little patter, and something emerged from the fox-hole.

For a moment, John's heart lifted: perhaps it was the black paw of the vixen, come to accept his good will – but, no, it was too sharp, and then it blinked and resolved into a crow. The bird crept forward, a cautious, spur-heeled stride, its eyes not on the bread, but on the sky above.

John stayed still, making no sound.

The crow snatched at the crust and scurried back into the hole, not using its wings for speed but trotting at a pace that should have been comical. But there was something about it that stilled any laughter John might have felt.

If the fox was still in there, it would surely have eaten the crow; foxes ate anything, and certainly wouldn't refuse a mouthful of meat that invited itself into their very nest. And just last week the fox had been there.

He'd never heard of a crow driving a fox from its hole, not outside the kind of moral tales that Matthew enjoyed and John found illogical. A bird would have to show the frenzy of desperation to do it – or have something after it that the fox was too wise not to flee.

A crow nesting underground. It might be that birds wintered

in burrows, but crows were a year-long bird – and he didn't think that was what he'd seen.

Agnes Smith hadn't been to Gyrford's square since she was a young woman. She didn't like to complain, so all she would say was that she knew her nephew had many folks to think of and she wouldn't like to get in his way. Tom and Jedediah both knew well enough what she meant by this: the Gyrford smithy drew strangers from around the county, and not all of them were polite enough to refrain from gaping at her ox's shoulders.

Those who knew her had always liked her looks. Even a more commonly built woman than Agnes would have felt plain growing up beside Constance Smith, but in truth, Agnes had a sweet face, and as an old woman she wore her wrinkles as gently as a silken wrap. But she didn't like to be stared at and was more comfortable with dear Tom and his family, caring for Constance and making herself useful in any little way she could, safe in the knowledge that she'd see no one who thought her mis-made.

Jedediah had meant to stand against dragging her back here. She was as much an Attic as she'd ever been a Smith and she deserved her peace. But the next day, as soon as the gossip reached her, Agnes wrapped herself in the biggest shawl she had and set off on her own.

Corbie was a late riser for a working man. As Agnes entered the square, her walk the same long-legged, diffident scuttle it had been in her youth, she saw only the Smith men in the forge, and on the bench beside it, Molly and her best friend Mary Anne Morgan, who had come to ask Molly if she could help at all. Agnes saw Mary Anne only occasionally, but she was inclined to love anyone who was pleasant to dear Jedediah and his young ones.

'Good day to you, Mary Anne, dear,' she said, taking Molly's hand and stroking it. 'What a treat to see you. Why, you've grown up most pretty, dear, *most* pretty.'

Mary Anne was a little shy and not used to compliments full of such awkward directness; she couldn't think of anything to say but, 'Thank you, Mistress, that's – that's kind to say.'

'Why, thank you, dear,' Agnes said, in delighted relief at being greeted with a compliment. 'My, what a good girl.'

'How do you, Auntie?' Molly said, standing up and kissing her. She was familiar with Aunt Agnes' ways; her life of retirement, revolving mostly around the care of Constance, had left her a little out of practice talking to folks who needed less reassurance than Constance did. Molly had adored her when she was little, for Agnes' manner was very well suited to small children, and while the twins were still young enough to find her fussing tiresome, Molly was growing back into seeing the kind intentions behind it.

'Well, darling, this is . . .' Agnes, unable to find words that would neither insult Corbie nor dismiss Molly, gave the sentence up. 'How are you, my dear? How do you bear things?'

'Auntie.' Jedediah came out of the smithy, cleaning his hands and full of concern. 'I didn't look for you here. I thought we could find some meeting-place better suited to your comfort.'

'Oh, dear, I hope I'm not underfoot,' Agnes said. She was bigger than Jedediah, but held herself folded down in a way that made it easy to overlook this.

'No, no,' Jedediah said in haste, 'of course I'm glad to see you. I just don't like to see you put out.'

'Well, dear . . .' Agnes looked around in discomfort. 'Mister Mackem would see me, and – well, he could come to Tom's house on his own if he grew hasty. He never was a man to keep waiting.'

She was absolutely right. Jedediah had just hoped that after four decades living as the favourite auntie of the Attic clan, she'd not have remembered so fast how you needed to jump between Corbie and Constance.

'Well, I'm glad to see you,' was all he could find to say.

'Oh, Mattie darling!' Agnes exclaimed, catching sight of Matthew, who was still wearing bandages. 'Oh, you poor *dear*! Oh, dear, I heard something of this, but I did hope folks might have – have remembered the tale worse than it was. You poor *love*!' She reached out to him, but her arms locked mid-air, still as rocks, and after a moment she let them drop. 'Well, darling, I reckon you're too sore to hug, you poor boy,' she said sorrowfully. 'I've some salve for you, and a pot of Tom's tincture for the pain. That is, I took them, and I'm sure he won't mind – oh dear, Jedediah, I hope you don't think I've overstepped?'

Jedediah had opened his mouth to reassure her when the door crashed open.

'Well, well!' Corbie's voice was a blare of satisfaction. 'I see there's guests today!'

Agnes stood, head lowered a little, hands holding each other tight, waiting for him to speak to her, but Corbie took in her posture and, with an irritated grin, turned his attention to the bench.

'Well, good day to you, Princess,' he said, making a bow to Mary Anne. 'I thought someone'd taken the sight from my eyes for a moment and I dreamed you, for never did I see such hair as yours. Why, there's butterflies just out of their silken cocoons would see the silk on your head and forsake their freedom, just to land upon you. You should be crowned with them, I swear.'

Mary Anne did indeed have unusually fair hair, but she'd also had an angry father and wasn't fond of loud voices. 'I . . . thank you, sir,' she said, standing up to curtsey. 'Molly and I were just about to . . .'

'Oh, now don't let my poor manners chase you away,' Corbie said, sounding wheedling.

Agnes stood still, waiting for him to address her.

'Mister Mackem!' Janet hastened from the house. 'Good day, dear,' she added to Mary Anne, and seeing the girl's distressed blush, said, 'Mister Mackem, you can reckon your age at eight-and-thirty, or you can reckon your age at eight-and seventy, but that's a girl of seventeen, and at either age you'd be acting the old goat. I'd hoped for better sense from you.'

'Shrew,' Corbie said, somewhere between enjoyment and rancour.

Matthew scowled; he regarded his Janet as brave and hated it when men didn't admire her for it, but wrapped and doved as he was, he couldn't think of anything useful to do.

'An ill-mannered old goat at that,' Janet went on. 'Here's Agnes Smith, the good woman, come all the way to see you, and do you intend to greet her like a Christian?'

'God help us,' Corbie said, 'but you've a tongue on you like a flail, woman. I'll tell you what: once Agnes has settled back in with her piss-poor housekeeping, you'll find yourself another roof to rail under. At least one of you knows when to shut her mouth.'

'I – I'd be glad of Janet's help, Mister Mackem,' Agnes said in a quick murmur. 'I'm sure it'd be an ease to you, once – once things were settled.'

'Ah, so we're to have no fuss at your coming back?' Corbie said. 'Well, well, I reckon some things do come easy in life. Not the things we want, alas for us, but what we can, we do.'

'Mister Mackem,' Janet said, and Jedediah tried to catch her eye; taking this tone with Corbie never ended well. Janet was too angry to notice: Mary Anne was a pet of hers, and she was very fond of Aunt Agnes as well. 'You'll mind your manners, if you please. You may think me a shrew if you like, but Agnes deserves better, for if ever God made a virtuous woman it was Agnes Smith, and on the subject of virtue, Mary Anne there neither asks nor likes your attentions, so if you must court without care . . .' She had meant to be firmly reasonable, but she had a headache, her husband was injured and so absorbed in trying not to complain that he was hardly talking to her at all, and Father was looking pale and tense and sometimes her tongue ran away with her. 'Then,' she finished, 'I suggest you seek your similars, and to that end, the neighbours down the lane have a sow penned in their yard – and I hope you catch the ringworm.'

'Do you know, Princess,' Corbie added chattily, 'I had a sister-in-law could call on crows – birds of all sorts. She showed me a bit, back in the times gone by; you don't remember Mabbie Smith, do you?'

'N-no sir,' Mary Anne said, shrinking back a little. She'd heard as much gossip as everyone, and the word was that Mister

Mackem was a splendid farrier and pleasant in his manners. In this light, it was hard to excuse the anxiety she felt as his eyes ransacked her body.

'Such a noise it was,' Corbie said. He gave just a glance to Janet: clear-eyed, almost mischievous, as if he had a pleasant prank in store for her. '*Kra, kra, kra* – you never heard the like. Of course, she could sing prettier songs too. I always liked a robin's tune, but she said they weren't for singing, for robins fight each other worse than barn-cats, and with more swearing besides.'

'Mama . . .' John had been standing silent through this whole exchange, but that *Kra, kra, kra* was troubling him: it wasn't fey, exactly; Uncle Corbie looked remarkably mortal for a man who'd been locked up in a tree for so long. But it was too accurate. John had known men who liked to mimic bird calls, but Uncle Corbie could outmatch them all.

Grandpa and Dada assumed that the bird business was just a fey touch, as whimsical as anything else the People did. But John didn't think the People went by whims, or at least, not without some kind of cause.

Give them the crow-killer so they do not flee, Ab had said. *Make them take us back.*

Us.

And then Ab had seen Dada put iron around Uncle Corbie's neck and had taken it for harm.

Break not your heart. You shall not know your kin.

It came together too fast, making John pant with dismay. Ab had given Uncle Corbie one of its gifts: the gift of being spared the painful knowledge that his family were the kind of men who'd put iron on someone. The People hated iron, and Ab, by the sounds of it, had always had trouble distinguishing what it wanted from what you did.

So it had taken that knowledge out of Uncle Corbie's head, and so thoroughly that a few other things had gone with it, like the fact that Corbie's kin weren't birds. It had pulled out the Smiths' humanity along with their kinship, like a careless gardener tugging up clumps of soil along with the weeds.

But it had had a preference for crows, a wish to be taken in by them – though not a requited wish, if the crows were braving fox-dens to hide from it. He hadn't seen a single crow in the sky.

Ab loved crows, and Ab would not have borne with a fellow-prisoner it knew to be a man of iron.

So what was Uncle Corbie to do? There were crows in there, and there was nothing to do but be one of them. Ab was muddled in its thinking, and if Uncle Corbie could sound like a crow, even a little bit, it might accept him as one himself – or at least, as something like Ab, a would-be crow who wasn't to blame if he didn't get it quite right.

John almost stopped on that thought, but then another came loose, worse than before: Uncle Corbie had made Aunt Mabbie train the birds to entice Ab. Before she'd left Gyrford for good, he'd heard her coax the crows.

And what could be simpler, in the tongue of a bird, than to say, *Come to me*?

'Mama, get inside!' John shouted. The air above them was flexing.

There were feathers then, twists of black draggled as hair, and something struggled down towards them. It wasn't a crow;

there were eyes to it, black and craving, and wires of darkness squirmed around it in an airborne pulse that moved closer, closer to them all. John stared wildly up, and the sky beat like wings.

'Heaven help us,' Corbie said, quite calmly. 'Agnes, do mind yourself.'

The sound he made then was almost clearing his throat – that was what Mary Anne heard, and anyone else Corbie chose to wield this power before. It certainly wasn't anything like a command: *Cast yourself on the one I name.*

Janet wasn't in the smithy yet, she was ushering Molly and Mary Anne ahead of her, for Mary Anne had frozen in fear and Molly wouldn't go without her. John was so busy trying to hurry them that he didn't see, until it was too late, where the blackness was aimed.

Uncle Corbie's eyes rested on Mama, bright blue, quite steady, with the relish of one outplaying a friendly challenger – as the thing landed, talons bared, on Agnes' shoulders. The impact made no sound, but it struck so hard that it knocked her to her knees.

I must have my friend. The voice spoke through the bones of everyone in the square. Doors were starting to open, folks staring out from homes or shops, witnessing a dreadful attack by one of the People upon a mortal woman.

'Molly, Mary Anne, stay back!' Matthew yelled. 'Johnny, fetch a punch, one of the finer ones – Janie, Janie don't—!' For Janet had run straight to Agnes, trying with all her strength to pull the thing loose.

Ab writhed against Agnes' back, for Janet's wedding ring had a core of iron to it, but it was only a narrow strip and it hadn't the power to move the great clamping mass of what was digging themselves into Agnes' ageing skin.

Jedediah was at the smithy wall, taking down tools. His hands worked without thought, selecting a torc, narrow tongs, a set of clippers – he'd have to pick the thing up strand by strand and cut it like a net. Feeling had drained out of him; he couldn't afford it. It hadn't happened since he was a child, but here he was again. He just needed to get the tools to cut the—

'Hey now, kind friend!' It was Corbie's voice, so loud that the silence after it rang like a bell.

Everyone stopped. Ab stopped. Agnes shuddered, her arms pulled backwards, the grappling mess across them suddenly still.

'That's enough now,' Corbie said. He cleared his throat again, or did something like it, but nothing anyone human could understand. After that, he reached into his pocket and pulled something out – a bullroarer, Jedediah saw, a plain wooden one on a short thong, and he swung it in the air, circling it over Agnes' head like a censer.

The sound was a sharp-edged drone, and everyone watching would swear that it was this that made the thing release Agnes Smith; no matter John Smith saying that by the time Corbie swung his instrument, Ab was already gone. They knew what they'd seen.

Agnes lay clutching her torn shawl, frantic to cover up her back, her powerful shoulders that she tried all her life to hide now bared to the world.

'Glory be!' someone exclaimed – Parson Green, by his voice.

'A prayer of thanks, good friends, for our good helper Mister Mackem.'

Jedediah stood very still, watching the world pray for good Corbie Mackem, who saved a poor touched woman from horrors.

John pulled on his sleeve, whispering, 'Grandpa? Grandpa!'

Jedediah patted his shoulder; he had a pretty good idea what the boy was going to tell him. And no doubt he'd have worked out some fey explanation for how Corbie had done it; John was clever that way. Jedediah would have to listen to him, but in this moment he didn't need an explanation. It was there in Corbie's white-blue eyes, fixed cheerfully on Janet, with the good humour of a man who has, fair and clear, bested his opponent.

Bodies can break, Jedediah thought. *Neighbours all around and they never saw who he was. I don't want to be a murderer, but I don't know what to do. Please, God, give me some other idea.*

Agnes moved into the smithy house without a word of complaint. So far Mister Mackem hadn't said anything about Constance, and her hope was that if she didn't say anything, he wouldn't think to.

As Corbie sat in the smithy, delighting passing customers before his increasingly silent son and grandson, John slipped off to the kitchen, where Molly was showing Agnes where things were kept these days.

'Johnny, darling,' Agnes said as she saw him, 'how do you bear up, sweeting?'

'Mostly I'm sorry for you,' John said. 'You know, Molly cooks much better than Mama. If you wanted to take some time to be with Granny, you could just go and Molly could cook. I don't think Uncle Corbie would know the difference.'

'Well, thank you, John Smith,' Molly said. 'I always did want a little brother to speak on my behalf.' Molly was in fact very attached to Johnny, who was a tender and affectionate brother when he wasn't being high-handed, but some day he'd be elder farrier. Molly held the increasing suspicion that she didn't want to marry: a husband and children just meant more folks to cook for. She was thinking more and more that what she'd really like was to train for something independent; perhaps Aunt Pell would teach her midwifery. But if that were the case, the man in her life ordering her around would be Johnny, and she felt it would be a good idea to make sure he didn't get too full of himself.

'I only meant—' John objected.

'I will cook for you, Auntie,' Molly said in haste, turning back to Agnes. 'Of course I will. I can tell him you've gone for this or that if he asks where you are. I just reckon that if it's my work, then there are boys in the house who need to let me offer on my own account.'

'Well, aren't you a pair of dears?' Agnes said, anxious to pacify any bickering, and Molly gave her a hug.

From beyond the kitchen, the rookery tree creaked. Its inhabitants had been Gyrford residents for generations, but the nests today were bare.

'Mind you,' John said, in answer to his own train of thought, 'his birding isn't foolish. Take Grandpa: if he's like any bird he *is* like a rook, isn't he?'

'I wish you didn't think that,' said Molly dolefully. Uncle

Corbie had dubbed her Sparrow. While Molly was one of the prettiest Smith women if you went purely by features, she had little admiration for her own looks: she was the sensible one to whom fell most of the dull responsibilities around the house. She couldn't *stop* being sensible, because if she did they probably wouldn't get regular dinners, but it wasn't the identity she'd have chosen for herself and she was rather hurt that Uncle Corbie had picked so very dowdy a bird.

'I don't know why you should mind,' John said, giving her a comforting pat; he was rather proud of her good sense, which he saw as a kind of cunning instinct. 'Sparrows are the pleasantest of birds – they're kind to each other, and even help each other at their nests.'

Molly felt herself accurately observed and thoroughly depressed. 'He should name himself, then,' she said with oblique resentment. 'Isn't Corbie supposed to mean crow? But none of the crows want him.'

John nodded; they knew that because they'd met a travelling man from the North once who'd called the crows pecking in the square 'corbies'.

'I don't think there's much to it,' he said. 'All the Mackems give nicknames. Most likely they just heard the word and thought it a funny shortening for Caleb, and that made him think of crows when it came time to trick Ab.'

'Well,' Molly said, 'I like rooks better. And I wish they'd come back.'

John missed the rooks too; he also couldn't help suspecting that with more birds about Corbie might be warier, and less likely to hurt poor Auntie.

'You're not . . .' he began, then changed his mind. He'd been about to say that she wasn't unlike a rook either, by which he meant she was clever and helpful, but he remembered just in time that she might not take it as he'd intended. 'If you were a rook, Molly,' he tried instead, 'where would you fly off to these days?'

'Ab's wood, I suppose,' Molly said; it was a typical Johnny question, but not, to her mind, a very difficult one. 'Ab wouldn't like to be back there; no one likes a place they suffered. I'd go where Ab wasn't.'

John stood, kissed Molly on the ear – he was aiming for her cheek, but too preoccupied to hit the mark – and went off. He forgot to say goodbye, but Molly was used to that happening when John had a thought in his head. She sighed, tucked her sensible brown shawl around her sensible brown dress and went back to her duties, stepping a little quietly in the hopes that she and Aunt Agnes could work together without Uncle Corbie hearing their conversation and bursting in to chuckle at them.

The fence around the trees was almost a sight of home to John. Dada had worked it, and the lines, simple curves with a grace to them like the rib of a leaf, were almost like hearing his voice. John hadn't realised how upset he was about Dada's injuries until he found himself looking at the fence; the woods were right there beyond him, with an odd, corrugated feel to the air like nothing he'd ever scented, and he really was interested, but he kept staring at the ironwork. Dada must have worked for weeks to make so many of them. They were so even, so carefully done; Dada had a way of bringing the hammer down with the force of a felled tree, but so precise and steady in his movement that it wasn't fearsome to watch, but calming.

John realised he was sniffling a little, which was quite beneath his dignity, even if it was just him there. Dada said that disjointed arms mended quicker than broken ones; that God willing, and if he was careful, he'd be quite all right in no time. And Grandpa said if Matthew wasn't careful to rest then he'd chain him to the lintel, and if that didn't work, he'd go to the magistrate and blame him for every petty crime in the county to get him safely locked in the stocks for the next three months.

Three months was a long time to worry about your mauled father.

John braced his foot against the fence to hoist himself aloft and was almost over when he felt a pinch on his ear so hard that, for a moment, he could hardly see or hear: his entire world filled up with the grip of iron fingers dragging him away from the woods.

'Get *off*, Aunt Pell!' he shouted. 'Even Grandpa would—'

But then, still gripping his ear, the hand jerked him upright and he saw, staggering, that it wasn't Aunt Pell at all. It was a tall man, his hair a warm grey and his eyebrow quirked up over a fierce, amused smile. So like Corbie Mackem in the face was he that John, confused by the pain, almost called him by that name – but no, he was older, threescore or so, and he looked at John with a sternness that was, if less volatile than Corbie's hard-edged laughter, no less implacable.

'Well, now, my lad,' the man said. 'I reckon your father'll want to hear of this, and if you don't want your arse slapped you'll stay off such places in future. Can't you see the ironwork?

That's fairy-smithing, my lad. There's things beyond there that aren't for boys to trifle with.'

John was furious to find that he was afraid. The fingers on his ear were still gripping hard, throwing everything into confusion. He wasn't used to being hurt; the Smith men never raised a stick, or even a hand – in fact, nobody in the family hit him except Mama, and she only ever dealt a quick slap that didn't hurt much. This fiery pinch, inflicted by a man who wasn't even excited about it, frightened him: it was like being in a foreign land where everyone spoke the wrong language.

'My father will – will tell you to *let me go*!' John shouted, sickened by the thought that he couldn't even threaten that Dada would hit the man, bandaged as he was. 'I *know* that's fairy-smithing – my father's the one who *made* it!'

At that, the man did let go.

Heat surged through John's ear; he wanted desperately to rub it, but he refused to give the man the satisfaction.

'You're the farrier's son, are you?' the man said. He didn't look at all intimidated, though, just alert. He bent his gaze on John with a probing intensity.

At that, John cupped both his ears. 'Yes, I am,' he said angrily. 'I'm John Jedediah Smith and you may *not* grab my ears again. I was on farrier business, and you should beg my pardon.'

'Oh, farrier business, is it?' The man looked amused again. John took a step back. 'I reckon that's why you were climbing fences. I know when I send any apprentice of mine out on a job, I always forget to give him a key to the gates.'

'Who are you?' John said, not liking the sound of this.

'Stan Mackem's my name, John Jedediah,' said the man.

'Come by the word of your penman grandfather. Why he couldn't send you with a message is beyond me; you're lively-limbed enough – but that's Smith manners for you. Come along, you'll take me to the smithy now.' He took hold of John's shoulder; his fingers dug in, hard-tipped and tough.

'I'm not called on to do anything you bid me,' John said. 'You're not my father, nor my elder.' He made an attempt to wriggle free, but Stan Mackem just gripped him harder, until the pain in his shoulder frightened him into angry submission.

'For a lad who doesn't want his arse slapped,' said Stan, steering a rather stumbling John towards a waiting horse, 'you've a queer way about you. Come on, John Jedediah, up you go. We're off to Gyrford.'

Jedediah was in a low mood that afternoon. Corbie had been entertaining the village left and right, put in an excellent temper by Agnes' cooking and sharing out helpings to any passer-by who looked curious – to the silent dismay of the Smith women, as they'd intended the leftovers for supper and would now have to spend more hours over the pots.

Even Celdie and Vevie were cooking now. When Corbie grew too agitated at their chatter he would wade among the girls, swiping around as if at birds, and while none of his blows had landed – yet – he struck out hard. The kitchen was one of the few places he mostly stayed out of, and the twins had huddled in there along with Molly and Agnes. They weren't even singing as they worked now, for it annoyed Corbie; they whispered to each other in the made-up language they'd used as inseparable toddlers, and when Molly gave them tasks they didn't tease her. Matthew had encouraged them to go for long walks or visit friends, but they didn't go: it was bitterly cold, and they were so much in the habit of walking or visiting for the fun of it that they didn't quite know how to do it when they'd lost their joy. They had turned in on themselves and didn't want to stray too far from their mother.

Jedediah, seeing Agnes' hands full of dirty bowls, went to open the door for her. 'You know,' he said quietly, 'you might cook badly. Let him tire of your housekeeping the quicker. Then he might let you go. Would your arms let you do that? It's hardly poisoning.'

'I couldn't do that, dear,' Agnes said, dismayed. 'You and the children eat the same as him.'

'Auntie, let me take those,' said Molly, appearing in the doorway. Being responsible for most of the cooking had always got on her nerves, but since her aunt's arrival, she'd become a fast, silent helper, lifting as many jobs from her hands as she possibly could. 'Grandpa, there's a letter for you.'

'Oh?' Jedediah exchanged a glance with her: Molly did not need to say that she'd refrained from bringing it to the smithy and irritating Corbie with Smithish literacy. 'Good girl. Who brought it?'

'A packman.' Grander folks had servants for their errands, and the Smiths and their friends tried to hire the hungrier children of the village to run messages. A packman meant it must have come from some distance. 'Said he'd come from the inn in Mayton.'

The missive was short and to the point.

My dear Jedediah,

I always provoked your father, and also the fey Ab was angry when I was born that it was not able to blight me with gifts. It is best I be away a while lest I make matters worse for you.

Your Janet can manage the midwifery. Do you tell the women to pass along the word that they must go to her and not me. She may stay out of my stores, thank you, and ask Tom Attic if she needs more.

Letters to the inn at Mayton will reach me, though I do not stay there. I brought all the innkeeper's children into this world and he is disposed to favour me.

My love to Sister Agnes, who I am sorry not to see. But she knows well that there are times a fire does not need one who stirs the coals.

I am sorry to be away, but it is for your good, and if I do not care more for your good than your company then that would be a shame to me.

Your fond aunt,
Pell Smith

Jedediah held the letter in his hands, looking at the big, neat letters pressed hard into the page. Of course she was right, he told himself. Her presence did irritate Corbie, and when he was irritated, he made others feel it. And she was right about Ab, too; it hadn't bothered her for seventy-some years, but that didn't mean it wouldn't start.

His heart weighed heavy, like a jug suddenly filled, and he told it to behave itself. He was a father and grandfather; he hadn't been anyone's child for a long time.

It was while he working this thought that he heard a clatter in the square and a shrill voice.

'So that's my *home* there, and if you don't let me *go* and dismount on my *own*, then it's just an *insult* to the kin who taught me riding, and if they take it amiss, you'll only have *yourself* to—'

'John?' Jedediah called, setting the letter aside in haste. There was no mistaking that treble haughtiness.

'Well, now,' said a voice from atop the horse, raising itself about John's indignant protests. 'Uncle Corbie, I'm glad to see you well. How are you, Cousin Jedediah? We've more than enough to settle between us.'

Age sat well on Stan Mackem. The day Ab had burst from the tree he'd been a gangling lad, not quite grown into his long, solid bones. Now he was robust and sturdy, a healthy tree of a man. If he lacked Matthew's height and bulk, he was still big by anyone's standards, and while the hair on his head and arms was less violently red these days, the arms still held plenty of vigour, and his creased pink face spoke of solid meals and a life spent outmanning the weather.

'Well now, Cousin,' Jedediah said, coming forwards. They'd had dealings at the border now and again and stayed on the right side of civil; this was a time to appeal to kinship if any was. Perhaps, if Stan was willing – perhaps if Corbie had an inclination to return to Tinsdowne – perhaps there was a way out of this with his soul unstained. Perhaps. 'I'm glad to see you in good health.'

'Now then, Cousin Jedediah,' said Stan. He was no awkward boy any more; he expressed his doubts about Gyrford not in jerky outbursts, but in a quick, up-and-down glance that took in the scene within a moment. 'Caught your lad here trying to climb a farrier fence – this is your lad, I suppose?'

'I told you I was!'

'He is,' Jedediah said, managing to sound more dry than worried. 'You can let him go now. I don't reckon he stole your purse, and as to fences, I'll have that out with him.'

John was down from the horse before Stan could say anything else about it, but rather than running off, he rallied. Turning, he gave a bow that was just on the side of manners and said, with the air of a host, 'I was brought up to believe there should be good feeling between kin, Cousin, so I'll forgive the matter of my ear, and in return, I reckon you don't intend to pinch it again.' Behind his posturing he was actually quite afraid that Stan would do just that, but he had his credit to maintain and this was a way of telling tales without admitting it. 'Welcome to Gyrford, and we hope you'll behave yourself.'

It was a nervous moment. Matthew hissed, 'Johnny, manners!' and Jedediah went stiffer still. He wouldn't shame his grandson in front of any Mackem, not for anything; at the same time, he wouldn't mind shaking the boy himself – perhaps later, when no one else was around. Perhaps.

Stan, however, showed a burst of Mackem spirit: he didn't laugh out loud, but he did grin, a big, wide chuckle that showed a mouth still in possession of all its teeth. 'You'll have no trouble keeping that one to the task, Cousin,' he said to Jedediah, and then to John, 'You've a little to learn of respect, lad, but never mind. Better iron in the core than gold in the gilding, eh?'

'I don't know that saying,' John said, distracted. 'Is it a Mackem one?'

'What's this, Magpie?'

It was an explosive voice, slapping hard against the smithy walls.

Corbie peered out of the smithy door and shaded his eyes, an elaborate mime of dazzlement. 'Who talks of Mackems in this Mackem-forsaken county?'

As he saw Stan Mackem, though, his half-scowl set, hardening like iron losing its heat, too dark to bend.

'Ah, God help us,' he said. 'Rooks every which way. Someone needs to cut down this house.'

Stan dismounted from his horse, holding the reins in a loose hand. His face had been quite cheerful before, but as he saw Corbie's addled glare, it settled into a stern caution.

'Good day, Uncle,' he said. It was an authoritative greeting, years of eldership ringing in its notes, but he spoke quiet nonetheless. 'How do you? I reckon you won't remember me. I'm Stan Mackem, son to your brother Dunstan.'

Corbie shook his head as if it offended him. 'Rooks every which way,' he said again. 'I had a brother, God help me. Two of them. Elder and Sweep, and sweep me out they did, indeed. No doubt His Majesty's settled well enough in splendour and comfort.'

Stan kept his gaze on Corbie. 'Your brother's grown old,' he said. There was something about how he spoke, Jedediah realised quite suddenly, that was a little familiar: the plainness of his words, the shortness of his sentences, the calm tone that wouldn't upset you. Folks often spoke that way to Constance. It was a thought to twist his stomach. Corbie would have raged against it, reduced to the same soft-speaking needed by his despised wife – but it didn't feel like justice. The folks who spoke to Constance that way had loved her.

'I am elder at Tinsdowne now,' Stan went on, quite level. 'Your brother lives there still. We see to his wants.'

He had been about to say something else, but Corbie exploded again at this – or rather, in Stan's broad direction, not looking at anything in particular. 'I had a brother,' he said. 'Ah, his wants were seen to, all right: born to an eldership, he was, given a wife on a fine trencher, he was, a beautiful lass whose father couldn't wait to match her to the best of prospects. Ah, Tinsdowne could never do without His Majesty, could it? Some of us are born to it, and others are just filings off the end, damn him. I had a brother my elder, a king to my knave when he was young enough to piss himself.'

John moved over to Matthew. Dada's arms weren't as tight-bound as they had been, but they were still in slings. Seeing him fidget, John felt an anxious responsibility to make sure his father didn't go breaking himself.

'Never mind, Johnny,' Matthew said, misunderstanding the worried face. 'You stay by me and no one'll get your ears.'

'Well,' Stan said, turning to Jedediah and looking rather upset, 'I see you didn't speak too high when you called him "something touched". What set his mind against his kin like that?'

The question was so unexpected that Jedediah found himself hard up for words. 'You'll have to ask that back at home,' he said after a moment. 'All I can say is that he wasn't glad to be sent here.'

'Oh, come along,' Stan said, impatient at the suggestion

Corbie's anger at his Mackem kin might be of mortal origin. 'What have you done to ease him?'

'Well, we haven't stabbed his ears with iron prongs,' Jedediah said, finding his own voice rising.

'That's enough.' Stan spoke with a sharp clip. 'I know you were fond of your mother, but when a man isn't here to speak for himself, I'd hope you knew better than to rake over old grudges. Here's your father before you: what *have* you done for him?'

'I had a wife,' Corbie said, apparently to the air. 'Pretty as an angel and clever as a half-squashed beetle. God knows how I deserved to be shackled to such a prodigy. There's creatures less ghastly under rocks and logs.'

'We can't put back what the fey took,' Jedediah said, growing harder-edged. 'That's a lesson you and yours might learn, if you cared to.'

'So you've not done a thing, have you? Just scrawled away to me, I see.' Stan's eyes were like Corbie's: a pale blue starred with white, bright and sharp. At that moment, they looked very cold. 'Well, if you have it in mind to unburden yourself, Cousin, you can make other plans. We've my father to care for already. Corbie's your elder, and if he thinks you birds, he at least knows his iron.' He nodded to a snare-trap sitting on the anvil that, until very recently, had been Matthew's. 'That's a Mackem snare if ever there was one. He can work, he can live, and if you can't care for a touched man, then I don't know how you can call yourselves farriers and hold up your heads.'

'Elder?' exclaimed John, furious. *Nobody* spoke to Grandpa this way. 'The elder here's my grandfather, Cousin, and you should mind your manners!' Having said it, he shrank a little against Matthew just in case Stan decided to go for his ear again.

'Oh, indeed.' Stan didn't reach for John; he kept his eyes on Jedediah. 'Show me your wrist.'

'What's that?' Jedediah's voice grew flat. He could feel it beginning to itch: the long-healed burn Corbie had, in a moment of roguish annointment, stamped upon his arm. The Mackem brand of a journeyman farrier, never crossed over with the brand of a master.

'Show me your wrist,' Stan said. He stood firm on his feet. 'I knew you a journeyman. If you have the mark of a master there, let me see it.'

Jedediah was very still. *You lock your voice in your throat; you hide your thoughts behind your face. You stay quiet when the roar begins.*

'I thought not,' Stan said. He didn't bother to show the scars on his own wrist; he was poised, a fighter sure of his ground. 'Corbie Mackem came to you a master farrier, Cousin Jedediah, and he served as elder until mischance took him away. You never gave a master-work to anyone.'

'Who should he give it to?' John demanded. 'No, Dada, don't hush me, it's fair! He had no elder to accept any master-work he made. He's been elder for ever here. Go in the smithy, you'll find a dozen pieces of his good enough for a master-work!'

'He could, lad,' said Stan, a little less fierce, as if explaining a harsh truth to a child too young to deserve it, 'have sent to Tinsdowne. He had kin there. My father was hearty and strong then. He'd have known a master-work, and if a father isn't there to approve it, an uncle will do just as well. But he didn't, lad. He took the eldership as a journeyman because he wouldn't stoop to ask a favour of his father's folk. He chose a journeyman's life, and that's what he has.'

'I'm elder of Gyrford,' Jedediah said. His voice was like ice: cold and hard, and under a strong enough blow, ready to break. 'We don't brand here. This place isn't under Mackem ways.'

'We can take it to the clans if you like,' Stan said, almost calm now. It was the relaxation of a victor, a man who sees nothing insurmountable in his path. 'See how many elder farriers cast their lot for a son who usurps his father. Or we can take it to law. Or both. My reckoning, Cousin, is that you'll find this is Caleb Mackem's smithy.'

He looked at the faces around them, noting their dismay without satisfaction. 'No doubt you can stay here,' he said. 'Serve under Corbie. You can even keep the name Smith. But you'll have to swallow your pride, Cousin. You can give Corbie the respect he's owed and serve under him, or you can not. And if you don't, then the clans will be against you. You won't have a hand's turn of help, nor a word of lore. It'll be the end of the Smiths, lad.' He said this to John without malice, just a plain delivery of fact. 'It'll be the Mackems' smithy, this place, and none the worse for that, for by the rights of names and lines, it's been a Mackem place all along. You want Smiths in Gyrford, John Jedediah? Mind your elder. And that elder stands within your smithy, and it isn't your grandpa.'

Over the next few days, Stan Mackem found himself living in the Smith household, surrounded by a kind of chilled courtesy that he didn't like.

'Don't you even sing in the smithy?' he asked.

'We do,' Jedediah said shortly, 'but the best voice is Matthew's, and he's got other uses for it.'

This was true as far as it went. Matthew felt bad about not being able to work and had taken to giving out advice for the asking to anyone who'd felt unable to pay for a survey. It was small things – cream drunk from the milk churns, chains of flowers leashing back tree-branches until they stood like bright-petalled prisoners, murmurs in the hayloft that sounded entirely too erotic considering that the words spoken were mostly about the crackle of the straw and the strewing of the dust. But the fact was that nobody felt much like singing.

Corbie joked with the customers and swatted at the 'birds' around him. Jedediah stood silent. He'd had a word with Molly and she'd had a word with Mary Anne; if things got too bad, she would take the twins and leave. The farm was managed by Seth Twine, a sensible man who owed the Smiths more than one favour, and he had no liking for men who frightened children; he was ready to make house-room for the Smith girls if need be.

But for now, Molly wouldn't go. All she'd say was, 'I'm Smith as much as anyone, Grandpa. Send me away and I'll reckon you think ill of me.'

There was just a flash of fire as she said it that gave him a quick shock of grief: this was the face that had said to him, with Louise's voice, that she'd ride with him to protect his mother. But then he saw it was Molly again, and he remembered how to bear grief down: you planted your feet and you did what you had to, and if that was his rule, he had no right to forbid Molly from making it hers.

But it couldn't go on. Every evening as he supped on Agnes' cooking, it was the best food he'd ever tasted: seasoning and fear in every perfect mouthful. She hid in the kitchen, whispering to Molly, shawled and bundled as ever Constance had been. And somewhere there was Ab, answering to Corbie's call, a dire fey that Corbie would never let them put to rest.

One day when Matthew was out examining a light case – Minnie Hinton's kittens had been replaced with mewling clumps of dandelion root and she couldn't spare such a litter of mousers – Jedediah took John aside.

'Look you, lad,' he said, 'can I trust you?'

'Of course, Grandpa,' John said. 'I'd never be Uncle Corbie's man. You're my elder, I don't care what Stan Mackem says.'

Jedediah would have liked to enjoy the loyalty, but that wasn't what he'd meant. 'I mean, John,' he said, trying to be unmistakable, 'that I'd like Corbie out of the smithy and I need to know if I can trust you to take him, without you do anything silly, mind. Bring Franklin with you for safety and take Corbie to survey some place with no troubles – keep him busy awhile. Can you do that? If you can't, best I know now.'

'Of course I can, Grandpa,' John declared, 'and you needn't speak slow as if I were Thomas Brady. There's nothing easier.'

'I know,' Jedediah said, 'but the question is, can I trust you not to make it difficult?'

If Grandpa hadn't looked so tired, John might have raised objections to this confusing question, which would have given Jedediah fair warning of John's approach to the difference between simple and complicated. But he did look tired, and John felt bad enough for Dada without Grandpa to feel bad for as well, so he said kindly, 'Of course, Grandpa. It won't be difficult at all.'

Franklin had Thomas with him again when John went to collect him, carried upon Franklin's shoulders so that Corbie, following the 'Magpie' out of curiosity for its flittings, made some remarks about treecreepers carrying eggs on their wings. Franklin himself was so glad to oblige Mister Smith that he did not interrogate John, assuming that the destination had been chosen by Jedediah. He was a little ill at ease – Corbie Mackem had frightened him as a child, and hadn't changed a hair since those days – but if it gave him a chance to aid Mister Smith, he'd do anything at all.

'Mister Thorpe,' said John, quite cheerful, 'we're off to the stone wolves. It's a fair distance, so we'll be some hours. Now, keep Thomas at a distance when we get there, so please you? He's a little young for such things.'

Thomas, hearing his name, gave John a thoughtful wave from atop his grandfather's shoulders, letting himself be carried off into the blue, safe skies where folks were certain to look after him.

'You don't want him back,' Jedediah told Stan. 'You reckon he has a right to this place. All right, we can't force you to take him. But he's not to elder here. Take it to the clans if you like. I'll ask what they think of one clan forcing out another that's been part of this place centuries back. I don't reckon many of them will like the notion that marrying your daughter to another clan's lad means losing your clan's name.'

It wasn't just crows that were missing from the countryside. The hedges didn't rustle; the skies were quiet; the woods were empty of every sound except the keen of wind through twigs. At one point John found a sett, but the midden beside it was dry and flaking, and wherever the brocks had gone they weren't there making use of their home.

'Mister Thorpe,' John said, 'how are the Bellame woods? How's the game?'

Franklin bounced Thomas on his shoulders, but his face was grave. 'Crowded,' he said. 'Crows and ravens, and you hear the foxes shriek and quarrel even in the daytime. I reckon they've come in from other places till it's close to war of beast on beast. I don't like it.'

Franklin was one of the few men John knew who never swore, and he had an aversion to complaining that amounted almost to a fear. To hear him say *I don't like it* was enough to chill anyone's bones.

'I don't reckon you're a blind man,' Stan told Jedediah. 'No spider set your eyes askew. I've been here a bare few days and I see the village listen to him, like his work, like his company. If you don't, that's your own business, but I reckon you'll have a hard time eldering with him here. Not unless you cast him out to starve – and see how the clans and the world like you for *that*.'

⋆

'Ah!' Corbie exclaimed as they emerged from a shaded path of trees, and the white wolf gleamed from the hillside before him. 'My greatest work! Or my largest, at any rate, Magpie mine.'

He didn't quite address John, but spoke as if to a bird on his wrist. He'd been like that all the way; the treecreeper hadn't interested him very much, but he'd made passing comments to John much the way Franklin sometimes talked to Soots.

The chalk of the hill was clean: the Hawton folk kept it that way. It was a tradition by now, and John had the sense that Jedediah wasn't very pleased about it. Well, John could see why: Grandpa had a fine hand for draftsmanship these days, almost as good as Dada's, but this was very much a child's drawing, all teeth and stick legs and a jagged tail raised fierce as a pike.

'I heard,' John told Franklin, 'that it was Jedediah Smith who did the drawing for this.' He'd noticed that if Corbie heard you say something, he'd take it in sideways: he wouldn't act as if you'd addressed him, but it would put an idea in his head anyway.

'Ach, I had a good notion with that one,' Corbie said, looking a little angry. 'Beget sons with your slate-pencil, Clem Smith, and see how many your wife bears!'

Thomas only knew a few words, but he knew a tone when he heard one. Whimpering, he tugged at Franklin's hair until Franklin swung him down and held the lad on his lap, bouncing him gently and whispering, 'Never mind, my little man. Grandpa's here, little man.'

'I only wonder,' John said, as if to no one in particular, 'how it is that a farrier should have it in his mind to master the People. Crush them with iron, you know, or fright them with chalk, or chat away to them like a crow so they do your bidding. It's not the kind of fairy-smithing I learned. I do wonder how it's done?'

'Ach, edge and hedge and flitters of nothing,' Corbie said, angrier than ever. 'Look you there what rises from the ground when it's not set a guard over!' He made a gesture towards the stones.

John had seen the sarsens many a time; they were a place he was only allowed to view from a distance, thrumming grey and misted with lichen. In Corbie's day they had crept, but since the chalk wolf, folks took the long way round them and forgot about them the rest of the time.

But the wolves weren't ironed; nobody had chained or collared them. They'd just gone down on their haunches, submissive to the loom of a greater wolf. They were still alive – well, not alive in the mortal sense, but they were what they had always been.

In John's opinion, it was time he had a proper look at them. He'd wanted the opportunity for years and here was an excellent time to ask: it would occupy Corbie all day, as requested, and John could try to get answers from him about anything he learned. Even if the answers came askew, that would be something.

'Mister Thorpe,' he said, 'stay you here with Cousin Thomas, if you please. Uncle Corbie, there's a treecreeper here needs your company.'

'Burden yourself with eggs on your wings,' Corbie said, stretching out on the grass, hands under his head in luxurious laziness. 'God help my poor old back. Does a man good not always to be tap-tap-tapping at his work.'

'John?' Franklin said, seeing the lad sighting upon the stones with a familiar and worrying intentness. 'Is this what your grandpa bid you do? Are you sure you're safe, up close to them?'

John slipped off his boots; there were iron nails in them. He emptied his pockets. 'Mm,' he said. He didn't really mean to lie; he just hadn't taken in Franklin's questions. The circle was too fascinating.

'John,' Franklin said, as close to stern as he got, 'do you do this by your grandpa's leave?'

'Eh?' said John. 'Oh. Yes, yes I do. Grandpa said he trusted me.'

Barefoot and ironless, he cat-footed it towards the stones.

'How in the name of Heaven,' Jedediah asked Stan, 'do you expect a man to be master of a forge where every soul under its roof is a bird to him? What's the village to make of a place where the elder can't hear a word said by every man under him? How's a man to live surrounded by birds, come to that? Think it's a happy life for him?'

As John approached the stones, he felt the back of his neck prickle. He'd expected to like them; from a distance there was something comforting about their calm sweep, and he had always felt most himself in places friendly to the People. It was like watching the world glitter, jewels of wood and flesh to be found under every leaf.

That was what he'd thought he'd feel here, standing by the circle. The stones were warmer than they should have been in such bleak weather; even without touching them, he could feel a pliant heat coming off them as if veins ran through their stiff crystals. But they weren't welcoming. Something blocked him, and he couldn't get past it.

As he tried to step within the stone circle, the ground under his feet felt unstable, as if he couldn't quite remember which way was up. Without meaning to, he sloped sideways, staggering a few paces.

He caught himself just before he fell, trying to find his way upright. Then he took a step, but the sky above looked at him cock-eyed, and the next thing he knew he was slewing sideways again.

'Don't push me out,' he said, or he tried to, but as he spoke, he felt his teeth start to buzz. It was the most uncomfortable thing he'd ever felt, a crawling, nasty itch that got right inside him; if he stayed here another minute his teeth might start slinking around his mouth just to get away from it.

'All right, all right,' he said, and stopped trying to get in. Instead, he approached the outer edge of one of the stones.

There it was: the moment he changed his intention, the dizziness stopped. He laid his hand on the sarsen wolf and it didn't throw him: it stood massive as a mountain, sharp muzzle pointed skywards, still slightly warm to his touch.

John turned his eyes to the chalk wolf opposite them. As he looked, he thought he felt something: a kind of cringe under his palm. The stone didn't move; it was hard and rough as ever. There was just something in its rigidity like a locked muscle; the frozen stillness of a beaten hound.

It wasn't confusion; it wasn't Ab. He was touching a stone full of fear.

'It's just a picture,' he tried to whisper to it. Setting the wolves on the wander again was the kind of thing Grandpa would have very stern words about, but he wasn't thinking about that. The crag of rock against his skin was like the bristle of terrified hackles.

John looked away from the chalk wolf, stared at his bare feet. 'I won't hurt you,' he said. 'I'm not very fond of the man who cut that chalk wolf.'

You couldn't say the stone relaxed. It just smoothed a little, like ice thawing at the edges.

John looked at the jagged white figure cut into the hill with slicing iron, at Corbie, watching him with a ferocious grin. He thought of the screaming creature Corbie had smashed on the anvil. He thought of Grandpa's face, still as a stone, when Corbie raised his voice.

'Do you think,' he said, finding himself confiding in a block of sarsen with more fellow-feeling than he'd quite expected, 'that when we get home, Grandpa will have talked Uncle Stan into taking Corbie away? Because I don't think he's good for the land here. I don't think he's good for this place.'

Stan said to Jedediah, 'Well, we can see about that.'

Crows were leaving the skies faster than ever now, and other birds with them. They invaded the underground citadels of the rabbits, driving them out to plague kitchen gardens; folks were starting to go hungry as the homeless coneys fled from shelter to shelter, devouring everything from dinner vegetables to medicinal herbs. Crows filled the chicken coops, stealing grain and frightening the layers up to the treetops, where they sat in awkward disarray, their dropped eggs smashing on the ground below. Moles hounded from their townships burrowed frantically in any soft ground they could find, heaping piles of dirt in the harvested fields and leaving hollows beneath, ready to break under a step and snap a leg with the fall. Displaced brocks gave up on their usual wormy feast and took to striking at any stray cat that passed their way.

This was worst of all, for the majority of county cats were working creatures, not cuddlers, and they weren't stupid either. So, in the common way of cats who feel their circumstances unbefitting, they took themselves elsewhere. Gone were the purring flocks crowding Janet's door; gone were the rangy, darting pouncers that kept down the mice and rats swimming filthy-furred through the golden harvest of grain. Unhunted, the rodents made merry; farmers opened grain bins to find fat piles of writhing bodies, and a year's store of corn and wheat, all that sweat and ache and grim-backed patience, began to diminish. Gyrford's winter supplies were sinking down a million tiny sharp-toothed throats.

Cold iron holds off the People, but when the People set animals a-running, there's no talisman or charm that will turn them back. Matthew had been quietly advising for days now, and was growing so upset that Janet had bandaged his arms back into place to stop him trying to pat shoulders in helpless sympathy.

Ab was a plague, and the cause of plagues, and Corbie wouldn't say where it had gone. John had, behind Stan's back, suggested that if things got too bad, they might threaten to throw him in the forge to make him tell.

'John Smith!' Matthew exclaimed, too shocked to 'Johnny' him. 'What in the world put such a wicked idea into your head?'

'Church,' John explained.

'What – the – John Jedediah Smith, it's a *dreadful* sin to tell such lies!'

'He did!' John insisted. 'Parson Green sermoned on Saint Phocas, you know, who was roasted in a kiln and then boiled. He talked of Saint Ignatius as well, but we haven't got a lion. I didn't mean we'd *really* throw him in the forge, Dada,' he added, in an attempt to be comforting. 'That would make a terrible mess.'

Matthew looked at Jedediah in utter woe; Jedediah was better at stamping out such appalling talk. But Jedediah only looked at John for a moment, then gave a rather sad laugh, ruffled his head, and said, 'Won't do, lad. Not one of your best.'

Stan Mackem wasn't a fool; he was aware that the birds and beasts were disappearing. He'd tried to discuss the matter with his cousin, but Jedediah was immovable in blaming Corbie.

'Come now,' Stan reasoned, 'the man's here to stay. You'll have to find some other means.'

'Any means we try, he'll undo,' Jedediah snapped. 'Look what he did to the scrubland.' This was another recent triumph of Corbie's: he'd dug over the rough patch known for its tiny white midnight fires, extinguishing them for good. This had been a relief to the more fearful villagers, and a disaster for Tom Attic, who had thereby lost a warm place to grow the liquorice root he used for his best skin salve.

'Oh, now,' said Stan, impatient, 'if a holding can't do without pagan physic it's no holding at all.'

'Forgive me,' Jedediah said, so angry that his voice had no expression at all. Tom had worked decades for his skill; Mister Attic used to say Moorish physicians cured sickness with herbs, but the herbs here were different and they'd had to learn anew from pure trial and error. 'I thought it was a Christian man that went to cure a woman's wits with a knife in her ear.'

'You don't still harp on that string?' Stan exclaimed, angry in turn. 'That was Corbie's clumsiness, not my pa's. I was there too, Jedediah Smith. Pa was sorry ever after for that mistake. He told us over and over, *Never work cures with hands you aren't sure of.* I'm sorry for your ma, may she rest in peace, but if you'd hold that grudge over the good of your father, I say he was right to leave you a journeyman.'

Matthew, at this point, intervened before either man could punch the other – or before anyone could let slip that Constance's peace was not among the dead and buried. Even the Smith children knew better than to let Corbie or Stan know she was still alive, and he would never have found out if he hadn't attempted to reason with John.

John was looking for the birds. The skies were cold without their chatter, and they must be somewhere. The only place he knew for sure he could find some was at Godfa Tom's. Auntie Agnes, along with two of Godfa Tom's sons, had made him a sturdy storehouse for his salves and potions, well-roofed against the rain and well-lined with straw against the frost, and John had always loved to stand there, inhaling the many scents contained within the shelves of pots.

It also had the advantage, if you were a crow trying to hide, that its owner was a tolerant man who wouldn't have the heart to shoo you out.

John couldn't talk to crows, which was a great annoyance to him; Uncle Corbie had the knack, but he had done it so fast John hadn't had time to pick it up. Still, crows were clever creatures and he felt it might be worth a try: Dickon Attic, Godfa Tom's grandson and apprentice, was a friend of John's and fond of feeding them, and perhaps together they might learn something.

When he set out, then, he'd expected to be alone. Having Stan Mackem join him was such an annoyance he could barely bite back his complaints; now he'd have to pretend he was headed somewhere else, for he knew as well as anyone that Granny Constance was not to be upset by any more Mackeming.

'Well now, my lad,' Stan said, not unfriendly, 'don't you think you might try to get along better with your grandpa? They say you're a little touched yourself; I'd have thought you'd find some things in common.'

Stan had been raised more to frankness than delicacy, and this was not a good start. 'They say Dada's a fearsome man who once thrashed a giant to death with nothing but a hazel twig,' John said retorted, 'when Dada never thrashed anyone in his life.'

'Yes, I can tell that from your manners,' Stan said, quite amicably. 'Come now, let me help you with this next job and we'll see if we can agree on something.'

'No.' John glared at the road ahead of him and sped up.

Stan, whose legs were longer than John's, was not to be out-paced. 'Come along, lad,' he said. 'What's the work today?'

John considered saying that he had slipped out with a view to avoiding work, but Stan was a man of proven violence against naughty boys, and he was undergoing a rather panicky inner debate when he spotted Walter Stryde, a garrulous ditch-digger who sang while he dug and stopped digging to exchange news with every possible passer-by. Jedediah, in his less charitable humours, was of the view that Walter must have two calluses, one on his chin from resting on his shovel, and the other on his tongue from chattering about every soul's business but his own. He was there, however, and he was never opposed to conversation; John took a chance.

'Hey now!' Walter exclaimed, with the cheerful interest always inspired by the sight of a new soul to talk to. 'What's the news, young Mister Smith?'

'Mister Stryde,' John improvised, 'I've a message from Grandpa. He says – he says that with all the loss of beasts of late, the county needs surveying. You're to come to the smithy, so please you, and tell what you've seen by way of creatures while you dig, and also to bring your shovel so he can look it over and be sure it won't do more harm than good.'

'Well indeed!' exclaimed Walter, fortunately pleased enough at the opportunity for further chit-chat that he didn't question John's proposition. 'That I'll be glad to do, and happy, and I hope he'll be so good as to wait till the end of the day. There's your Tom Attic up the way, and I've sworn to bring him the Lady's Smock I grub up, and the ways of drying that fellow has are such as I couldn't say, but I know he likes to begin day-fresh. No doubt your good grandpa'll understand; always the best of friends, they were. Does you good to see a boyhood friendship last out the years.'

'That's the fellow your Aunt Agnes stayed with, is he not?' Stan said. 'Pagan man, isn't he?'

'Ach, he was baptised well enough,' put in Walter Stryde; such prejudices as he had were against those who wouldn't stop and gossip with him, and the affable Tom Attic was not one of them. 'So was his dada once he settled here; never missed a Sunday sermon, old Mister Attic. Never was a drinking man, mind. Don't know how they get by so dry, those Moorish lads, for I heard tell their countries are mightily hot.'

'Mister Attic's a good Christian,' John said, a little formally. 'He stood godfather to Dada, and Dada said his spiritual counsel was most sensible.'

Stan shrugged this off, evidently not seeing doctrine as an essential aspect of paganism. 'Not complaining about losing Aunt Agnes, is he?' he asked, getting to his point. 'She's Corbie's sister, and if he feels the need of her back home, Attic's no rights in the matter.'

'Now, for my part,' Walter said conversationally, 'I'd want my wife back before my sister. I've heard the lasses say that our Mister Corbie has an eye, and could be he'd rather burn his coals in other hearths, but still, a wife's a wife, eh?'

'What's that?' Stan pulled John to face him. 'Don't tell me your great-grandmother's there too?'

John was fond of Granny Constance, who petted him and allowed him to discourse on whatever subject had current hold of his mind. She didn't say much, but she fell very comfortably into his chatty rhythm and could be relied upon to say 'Lovely!' or 'Dear oh dear!' at the right moments. Their conversations might be one-sided, but their affection was mutual: Constance, who still found expressing herself with words rather difficult, liked to let him talk, and John could tell when someone's enjoyment of his company was sincere. He didn't know much about Uncle Corbie's relationship with her, but he had the strong instinct that they must be kept apart. Dada and Grandpa had been very careful not to mention her name in Corbie's hearing – or Stan's.

He glared at Stan and said nothing.

'Come on, lad, speak up,' Stan said, giving him a light shake. 'Is she alive still?'

'If you don't know who lives and dies in our holding,' John said, as close to Jedediah's clip as he could manage with a voice still mostly unbroken, 'then I reckon you should ask the man who holds the forge. I'm just an apprentice, and Grandpa never stops telling me what's not my place.'

'Ah,' said Walter Stryde helpfully, 'your Mister Smith, now, he's not the most jolly of talkers. Pity, that, or I think so. Doesn't speak of his mama much, indeed he doesn't. Then again, folks don't these days; I don't reckon I've seen her since I was a lad. Lovely woman she was, quite took your breath away. But you know how it is when folks live quiet and don't do much; there isn't so much news to share of them. Now me, I hadn't thought of her for years, and that's a thing, for I'm a friendly fellow. But she must be alive, for we've had no funeral come by for her, and touched or no, I don't reckon she'd melt into air when her time on earth ended; a body's a body, for the most part, and I never knew Mister Smith to neglect a funeral when there was one to be held. Even pays for them sometimes if the family can't afford to bury the departed, so Bill Munday tells me, and you'd think the sexton would know if any man did . . . Well, Godspeed to you, sir, and never mind. I don't begrudge a man in a hurry. Never did. Doesn't do, for there's folks'll chat pleasant and then hare off sudden, and we are what we are, so the holy writ says. I think it's the holy writ; Parson Green'll know—'

By this point, Walter Stryde was talking to himself. Stan Mackem, John's shoulder held in a firm grip, was heading up the long lane that led to the Attic property.

Once, long ago, Stan Mackem's father had snatched Constance Smith from a quiet garden; he had trussed her to a tree and stabbed her ear with an iron spike.

If John had known that, he might have fought free and run for help. But it wasn't a story Jedediah liked to tell. Matthew knew, because he'd asked his mother why Granny's ear was deaf, and Louise had told him the story of how brave his dada had been to rescue her. She told him many such tales, for in truth, she had worshipped her husband. Quietly, teasingly – she always wore her feelings lightly in public – but in the soft intimacy between mother and son, she often recounted to Matthew how she had once upon a time been a poor lonely scrubbing-girl with sore hands, and one day a man from far away had come to the farm. He was daring and skilled and full of learning, able to read a page or a field or a face with just a glance of his bright eyes, but generous and good, kind to children and patient with beasts, and he looked down on no one for their ignorance or their empty pockets.

The tale of Constance's shield ear, for Matthew, had been mixed up with those moments on his mother's lap where she spoke to him of his father's valour and virtue, and her warm faith that he would be another such man. He hadn't shared those stories with John; they had felt too private. Johnny meant well, but he asked awkward questions and Matthew didn't want him tugging on those memories – and besides that, John had never asked why Granny Constance had a deaf ear. He just took it for granted that this was how she was.

So John had no way of knowing how easily Constance could be snatched from a garden where she sat by a sparkling stream, admiring the light on the water. He didn't know how easily she could be frightened into submission.

Stan Mackem was a little startled when he saw Constance, but she was alone, reciting a quiet litany of prayers. Agnes had always said theirs was so pleasant a life that it was good to spend some time giving thanks, and with Agnes absent, Constance was evoking her presence as best she could. Her tone, as she spoke of God's will being done on Earth, was copied exactly from her sister's: Agnes prayed as if she was sorry to bother God when He was no doubt very busy.

'Come along, Mistress,' he said to her. 'We're off for a walk.'

'No!' John exclaimed. 'You leave her alone!'

Stan Mackem didn't bother to argue; he just took hold of John's ear and said, 'Now don't you make trouble, lad.'

The pinch wasn't as hard as the first time; it was more a gesture of authority, like pulling the collar of a dog. Jedediah sometimes did the same thing, although with lighter fingers. It wasn't the pain that silenced John: it was the flick, flick, flick of Granny Constance's eyes, a frightened skitter that he'd never seen before.

Granny Constance had lived with the Attics all his life. He knew that she had a love of peace: if a family quarrel rose, someone would take her quietly out of the room. He knew too that she found things muddled; Dada said she had trouble telling her own ideas from everyone else's. John felt more than that was mixed up, that the whole world sat in her lap like a tangle of yarn she couldn't quite unpick. But mostly she was calm – a fragile calm, maybe, but she could make herself understood and follow a lot of what was said, and her moments of upset were only when other folks were out of sorts too. He'd always thought of her as one of those touched folks who was pretty much all right.

He'd never, until this moment, seen what Dada had meant when he spoke of her being frightened by the suffering of others. It was like seeing a great blast shatter everything around it, a blare of misery that drowned her out until there was nothing left but a wild wish to understand that couldn't fight through the pain.

'No,' she said, her voice rising high, 'no, no no no!' She smacked at her head, landing a hard blow on her shield ear which, once upon a time, Mackem men had stabbed to destruction.

'*NO—!*' Constance wailed, stretching the word until it lost all meaning except a cry of anguish.

John swallowed. Her cry rang in his heart. 'It's all right, dear,' he said, smoothing his face so it showed no pain. 'Never you mind, there's a good Granny. It's all right. You can hold my hand if you need to be steady.'

'That's right,' Stan said, and John didn't open his mouth to contradict. 'You come along with me, there's a good woman.'

It was a long walk to the smithy, and Granny Constance had to stop several times on the way. By the time they reached Gyrford, John's curls stood out around his head like a wilting daffodil, so often had Constance petted them by way of reassuring herself.

'Cousin?' Stan called, still holding Constance's elbow with a firm grip. 'Come out, will you? We've things to settle. Come along.'

Constance, released, sat herself on the bench outside the smithy, combing her hair with her fingers and rocking a little, reciting the Lord's Prayer in Agnes' apologetic tones by way of comfort.

'Mama!' John yelled at the house. 'Mama, come out here and tell Uncle Corbie to go away!'

Stan pushed the door open further. Corbie stood in the centre of the smithy, big and cheerful as ever; Jedediah was in the middle of adjusting Matthew's bandages.

'Good, you're all here,' Stan said. 'Now look you, Cousin Jedediah. I know you hold it sore that your ma came to harm. It's a long time to blame a slip of the hand, but it's time to make peace now, and that's all there is to it. Could be your ma doesn't think very clear, and I can credit that your pa never begged her pardon. But he'll know her, won't he? He sees Matthew's wife as a woman; he should see his own. Let him beg her pardon, and then for pity's sake you can let go of the grudge. Then perhaps we can get somewhere.'

Matthew and Jedediah stood, frozen. From the square could be heard a quiet sound: Janet whispering, 'Come away, dear. Come with Janet, darling. Come, let's be quick . . .'

'Birds every which way,' Corbie said. His voice was loud as a slap. 'You there, Janet Smith, what do you mean by mousing about outside? If you've food or drink for me, bring it in like a Christian!'

He might have said more, but at that moment, the men in the smithy heard a whimpering.

It was a sound familiar to Jedediah from his childhood, and while he hadn't heard it for decades, it wasn't a sound you forgot.

You don't ever forget the sound of your mother crying.

There was a long moment, broken only by Constance's frightened sobs.

'Dear God,' said Corbie, 'don't tell me I'm not a widower yet?'

'Leave her alone!' John shouted.

Corbie put down his hammer.

'You leave her be,' Janet said, drawing up as tall as she could, though she wasn't very tall. 'She doesn't want to see you – and you, Stan Mackem, if you dragged her here along with John, you should be ashamed of yourself too. How would you like if someone had done that to your mother, God rest her soul?'

'God save us all from the shrews,' Corbie said, 'and the simpletons too, God help us. Well, so the fair maiden has been rescued from the black hand of paganism. Come along, Constance my pet, let's have a look at you.'

He spoke with real anger in his voice, as if Constance's wilful refusal to die was just another one of her unreasonable habits that had been laid upon him like a yoke. So hostile did he sound that Matthew unobtrusively loosed his right arm from its sling and then, changing his mind, put it back and loosed his left. He'd never work iron again if he knocked his right arm about before it healed, but perhaps he could spare his left. If he had to. A one-armed man could still work.

Corbie strode out to the bench with a kind of outraged brutality in his stride. He looked unbreakable, a knot of fury – right up until the instant he saw her.

The sight of Corbie cracked Constance in two. She curled up on herself, covering her eyes, her ears, her thin hands too small to conceal anything of the horror she had become. There was no self-consciousness in her frantic little gestures: Constance had never known she was beautiful, and she didn't know what her looks meant to folks now. But the sight of Constance drained Corbie's face to a dense, sickened grey.

Constance Smith, in her youth, had been beautiful beyond all women: pristine, silver-perfect, lovely enough to break your heart.

In old age, she was become terrifying.

Ab had given her beauty, but it evidently hadn't thought all the way into the future. And beauty is only skin-deep.

It was the skull you saw now. Constance's skin still gleamed like a snowdrop. Her hair was moon-bright, and her teeth, in their receding gums, sat in a perfect row, gleaming bare-rooted in their skull. Nobody forced Constance to eat: her skin sat flat against her bones, falling in wreaths around her twig-thin neck like a set of slashes. Above her knife-sharp cheekbones, her silver eyes glowed within their sunken sockets, bright as stars within a deep black sky.

Those who knew Constance looked at her and saw a gentle grandmother, a woman with a shrinking bladder and shaky legs who needed an arm to support her on her frequent trips to the privy. Her hands, narrow, breakable, with knots at the joints like galls in a twig, were familiar to John from all the days she'd stroked his hair. He knew the feel of them, the way the girlish skin slid loose as she petted him, the time-hoarsened voice that would murmur tenderly over him. But she was three-and-eighty: if she bent her head over someone to dote on them, you could count the bones of her spine.

Being loved was all she really cared about, and defiance had never served her well. Even now, with her husband before her, she held her fingers over her mouth in obedience to some long-remembered warning not to trouble Corbie's ears with her damned keening.

Corbie swallowed. 'Thought I'd married an idiot,' he said, 'not a demon.' He raised his arm; Constance cowered as he beckoned Janet. 'Lock her out back, will you?' he said. 'We've cages out there for the monsters.'

'I'll do no such thing!' Janet said, breathless. 'She can go back to Tom's, or she can bed with Agnes here. Come along, Constance darling, let's get you inside. Come and see Molly, there's a love; Molly will be very happy to see her Granny Constance.'

'I bid you do something, Shrew,' Corbie said. 'Do you mean to do it?'

Janet turned to him. 'I do not,' she said. 'And if I'm a shrew, you mind my bite.'

'Well, well.' Corbie covered his mouth as if to cough. *Kra, kra, kra*. 'It's a pity,' he said, 'when a man's beset by women. And this one, I don't like. I think she'd be better off the ground, at least for a while.'

'Mama,' John said, suddenly too scared to shout, 'Mama, come into the smithy. Mama, come now—'

There was a silence for a moment – not a hush, for everyone had something to say, but a blanketing smother pressing their throats closed as if, for a moment, something around them had drunk down all the air. The sky was white, and as John dashed his eyes from one corner of it to the other, he saw smoke.

The smithy chimney was active all day, a tumbling billow of charcoal dust, and it fountained up straight and steady as ever. The People didn't touch forge-smoke. But the houses around the square had hearth-fires and their columns of smoke began to bend, closing down around the square like the fingers of a fist.

When they touched each other, they began to swirl, smoky feathers eddying away from the tumbling whirlwind, angelic shadows of wings around a coiling body of dark, twining wreaths.

'Mama!' John shouted.

Janet saw the crow of smoke reaching its claws down towards her and she might have escaped it, but she stopped to pull Constance to her feet, push her, gently, into the smithy, to say, 'In you go, darling, there's a good—'

And in that moment, the smoke-wrought talons of Ab grabbed Janet Smith and lifted her high in the air.

Janet was a brave woman. She didn't scream as the smoke tapered to points around her chest, the tips of them glowing with burning trickles of light, like heat creeping through paper. Above her, Ab was all eyes and muddle, a tumbling cloud of darkness. It shook her with the rough insistence of a child contending for a toy.

I must have my friend, it said.

'Janie!' Matthew yelled. His voice, normally a harmonious bass, rose almost to a shriek. 'Janie! *Janie—!*'

'Now, darlings, I'm all right.' Tears ran down Janet's face; the thin courage that rang through her voice made Matthew want to burst into tears of his own. 'It's all right, Johnny lamb – ah!' Janet said, almost managing a soothing croon, and then gasping as the talons tightened. 'I won't say I'm comfortable, but never you fret about Mama.'

'Kind friend, do you put her down *at once*!' John screamed. 'That is *my* mama, not *your* mama! She does not have your friend, nor *is* she your friend, for you are hurting her and it is bad courtesy! Uncle Corbie, call the kind friend off my kin!'

'For God's sake, man,' Matthew said, gathering himself enough to accost Stan. 'I can't shoot like this. Get the arrows.'

'Jedediah, how's your aim?' Stan was hurrying into the smithy. 'I can do it if you'd rather mind your mother.'

Constance was curled up in the corner of the smithy, shaking beyond control. Jedediah gave Stan an angry nod and knelt over her, covering her with an apron. 'It's a dream, Mama,' he said helplessly. 'Put your shield ear up; stay safe, dear.'

'The bow's here,' Matthew said, too frantic to speak soft. Stan had to fire before Ab shook Janet hard enough to break her spine. 'Johnny, get behind the string.'

Corbie watched with innocent interest as Stan pulled the arrow back, loosed it with a firm flick. It was a good shot, striking straight through what, if the thing had been a crow, would have been its head.

Little coils of Ab winced away, but it didn't retreat and it didn't release Janet, just twisted deeper, the shimmer of a whirlwind beginning to spiral up its formless self like a cup taking shape under the fingers of a potter.

'It'll rip her.' The voice was Corbie's; he spoke with mild indifference. 'What a pity. There'll be no fur left on that shrew once it gets to whirling. I suppose someone who knows what he's about had better do something.'

He reached towards one of the benches, picked up an object – a poker, not quite finished, of no special workmanship.

'Best to set the woman down,' he said, swinging the poker to and fro in a complex pattern. He coughed again: *Kra, kra*. 'I'd like her set safe on her feet now.'

The whirlwind dropped, forgotten. Its grip on Janet weakened, wavered.

Matthew ran forward. It was only when he was underneath her that he remembered his arms were too injured to catch her. All he could think to do was cast himself down, stretching his body across the cobbles like a pallet.

The air slackened all at once. Janet dropped and, by the grace of God, as Matthew would always say when re-telling the story, fell hard across his chest.

It was a breathlessly painful landing, but Matthew's ribs absorbed most of it; the two of them lay together on the cobbles in a tangle of limbs. Matthew just about had the strength to raise his hand and cradle the back of Janet's neck.

'Well, well,' Corbie said, watching as the dark threads of smoke melted away into the cold air. 'Good thing someone keeps his head, eh?'

Constance was huddled against the wall, her deaf ear turned outwards. Her whispered prayers were the only sound over Janet and Matthew's gasps.

'Mister Mackem,' John said to Stan, regaining his voice, 'don't tell me you didn't see that. Don't tell me you don't know that Corbie of yours did it on purpose. That wasn't poker-work, that was *calling*, and don't tell me you don't know it. We have a Bible in the house and I'll bring it out for you to swear on.'

Stan looked around, at Corbie's angry smile, at the toppled bodies in the square. At Jedediah's eyes, staring at him hard enough to bore through bone.

'I'm no liar, boy,' he said. 'I know that wasn't any Mackem trick with the poker. And if you say it wasn't Smith either, well, I'm no Smith to say you nay. But what would you have of me?' His voice was taut, and he stared at Jedediah with the same hard gaze. 'He's your sire, man. Don't push him off on me.'

Jedediah wasn't in the smithy. He wasn't anywhere – or at least, nowhere they could see him, and Matthew didn't dare leave Corbie unattended to search.

Janet had never seen Jedediah admit to distress. She remembered a story Matthew had told her once: he was very young and newly apprenticed and Jedediah had missed his stroke with the hammer and broken his finger so badly the bone showed through the skin. Jedediah had turned his face aside without a sound, and after a ghastly silence, had said, very nearly steady, 'Never mind, lad. Time you learned how to set bones anyway.'

Jedediah hadn't told her where he was going, but she checked in his bedroom – a liberty she didn't usually take – and saw his leather pallet was gone. She knew of a few places where you might, if you had a mind to, set up a pallet on some smooth and sheltered earth – she had visited some of them, because life is sometimes the more thrilling for a little sneaking around with your own beloved husband. And if Matthew could find such hidden spaces, Jedediah could too. There was nowhere in this holding that her father-in-law didn't know.

The place was between tall hedges; the branches were so ivied over that even in winter, you couldn't be seen within. From the outside it looked vividly green; from within, it was brown and dusky, the choked branches furred with ivy roots. Jedediah was sitting here, hunched on the ground, his elbows resting on his knees, his pipe hanging loose from his hand, unlit.

Jedediah looked up at her. He could have made a remark about getting no peace; it would have been natural enough. But he didn't.

Janet sat down beside him, and the two of them rested in silence for a while.

'Used to be,' Jedediah said in the end, 'there was a path in here. You could walk from the Gillams to the Tauntons with your head sheltered. The Tauntons didn't keep it clear. Now it's grown over, mostly.'

Janet didn't say anything. Her heart hurt in her chest at the sight of him.

Jedediah stared at the ground. Sixty years old and hiding in the hedge like a child.

'I don't mean to trouble you, Father,' Janet said, 'only . . . Well. Let's say I have a liking for your company.'

He couldn't look at her. It was shaming to be found here, but he discovered he wasn't surprised. His family knew things about him, and they had never mocked.

'If I step down,' Jedediah said, 'we might make a case for Matthew as elder over Corbie. He's a master, and his wits are clear.'

Janet nodded, a slow nod to show she'd heard him rather than an agreement.

'I know,' Jedediah said. 'No good. He's a master because I made him so, and I didn't have the authority.' He gazed at his empty pipe. 'I'm sorry, lass.'

Janet didn't ask why he hadn't gone to another farrier clan to accept him as a master, but he said, regardless, 'Stan's right: I should have swallowed my pride. I could even have gone to a Gowan master, or a Faber one, if I didn't like to ask the Mackems.'

She rested her hand on his shoulder and he didn't shrug it off. 'I reckon you had enough to think of with Corbie vanishing like that. Why upset the holding, making a business of it and telling them all you weren't a master, when anyone could see you knew the work? I've never seen you make a journeyman piece in my life.'

Jedediah sighed. It was as if all the force was going out of his body. 'I was happy,' he said. 'That's what went wrong. I was new-married, and then we had Matthew. I was too happy to think of troubles ahead. And then later . . .' He didn't look at her. 'I was sad.' His voice was hoarse with the strain of admitting it. 'Then,' he hastened on, 'I was busy. You get old. Happens sooner than you look for it.'

At this, Janet smiled with light sarcasm. 'A child to think of? What kind of man lets that crowd his mind? Why, you were a positive *father*, for shame.'

Jedediah laughed, one short, sorry syllable.

'Matthew'd hate to be elder with you living,' Janet said. She was serious now. 'You know he would.'

Jedediah sighed again. 'I'd hoped to live a decade more,' he said. 'Even half a decade. Let Johnny grow to a master. There's one doesn't mind saying what's what. Matthew's . . . humble, for an elder. But he and John could man the place together. Don't tell Matthew I said that, mind.'

'I can see it.' Janet's smile was tender now. 'Matthew could stand in the back and nod when John speaks, and everyone would think Matthew a fearsome sage. Not that he isn't, of course. A sage, at any rate.'

'Well,' said Jedediah, so brisk he sounded almost normal, 'that's gone now. Matthew'll have Corbie to manage. Could be I should go away. He'd be easier to manage if I wasn't there thorning his side.'

'Don't,' Janet said. 'Don't leave us.'

Jedediah was staring into space. 'Franklin'd have me,' he said, 'Pretty sure of that. He's alone in his cottage since Francie wed. I'd stay near Gyrford, out of the smithy, out of his sight. I'd be there for you to visit.'

'Father,' Janet said, holding his shoulder tighter, 'I don't go to tell you your business, but I'm pretty sure that if you stop now, you'll die.'

'Could chop logs. Stay strong.'

'You'll die without the holding to care for,' Janet said. 'I speak with respect, Father, and I love you very well, but I don't think you'd know how to stay alive if you didn't have the world in your care. I know you're no woman in labour, but I know nursing.'

Jedediah turned his head away. His voice was stuck in his throat, his eyes a little hazed, so unfamiliar a feeling that for a moment, he thought age had come for him, that he was going blind.

He'd long ago forgotten how to cry.

Janet was staring ahead, as if caught by an idea. 'It's a thought, though,' she murmured. 'Not much of one, but then, a thought's a thought.'

'What?' Jedediah spoke with something like his old brusqueness; it was a comfort, of sorts, to be irritated at the girl as if nothing in the world was wrong except that his son's wife was a chatterer.

'No, no, never mind,' said Janet, waving her hand. 'It's only a thought.'

'*What's* a thought?' Jedediah demanded.

'Then again,' Janet said, 'I might as well. A visit does no harm in any case, and it's good to exchange tales and notions.'

'Janet Smith,' Jedediah said, 'tell me this moment and stop . . . *magpieing*.'

'Now, Father,' Janet said, laying her head on his arm, 'there's no need for that.'

Jedediah thought for a moment, and then patted her hand. 'If you mean to annoy me out of my gloom, lass,' he said, 'you need more respect for your elders.'

'It worked, though, didn't it?' Janet said. She kissed his rough cheek. 'No, it's only that I had a notion to visit Tinsdowne – I could see the lie of the land there, and bring Shibbie for a visit.'

Shibbie – or, baptismally speaking, Bathsheba – was the daughter of Stan Mackem's nephew Lazarus, so named because he'd been thought dead at birth until revived by the skill of the midwife. Shibbie, as a result, had been reared in a family where midwifery was the crowning ambition of a woman's life. Janet didn't know her personally, but midwives talk to each other, and the word was that Shibbie was dedicated to her trade.

'Why?' he said.

Janet shrugged. 'Stan likes her in particular, I hear. He had only girls, you know, and those who lived married away. And you know how Molly can talk you round when you're out of temper . . .'

'Don't you misjudge our Molly, lass. She's a good girl, that one. I listen to her because she has sense.'

'Well, there you go,' Janet said, giving no indication she considered Jedediah Smith above such things as grandfatherly weakness.

A dispute would have been invigorating, but he didn't quite have the energy. He'd thought, for a moment, she might have had one of her flashes of insight, but all she had was a hope. He might give way to Molly on occasion – maybe oftener than that: she was so good a girl – but there was no reason to suppose Stan Mackem had such inclinations, certainly not strong enough to persuade him to take Corbie away from them.

Not enough to give Jedediah a reason to let Corbie live.

Janet was right; he wouldn't live long if he gave up the smithy. It had kept him alive after he lost Louise; he'd wither like an unshelled snail. If it would solve anything, leaving his home and fading away, well, he'd lived a longer life than some. But his own death wouldn't save his children.

Not *his* death.

'Haven't we enough Mackems underfoot?' he asked.

'It's a good question,' Janet replied, 'but I reckon perhaps not.'

'Well,' said Jedediah heavily, 'if you think Stan has a soft heart for her and she can talk him round to anything, by all means go, lass. If it's my leave you have to ask,' he added bleakly, and then stopped himself. The world didn't need complainers.

'Don't be away too long, though,' he added. It wasn't easy to say. Janet could say *I love you* as easily as sprinkling salt; he didn't know how she had the knack of it. 'Do you come back soon,' he managed. 'You'll be missed.'

Janet had meant to leave the very next morning, but word came in the middle of the night that Francie's baby was on its way.

John woke at the sound of her footsteps and went to find her in a haze of instinct – he'd been having bad dreams, and Mama was safety – but she stroked his cheek and said, 'Go back to bed, sweeting. I'm away to Francie's childbed.'

'Don't let her get ate,' John had mumbled, not quite awake enough to be clear on the usual dangers of birth, and had fallen back asleep and dreamed of Thomas Brady and how anxiously Cousin Anthony had hovered over Molly as she dandled her new cousin.

The next morning, Matthew rose early; it was frustrating to lie beside Janet feeling the warmth of a body he couldn't put his strapped-up arms around, but sleeping alone was more disheartening still. Corbie had walked off in anger; he was of the loud opinion that he couldn't be expected to loiter in a house containing such a monster as Constance, although he was equally loud in his objection to letting her go home.

John hid in the garden, for Molly was furious with him for not preventing Stan Mackem from dragging Granny Constance here, and the twins, who usually differed from Molly just to keep things interesting, completely agreed with her. His father, meanwhile, was very sorry to learn that he'd taken Corbie to the stone wolves, a decision anyone could have told him might lead to dreadful things – and Dada being very sorry to hear you'd done something was a serious disgrace.

With the kitchen full of girls who thought him a very poor figure and the smithy holding a father who was being painfully forgiving, John retreated to the safety of the outdoors. It was there that Jedediah found him, gnawing on an apple foraged from one of the trees.

'John,' he said. He didn't share the girls' anger; he was too absorbed in his own failures to blame anyone else's. And there was something comforting in the company of a lad who was almost as faulty as he was.

'I'm sorry about Granny Constance,' John said into his apple. His voice was rather small. 'But if you mean to scold me, Grandpa – well, you can, I reckon, if it'll relieve your feelings. But if you think it's for my good, I should tell you Molly's already taken a turn, and then Vevie and Celdie together. And then Molly again.'

Jedediah almost laughed. It was a small warmth that John didn't stop being John. 'Nay, now,' he said, 'that sounds enough scolding to me. You mind our Molly, though. She's a good girl.'

John sniffed a bit. 'Would you like an apple?' he said, as to a fellow-sufferer. 'I can find you one.'

Jedediah took out his pipe, tamped it down, but didn't light it. He stared at the bowl. 'I'll tell you what, John,' he said after a moment. 'I was in trouble enough at your age and I didn't care for it. I don't say you don't deserve it, but it's no great joy.'

'I don't mean to deserve it,' John said. It was the pitch of a twelve-year-old, a light little treble, but there was a depth of discouragement to it that Jedediah truly didn't like to hear. 'Folks say I should do my duty, then when I try they say I overstepped – and it's not as if anyone *else* has a way of doing duty that doesn't mean minding Uncle Corbie even when he hurts folks. The stones bristled when I just *looked* at him. Even the sarsens don't like him.'

Jedediah sat in silence. Then he put his hand on his grandson's shoulder. 'John,' he said, 'I'd like your view on a job.'

That brightened John up as nothing else could have. 'What can we do for you today?' he said, very much in Matthew's customer-greeting tone. 'Well, what can I do, but I'm sure everyone else would help too. Except Uncle Corbie. And Stan Mackem. I will, at any rate.'

Jedediah waited to see if John had finished.

'Tell me, Grandpa,' John persisted. 'Come along.'

Jedediah cleared his throat. A time might be coming when he wouldn't be here. His mother was cowering in her bed; Agnes drudged silently in the kitchen; his granddaughters had stopped singing. Matthew would train the boy, of course, but it'd be good for John to have as much time with his elder as possible. Just in case.

'So, there's Anthony Brady,' he said. 'What with one thing and another, we've had yet to think of the pig he met, and what came after. You remember, though, what he said befell him before the pig?'

'Mists,' John said readily. 'I said the same, you know.'

'Aye, no doubt,' Jedediah said, turning the pipe over in his hands. 'Now, once there was a fey in those mists – before your time, before your father's, even, when I was a young man. But it was a child-stealer.'

'Ooh, Aunt Pell talked of that!' John burst in; he'd never been good at waiting for the story to be told. Child-stealing People were a thing more often feared than seen, so the prospect of seeing a real one intrigued him too much for John to remember that he was, himself, a stealable child. 'She said you killed it.'

'Cut off its head,' Jedediah said briefly. 'But that's unsettled ground there, always has been, near the wolf-stones. Could be it's grown back.'

'Like a mushroom,' John suggested. 'You know,' seeing Jedediah's blank face, 'you cut a mushroom and eat it, and then the roots fruit again another year. They're hard to get rid of once they're bedded in.'

Jedediah found he couldn't fault the analogy. 'All right, more or less. So, we can't have a child-stealer back, can we? You and I must go and see to it.'

'I don't suppose it'd eat Uncle Corbie?' John said with more hope in his voice than really befitted a Christian youth.

Jedediah raised his pipe to his lips, put it down without lighting it. After a bit, he said, 'Don't think so. I was a younger man than him and it didn't try to steal me, just to frighten me away so it could steal children. Big man like him – don't reckon he'd be to its taste. And do you stop suggesting murder, John. It – it upsets your father.'

'Oh well,' John said, and then he stopped. 'Grandpa,' he said, 'don't you wish we could call Ab? The way Uncle Corbie does, I mean?'

'I wish he couldn't,' Jedediah said dryly.

'Yes, but he can. And if we could call Ab off, then he wouldn't hurt folks so easy, would he?'

John's eyes were dark, all sparkling pupil. He wasn't staring, not exactly, but he had a look that didn't quite see his grandfather.

'John?' Jedediah said. 'What have you in mind? It answers to none but Corbie.'

The words recalled John from wherever he'd been. He glanced at Jedediah, started to say something – and then the glow went out of him. 'You'll only stare,' he said.

'What's that?'

'When I say things – you know, folks say I go starey, but *they* stare at me too.' The words were quiet, but there was a weight to them. It was Janet the boy resembled most, but there was something in the drop of his head just at that moment that spoke to Jedediah of Agnes, of her great hunched shoulders that she covered, winter or summer, in a thick shawl.

He sat for a moment, his heart sore. He'd wished so much for Matthew to feel safe in the world, and when Matthew had children, he'd taken to fathering them so easily. John was right, though: they did watch him, and usually with some nervousness. They couldn't help it; not when John got sudden ideas and ran towards things he shouldn't touch. Good God; Jedediah had told him to take Corbie somewhere innocuous and John had taken him right to the stone wolves; it was only by God's inexplicable grace that something truly bad hadn't happened. They had to watch John, but the boy knew they did it, and if he didn't like to be treated as unsteady, well, he couldn't be blamed for that.

Just because a thing was true didn't mean that it wouldn't hurt your feelings.

'All right,' he said, 'I won't stare. I'll look at my boots, all right? What have you in mind? Let's . . . let's call this your chance to show me you do have some sense.'

Jedediah hadn't expected this to work as well as it did: John threw small, strong arms around his shoulders and gave him a hug. 'That's most good of you, Grandpa,' he said. 'You can do that more, if you please. So, it's this: Uncle Corbie calls as a crow, yes? But we don't speak Crow. But suppose there was a stealer there by the Lendens? Might it not call to a crow-chick? And if it did, well, might not Ab hear? After all, how many ways to say *Come here* does a crow need? If Ab heard something say *Come here* in Crow, even if it was another fey, might it not come to see what was afoot? And then we'd be there without Corbie, and we could – well, we could try to have a word, at least.'

Jedediah's boots were well-worn leather, hard-stitched and hobnailed, broken in around his feet until he hardly felt them. They were not, however, good at giving advice.

'That's a – wild risk, lad,' he said in the end. 'Many ways it could go wrong.'

'True enough,' John said equably. 'To begin, it should be me who goes into the mist – it saw you before, and if you cut off its head – you must have been a fierce young fellow, Grandpa! – so I'll need to get a crow and . . .'

'Oh no.' Jedediah raised his head to glare at John – but no, he'd promised not to. 'Don't you dare,' he told his boots. 'You're young, John, and I'll not have you go up to a child-stealer alone.'

'I wouldn't be alone,' John said. 'That is, you'd have to stay away, but I could get some help.'

'Who? You recall, I hope, that your father can't move either arm?'

John's voice was hurt. 'Of course I do, Grandpa. I'm very unhappy about that, and you know, I reckon Uncle Corbie could have stopped it if he'd had a mind to. He didn't even think to. And even if he didn't know it was his own grandson being cracked about, or even a man – well, you shouldn't let a bird be pulled apart either. It's not *kind*.'

Jedediah swallowed, remembering how helpful John had been when they'd put Matthew's arms back into place. He'd carried the cider, patted Matthew's back, said, 'There now, Dada.' And Matthew had mumbled back, 'Thank you, Johnny, love. Never you fret,' and hidden his face against the bench so that his son wouldn't have to watch as he tried not to scream – but John wouldn't have it; he'd squatted down and said frankly, 'I find a good shriek takes my mind off it when I'm hurt, Dada. I'd sing out if I were you.'

'All right,' Jedediah said. His voice sounded harder now. 'Whose help do you plan for?'

Tom Attic had prospered as a cunning man. These days he was no spry and lively lad; decades of Agnes' good cooking had put a comfortable belly on him, and the willingness of many children and grandchildren to fetch him things had allowed him to become slow. But his eyes were as alert as ever, and they missed very little when it came to his neat-tended herb beds, his orderly stores or his physic jars – which had the profitable advantage over many that, having been tested upon himself, they tended to work. These days they nestled amongst the shirring blackness of a million feathers, but Tom didn't mind the crows hiding in his storehouse. His grandson Dickon, who served as his apprentice, was a patient lad who enjoyed feeding them, and in truth, Tom felt these days that any kindness could ill be spared.

He kept as cheerful as he could, but he was heartsore at the depredations of these Mackem men. Agnes and Constance were as much his family as Jedediah's, and worse, Jedediah would blame himself instead of shouting at Tom like a reasonable man.

The fellow had always been stiff about taking favours, even ones you liked to do, so Constance's snatching away had to sit unexpiated on Tom's conscience.

So when Jedediah's grandson turned up asking for a loan of a crow from his storehouse, Tom was entirely willing. He would have rather liked to provoke Jedediah just to get the fellow to harangue away some of his distress, but Jedediah always had been awkward about allowing himself to be comforted, the old fool. The crow would just have to do.

Cissie Lenden came out to greet Mister Jedediah's grandson at the boundary of her farm. 'My dear young sir,' she said, 'I do hope your reverend grandfather isn't hurt? These are such times, oh dear. I do hope he's well?'

'He is, Mistress,' John said, as politely as he could. 'He's kept busy.'

'Oh, he is, that he is.' Aunt Cissie sighed. 'He's too good a man for this world, I fear.'

'Yes, I know,' said John shortly. He was very much on Jedediah's side, but 'too good for this world' was over-salting the broth rather; Grandpa could be quite annoying sometimes. 'But it's me here today, and there's a notion I have to try. Can you help me? I have a task to perform and if I lay a chain around your feet' – she was sitting so attentively he had already begun – 'you should be guarded enough. I have here' – he lifted it from the bag and passed it into her delighted hands – 'a tone drum.' He produced a carved oak stick from the bag. 'It plays different notes when you strike it here – and here – and here, see?'

The tone drum was his own invention and he was rather proud of it. He had taken an interest in what you could do with a bell other than just ringing it, and this was the result: an iron bell with no clapper, flattened out until it was wide as a pot, with dips in it carefully worked to ring out different notes. It was good for only a very simple harmony, but the People appreciated any kind of music.

'So if you can strike it for me, like this . . .' John demonstrated a five-note phrase, 'then that'll put something in the air I can hear my way back to. So I won't get lost.'

'Well, that's quite the idea!' Aunt Cissie exclaimed. 'I never heard the like – I thought you were fiddlers at the smithy.'

'We are,' John said, and not wanting to get into all that, said firmly, 'Grandpa thinks this a good addition.' This was true, as far as it went. John played pretty well, although folks sometimes said his style gave them queer moods, but Grandpa only let him play at home, saying that if the holding needed jigs to set the stones a-dancing, John would be the first man for the job. That was another reason John had invented the tone drum.

'Well, no doubt he's right,' Aunt Cissie said, meaning only to compliment Mister Jedediah's taste and not his censures, and struck at the bell in careful rhythm.

'That'll do, Mistress,' John said. 'But just wait you on my signal before you begin on it, if you please?'

The field of the mist-mother was clear-aired, a little frosted. John felt the yielding crunch of every step; the slopes around him were dulled with ice. Under his arm, the basket holding the crow clattered and squawked.

'I'm sorry about this,' John told it. 'I know it's been a long journey for you. Come you back to me after and I'll take you somewhere safe. But I need to call on someone. Just . . . well, I am sorry about this.'

And, with a sense of heavy contrition, he tweaked the crow's tail. It squawked in pain, and then turned upon him, ready to peck – only to find a seed dropped into its beak.

'I am sorry,' John said, stuffing it back in the basket and dropping in a handful of seeds more. 'I just needed you to sound upset.' Thin tendrils of white were already unfurling from the ground like streams of smoke from a kindling flame.

Well, John thought, standing a few minutes later surrounded by whiteness and damp, *I wasn't sure that would work*.

'Play the drum, if you please, Aunt Cissie,' he called. 'And so please you, don't listen if any voice calls for you. That's very good.'

'Why, thank you dear!' The exclamation was genuinely glad, and John half-wondered if he should mention that to Dada as an example of the Christian kindness Dada was always counselling – but when he looked at the mist, he could feel a chill. Not the vigorous nip of a dry day, but a soft, coaxing curl, twining around his hands, lifting locks of his hair, cupping his face. A depthless, gleaming blank.

The thin, sweet taste of milk, or something like milk. Coiling snakes of mist.

John was just starting to grow tall. Grandpa had remarked on his appetite, or Mama had – he wasn't sure, just at this moment. He was hungry much of the time, these days, and someone – was it Mama? – had said to let him eat as he liked, for he'd need it to grow . . .

Things were wisping around him, not random swirls, not like proper mist; more like . . . tongues? Snail eyes? Once, on a windy day, Mama had taken a ribbon from her hair – no, it was Molly, he was sure it was Molly – and had let the bright scrap dance on the air: it curled and tangled, but at one end, it was still, where Mama was holding it – no, Molly, it must have been Molly, why was he thinking of Mama?

The thought was hazing around John that perhaps he should put on his torc or swing his bullroarer; Mama had – no, *Grandpa* had made sure he came equipped. He couldn't feel the ground beneath his feet; he was too cradled, too carried along. And he was right, now he thought of it: the hanks of mist spiralled as they stroked around him, but they weren't floating free. There was another end to them; something had hold of them. Something was casting them like a fisherman – or sending them forth like snakes' tongue – or—

He was hungry. That was something he felt for sure; his belly was so empty he could cry. The milk in his mouth wasn't quite sweet; there was a bitter clamp to it in the aftertaste, a running red echo of salt, but it was sweet when he tasted it first, and if he kept his mouth open, the sweetness kept flowing, and he was hungry, hungry enough to sit down and weep.

Somewhere, there was the thought that none of this was right, that something dangerous was happening to him – but it wasn't a thought in his head; it was floating above him, coming loose.

Detached, now growing distant, was the feeling that everything was wrong, that he was being bound, encased like a web-caught fly. But he was so light, so cradled, so warm, so safe.

Well, of course you are, darling, said Mama. There she was, just visible through the mist. *What else should you be?*

Mama? John asked. The words didn't come from his mouth.

Johnny, love, said Mama. Her brown curls were unloosed; a few fine strands of grey tumbled through them, bleeding white into the mist. *There you are. There's my fine man.*

Mama, why isn't it raining? John tried to ask. His clothes were wet; he shouldn't have felt so cosy.

Why should it be? said Mama. *You must be tired, lambkin. Come, sit with me for a while.* She smiled. Her teeth, pearl-pale, were melting a little at the ends, tipping themselves into sharp, wavering points.

'I'm . . . I'm too big to be called lambkin.' Those words did come out of his mouth, John knew, but strangely: at once muffled in the soft air and terribly loud.

Well, I can't call you a sheep, said Mama. He didn't hear her laugh, but the curls of her hair shook merrily, and the curls of mist shook with them. *You wouldn't like it. I could call you a shearling if you like? My poor man, you look so hungry. Come to Mama.*

It sounded true; that was how Mama talked in his memories, all of his memories, lying atop each other: twelve years old, telling Mama he was nearly a grown man; six years old, wheedling apple peel while she made a desultory attempt at a pie; two years old, overtired and bruised from a fall, crying and stumbling into her arms.

Somewhere distant, he could hear the clinking of a pot. John shut his eyes, tried to fix his mind on it, and now it was sounding clearer, more distinct, much closer than made any sense in this trackless immensity of soft white nothing. It wasn't quite in time: it lacked precision, as if the player couldn't feel the beat in their bones. One of those folks who didn't have what Grandpa called 'an ear'. It was imperfect and frustrating and definite and *there*, a real sound in the blur.

Johnny, said Mama. *Lovie.* Her voice was caressing, fond, a little playful. It was how he would have spoken himself, if he'd tried to show a stranger how his mother talked.

John wanted to say to her, *Mama, I'm hungry*, but he felt he shouldn't, though he didn't know why. He was growing frightened, a queer fright that ran along his backbone and chilled him deep, but he kept losing it. His body was warm and weightless, and there was no hurry and nothing wrong and he could rest as much as he liked, and then, when he pulled his mind back against it to make sure, there it was again, this icy column of fear – then it melted away and he was warm and he didn't have to be grown-up, and if he asked, his mama would feed him as much as she liked . . .

Someone was playing music, rather badly; a dull, metallic twang, like stones dropped on an iron plate. *Drop. Drop. Drop.*

John tried to listen to it: it was plucking the fear at his back, sending him thrumming like a harp-string.

I don't know, lovie, said Mama. *I don't know what to make of you when you get like this. It's a pity. It's disappointing, if you want to hear the truth.*

The hurt of that shook him hard, echoing through his flesh in a discordant clang. It was a ghastly pain, utter heart-hunger, the burn of tears in your throat before you shed them. Had she ever said that? She said it with such tenderness, but there was a precipice beneath the words: if he didn't make Mama love him again, he'd be utterly alone and he'd starve and no one would ever care for him . . .

Everything in him yearned to run to her, to beg for mercy. *Mama, love me, Mama, please, I need you, please, don't take the world away—*

Behind him, almost in rhythm, went the *drop, drop, drop* of that instrument someone was playing so badly. As the sound clouded back into his attention again, he heard other things: the hiss of falling rain, the dull crack of thunder. It was raining – it should be raining on his head but the water drops couldn't find him. He was lost.

No you're not, said Mama. *Come here, darling.*

John was almost reaching his hand out; there was a fear in him somewhere and he was almost ready to listen to it – to discard it so he could go home, he needed to go home . . .

There was a croak from the basket – no, not a croak, a plea: the hoarse, ravening squawk of a baby bird begging scraps from its mother.

Mama flickered.

For just an instant, her features slipped: her nose smudged to a black point and her eyes came adrift as if she didn't remember who she was – but then she was there again, holding out her hand.

Drop, drop, drop ran the music.

John closed his eyes, listened to the chiming tap of iron, the hungry cries of a full-grown crow crying for food like a fledgling. He wasn't sure of many things just now, but he was sure his mama didn't have a beak. And she didn't make him feel like he'd tear apart.

In that thought, he remembered the words he'd meant to say; he couldn't remember why, but he did remember what they were. 'Kind friend!' he yelled. 'There is justice in the crows of the air! Come to me to save the crow!'

Hush. Hush.

It was a silence that built, gathered itself up in beats, until, like the pounding of a heart, he could hear it coming: the hush of air, the beat of wings.

John looked up. Above him, mist-smeared and soft-edged, beat great black wings, feathers gripping the sky like skeleton hands.

Mama looked up, but it wasn't Mama now; it had forgotten its brown curls, its blue eyes. It was a tangle of clouds, feathered white and frothing into the shape of a woman, then a bird, back and forth, writhing within itself, knotted as a dropped skein.

The dark shape above stooped, circling around the heads of the mist-thing. The cries that came from its throat were guttural, plaintive, ear-cracking.

When John looked back, there was Mama again – she'd found her brown hair, although her eyes were black now, but she waved her hand at the sky with a gesture of brisk dismissal almost Janet's own.

Shoo now, she said upwards. *You're not mine.*

The crow in the basket stopped its entreaties. It went very still and silent. Up above, the winged figure froze, hanging, weightless and massive, halfway through a stroke against the sky.

Lightning.

Yes, it must have been lightning: a bright flash illuminating everything, a split-second of fiery silver. But then it was gone again – except it wasn't, not entirely: the mist was glimmering now, its droplets lit up like the gleam of sunlight on the back of a rose-chafer, a copper-green brilliance bejewelling every speck, and when he moved his hand through it, it left a trace behind him, like drawing a trail through pondweed. The taste bit his tongue: piercing sweet, icy-cold.

John looked up through the mist and saw the swaying mass, not a crow any more, but a four-legged figure, green as a lake, curved as an egg, an earless horse-head as tall as a man, and below it, massive, shaggy, long-fingered paws planting themselves down on the ground.

Johnny! screamed Mama – and then the paw came for her, wrapped itself around her body, its grip crushing away her features, until Mama's hair and eyes and mouth were all gone, leaving nothing behind but a writhing grub of a thing with tattery scraps of mist dripping water down the giant fist.

John dropped everything, ran towards her, shrieking, '*Mama!*'

The creature – *drowie*, he knew the word; suddenly he *knew* the word – the drowie lifted up the squirming maggot that was no longer Mama and placed it to its mouth. There were no lips to suck, only matted heaps of green, moss and slime and sodden, glimmering rot, but as the Mama-thing touched them, the green slid back and like a cat baring its claw, out came a beautiful mouth, pink-lipped and pristine and ready for its kiss.

John grappled in his pockets: there were no weapons there except the bullroarer. He pulled it out, ready to swing it.

There was a soft sucking noise, slight as a whisper, and the Mama-thing slithered within the drowie's lips and was gone.

The drowie withered back into itself, shrinking its limbs like a touched slug, until it was once again a creature of black and feathers, hovering in the sky, utterly still.

The mist was lifting. The day was cold, but it was burning off now: every second that passed, the sheltering smudge between his gaze and Ab's thinned.

John's eyes were full of tears and his mouth was full of sweetness. The bullroarer dropped from his hand. Above him sat the Ab-thing, resting on nothing.

'Kind friend,' he said, his voice almost soundless, 'you have saved the crow. Will you speak with me?'

It wasn't a crow above; it hadn't the shape now. The mist was gone, but not the blur. Ab hung in the air, eyeless and undefined.

Where is my friend? it said.

The voice wasn't what John had thought to hear. As Dada had described it, Ab had been lively, courteous, full of vigour if a little misguided. And in the graveyard, he'd heard it again, but it had been speaking to Corbie; it hadn't felt like this.

This wasn't the voice of a courtier from some fairy ball, nor the charming trickster coaxing you off your path. This was a fish-hook in your mind. It slid in and it held, and it pulled.

There was no relenting in this voice, no pause for you to respond. It pierced inside you and tugged until you did something, *anything*, to give it an answer.

Whether it was high or low, he couldn't say; it was pure *voice*, neither man nor beast. But now it was speaking to him, and it bored through him with a demand that blotted out the world.

He could give it the crow – if he gave it the crow, maybe it would stop.

He'd promised the crow he'd protect it.

'W-who is your friend?' he asked. He could hardly hear his own voice with Ab's still echoing inside him.

The shadows shook like a denying head, so fast that wind slapped him from side to side. *I must have my friend*, it said.

'I think,' John said, 'you have saved many, by your latest act. You consumed a thing that stole the unwilling. You—' Heaven help him, what could he say? It was true, in a way; the mist-mother had come to his call, and if he hadn't summoned her, she might have come back some other time when no one was prepared, so Ab had truly been a friend to everyone in putting an end to her. But if he said that, Ab might haunt all of mankind till Doomsday.

'You did a kindly act,' he said, feeling desperate now, for any moment, Ab would talk to him again, and he didn't think he could bear it. 'Thank you.'

His foot, seeking purchase on an earth that existed only to echo back Ab's plea, tapped against the torc by his foot, and John remembered that he was supposed to be a farrier.

'Oh, look,' he said. 'What have I here?'

No! Ab exclaimed, and John thought it might tear the skin off his hands to finish the gesture, but he put the torc around his own neck.

There was a roar of wings, but Ab didn't vanish, not this time. It pulled itself back, dripping black splashes that singed the ground at John's feet: where they fell, everything died, turning at once to stone. Rocks stood around him, topped with grey, rigid grass-blades, the life and movement of them sucked dry.

'Kind friend,' John said, starting to panic, 'don't do that, please. Don't – um – don't cry. Please, stop.'

Another great splash fell before his feet, leaching colour out of the earth, turning clover-leaves rigid as crystal.

'I – I don't think it's me you want,' John said, panting. 'Find a friend, if you feel forced to, but you miss your mark if you think it might be me . . .'

Ab might have made Left-Lop alliterative, but John's attempt didn't work now. The darkness hung over him, splashing stone. The torc kept the drops from landing directly on him, but everything around him was greying over, and now he remembered Aunt Cissie was still nearby, tinkling away on the tone drum. There was no saying the blackness wouldn't fall on her.

'I – I need to go this way,' he said, pointing to the path away from her. It led back to the Attics', if you followed it long enough. At that thought, he opened the basket and threw the crow into the air; the poor thing had done as he asked and he shouldn't keep it here any longer. It thrashed to find its wings, then headed Attic-wards, faster than he'd ever seen a crow fly.

Justice in the crows of the air, Ab said, gathered itself into something more feathered than before and set off after it.

'Oh, no, no!' John shouted. He'd only meant to direct Ab away from Cissie, not towards the Attics. 'Kind friend, *stop*!' And as fast as his earthly, inadequate feet could carry him, he set off in pursuit.

*

Folks often thought John might be a little fey, and he sometimes thought they could be right, but as he panted down the lanes, rocks catching his boots and sweat pouring down his face in the cold November winds, he felt entirely too mortal.

Dark splatters were hitting the ground ahead of him, freezing everything to rock where they struck. John tripped over a stony thistle, gouging his leg, but he didn't have time to do anything about it; he would just have to bleed into his boot. He struggled on, little red droplets pattering over the ground between each sudden puddle of stone.

'Godfa Tom!' he yelled as the house came in sight, 'Dickon! Mistress Tippit!' The crow had outpaced him entirely; Ab hovered over the storehouse, weeping tears that slapped down on the roof, petrifying the slats where they struck. John, running gasping through the gate, saw with a stab at his heart that Godfa Tom's prized herb-beds were stone-cropping as well: the rosemary was a tower of spines and the lambs-ear a handful of rough jags.

At John's cry, Tom himself appeared in the doorway – and John shrieked again, 'No! no, stay inside! I didn't mean come out! Godfa Tom, I'm sorry, this one is my fault, but you have to—'

He leaped back, for Ab, circling the storehouse without success, had turned its attention back to John. A furling bubble of darkness smacked down at his feet.

'Stay inside!' John shouted.

Godfa Tom might be slow-moving these days, but he was still quick of mind. 'Tippit? Tippit, love!' he called to his wife, 'get in the kitchen, sit under the table. Dickon, come here!'

At the sound of Tom's voice, Ab began to shake in the sky,

feathers fraying like an image rippling when the surface of water is broken. *I must have my friend*, it said.

John, frantic, cast around: if Ab didn't stop weeping, it would splash him eventually, and he was far from sure his torc would be enough to protect him. Standing under a tree would make at least a breakwall between him and the spatters – was there a right one to choose? *Beware of oak, it draws the stroke*, he thought wildly, but no, that was lightning. Godfa Tom kept an alder tree at the edge of his garden for the leaves; Pell used them for nursing mothers – it would have to do. But it didn't have many leaves left. It was nearly winter.

Standing under a gap-toothed lattice of twigs, John saw Godfa Tom reappear in his doorway, with Dickon by his side. Dickon, usually a phlegmatic boy, looked wide-eyed and shocked, but Tom's face held steady.

'What do you need, John?' he asked. 'Tell us what to fetch.'

'It's – it's all right, Godfa Tom,' John said distractedly. Darkness splattered against the alder's branches; there was a crack and a whole spindle of stony twigs smashed down at his feet. 'This is farrier work. You stay safe.'

'Don't be silly,' Tom said, sounding unusually fierce. 'It's not the first queer sight I've seen: I grew up with your grandfather, and it's *my* garden stoning over, lad. Tell me what to do.'

John thought desperately. If he'd been at the smithy, there were any number of tools he could have used: the iron arrows, the slingshot, the weighted net – and he *must* get Ab to the smithy, where they could trap it. They couldn't give up. Even if Corbie called to it again, they must at least try to capture it. If he could lead it there . . .

But he didn't have *anything*. He'd dropped his bullroarer in the field; he'd left his iron drum behind with Cissie Lenden.

What did Ab want for a friend? Did it want something like itself? No . . . surely it couldn't be that simple, not when Clem Smith had struggled his whole life under the weight of Ab's love? But then, Clem hadn't known anyone Moorish.

'Godfa Tom,' he shouted, 'I need to borrow the looking-glass! Can I—?'

Before he'd even finished his sentence, Tom had given Dickon a light push and Dickon was off like a hare. The looking-glass was a queer treasure Godfa Tom's dada had brought over from the Africs: a palm's-width across, with some kind of silver gilding on the back that showed your face sharper than any polished metal you'd find in England. The Moorish craftsmen had been pretty clever to make such a thing, John reckoned, and he wished he could ask them about it, but he didn't quite like seeing his own face in its pristine depths. Water might be wavering, but it wasn't so eerily precise.

'Kind friend!' John yelled as Dickon reappeared in the doorway, a little out of breath. 'Hold off! Let him bring me something that may show you a friendly face!'

Ab, at that moment, was more a scatter of spines overhead than anything coherent, but at that thought, it coalesced into a pair of bright black eyes.

I must have my friend, it said.

'That's all right,' John said, a little shakily. 'Dickon, let me have that and I'll – we'll – we'll hurry back to Gyrford square, where – where I shall be able to show you.'

The glare hung above him, unblinking. Silence shivered

around them, empty of birdsong; even the wind hushed as if a hand had pressed it down.

'Borrow Posy,' Tom said; the plump, elderly mare was used to John, having endured a great deal of shoeing practice. 'You'll get there the quicker.'

'I can't,' John said, conscience-stricken, unable to take his gaze from the black eyes, big as pot-lids, twenty feet above his head. 'What if something befell her?'

'Then perhaps Jedediah won't kill me for sending you off on foot,' said Tom, holding his nerve extremely well, John had to admit. 'Dickon, fetch her, there's the lad. John, take Posy and get the lot of you out of my garden while there's still some garden left.'

Posy huffed and shuddered her way down the paths, turning corners joltily, almost unseating John, who was gripping with his knees as hard as he could and holding tight to the looking-glass to keep it safe.

Above him rolled clouds of feather and eyes, still pleading for their friend.

Posy stopped in Gyrford square and John looked around in a fever, but Grandpa wasn't there. Corbie was sitting on the anvil, chatting away to their neighbour Alice Brady – or rather, attempting to flirt with her and getting nowhere, for Alice, being the widow of Anthony Brady's late brother, was of the firm opinion that one husband had been more than enough. John just had time to realise that if Alice were there, Francie's baby must have arrived safe – and what was even worse, if Ab noticed his new cousin – for Ab had a habit of inflicting its good will on babies . . .

'Dada,' John yelled, 'Dada, the kind friend's joined us!'

Matthew forgot everything. 'Johnny!' he called, running from the smithy to his son. 'What are you about?'

I must have my friend. The clouds were darkening; in a few seconds, they had tumbled from grey wisp to black knots, and then they were eyes again, staring down at Matthew.

'Keep it from the Bradys—' John began, but found himself smothered. Matthew had seized him, folding his broad back over John so that no inch of him was visible from above. 'Dada, let go,' John exclaimed, muffled. 'I have a plan—'

'No doubt,' Matthew said, but he spoke less softly than usual; keeping his arms around John, he ran back into the smithy, forcing John to stumble ahead of him. 'Let's go.'

'Dada!' John emerged desperate from his father's grip. 'I need to do this quickly – it wants its friend, yes? See, I have Godfa Tom's looking-glass. Let it look at itself – it might like what it sees, and even if it doesn't, it might see what it wants. Don't take its eyes off me, think of what's to do in the Bradys' house!'

Corbie was in an ill humour. Alice Brady's husband had beat and starved her, and it was only thanks to Anthony that widowhood hadn't left her destitute. Under Franklin's guidance, though, Anthony had been thorough: Alice now owned land and flocks and had young men in her employ, managing it all with a foresight and care that meant her lads looked up to her, her neighbours respected her, her animals adored her and no man would ever again be free to lay a finger on her against her wishes. Her pleasure in life was her stock, and her joy was her nephew Thomas. Alice was in no mood to be distracted from the recent arrival of her niece – a delightful little girl the Bradys had named after her, no less – by unwanted attentions. Corbie had not enjoyed being told that she had goats enough in her barnyard and no wish to meet one in the smithy.

'What's this, Magpie?' he roared. 'Have you been to trouble with things that aren't yours to trifle with?'

'Yes,' said John, rather hysterical, 'and I think half your mind understands me. Call on Ab by all means; I'll learn how to call too.'

There was no warning before Corbie threw himself upon John. The weight of him knocked them both to the ground. John's breath was pushed from his lungs; if he didn't breathe soon, he was going to die.

'Matthew!' shrieked Alice, but Matthew had already turned back to see them grappling: John with a package clutched against his chest, and Corbie snatching at John's shirt, his hair, his face, as if grabbing in the dark for what John held. The swings were wild, but as John struggled for breath, they found their mark. Corbie dragged the looking-glass from John's small hands.

Matthew was a gentle man, but he'd seen too many loved ones terrorised – Aunt Agnes and his grandmother, and his Janet, the light of his heart, hauled into the air to be mauled by smoke – and now Corbie had set upon his son.

Matthew's arms might be crippled, but his legs worked. He ran four steps into the smithy and swung. The kick caught Corbie full in the belly and lifted him a foot into the air before he crashed down again.

Corbie rolled across the floor. He lay there for a moment, doubled over, breath groaning in and out of him.

Then he sat up and pointed. *Kra, kra, kra*. There was no effort to hide it this time: he called crow-wise, his hand pointing at Matthew.

John had heard that cry before; he was sure now what it meant, down to the last tone. *Attack*.

'No!' he cried, struggling up again. Air scraped into his chest in a screeching drag. 'Dada, get back!' The looking-glass was still in Corbie's grip, so John did the only thing he could think of: he tightened his throat and, pointing at Corbie, called, *Kra, kra, kra*.

All farriers could carry a tune, but the Mackems cared less about it than some clans: they were chanters, not carollers. But Jedediah had played singing games with John since he was old enough to sit upright. It was difficult to imitate a crow's creak precisely, but John's throat was already good and hoarse from Corbie's blow.

Ab heard. It wavered.

Corbie froze – then with a lunge, he was on John again. 'Don't hear trickery!' he shouted to Ab. He pointed at John again and his call, this time, was different: a long, bending *Ha!* sound, and John didn't know what it meant, and Ab was flowing now, eyes whirling black on black, from Corbie to John, from John to Corbie.

Matthew was between them now, trying to block John from Ab's view. 'Not the boy!' he shouted; when the People were confused, sometimes they attacked the one confusing them. 'Kind friend, be after me if you must! Not the boy, me!' And, newly inspired by his ability to kick folks, he made for Corbie.

Matthew wasn't fond of violent sports. He didn't even like horseshoe-toss all that much because his training had made him too good at it for anyone else to have fun; he secretly preferred skittles, where he had an honest chance of losing. But he knew how to play football, and that meant he knew how to whip a foot between a man's legs and trip him.

Corbie, falling, was still holding tight to the looking-glass. He landed on his elbows, the glass right before his face.

Ab flowed towards him and stopped above his head. Corbie flipped the glass over as fast as he could, saying, 'No oh no – no, don't hear trickery, don't hear trickery—' But it was too late, for Ab had seen what it held.

'What is it, kind friend?' John asked. He supposed Corbie would see his own face, but if the fey twist in his head had worked within the looking-glass – if it counted Corbie as kin to himself – then he'd have seen a bird. And Ab knew what bird Corbie had seen in his own features.

Cuckoo, it said.

Corbie covered his face. 'No,' he said.

The birds of the air love their own kind. But there is no justice in the cuckoo.

Ab's dark feathers began to bristle until a thousand filigree knives filled the sky.

Corbie lay on the ground, arms over his head, helpless.

John didn't think about what to do. He acted on pure habit: farriers protected folks from the People. So he ran over and snatched up the looking-glass.

'Kind friend!' he yelled, looking up into the eyes hovering above him. 'Look you here, kind friend!'

Ab's eyes blinked. Trails of thickened air ravelled off in skeins as its eyes began to silver over. The looking-glass couldn't take its image: there was nothing in the reflection but the empty sky above.

The looking-glass couldn't reflect Ab; Ab had reflected the looking-glass.

I must have . . . came the voice, in a kind of sob, and there was a burst of pressure, so hard it slapped John to the ground. Splashes were falling again, but not turning to stone this time; they silvered, reflecting back the white skies with a mirror shine. Light splattered against the sun – and then Ab was gone.

'Johnny,' Matthew said, running forward. It hurt, but he had to put his arms around his son. 'Johnny, well done, *well done*, my man. That was fast thinking. Oh, and you're right, we have a new cousin; Francie's had a girl, a lovely little lass, and untouched, thanks to you! Johnny, *well done*! Are you hurt?' he added, tipping John's face back to look at him. 'I wouldn't say this most of the time, but if you want me to, I will kick him again.'

The threat, however, didn't reach Corbie, who had dropped his hands from his face, a little tentatively – then, seeing a world temporarily devoid of Ab, rolled over on his back.

His hearty laugh rang off the walls of the square. 'Glory be! It's a Smithed place here, old Gyrford, and books and letters and no damn memory at all, and yet someone's got a fairy-servant into their midst! What hill do you come from under, Fairy-pie? How did they catch you? Come along, Maggie-fey, tell an old man how they got themselves a fairy-servant!'

*

There were old Mackem tales of it, told in chants: Jedediah, with the stern conviction that he had no excuse to deny his boy knowledge just because he himself hadn't had the kindest teacher, had taught them to Matthew, and Matthew, a lot more cheerfully, had passed them along to John. Matthew liked to sing them, as long as no strangers were listening, and John had a tendency to harmonise without being invited that Jedediah found perversely satisfying, for you weren't supposed to do that with the old Mackem memory-chants.

So John knew the story of Old Lilly Whisht, whose man of magic had followed her footsteps, sown her seeds, cropped her corn, spun her silks and generally made himself useful until the day Old Lilly offered him a gold coin she found under a stile, upon which the little man had taken himself off, haughty and huffy, flaming with fury, and generally showing all the signs of a labourer who took exception to his hire.

He knew the song of the Man of Pelmere, who hated his neighbours dire, being given over to vice and ire, and who had worked unnamed works to master a fey to serve his wicked way, which had worked upon them seven tricks, involving making them too sick to be nursed (that being trick the first), making their good cows gore (trick number four), and generally being unpleasant, until for the seventh trick the fey baked the unfortunate neighbours in a pie and served them to the Man of Pelmere for his supper, which settled matters once and for all, for he burst from over-eating.

And there was the story of a farrier of sage and shrewd sense who had cozened and coaxed a little fairy-man into doing his bidding, chasing off other fairies that were annoying his neighbours without the use of iron, thus presumably saving himself a great deal of work.

Maybe Corbie Mackem didn't believe that any mortal could have got Ab to turn from him like that, or perhaps, in his hazed way, he could feel John was what Matthew tactfully called 'a little out of the common', and took it to mean more than it did. Or perhaps he mistook the Moorish looking-glass itself for something fey, Corbie not one to believe that foreigners and strangers could get up to cleverness he himself couldn't understand.

But before the day was done, it was clear to everyone that John Smith was, in the mind of his Great-Grandfather Corbie Mackem, a fairy-servant possessed of powers, taking the form of a Magpie but capable of speech, and altogether just such a fey creature as any man would wish at his service.

And Corbie's view of all fey creatures was that he was put upon this earth to master them.

Corbie no longer left the house unmasked. He'd helped himself to a wicker-and-wire hood intended for Lord Robert's beekeeper and wouldn't give it back no matter how they protested that Lord Robert's beekeeper resented being kept waiting for his order.

He paid little attention to anyone else now; his mind was focused on the fairy Magpie he was certain lived in their midst, and in particular, how it might be bent to his own bidding.

Stan Mackem was of the view that John should simply stand up for himself more, but Matthew and Jedediah feared to allow it. Corbie might not dare call on Ab now, but he was still the elder of Gyrford by law, and he had no compunction about smashing aside any bird that hindered his great project. Jedediah was willing to take some slaps if it would protect Johnny, but it didn't: any interference made Corbie rougher and angrier, and it was as likely to be Agnes or Constance, or John himself, who bore the brunt of it.

They tried, but Corbie had a way of appearing suddenly. John might be minding his own business, scooping charcoal into the scuttle, and Corbie would rush up behind him and leash his arm in a Mackem rope-knot, examining it with chant and sign in order to find out why this fairy-man was able to handle an iron shovel.

John might be sitting in church, listening to the sermon with about half his attention and dispersing the rest of it upon the windows, carvings and wood-knotted pews of the building, only to find a worked crucifix shoved up against his mouth just as he was trying to say 'Amen', Corbie being of the view that it was necessary to test if the Smiths' fairy-man had any infernal alliances. (He had a moment of doubt as John spluttered in fury at the hard metal squashing his lips against his teeth, but then John snatched the cross, kissed it with more defiance than devotion, and treated the congregation to an incensed rendition of the early verses of Matthew Chapter One at high speed. That chapter was one of his favourites, for he liked the sound of all the names, but Matthew – that is, Matthew the smith, not Matthew the apostle – intervened gently before he could get to Salathiel and Zorobabel, or even Aminadab, and John sat down, complaining bitterly that being interrupted even when he was speaking sacred words was too much for anyone, and if he was supposed to follow the Fourth Commandment, his father ought at least to *help*.)

John might playing in the square, kicking a ball around with the other Gyrford lads, when, much to his friends' amusement, he found himself collared and offered mortal food by way of binding him to this earth – and when he said he wasn't hungry, Uncle Corbie, being a practical man, simply pinched his nose until he opened his mouth. To do such a thing to a twelve-year-old in front of other boys is a crime according to any law of nature you could name, even if it hadn't hurt, which it did.

And the neighbours of the village, being admirers of Corbie, were growing inclined to blame the Smiths, especially over John's attempts to avoid Corbie. Ida Pearce thought that if they couldn't control a poor addled man in church then they should at least leave their impious son at home, where he wouldn't bother Mister Mackem. Micky Carpenter said that he'd found John Smith sitting right at the top of his best pear-tree, and when he'd told the lad to come down and stop coming onto a man's land without asking, the boy had given him such impudence – his father should have leathered it out of him years back.

Matthew went so far as to plead with Stan behind his father's back. Surely, he begged, they could care for Corbie in Tinsdowne, where there were more men to manage him and he wouldn't think any Mackem child a fairy? Stan would say only that they had Mackem cares to attend to and the Smiths must carry their own burden, and remained so obdurate on the subject that Matthew and John spent much of the following day in the church, Matthew in struggle with his soul because he was having truly unChristian thoughts about his kinsmen, and John because he was hiding from Corbie.

Corbie worked away at an iron-weighted bird-net, a giant bird-cage and shears to crop a Fairy-pie's wings, and while he worked, whenever he saw John in sight, he spoke to him of the great things they'd do together once they came to an understanding. They'd make Madam Alice Brady a little more natural in her ways towards a pleasant man. They'd shake the birds out of this house, driving out the Rook and Dove and Sparrow and shrewish women. They'd free him from that demon he was shackled to at the altar when he was just a boy, far too young and foolish to know the monster he'd been bedded with. They'd send her right back to Hell, where she belonged.

Janet drove herself to Tinsdowne. The large village sat either side of an old Roman road, one of those straight ones that got you across the country good and fast if you didn't mind staring dead ahead for hours at a time. It was market day, the stalls set out in the square surrounded by big, well-timbered houses, and shouts arose on all sides: *Goooood cloth, fine colours, best weave! Chickens and geese, chickens and geese! Will you have some cheese now?*

The Mackem smithy, unlike the Smiths', was not quite at the centre of things. A sign, carved in oak and ornamented with an iron bracket so ornate it was positively curly, pointed a wooden finger down a side street. The finger was quite realistic, if a bit cracked from age, and while there was no name on the wood – the Mackem objection to literacy evidently extended to their signposting – there hung beneath the pointing hand a plate stamped with the Mackem emblem.

Like the Smiths', this emblem bore a crossed hammer and tongs, but the design was more elaborate. In place of the Smiths' pentangle sat an anvil; the Mackems had never been great believers in the abstract, considering the endless knot too close to astrology, written words and other such flummery. The Mackem anvil, also under a hammer and tongs, sat within an interlocking pattern of seven horseshoes. The number might have been a reference to the seven metals – Mackem chants sometimes referenced the ancient pantheon of copper, tin, lead, gold, silver, quicksilver and iron, and 'hammering quicksilver' was an old Mackem saying for 'wasting your time' – but the Mackems wouldn't swear to that; some reckoned that whichever lad drew it first just found it an easy number to fit around the pattern. From a distance, the interlocked circle looked rather like a Clementing wreath.

The Mackem forge had a well in front of it, and a larger space for the work than in Gyrford. At one corner, leaning his chin on his stick and watching the world go by, sat an aged man: Old Dunstan Mackem, he must be, Jedediah's uncle, the patriarch who was no longer elder. There was a man around Stan's age who must be his brother, doing something at the forge – Esau, that was his name. And in the centre of the smithy were three lads, each as red-headed as the next, gathered around another man, middle-aged and cheery, who was demonstrating something with the occasional joke, judging by the laughter.

That must be Lazarus; he looked very much like his Uncle Stan. That Mackem face persisted down the generations – or it did in Tinsdowne, at least; Jedediah had always had more of a

Smith look. Janet, who liked to trace family resemblances, thought he looked something like Constance, or what Constance might have looked like if she hadn't been struck down with beauty.

As Janet tethered Dobbs, Old Dunstan noticed her and raised a shaking hand. 'Well, Flower,' he said, a little quavery, 'have you need of ironwork?'

Esau, the senior man in Stan's absence, turned from the forge rather quickly. 'Good day, Mistress.' He spoke with the bounce of all the Mackem men, but his greeting was quite civil. 'How can we serve you?'

'Oho,' Old Dunstan said, chuckling as if Esau had made a very sly and naughty joke, 'oh, no doubt you'd serve her – and you a married man.'

Janet blinked. She'd supposed Old Dunstan must be getting frail if Stan had succeeded him, but she hadn't expected this.

Esau patted him on the shoulder and said, 'Pay him no mind, Mistress. What can we do for you?'

Dunstan snickered again. 'You could do more than you should, I'm sure of that.'

It was the tenderness with which his son patted that spoke louder than any words could have. Old Dunstan wasn't just old. Esau was speaking to him the way she spoke to Constance. Age hadn't broken his body; it was his wits starting to fray at the edges. She wondered if he even knew he wasn't elder any more. He spoke to Esau with the jovial authority of a leader; Esau spoke with the mildness of a carer in return.

It was so with his ribald comments, she guessed: some men made remarks to play with you and some did it like dogs pissing against a post, but Old Dunstan wasn't quite like either. By all accounts he'd been a faithful husband. He was laughing now as if he couldn't quite help it: other things had slipped away and stopped distracting him from the fact that folks were mischievous and double meanings were very funny.

'Never you mind me,' she said to Dunstan, and found herself adding a wink. She objected, on principle, to the Mackems – Old Dunstan himself had deafened Constance's ear back in the day, or at any rate he hadn't been quick enough to stop Corbie – but it was hard not to talk kindly to a man who was now so old and shaky and giggly and helpless. 'I know an old cockerel when I see one, but I get my feathers trod in another barnyard, thank you.'

Dunstan might not have the strength of body for a loud laugh, but he hugged himself with one arm and shook, so amused that a tear trickled down his face.

She thought she saw Lazarus Mackem's face soften a little as she turned to him. 'I beg your pardon,' she said. 'No, I'm not here for ironwork. I'm Janet Smith, Matthew Smith's Janet, from Gyrford. I've had word that your Shibbie is a good midwife, or learns to be, and as your Stan is with us, I thought, why not come and fetch Cousin Shibbie too? I'd like to teach a bit and learn a bit, and this way, she could travel back when Stan does and save herself some trouble.'

Laz's look stiffened; he regarded her with an assessing eye. 'Gyrford Smith, eh?' he said, sounding politely wary. 'How does Stan with that old hawk of yours?'

The mention of birds gave Janet a bad moment – but no, he wasn't referring to Corbie and his birdy ideas; Father did sometimes have a fierce, raptorish stare. He usually did it when he felt on the defensive.

'He's well and hearty, thank you,' she said. 'Father's kestrelling over his holding and staying atop the winds,' she added, determined to extract a compliment from the comparison, and Old Dunstan snorted into his scarf. 'As always. No doubt Stan does the same here. Much alike, those two, I'd say.'

Laz raised his eyebrows at that, but he didn't argue. 'Glad to hear it,' he said. 'Well, my Shibbie's free to go if she likes. Harry!'

'Yes, Pa?' The youngest-looking of the boys came smartly to attention; they'd all been listening with interest to the conversation. Janet wasn't sure if 'Harry' was the merciful nickname for something appalling, or if Laz had just liked his sons well enough to give them reasonable Christian names.

'Fetch your sister,' Laz told him.

His brothers grinned at him – evidently sister-fetching was not a favoured job around the smithy – but Harry only smiled a little ruefully and took off with a prompt, 'Yes, Pa.'

Janet looked around. The smithy was quite full of men, but they were all at ease with each other.

'Danny,' Laz told another of his sons, 'get some feed and water for her horse, will you? Shibbie or no Shibbie, she's made a journey here and she'll have to make one back. Where are your manners, boy?'

Shibbie Mackem came in her own time, and when she appeared, she didn't curtsey to Janet but gave a short bow and drew herself up, looking at her cousin with an appraisal quite as frank as Janet's own.

Shibbie wasn't a big lass; she was taller than Janet – though that wasn't saying much – but she made the most of it. Her face was fully Mackem, and the worked iron pendant around her neck had the Mackem emblem on it, but where her menfolk were solid and heavy, she had an elbowy, sharp-hipped quality to her, a skinny girl who hadn't finished growing yet and was offended with gravity for knocking her around just because her knees and shoulders weren't quite where they should be.

'Cousin Janet,' she said, with a slight edge of defiance, challenging Mistress Smith to upbraid her for using so familiar an address to a senior midwife.

'Ah, Cousin Shibbie.' Janet had been a girl with notions herself in years gone by. 'What a pleasure to meet you at last. I've heard fine reports of you. They say you're a hard worker, and as keen to learn as anyone could ask.'

Shibbie tossed her head, not about to submit to the compliment. 'I like to learn,' she deigned to admit. 'All I wish is that every old midwife had things to teach worth the learning. If I think a method is nonsense, I'll say so, you know.'

'Shibbie,' said Lazarus, with the kind of weary sternness Janet heard whenever Matthew tried to rein John in, 'you'll be fit to correct your elders when you're trained and grown. Show some respect.'

Shibbie tossed her head, but she flushed as well, and Janet felt a twinge of unexpected sympathy. Janet had been a fanciful girl with a respectable mother and she knew from experience how much such public reproaches stung.

'She's quite right, mind,' she said, feeling it was time to start managing this girl. She wouldn't have put up with half so much disrespect from one of the Mackem adults, but Shibbie was at that age where you feel much older than you are and desperately wish the world to know it. 'It's the safety of mother and babe that matters, far more than the pride of the midwife. If we don't keep our wits sharp, it's a bad day for the women and children.'

'Hmph,' Shibbie said, still making what she could of her inches to stand tall over Mistress Smith. 'That's well enough, but if I do a good job, I won't pretend I haven't.'

Janet had come to Tinsdowne ready to dislike the whole pack of them – to speak soft and ply them to her wishes, yes, but still to dislike them. It was a little vexing to find that she enjoyed Shibbie's spirit. Janet wasn't one to ignore a slight, but she felt an amused appreciation for impudence.

'That's the way,' she told Shibbie. 'A midwife needs a backbone or she'll never last the years. Now, will you come with me to Gyrford as a guest, or must you stay in Tinsdowne just to prove you won't be told?'

Shibbie considered for a rapid instant, her elbows pinched tight against her narrow, curveless body, before saying, 'Of course I'll go. I already said I would, didn't I?'

'Hey, now,' said Old Dunstan, reaching out. It wasn't a lecherous grasp; he stroked Shibbie's hair as if soothing a baby. 'Who's to go, my lambkin? Won't you take Grandpa?'

At that Lazarus and Esau looked at each other.

'He likes to be with the young ones,' Esau said, a little awkwardly. 'And it was his way to go about. Before.'

Janet had not planned on taking the old man on her

mission – what if Constance recognised him? It was he who'd overlooked her. She didn't care what Stan Mackem would think, but if she couldn't keep him away from Constance—

'Well, I hope you have care for the elders as well as the babes, Cousin Janet,' Shibbie said, with the beginnings of an accusation. 'There's more to life than just the beginnings of it, I'd have you know.'

'Indeed,' said Janet. She was working so fast over the possibilities that she sounded a little absent, and that made Shibbie's mind up for her.

'I'll tell you plain,' Shibbie announced, 'that I reckon Grandpa should come. It's been too long since he made a visit. Cousin Janet, you'll take us both, or I won't come.'

There were elder midwives who might box an apprentice's ear if they felt it necessary. Janet had never been one of them, but she came very close for a moment.

Restraining herself with the reminder that Corbie Mackem would have succumbed to the temptation, she said, as brightly as she could, 'Very well, then. Let's be off; we haven't time to waste.'

Once, decades ago, the north-east Fabers had sent their parson to Gyrford's to reason together on the subject of how a man alone like Jedediah couldn't possibly raise a child as young as Matthew. It was against the laws of nature, being a task that God fitted for women. How, the visiting parson had asked, could a father shape a child so unformed? Why, hadn't they the lesson from God's creatures the bears? When cubs were born, they were mere lumpen muddles; it was the mother's tongue that licked them into shape. If a father bear had tried such a thing, he'd find himself raising formless abominations.

Jedediah had managed not to hit the man of God, who had no children himself and hadn't noticed how carefully Matthew remembered his manners that day.

'Matthew's nature is set,' he'd said as quietly as he could. 'He's no infant and I'm no bear. He'll shape himself within his home, and that's here with me.'

It had been a long dispute, and he'd never really persuaded the visitor. It was just lucky that Mister Haye, the Gyrford parson of the time, was a man of mild and incurious temper when it came to doctrine and considerable interest in the workings of God as expressed in the birds and beasts of Creation. Mister Haye was swayed mostly by Jedediah's undeniable contention that he was, indeed, not a bear. But in Jedediah's heart, that conversation had never really ended.

Matthew had cried his eyes out after that visit. He'd had nightmares for weeks. Jedediah had held him through every one, trying not to feel anything at all, stilling his heart and mind until he was just a voice saying over and over again, 'There now. There now.'

He'd learned that from Agnes: those were the words she'd said, all those times Corbie had made Constance cry.

But Constance was here, crying quietly no matter what Agnes said to her.

'We'll send her back,' Corbie told John cheerfully. 'Back to Hell where she belongs. I'll tell you what, Magpie, she's outlived too much already.'

Outraged, John declared he would never do it, but Corbie

only grinned. Once he had the Maggie-fey under his sway it would be a great deal more biddable.

Jedediah remembered the chalk wolf carved to frighten down the sarsens; the little scrunched-owl fey, screaming as Corbie smashed it on the anvil; a treeful of crows, flapping their wings for an eternity against the captive Ab.

No more of this.

Corbie couldn't live without hurting those he should have loved. So Corbie couldn't live.

No good in lying to himself: he'd have to have it on his soul that he'd killed a man.

The parsons said the lowest circle of Hell was reserved for the patricides, although where they put the infanticides, the men who destroyed their children, he wasn't sure. Higher up, probably. Perhaps they didn't have room for them lower down; there were, after all, more fathers who crushed their children than children who crushed their fathers.

If I burn, I'll burn a Smith.

Corbie was a cuckoo, in fey terms at least, and Ab could be called; Johnny had done it with a crow. He could borrow another one from Tom's hut; it would be good to see Tom anyway, before the end of things.

Catch a crow, call Ab. Be its friend for a moment; Grandpa Clem endured its friendship for decades. I just need to be its friend long enough to teach it what a cuckoo is, and why any just bird has to destroy them.

He'd have Ab after him then, but he was an old man and suicide wouldn't damn him any deeper than he'd be damned already. His family would be free.

That left only the need for something of a cuckoo. It wasn't the season for them, but Jack Lenden had been so afraid of changelings he'd fixed cuckoo eggs to every post on his farm. And Cissie Lenden would never mind if he took one. She was a loyal woman; he did her one favour in childhood and she'd looked up to him ever after. Some folks were like that. Her father had been frightening when the mood was on him, but in between times he'd been tender to her.

Get a cuckoo egg, then do what John had done: call upon Ab with a crow. It would be a long day on his feet, but that was what you had to do if you weren't dazzling. If you weren't full of boisterous laughter like Corbie, so bold in your sweeps that folks who didn't know you thought you a hero. Or if you weren't clever like John, mad but clever, somehow able to dodge in and out of Death's grip. If all you were was plain Jedediah Smith, then there was nothing for it but to step into the world and work until the job was done.

Use a crow to call a fey. Jedediah almost smiled as he set out on his mission of murder. Trust Johnny to think of that.

He couldn't see any of the Lendens on their farm. Across to the west, their pigs were grazing, dotted across the field in pink-and-gold humps. All of them looked pretty much like Left-Lop to Jedediah, but most likely they had their own characters. He thought of savage boars, of sows that ate their own litters.

It had been a long time since he'd been here. He'd avoided that field so many years, the place that might have been his home; when he did have to pass it, he tried not to look.

What would Louise have said if she'd been here now? Her voice was as clear in his head as the day he'd first met her; he could hear the edges of her smile in its echoes.

Louise, I've failed our children. If I don't stop him now, he'll kill Mama, and maybe John with her. I'm not who Matthew deserved.

She was a young woman in his mind, with the future still to hope for. *Well*, she said, *he made do. He's a good lad.*

Louise, would you forgive me if I kill a man?

What do you think I'll say? I'm dead, Jed. I'm just a voice in your mind. She sounded amused. She'd always been the only soul he could bear to laugh at him. *You wouldn't listen to me if I did forgive you*, she said. *You don't plan to forgive yourself, do you?.*

I'll go to Hell, love, he told her. *I'll go to Hell and you won't be there. I'll never see you again.*

To that, she had nothing to say. But she didn't have any better solutions either.

Jedediah looked down the hill at the storehouse Pell now rented for her tools, the home he and Louise had never lived in.

It was a misty day; the grass here always held the dew longer than other places. The edges of the house were a little faded; a memory roofed and doored in an unchanging field.

He couldn't avoid it the rest of his life, even when that time was measured in days now. He could go there, open the door – Pell didn't keep it locked, for no one would dare rob her. He could look inside, see a small, stone room that never sheltered Louise.

He could go to the end with one less weight on his soul. It would only take a minute.

★

The door was closed, and while the latch lifted, there was a lock added beneath it – not one of his workmanship, either. That was a little odd, but it wasn't very difficult to prise open; he would re-lock it before he left.

As he opened the door, his eyes took a moment to adjust to the darkness.

There were shelves of jars and boxes; he'd expected that. Janet carried a bag when she went out to a delivery, but he'd never asked what was in it; that was women's business. He'd supposed Pell needed more equipment, more space to store it, because she was an elder midwife, but that didn't make sense. You fit the tools to the task; the age of the worker has nothing to do with it. Pell had no more equipment than Janet did; certainly not enough to call for a rented house.

And the firepit had ashes in it, not old and crumbling, but wet. When he crouched down and touched them, he could feel the heat of suddenly doused wood.

The room was empty, but it was smaller than he remembered it. It shouldn't have been; he hadn't been a child when he saw it last. As his eyes adjusted he found the reason. The wall opposite wasn't a wall, but a set of panels, hinged across and lightly carved.

He'd seen carving like that before, on the box-bed Pell had given him, her wedding gift, where he'd never slept with Louise. The carpenter was a man from Hawksdowne, she'd said – Roddy Parsons, was it? Or Pearson, something like that. He'd been older than Pell, was long dead now. Pell had saved his wife and his only son from a bloody childbed; since then, Roddy had been devoted to her. 'Never fret about the cost, lad,' she'd said when she gave him the box-bed. 'Roddy Pearson's rates to me would barely pay a mouse.'

It wasn't the same box-bed, but it was the same workmanship, made to fit the house from corner to corner.

Jedediah stood very still. There was no sound coming from inside it.

'It's only me, Pell,' he said.

There was no reply.

'Come out, Aunt Pell,' he said. 'I won't tell Matthew you're here if you prefer. Come on, you must wish to box my ears for trespassing.'

The bed was quiet. There was just the tiny crack of a single straw from the pallet within.

'Aunt Pell,' said Jedediah, 'I can open the door of the bed easy enough. I don't wish to disrespect you. I don't know why you should keep from me. If you preferred to hide from the kind friend in this place than in another village, well, I can't think it the best plan, but I reckon you had your reasons. But I need to speak with you.' He swallowed. Pell was an old woman, not some strong adult he could lay his worries before, but you never stopped feeling young and unequipped no matter the years behind you. If he hadn't by now, then surely she wouldn't either.

'Aunt Pell,' he said, 'please come out. I'd like to see you.'

He'd expected another silence, but he hadn't quite finished his sentence before the crunch of straw made him jump.

'Oh, for pity's sake,' said the voice. It wasn't Pell's. It was delicate, sweet, a liquid flicker of sound clear as a robin's song. It was beautiful – and sounded thoroughly impatient. 'He won't go till he sees you, so you might as well give up dead-leafing in here. We're *spotted*, and that's that.'

Jedediah was too startled to speak. He'd never heard such a voice in his life. It wasn't just unfamiliar, it was . . . *unreal*, except for the fact that he could hear it. The speaker was a woman, but her words had the thin clarity of a piper's flute. It wasn't a voice of flesh – or at least, not the flesh of any land creature. On the word *spotted*, it had trilled, a shivering alarm-call. He'd heard such sounds sing out from the trees and hedges at a dawn chorus, but he'd never known a woman with a throat that could hold the voice of a bird.

Because he'd never met his Aunt Mabel. The second of Clem's daughters, the child gifted with the lovely voice. Mama hadn't liked to think of her, for she'd been sharp and quick-tempered; Pell had said only that Mabbie didn't care for company and had gone to live by herself as soon as she was old enough.

But Pell Smith had always loved her sisters. She'd always stood by the family Ab had left her.

There was no creak as the door of the box-bed swung open.

He didn't know what he'd been expecting – some feathered seraph or knife-beaked hawk – but what he saw was too ordinary to be believed. Mabbie Smith was an old woman well along into her seventies, small, wiry, wrapped up nice and warm against the cold. In height and cast of feature, in build and complexion, she looked very much like Pell.

'Well, Nephew,' Mabbie Smith said, looking upon him with a bright eye. Her voice was as brisk as Pell's, as sweet as a nightingale's. 'So that tomcat father of yours is back, is he? I always told Pell we should have done him thorough the first time.'

Jedediah sat on the stump stool in the corner of the room. He felt the need to.

Pell and Mabbie sat side by side on the box-bed, the door open wide now; within, small hooks held a couple of shifts, a shawl, some cleaning cloths, a comb: all the odds and ends an old woman might need if she were to stay a few nights somewhere.

'No need to faint, man,' Mabbie said. 'You knew you had another auntie somewhere.' It was a quiet, up-and-down chirp; you couldn't say it wasn't a woman's voice, but from a distance, you might have mistaken it for an ousel's chatter.

'Must be easier to talk unnoticed, the way you sound,' Jedediah said. It was the only thought that came to him; the rest of his head was entirely empty. Mabbie Smith sat beside Pell Smith with a casual intimacy, hip-to-hip, that spoke of decades in each other's company.

'Sorry, Jedediah.' That was Pell. She wasn't apologising very deep; it was a swift, practical acknowledgement that he probably had some things to think about. 'But Mabbie liked to live well away from Corbie, and from most folks. I thought you might like to meet her when you were old enough to keep a secret, but – well, by then it was clear enough what kind of father you had. I always knew we might have to do something about him. Best not to burden you if we did. I have to say, if there was anywhere in your holding I thought you wouldn't come, it'd be here. The birds did tell us you were after the cuckoo-eggs – wanting Ab to snatch Corbie away, I suppose – but I didn't think you'd come in here. Just goes to show.'

'What?' Mabbie's remark about how they should have done Corbie thorough the first time was crackling around the edges of Jedediah's skull, but he couldn't quite make himself think it through, not in this instant. What filled his mind more pressingly was shamingly childish: Pell had lied to him, and Mabbie hadn't wanted to know him. He could have had another auntie. He'd always liked having aunties.

Mabbie cocked her head on one side, a neat, quick gesture, but Pell motioned her quiet. 'If you like, dear,' she said, 'you could go now. Ask no questions and you'll carry no secrets. I know you understand that.'

'To hell with that!' The words burst out of Jedediah before he'd had time to weigh them. It took a slow, struggling moment before he was able to say what he really meant. 'This is my holding.'

Although it wasn't, not now, not if Corbie took it back.

No. It was. He'd lived his life here; he'd worked his days watching the land and minding the folks.

'Tell me,' he said, pushing himself forward, 'what's been to do in my holding.'

Some things were simple. Mabbie did not live in this remote house, not usually. She had a shack of her own near Mayton, out in the woods where nobody bothered her except the birds, and the birds, at least, fought honest and let their fights have an ending.

Of course she'd kept in touch with Pell. They weren't Mackems, were they? They could read and write.

Mabbie had done quite all right, thank you. She made a living as a cunning woman: if you could understand the birds then you knew what weather was coming, and farmers will pay for such knowledge. Besides that, crows and magpies were easy to befriend; you never knew when some fine merchant might stop to count his coins, and he'd never catch a black-feathered thief skimming up into the air with a scrap of gold in its beak.

Mabbie mentioned this in the same unblinking manner as she remarked that the birds could tell you which fruits were ripe and ready to pluck, or where the wild bees built their nests. She'd kept herself since she was a young woman, plainly regarding foraging for money and foraging for berries in the exact same light.

Mabbie said with equal matter-of-factness that she liked to visit her sister Pell, and it was easy enough, this being Lenden land and the Lendens themselves never troubling this place. She wore a shawl the same colour as Pell's, carried the same sort of crutch, hid her legs under a long skirt and limped along just like her sister. From a distance, anyone would think she was Pell Smith visiting her storeroom.

'And if it's midwifery they want,' Pell added, seeing that Mabbie was moving rather too fast for Jedediah's spinning head, 'they go to my cottage, and Mabbie doesn't visit there. I won't say we haven't had some near misses, but our luck's held – until now.'

'And,' Mabbie added, her voice clear as water, 'as long as we'd done no harm, it'd do no harm to be spotted.' She sat confident enough as she said that, but she wasn't able to say the word *spotted*, it seemed, without an alarmed little trill on the vowel.

Pell was the only soul she visited. She didn't admit to missing Constance or Agnes; Constance couldn't find her way and Agnes couldn't peck, and Mabbie's offhand view was that they couldn't get out of their cage but she wasn't about to step into it. This lack of indulgence for other touched folks struck Jedediah as a want of solidarity – but when he said something not very coherent on the subject, feeling a muddled sense of anger on behalf of his mother, she fixed him with a sharp stare and said, 'Didn't say I wouldn't mob for them, did I?'

'What do you mean, *mob*?' Jedediah managed.

'Well, dear,' said Pell, her voice no softer than it ever had been, 'that's the thing.'

BOOK FIVE

PELL

All right, listen, Jedediah. I know you're set back, but listen. We haven't much time if we're to keep you elder here.

Don't give me that look. Of course you must stay elder. And don't pretend you don't mean to; we know you've been after the cuckoo eggs here – not all the crows are out of the sky, lad; they've seen you.

Of course you were looking for a way to finish this. You couldn't put it on Matthew; too much heart, that lad. You did a fine job with him, I'll give you that. I've seen fathers enough, and it's not all I'd trust with their young, not without a woman. Not all, nor most. He's all right, your Matthew, and that should be said. But he doesn't want the eldership, not like this.

I reckon you did want it when you were a young man – not the way Corbie had it, mind, or the way he has it now. But you wanted it in your own way. Think you weren't playing elder when you took Cissie Lenden off the iron shovel? When you took Franklin Thorpe under your wing? When you got Constance and Agnes out of Corbie's grip? All those times you took a whipping and didn't run to Constance? Think I didn't see you, lad? You've been elder since you could think and act. What's elder work if not what you've been at all this time?

And we need an elder. One who cares for folks, and Corbie doesn't. We can't have that.

Look you, Jedediah, Agnes could keep Constance safe, up to a point – or keep her comforted at least, and you did what you could too. Mabbie was for doing away with Corbie pretty much as soon as you were old enough to hold a hammer, but then, Mabbie doesn't live with folks.

Constance and Agnes endured, and so did you, and by God he made sure you had plenty to endure. There's men'll kick a stone, and there's men who'll kick a body and blame the body when it bleeds. Why do you think he'd not have me about the place? I've always known what kind of man he was.

Corbie had his women, and that cheered him somewhat. Mind, I won't tell you how many girls I've had to teach to count the days, how to mix up the tansy and pennyroyal. You've no brothers or sisters in Gyrford and you can thank me for that, my lad, else who knows? Most likely, you and Constance and Agnes would all have been out of the smithy and some red-headed newborn 'prenticed in your place – if he'd had a boy, at least. He'd never have laid claim to a daughter; the poor mother could die in a ditch with a girl bastard and he'd barely notice, that man. I thought he might settle over the years, get used to the place, get to like you. Make the best of things. He's not stupid, that man, and I hoped he'd see the sense of it.

But there you go.

And then you go and get yourself a girl.

Of course it was bound to happen – and I'll give you credit, lad, I never had a girl come to me before weeping that Jedediah Smith left her in a mess. You never talked to me of girls you had, but I didn't think you a monk; if the girls hadn't liked you, you'd have wanted more counsel on how to court them. Agnes knew what was what, but she held her tongue; she'd never break a secret of yours, not even to me. You kept things to yourself, and you kept your life away from Corbie. You had that much sense.

But it couldn't go on for ever. I saw you run off to the Attics' house all the time; you liked a home, if you could have one without heartache. You were always a family man.

I knew Corbie paid you, and you didn't spend it on yourself, and then you took Constance and Agnes to the Attics more and more, and, lad, I know a good idea when I see one, but I knew Corbie wouldn't have it.

You were young, and young folks hope for the best, even you. But not in a hundred years, nor a thousand, would Corbie Mackem have you move his wife out from under him.

No, of course he didn't want her himself – but he didn't want to be outmanned. You were more of a man than he was when you were ten years old – a better man, at least, for I can't say that being more of a man is a good thing, men being what they are. But nothing you did for your mother could have done aught but anger him. You could have sent Constance off in a cart drawn by angels and replaced her body in the house with a sack of gold and Corbie would have been angry, and he'd have stayed angry till he died, and made you feel it till you wished you could die first.

Couldn't have that. Not to my boy.

Pell Smith gazed upon Jedediah, her face implacable with love.

Before he could fully feel the weight of what she'd said, she went on, 'And not to your boy either. I knew you'd be having little ones sooner than you meant to – knew you had a girl a year before you told me of her; nothing else could've made you look that happy. And when lads get that look about a girl, soon enough, they get children. I taught you what I could, but young men are what they are. What you'd bear to protect your mother was nothing to what you'd bear to protect a wife and young ones.

'He'd have made you bear it, too – think I didn't see you going ragged and drudging away? – and you'd have taken it to shield them. Enough is enough, we said.'

He looked at them, two small, withered women, wrapped up in sensible woollen shawls against the cold, and for a moment he didn't see his clan. He saw something unknown, a dark bedrock beneath his life he'd never known was there. A coven: sister-witches side by side. But it was just for a second, and it drowned in what he was feeling, which wasn't gratitude, or outrage, but a great, senseless flood of humiliation, warm and deep and soaking through his every pore.

He'd have made you bear it.

You'd have taken it.

They were right. He'd never had the strength to stop Corbie.

Mabbie caught his look, tipped her little head on one side. 'Don't expect him to chirrup,' she told Pell. 'He feels foolish for enduring the man.'

'Oh, for pity's sake,' said Pell, sounding exasperated; her note of motherly impatience didn't make Jedediah feel any less crushed. 'What else were you to do?' She tutted, a sharp, precise *tck* of dismissal. 'Men and their pride. Ask a woman sometime who's more of a man, the one who torments a distracted woman or the one who sweats to free her? Look at Matthew: whose son was prouder of his father, Corbie Mackem's or Jedediah Smith's? Ask him *that*, some time.'

'You might have asked me,' Jedediah said, his voice sounding more timeworn than his aunt's, 'if you meant to put him out of the world. I might have had views, you know.' He cleared his throat. 'I might have helped.'

'Tsh,' said Pell. 'You're a fairy-smith, my man. It wasn't your trade. Look at you today: you made up your mind to rid yourself of Corbie, and with every secret spot in the county in your memory and a forge full of hammers to choose from, you went traipsing after cuckoo eggs when you might have taken him somewhere quiet and cracked his skull like a sensible man. Half-hearted plan if ever I heard one. Nay, you don't think like a murderer, and you shouldn't try. Don't suit you.

'Now me, I've bloodied my hands many a time. Ask your Janet if she's never had to choose whether it's the mother or the baby outlives the birth. Life's a killing business, my lamb.' Her gaze on him was unapologetic, and while her face was lined, her eyes were clear as a hare's. 'Sometimes one of two can live, but not both.

'Some folks end up bloodsmiths.' She grinned, mirthless and fierce. 'But not you, my lad. You were always a good man. A fighter, you were, but not a killer. And that' – she waved a small, age-worn hand, to indicate the removal from the world of a man whose life didn't meet her approval – 'well, Jedediah Smith, that was women's work.'

Jedediah sat very still. 'Women's work,' he repeated.

Life's a killing business.

'Oh, don't take it to heart,' Pell said, sounding dizzingly ordinary. 'We just had to get him gone. It would have been simple enough, except that you happened upon us.'

'What—' Jedediah couldn't quite make it a question. It was a plain statement: the centre-point of his life had happened beyond him. Nothing was what he had ever thought it was.

'Look you, dear,' Pell said. 'Tell me what you remember, that day they overlooked Constance.'

Jedediah had a hundred things to say pressing on his chest, tight and writhing as a bag of tadpoles. 'I remember,' he said slowly, 'that they took Mama to Ab's tree. Corbie and Old Dunstan were to overlook her. Old Dunstan truly thought it would help, I reckon, and Corbie thought it'd settle things neatly for him – easy enough to pull her onto some spike or blade and feign mistake. So they took her to the tree and chained her.

'Then I came along and tried to stop them. I had Louise with me, and a fey spider; No One, it called itself. They wouldn't stop, so I set No One on Old Dunstan, and it blinded him – not for ever, but it turned his eyes around. I remember he fell, and someone ran to help him – Stan, most likely; he was always fond of his father.

'All was in confusion and one of them grabbed at the chain and it came apart – and Ab got out. Ab and some crows. It came out like a naked man masked with feathers.

'So I drove Ab back into the tree and sealed it up. You came along after that, I remember that – you said you'd heard a racket in the woods.

'After that we took Mama away – and Corbie came home. He was sick a few days, and sulky; I reckoned he was too angry to face anyone. He didn't come to the wedding, I remember that, and when we all went to bless the bed, there was a letter from him saying he'd left and I should take the smithy.'

He looked at Pell. 'It was strange that he'd leave me the smithy like that. I'd thought he'd contend with me for mastery all his days.'

'So he would have,' Pell said. 'If it hadn't been your wedding night, most like you'd have thought it over more. Nothing like a pretty girl to take a man's mind off things. That ran in our favour.'

It was mad, this whole business. Or so it should have felt, but Pell was so practical, so calm, that it didn't; it was an ordinary day outside, and this was an ordinary conversation. For such revelations there should have been a raging storm, lightning flashing through the chimney above, the world shaking around them. Not this common stone room still warm from the fire they'd put out.

'Well,' he said, trying to sound sane enough that she'd explain it to him, 'what did I have wrong?'

*

Oh, you put it together pretty well, lad. We had other ideas for how that day would go, that's all. I'd written to Mabbie when I knew you were to be wed, though nuisance that you were, dear, you kept it quiet till the last minute. You always did keep your heart behind your breastbone. Well, I can't blame you; better than getting it stamped on.

It wasn't that hard, when you think about it. Ab was in that tree; we all knew that. And we reckoned it'd have a grudge against the man that had locked it in there. And when Corbie locked Ab in the tree that first time, he'd tricked it in with crows, you remember that part of the history? *There is justice in the crows of the air.*

He'd made Mabbie wheedle the crows into helping him, you knew that. Poor Mabbie; she'd had her complaints about the birds before that day, but she's liked them better than men ever since, and you know, dear, I can't say that I blame her. Well, Mabbie did it, she wheedled the crows to help Corbie, for none of us wished Ab to lour over our lives another minute if we could help it, but she supposed the crows would just fly away after that – she never thought he'd lock them up in the tree too.

He hardly noticed at the time, I reckon. And if you can't understand the birds, perhaps it's an easy thing to forget. But it was a terrible thing if you couldn't, for they were all pent in there together. Ab made a space for them with what it had, but it was small and dark and time wasn't there, and a bird can't fly without time. Well, I don't understand it entire either, and Mabbie says she can't explain it in English, but when she put her ear to the trunk and tapped, she could hear them weeping.

So in the end it wasn't hard for her; she just had to sing back to them and promise them that if they helped her, and coaxed Ab to help her, she knew how to get them out.

If they got out, Ab would get out with them, so all we needed to do was weaken the chain, and then break it when Corbie was nearby. And we weren't a farrier's girls for nothing.

We didn't wish to hang for murder – I would have, if there'd been no other course, dear, but we reckoned there was, you see. Do you remember anything Corbie said, after the tree came apart?

Jedediah's head was aching. It made sense, some of what Pell was saying: the People do not like to be trapped in places, and if you let them out they may very well savage you, even if you weren't the one who locked them in. There was the case of poor old Hal Penton a decade ago; he'd tripped over a stone that held beneath it a white ermine with the eyes of a woman, and it had gone straight for his face. It had bitten his skin to stone, sinking in teeth so rich in fey poison that every bite turned granite, and by the time he'd staggered into the smithy with the vicious snow-white creature hanging from the stone tip of his nose, his head was so heavy he'd fallen right to the floor.

But Corbie had survived; he'd been shocked, knocked about, but he'd survived. Ab had stepped out of the tree, tall, masked in feathers, and Jedediah had driven it back. Corbie didn't vanish until days later – and all that time Ab had been back in the tree.

'Don't frown at your knees,' Pell commanded. 'Tell me: what do you remember about Corbie after he came out of the tree?'

'He was dazed,' Jedediah said. He was frowning now, and

realised, all of a sudden, why it all felt so ordinary. This was work; this was a fey puzzle to unknot. He should have been weeping or raging, or else perhaps kissing Pell's feet, but all he knew to do was try to think it out. He'd been labouring at this business all his life, and he wasn't sure how to stop.

'Dazed, is it? Try to remember, lad.'

'Well,' Jedediah said, 'he didn't say much. Only "What?", that I remember. Then you put him to bed and he wouldn't see anyone one . . . and' – he looked up – 'you wouldn't let his brother see him either. You wouldn't let Old Dunstan stop in on him.'

'No I wouldn't,' Pell said, with mild satisfaction. 'It's one thing to pass for dazed when everything's in confusion, but another to fool a man's own brother.' She lifted her chin at him, and Jedediah saw in her face no shame.

Well, dear, he was always a man who might leave sudden, your father. Nobody, not even those who admired him, would doubt that. And it wasn't difficult to write a letter and say it was at his asking; nobody in Gyrford knew Mabbie's handwriting.

Mabbie persuaded the crows, and the crows persuaded Ab, and that's all there is to it. Ab could change *anything*; it changed Constance and Agnes and Mabbie herself when they were barely born.

For Ab to change a crow to look like Corbie, just for a couple of days? Not difficult.

For the crow to *pretend* to be Corbie, now, that was a little harder. Crows can speak a few words of English if you teach them, but not long talks. But Mabbie managed that – she taught it to say 'What?' and 'I'm sick, leave me alone,' and 'God help us,' and that covered pretty much everything we could think of.

We'd thought Ab would get out, make an end of Corbie, and then the crow would take his place for a few days. They don't reckon time like we do, so we promised it would only have to stay until the church bell rang – you were to marry in a couple of days, after all, and when the bells started ringing, everyone would be in the church, or just coming out. If the crow was a little way down the road, then no one would be there to see it shed its Corbie-shape and fly off free.

And so it did. But you see, we hadn't reckoned you'd be there at the Ab tree, with your uncle and your spider and all the rest of it – but you in particular, Jedediah. See, you acted like a farrier.

Ab came out of the tree, and it grabbed what it could. That was Corbie.

You said Ab came out of the tree like a naked man masked with feathers. Not quite right, dear.

The feather mask, that was Ab.

The naked man?

Well, that was Corbie.

What it did with his clothes I don't know. I'd guess it was covering Corbie with feathers, starting at his face, and did away with the clothes to make room for them. Things were so confused at that point I reckon Ab forgot it was Corbie it had hold of and just reckoned it had a man.

But you drove it back into the tree, like a good lad. The mask went back into the tree, and it pulled Corbie with it.

Corbie's no bird, by the by, not in his mind. Mabbie says he's more tomcat than anything else, all scratch and piss, but he does think himself a bird, in a way. He had to, to shield from Ab. Ab had hold of his head, so he had to change what was in it pretty quick.

He was never stupid, that man, alas – not right in the head now, but not stupid. We heard of that looking-glass trick John tried. If Ab finds out Corbie thinks he's a cuckoo, not a crow . . . Well, he's right: he's a cuckoo if he's any bird. But Ab won't like it. We can use that, or hold it in reserve, at least.

In any case, that's what happened that day. We meant to let Ab take Corbie out of the world, but it took him into the tree instead, because you turned up. But the crow misled everyone, so no one thought much about it, and we decided to let be, for as long as Corbie was in the tree, he couldn't trouble us. It's a shame he didn't stay there. I reckon Ab got a taste of freedom and, in the end, thought up another way to get out. That poor pig. Pigs weren't meant to fly, bless them.

'Wait you.' Jedediah had been listening too long; he heard himself speak with a snap, the sure authority of a farrier. 'That's no plan. You meant to just let Ab out of the tree – and then what? Let it ravage the land again? Once it ate Corbie, then what?'

Pell shrugged, looking a little surprised it wasn't obvious. 'Well, dear, you were one-and-twenty. You'd have found a way to get rid of it somehow.'

Pell had not raised him to gape, but circumstances were what they were. 'Clem didn't.'

'No. Poor Dada. But you always were cleverer than him.'

★

After a long moment, Mabbie sang out, 'Swallow the worm down. It'll squirm the less once it's all the way into your belly.'

Jedediah looked at his hands. They were scarred, hard-palmed, the skin on their backs dappled with the years. They should have been shaking, but they weren't. When he curled them into fists, they held.

'All right,' he said, 'so enough is enough. My father's back, and he'll hurt my kin. And' – the phrase came to him before he heard the echo of Pell in his words – 'I can't have that. I'm no elder, so I can't send him away. Stan Mackem made that clear: I never made a master-work; I'm a journeyman working extra shifts. But I can't have him hurt them. I had an idea much like yours, to raise Ab against him, but I'd not like to murder if I can help it. Have you another plan, Aunties? I'll listen if you do.'

'The crows.' Mabbie's voice was a sweet note, sharp as a pin. 'Once you used the crows to warn him out of the county. You told Old Dunstan the crows would never forgive him.' She twittered for a moment, then recalled herself. 'Crows *don't* forgive: Mackems will remember that, Stan Mackem will remember that. He heard you say it, back at one-and-twenty. I can set them after Corbie, drive him from the county, drive him from the county.'

Jedediah thought it over, a quick set of flashes within his brain. 'Can't be done,' he said. 'They're too afraid of Ab – they're all in hiding.'

'Well, so you get rid of Ab first,' said Pell, a little out of patience with him missing the obvious.

He'd borne a lot today. He'd listened to his aunts talk of

taking his father out of the world with no more compunction than they'd have cleaned a pair of boots. He'd sat still while they told him, blithe as robins, that they'd had to take the decision for him, that he wasn't fit for women's work. He respected his elders. Pell had been a mother to him, almost. But this was just too much.

'How,' he shouted, 'do you think I'll do that? Do you think I haven't beaten my head over and over to think of how? "Get rid of Ab", like you'd sweep up a cobweb – how in the name of *anything* do you think I'll do that?'

'Well, as to that,' Pell said, with the maddening tolerance of a woman ignoring the fuss of a sixty-year-old toddler, 'talk to John and Matthew, of course. Talk to that Franklin of yours; I'd bet my other leg he'll help you. Don't try to do a one-man job when you've other men at your bidding. Talk to them, you fool. Talk to John in particular; he'll have some notions. Put your common sense under them and you might have something.'

Jedediah shook his head. 'I – I can't,' he said. 'They shouldn't know what I planned today.' He swallowed. If they could do it with crows, send Corbie away without murder, he would rush at the chance; the relief of it was sweeping through him with such passion he was embarrassed. But he'd have killed Corbie if it would protect John and Constance, whatever Pell said.

He was almost sure he would have.

'I can't tell them,' he said. 'They'd have to know you meant to murder and I can't do that to them. They – they're good souls. I can't – I have to shield them. I can't do that.'

'Oh, for pity's sake,' said Pell, and Mabbie scraped her feet along the floor as if preparing to fly away from such nonsense. 'You think they'll stop being good souls if they hear an old auntie was willing to bloody her hands? They won't, man. They'll help you.' She bent an eye on him, unyielding. '*Never made a master-work*, indeed. If you think your family isn't your master-work, Jedediah Smith, then you've forgotten to think like a farrier.'

BOOK SIX

SMITH

Franklin should have been at his work, but he was hesitant about leaving Gyrford. He wasn't sure why he felt so ill at ease about that, but Mister Smith had been away since dawn and he didn't feel quite able to go, so he was still in the square, discussing his new granddaughter's many perfections with Matthew, when the cart clattered in.

Holding the reins was the welcome sight of Janet, with an alert-looking young girl beside her – and then there was a figure he recognised.

Matthew didn't pay the old man much heed; he was too busy jumping up to kiss his wife. The red-headed girl was looking disgusted at the ardour of folks well over thirty, but the old man laughed in pure delight, then looked about him with shrewd, shining eyes.

For a moment Franklin was sitting again before a burning barn, held in the lap of a young woman stroking his hair, watching the man he worshipped speaking tensely to an elder. *You'll have to forgive me, Uncle. I've promises to keep.*

But Old Dunstan Mackem had shrunk through the years.

The bright intelligence of his glare hadn't dimmed, but it no longer pierced. He gazed at the kissing couple as if at a spectacle of jollity put on for nothing less than merriment of the whole world.

'Ah, I knew it,' he said, laughing so hard he could hardly speak. 'Nothing like a fine cock to fly home to, hey, pretty chicken?'

Janet, evidently not surprised by this remark, grinned back, saying, 'Now then, you old Peeping Tom, you keep your fine eyes to yourself.'

Dunstan, nothing discouraged, called cheerfully to Matthew, who looked a little startled by so bold a greeting, 'Well, now, so you'll be our handsome Chanticleer, then? Got yourself a fine flock of little ones, so I hear.'

'Um, good day, sir,' Matthew said. He wasn't a devotee of the old beast fables folks liked so well, such stories being full of torments and flayings – they'd given him nightmares as a child – and being addressed as the foolish cockerel of the tales by a man who nonetheless seemed well disposed rather threw him. He glanced at Janet, but she just winked at him in a manner more romantic than enlightening, so he gave it up. The Mackems were nicknamers; any new handle was probably a friendly gesture.

'Yes,' he said, invoking the safety of plain facts, 'I – we do have four children.'

Something in the word 'four' amused Dunstan so much that he bent over laughing, but before he could comment on it, Stan Mackem came out. 'Pa?' he said, sounding alarmed. 'What do you here?'

'Hardly had time to *do* anything yet!' Dunstan grinned, in the manner of a man given far too good an opportunity to pass up the joke. 'There's my darling lad. There you are, so you are.'

Stan gave only a glance at Matthew before stepping towards the cart. His voice was quieter than Jedediah had ever heard it. 'Shibbie, love?' he said. 'Why did you bring Grandpa? Is he unwell?'

Shibbie lifted her chin. 'He'll be none the worse for an airing,' she said, aiming for haughtiness but sounding just a bit hurt. 'As if I'd bring him *anywhere* if he needed rest. Why shouldn't he have some sport out and about, eh?'

'Oh, for my sporting days,' Dunstan laughed, and then, on the sudden, looked sad. 'Oh, my Stan,' he said, 'your ma was a fine woman.'

Stan moved quickly. 'Come on, Pa,' he said, reaching out to take Dunstan's fragile hand. 'Let's set you on your feet, find someone to make you comfortable.'

'And you a respectable man!'

'She wouldn't come without him,' Janet said aside to Matthew.

'Why am I Chanticleer now?' Matthew whispered.

'Tell you later. All to your credit, never fear. He needs a little looking after, but Shibbie's all for it.'

'Well, if he likes, I reckon we could—'

Matthew stopped, for Old Dunstan had given a reedy yelp of fear.

When Franklin turned, the figure behind him was a shock, even though he should have known to expect it: a faceless weave of willow, a flat plate interwoven with dark knots of wire, covered over with an iron-threaded hood as if some ghastly foxglove had grown tall and mighty enough to loom. It covered the head of a figure that stood with fists clenched.

'Oh,' Janet said with bitter courtesy, 'good morning, Uncle Corbie.'

It was only a beekeeper's mask, and on another man it might not have looked so sinister. Folks had unfortunately forgotten to tell the bees about the death of Lord Robert's beekeeper's brother-in-law and since then, the People had been crawling into their hives, donning waxen crowns and ordering away all the honey. The beekeeper should have had the mask, and then Matthew could have sorted the hives, but Corbie wore it everywhere now, only taking it off to eat – or to frighten Constance by threatening kisses when she was least expecting them. He had a sense for the moments most likely to make her heart fail within her.

Beekeeper masks were not a Mackem tradition but something Jedediah had learned from his Grandpa Clem, and Dunstan stared at it in bewildered alarm.

A slow chuckle rose from within the mesh – not a joyful laugh, like Old Dunstan's giggles, but the snarl of a dog seeing a foot set over its threshold.

'Well,' Corbie said, 'I see Time's run his plough over *you*, brother. Come to claim my holding, have you? Feel the need to add a little more to your honours?'

Franklin remembered Dunstan Mackem a strong man, authoritative and bold-spoken – Mister Smith had felt the need to stand up to him, he remembered – but not fearsome; he'd never had the feel of a man who'd whip you in temper. It gave Franklin a deeper pang than he'd ever expected to see the man turn aside to his son, clutching Stan's shirt with trembling fingers and start to cry.

Everyone was frozen for a moment. The Smiths looked at each other, standing around the man who might still, cuckoo or not, call upon Ab. If Corbie grew angry, the havoc he could wreak didn't bear thinking of.

'Now, Pa; now, Pa . . .'

Janet, who had not liked Stan Mackem one little bit, turned to look at him with a jolt of recognition: that was the tone you used to console a hurt child, the light of your life. 'Now, Pa,' Stan soothed, 'never you mind. Let's go and see where you'll rest.' Old Dunstan's quiet sobs faded and Stan said, giving him the tenderest of nudges, 'Hey, now. You can share my bed. Make sure I don't creep into anyone else's, eh?'

And Old Dunstan gave a tentative giggle.

'I don't know what you all think you're about.' Shibbie Mackem broke into the conversation, tossing her head in defiance at anyone who might call her great-grandfather addled or her great-uncle soft. 'Letting him speak to an elder like that. All right, Nuncle,' she added to Stan, although he hadn't upbraided her, 'I suppose that is Mister Smith? How do you do, Mister Smith? Where am I to sleep?'

Matthew started to say something, but Corbie decided to take off his mask, the better to grin at his frightened brother, and that improved his view of Stan and Shibbie.

'Well, so the shrew's back,' he said, 'and who's this?' He bowed to Shibbie, who reached for Old Dunstan, partly to protect him and partly for comfort in the face of Corbie's probing stare. 'Well, and here's a lovely sight for my saddened eyes. Hair like fire on a hilltop, bright enough to dazzle me. Ah, I always did love a red-headed woman.'

'Welcome to Gyrford, dear,' Matthew said to Shibbie, ignoring Corbie. 'I'm your Cousin Matthew, I'm Janet's man. You'll meet my young ones soon enough – oh, you're here, are you, Johnny?' John had been watching events for some time, but decided to step out when he saw Uncle Corbie upsetting the old man. If anyone was going to kick him again, John wanted to be there. 'This is your cousin Shibbie, love. Cousin Shibbie, this is our John.'

Janet stood very still, looking from one face to another: Stan Mackem, angry and defensive, shielding his father; Shibbie, holding her nerve in a crowd of strangers; Corbie, unmasked.

'Rook,' she said to Corbie, quiet and careful, indicating Stan. Then, indicating Shibbie, 'Pretty girl?'

'Well, there's eyes in the shrew,' Corbie said. 'Glory be, rooks every which way. Never did like the rattle of them. There's pestilence in that tree up over the smithy, I'll be bound.'

'Matthew,' said Janet, softer still.

Matthew looked at her, searching her face. Years of marriage rose in his understanding, and he covered his mouth.

Franklin, not being married to her, shifted his feet in discomfort: whatever she meant by this, it weighed heavy in her voice.

'Oh,' said John. '*Oh*.'

'What's all this to-do?' Stan demanded. 'Look you, Matthew, it's your father's father here – don't let him harry mine. Make an effort, man.'

'Oh, poor Dunstan,' Corbie said, his voice hard and happy,

'looks to me like Tinsdowne could do with some help. Always did have a yearning to see the old place again.'

'No,' Stan said, very fast. 'No, you are not asked for. Leave him be.'

'You see it, don't you, Johnny?' Janet said. 'I know I'm no farrier, but I'm right, aren't I?'

'Yes,' said John. '*Yes*, yes you are. It must be. Well, I didn't think of that!'

'Mistress Janet,' said Shibbie, seeing Stan's angry puzzlement and tilting her chin, 'I think it's poor nursing not to let an old man come in and rest. Hadn't we best be about it?'

'Janet?' Franklin said. 'What is it?'

Before Janet could answer, John jumped in with the enthusiasm of a terrier sighting a mouse. 'Cousin Shibbie,' he said, 'what would you say you were to Mister Stan? In relation, I mean?'

Shibbie was not old enough to ignore a provocation. 'I am his great-niece,' she said with dignity. 'His nephew Lazarus is my father, and son to his brother Esau.'

'Not a child or grandchild of his, then? Not by direct line?'

'Didn't I just say so, sir?'

'Well, then,' said Janet, 'now we know why Corbie's father was so glad to get him out of Tinsdowne at any price. Shibbie, dear, take Mister Dunstan inside, will you? There's food and drink in the kitchen; give him what you think best.'

'Well, not before time,' said Shibbie, and led Old Dunstan in by the hand.

Stan made to follow, but Janet stopped him, saying, 'He'll be well enough with her a moment, Stan. Wait you: this is for you to hear.'

'Janet,' Matthew said, quite softly, 'should we wait till Dada comes back?'

'The sooner the better,' Janet said; she had little sympathy for the man who'd questioned Father's eldership. 'Stan Mackem, the kind friend took out of Corbie's head the knowledge of his family, yes? Of his *descendants* – be a child or grandchild or great-grandchild of Corbie Mackem and he thinks you a bird. It's not all in the bloodlines, for he saw the same on Franklin; he thought Franklin Father's son, and I wouldn't call him all wrong. So we thought, when he called you a rook, it was just because you were kin.

'But Shibbie has the Mackem face just as much as you have. And he didn't see a bird; he saw a girl.'

'So?' Stan Mackem stood rigid.

Janet's reply was almost tender. 'So she's not his child nor grandchild. For nephews and nieces, he doesn't see birds – but he saw you, and he saw a rook.'

John was so eager to support the point that he didn't notice the sudden whitening of Stan Mackem's face. 'Father to son,' he said to Matthew. 'He looks *much* more like Uncle Corbie than Grandpa does.'

'It's usually not my business if a man begets a child on his brother's wife,' Janet said, 'but I can see why, if he does, his own father might wish him out of the village and married to another woman. Any other woman.'

She turned back to Stan, put her hands on her hips. 'If you're this much set upon a son's duty to a father, well, I'd say it's time to consider whose son you truly are.'

*

Jedediah was nowhere to be found. Someone needed to tell him, but he'd been missing all day. He hadn't said where he was going, only that he needed to go out and survey, and he'd been so low-spirited of late that nobody had liked to press him.

There was nothing to do but wait. Customers were scarce that day; Matthew had given everyone such good advice on so many small matters that none of them had grown into proper jobs. All they could do was sit and stare at each other.

Janet, returning from Francie's lying-in, broke up the awkwardness by reporting that the Mackems were all invited to board at the Brady house. It should suit everyone, she declared: Old Dunstan was known to like babies, and Shibbie could help nurse Francie, and there was room for Stan too, who would no doubt like the company of his kin. And, she added privately to Matthew, it would be a kindness to Anthony to take the favour: the poor man still hadn't forgiven himself over his mistake with the pig, and any amends he could make would be a balm to him.

That kept them busy for a bit. Shibbie did, in fact, show herself a capable girl; if she wasn't quite as perfect as her lifted chin would assert, Janet acknowledged that she shaped well for a novice.

Molly, identifying the adult most likely to support her, had hinted to her grandfather that she'd be interested in training. Jedediah had considered the matter for a long minute, then, getting out his pipe, said, 'Go on then, lass. If we're to have children, we must have midwives, and we'll need them with good hearts. Better you than most.'

It didn't sound quite the affirmation had Molly hoped for,

but after he said it, he kissed her forehead, then clapped her on the shoulder in the way he usually reserved for her father and brother, so to begin her training she'd gone over to Francie too. Shibbie was very pleased to take her in hand. She delivered long streams of information with a kind of rapid clarity that would have lost a slower thinker, but Molly kept up and Shibbie, after the first hour, acknowledged that Molly Smith wasn't stupid. By the second hour, she'd rolled her eyes at Molly over the ineptitude of grown folks, and if that wasn't a seal of approval, Molly didn't know what was.

Then it was noon, and Jedediah still wasn't back.

Matthew sat in the smithy, with Janet and John beside him.

'Darling,' Janet said after a compassionate silence, 'do you mind? Another uncle, I mean?'

Matthew gazed into the forge. It was hard to put into words what he was feeling about it. 'I always loved my Ditton uncles,' he said at last. His mother's brothers couldn't visit as often as he'd have liked, but they were warm and gentle men who had been very kind whenever he'd seen them. Matthew's Ditton uncles were kin, but any descendent of Corbie Mackem was *clan* – and until the day he'd had a son, the whole of his clan had been himself and his father: Jedediah and Matthew Smith of Gyrford.

He'd been so afraid, after his mother died, that someone would take him away. He still remembered standing at his mother's graveside, holding Dada's hand, the world so empty around him that he could barely feel the ground beneath his feet, and Dada's hand was the only thing keeping him from falling and falling for ever. Godfa Tom had stepped up to Dada at one point, offered to hug him, and Dada had stepped back. 'Don't,' he said, very quietly. 'Can't.' His face was a mask – but he hadn't let go of Matthew's hand.

Only when they returned home and shut the door behind them did Dada release him – and the cold had closed over Matthew's head. At that moment he had cried and cried, shaking and terrified, lost in the void, until Dada had picked him up and set Matthew on his lap. He'd seemed so big at the time, wrapping him in his arms. He didn't speak, just held on, very still, while Matthew cried his broken heart out.

In the end, when Matthew had run out of tears, Dada had leaned back a little to wipe his face with gentle, callused fingers. 'Are you tired?' he'd asked, but Matthew hadn't known what to say.

Dada set him on his feet, took him by the hand and led him into the smithy. 'Come on,' he said, 'I'll show you how to make a nail.'

And that had been their life together: he'd made nails, day after day, for Dada told him the first lesson was to make a hundred of them. Dada looked over his work, advised, directed, confirmed, and at the end of each day, he'd say, 'Good lad. Good work.' And the nails got more and more like real nails and then, one day, he'd finished his hundredth, and it *was* good. He could measure the time in strips of iron between that day in an empty world and that new day, when somehow, he'd got better – or a better ironworker, at least. He'd grown stronger in his arms and learned some skills and now he was a farrier's apprentice, who knew how to make a nail.

Other farrier clans had offered to take him in, and if they had, he knew they'd have taken his heart out of his chest and left nothing behind but an empty boy. He didn't want to be a Gowan or a Faber: he was a Smith of Gyrford. That was who they were, and that knowledge was what held his heart safe.

He hadn't *ever* wanted to be a Mackem.

'I like the Dittons better too,' John put in, and Matthew put an arm around him. 'But I think we'll have to get used to Stan Mackem,' John added, with cheerful insensitivity. 'Never mind. You know, I don't think he likes Uncle Corbie any better than we do.'

'Johnny, dear,' Matthew said. His voice sounded the way it always did: loving, patient. He'd rested his life on patience. 'Why don't you go over to Molly? You've more new kin to think of than . . . Nuncle Stan.' That was what Shibbie had called him: Nuncle, a word for uncles, but also just older men you were fond of. They could make it do. 'You haven't met your cousin Lissy yet,' he told his son. 'She's to be christened Alice, after her dear auntie, but Lissy so we don't mix them up. Go and see her, she's a darling.'

And with that, John was sent out into a world where he had loving kin in plenty.

As John entered the bedroom he saw a crowd: Molly and Shibbie were busy fixing an iron talisman in the window, while Cousin Anthony sat on the bed beside Francie, a small bundle held very carefully in his arms.

'Johnny!'

John was a bit dismayed, seeing Francie: everyone had said she was doing very well, but she was puffy-faced, her eyes dark-shadowed, her hair fraying away from her across the bolster.

'Are you all right, Francie?' he said in a bit of a blurt. He'd meant to come in very confident, perhaps give the girls some tips on how to set up the talisman, but no one appeared in need of his help.

Francie laughed; it was a tired laugh, but sounded grateful. 'Bless you for asking,' she said. 'You'll find this out when you have babies: visitors flock around to *tell* you how very well you are. You don't get asked all that much.'

'Well, there's gratitude,' said Shibbie, without lifting her eyes from the talisman.

'Carp at me all you like – it'll do me good – but carp at a patient again and you'll leave the room, Madam,' said Mama, a lot more severely than usual. 'You carry a body between your bladder and your backbone for nine months, then push out a head that size, and see if you feel in need of comments.'

Cousin Anthony, dandling his daughter, gave John the rather helpless look that men exchange when women outnumber them and start talking frankly.

'I'm better than I was after Thomas,' Francie said, seeing the look, 'and as these things go, that's no worse than anyone feels.' Her gaze kept moving from John to the baby, a constant *flick, flick, flick* of the eyes, as if Lissy was a scrap of metal on the coals that might, at any moment, melt out of shape. 'Woman to farrier, love,' she added, 'I feel as if I've been kicked in the belly, I'm torn in places I shan't name, and more of me feels bruised than not. But that's what we mean when we say the mother of a newborn's doing very well.' She gave him a weary smile; she and John had always been good friends.

Cousin Anthony shifted his arms a little and there was a bleat from within the blankets. 'Oh, look who's awake,' he said. 'Oh, now, there's a Lissy! There's Lissy-eyes!'

It seemed to John that fatherhood did something to people's judgement, or at least to their ability to talk sense. Still, he was curious about this new cousin of his. He would have preferred another boy, feeling that he was well supplied with sisters at home, but never mind; he did like his sisters, for the most part, and Lissy would hopefully grow up to make more intelligent remarks than the ones she was hearing just now. He edged over to peer at her.

'Here,' said Cousin Anthony, startling him rather by handing the bundle to him. 'Look, Lissy, here's your big cousin John.'

John wasn't used to being handed babies; with Thomas, everyone had been so busy crowding around that John hadn't taken his turn with the new little lad. It was one of those things folks did to his sisters without a second thought, planting babies into their arms, but for himself, meeting new neighbours was experienced more at a distance. He knew enough to keep Lissy's head steady, doing so ostentatiously in case anybody felt the need to lecture him, but he was surprised at the weight of her. He'd somehow pictured her light as a kitten, but Lissy wasn't like that at all: she was solid, compact, made of sturdy stuff.

'Isn't she a beauty?' Cousin Anthony said, unable to resist reaching out to stroke his daughter's face.

John had no desire to quarrel with the squashed little body

in his arms, but he couldn't help feeling that she pretty much looked like all babies, so he avoided the question by saying, 'Well now, Lissy.' He stopped. What else could you say to an infant that wasn't embarrassing nonsense? Since he'd always liked it when folks spoke to him man-to-man, he decided to extend Lissy the same courtesy. 'I'm John, and I reckon I'll be your farrier when you're older,' he said, 'so you needn't fret about that. I reckon you've enough to fret about, having got here the way you did. It's not all squashing, though. You'll have good times enough. You've folks love you already.'

Lissy had been dozing, but as John chatted to her, her swollen lids drifted open. Her eyes were an odd smudgy blue and she wasn't clear what to do with her face; she chewed on her mouth with a sleepy smacking noise. Then her lips crooked down in a profound pout and her forehead rumpled till she looked like nothing so much as an offended old magistrate. She bleated again, an unhappy little goat-sob, then began to cry.

'Hey now,' John said, a bit alarmed, 'no need to take it amiss.'

Lissy was starting to thrash her head to the side, casting around with a desperation quite in excess of any crisis John could imagine afflicting her. Then she turned to the other side, fastened her lips on his hand and sucked with a muffled little moan.

'There now, sweeting,' Cousin Anthony said, lifting her out of John's relieved arms. 'Who's a hungry lass?' His tone was soothing, and John would have expected Lissy to be reassured, but Lissy was having none of it. She squirmed in her father's grip, turned her head aside again and wailed.

'I'm sure you'll be fed in a moment,' John told her, rather discomfited.

'Hush, now,' her father soothed, passing her to Francie; she raised her shift – John turned politely aside – and the sobs were replaced by a little mumbling rhythm.

'There now,' Cousin Anthony said, gazing rapt at his wife and daughter. 'That's a good girl.'

'That's . . . forgiving of you,' John said. Anthony had been close to despair over his mistake with the pig; at least Lissy was cheering him up.

Something about her was plucking at John's mind – not quite an idea yet, but it felt like it wanted to be. 'Didn't she know your voice?' he asked, more or less at random.

'Ah, she does, the good girl,' Anthony doted, 'but sometimes only Mama will do, eh pretty one?'

'You were the same, Johnny,' Janet contributed. 'That's babies, even after they're weaned. You were glad enough to go to Dada or Grandpa, but Anthony has the right of it.' Like John, she felt sorry for Anthony: she'd made mistakes enough around the People in her own day, and it didn't do for a well-meaning man to berate himself.

'So . . .' John tried to gather his thoughts. 'Lissy's like any baby?'

'Oh, now, don't say that to her,' Francie said with a soft little laugh. She didn't raise her eyes from the scrap at her breast. 'Like any baby, except the best of them. Lissy and Thomas both – and you too, in your day. You were lovely.'

'All of us,' Janet said loyally. 'Even Grandpa must have been the sweetest of moppets, once upon a time. Not that—' She restrained herself; Shibbie was a Mackem, however intelligent, and it wasn't fair for a teacher to traduce even so poor a father as Corbie before his kin.

And there it was. John could see it all clear, except some small details. He could have kicked himself for not seeing it sooner – except he couldn't have.

He opened his mouth to tell his mother what he'd just realised – but no, with so much trouble over the eldership, he was going to tell Grandpa first. Whatever anyone said, his elder was Jedediah Smith: John would do the duty of a farrier and bring his news to his elder.

'Well, I think I should be off,' he said. 'My compliments – she's a – a very good baby.'

Anthony actually laughed. 'Never mind, Cousin John,' he said. 'Babies looked alike to me too before I had any. You've been very kind.'

'Mm,' said John, preoccupied, 'excuse me, Cousin. I think . . . yes, I think I'd best be off.'

If there hadn't been a baby in the room someone might have noticed his manner, but John was out of the room and heading for the side door without further comment. Business acquaintances came to the front door; using the side was the family custom.

So nobody saw, as John Smith stepped out into the cold day, that a blanket dropped over his head, and a large, cheery figure carried him away like a thrashing, fulminating package.

By early afternoon, Jedediah was still absent.

When Matthew knocked at the Bradys' door he wasn't holding out much hope that Jedediah would be there; they'd given John firm instructions not to take it upon himself to break the news of this new-found brother to Grandpa and there was no way John could have held in such a discovery. If he'd been there, John would have raced out of the house exclaiming that he'd been told not to tell Grandpa, but it wasn't within mortal means to say nothing all day, and so *someone* had to say something and he'd brought Grandpa along for the purpose.

Matthew badly wanted to see his father, but Jedediah wasn't there.

And neither was John.

Janet searched the house, then sent Matthew to search the lanes of Gyrford. Franklin remained to guard the smithy, although there was nobody in it just now; even Corbie had wandered off somewhere. All of them had moved from puzzled to worried.

So it was Janet who discovered Agnes weeping over the still, pearl-white body of her sister.

'Agnes?' Janet said – then realising what she was looking at, she flew to their side. Constance was laid out on the bed they'd shared, eyes closed, unmoving. She might have been asleep, except that she was lying with her hearing ear tipped upwards. Since the day she'd been deafened, she always rested with her shield ear uppermost.

'I can't wake her!' Agnes exclaimed. She lifted Constance easy as a babe; bone-narrow limbs lolled from her great arms. 'Janet, I thought she'd just come to lie down for a little peace. Constance? Constance, darling? I can't wake her!'

Janet felt a moment of utter horror, right in the pit of her belly. For a moment she'd thought Constance was dead, but this wasn't how corpses looked: her mouth and eyes were closed. She was deep asleep, her carven skull elegant and gaunt as it rested in the crook of Agnes' arm, but no matter how they shook her, she didn't wake.

'Lay her down,' Janet said, feeling a little sick. 'I need to smell her.'

Constance lay limp, silken white hair trailing soft and sheening around her.

As Janet bent to her lips and inhaled, the last hint of colour drained from her. 'We need Tom,' she said. 'Agnes, dear, send someone for Tom – not you, we must all stay on the spot; ask a neighbour – anyone'll do. Never mind Corbie; I'll take the beating if there is one.'

'What is it?' Agnes was locked to the spot, struggling with her own limbs: hurt was being done and someone had to prevent it, but she didn't know how.

'From the smell,' Janet said, her teeth chattering, 'one of Tom's drowses. He's given her hemlock.' The horror was that Agnes had brought it to ease Matthew's pain – but Janet would have drunk it herself before telling Agnes that. 'We lock drowses away,' she said instead. 'We should have remembered Corbie would know where to find the keys.' She drew a breath through a throat thickened with fear. 'Agnes, darling,' she said, 'we know Corbie wanted rid of Constance, but she may come through this if he didn't give her too much. I never heard the man knew his physic. But we need Tom, this very moment. And Father, if we can find him. We can send the cart.'

It was only when the two of them ran down to the stable, tears blurring both their faces, that they discovered the cart was gone, and Dobbs the horse with it.

Jedediah was elsewhere and Johnny was gone.

Corbie, leaving behind a poisoned wife, had taken the cart and the fairy-servant he thought would save him from Ab and gone on the road.

It was Franklin who dragged Stan Mackem from the Bradys' house. Matthew followed him, unable to do any dragging; he was close to weeping for Granny Constance himself, but the taking of Johnny had dried his eyes to burning embers. He almost danced with impatience as Franklin sat Stan at the Smiths' kitchen table and said, 'By your leave, sir, we need your action, and we need it now.'

'I'll risk a feud,' Matthew panted. 'I'll be shunned by every clan from here to John O'Groats – he's taken my son. He's taken my *son*.'

'What would you have of me?' Anger had opened Stan Mackem's face; he stared at them both in furious confusion, grief intermixed with it, and shock. In that moment he looked young and lost. '*I* didn't take your son, or dose your grandma. Don't tell me you can't mind your own forge and family and then put the blame on me for it.'

'I'll kick you off your chair,' Matthew told him. 'I'll kick your skull till it cracks. I'll *stamp* on it.'

'Matt, no.' It was Franklin who pulled himself together. He loved Constance and John very nearly as much as Matthew did, but something else was holding him. Jedediah rejected the notion of debt, but this was the kitchen where Mister Smith had, again and again, set a bowl of food before him, a handful of currants, a brisk kindness that had given him a place in a world where he wasn't sorry he'd ever been born.

Matthew was angry. Matthew wasn't used to being angry and he might not be good at controlling it, which meant someone had to think.

'Matthew wants his son,' he said to Stan, and found that his voice was almost calm. 'You'd want the same, and most likely you'd kick in a head or two too, so let's not blame him. But we have to settle this, and we have to settle it fast. By the time Mister Smith comes home it might be too late; we have no idea what Corbie might do to a boy he thinks a bird-fey. You'll forgive me, Mister Mackem, but we can't have that.'

Stan Mackem had taken too many blows to his world in the past few days and now he had two large men looming over him, threatening him as he'd never been threatened in his life. Customers might lash out in your smithy, but he was not used to being alone. 'What in God's name do you think I can do about it?' he shouted. 'He thinks me a bird too! Cuckolding my father doesn't make him my charge!'

'It makes you a farrier,' Franklin said, with the kind of quiet matter-of-factness that had warned many a poacher in his Lordship's forest to go and hunt for his dinner somewhere safer. 'If Corbie tries to hurt John, we'll need a farrier to stop it. Janet's gone for Tom Attic and someone'll need to mind Constance till they get back; that should be Matthew.' He turned. 'I know you're no physician, Matt, but you know more of it than me. Your knowledge and Agnes' arms is the best we can do till Mister Attic or Mister Smith get back.'

Matthew, torn between the desire to murder Stan in lieu of getting at Corbie and the fact that he was, most of the time, a pious and well-meaning man, nodded. Granny Constance was dear to him too, and Franklin was right – not least in the part he was too kind to mention: with the cart gone, horseback was their only choice, and Matthew, wounded as he was, couldn't hold the reins.

'Now,' said Franklin, taking Stan and lifting him up with only the slightest echo of iron in his grip, 'we have my horse, and we have yours. I can track and you can fairy-smith, so you and I, sir, will go after Corbie Mackem. Once we find him, I'll turn off and seek Mister Smith, for we need our elder in such times as this, sir. You'll bring Corbie back here: poisoning's a hanging crime and if I didn't care for Mister Tom Attic's good name and good physic, we might even call it bewitching. Perhaps it need not come to that, but I wouldn't like to force the subject. I reckon the quicker we get him back, sir, the better.

'Go on, Matt.' Franklin was already at the door. 'Never fret. You care for Granny Constance – she needs you.' He'd sworn, when he was young, that he wouldn't grow up to be a shouting man. It was with quite a mild voice he said, 'On my soul, Matt, we'll find your boy.'

When Franklin was thirteen, Jedediah had called him into the smithy. There was a dog sitting, alert and devoted, beside him, which Franklin supposed he was minding for someone; Mister Smith was good with dogs, but he'd always insisted he'd never have one of his own.

Mister Smith looked him up and down, practical as ever. 'Now,' he said, 'you'll be getting quite a man soon enough, and you'll want to keep yourself. Bright lad like you could do with training. As it happens, I had Edgar Mann in here the other day with his horse. Forester for Lord Robert. You haven't met him, I think. Skilled man, not ill-tempered. He's on the watch for an apprentice, so I told him about you. Reckons he'll take you, if you have a mind. Like to be a forester, would you?'

Franklin opened his mouth, closed it again. Forestry was a rank of life far above his: you had to manage the woods and the boundaries, know the land, learn a little of the law. A forester could hold his head up alongside anyone. Nobody would take Joe Thorpe's boy for that – but if the farrier spoke for him . . . ? But no, it was impossible. There would be an indenture to pay. Mister Smith had found him work for years, but the little Franklin had saved wouldn't cover a quarter of it. There'd be food to buy, firewood, clothes that fit him; no matter how frugal he lived, his purse weighed light. Franklin felt cold with longing. Learning skilled work out in the woods, being a clever man; it was all out of his reach. It was kindly meant, but he wished he'd never heard the possibility, so he'd never have to grieve over what he couldn't have.

'I – I thank you for your good word, Mister Smith,' he said, trying to sound steady, 'but I fear the articles would be beyond me. I do thank you, though.'

''Course it's beyond you,' said Mister Smith, 'for now. Not beyond me, though. I've enough put by, and I can 'prentice Matthew myself. You work hard and become a forester, you'll prosper, then you can settle up with me when you've got the money. Or if you can't, never mind. I can spare it.'

Franklin was almost too astonished to speak. He wanted desperately to say yes, to just grab at this chance, but – surely he couldn't? Mister Smith had a wife and a child and a home to keep, and Franklin had no claim.

'It's . . . so kind of you,' he said. The dog, which was flop-eared and sweet-faced, tipped its head in concern and gave its tail a sympathetic thump. 'But truly, I couldn't . . . you've . . . you've been so good to me.' Mister Smith made a slightly irritable gesture, brushing that aside. 'I couldn't see you pinched if things changed for you. It wouldn't be right.'

'Wouldn't be right my hind foot.' Mister Smith's voice was crisp. 'I can keep myself, lad. Wouldn't offer if I couldn't. What I would like to see is my money set up a forester with a head on his shoulders instead of letting it sit under a stone like some parable the parson'd go on about. I need good foresters in this county, lad. The People love the woods. You should be more worried I'm trying to buy you for an ally, not that I'd beggar myself out of charity. Have you any dislike to the work, is what I'm asking?'

'No, Mister Smith,' said Franklin, feeling a little wild, the word 'ally' ringing in his head. 'Not at all.'

'That's fine then. I'll talk to Edgar Mann, pay the articles, then tell you when and where he'll look for you. You can be there when you're wanted and make yourself useful, or you can not be there and make me look a fool. Up to you. You'll need a dog, though.' Mister Smith snapped his fingers twice and the dog trotted up to Franklin, sniffing his hand agreeably as if the world had not been upended. 'He's yours. Hasn't a name, but I reckon you'll think of one.'

'M-mister Smith . . .' Franklin attempted. 'I – you have been the best of—' He was trying to find a way to say the words that almost choked him, full as he was of a sudden future, but Mister Smith gave him a bit of a glare. He drew a deep breath and tried again. 'I shall make the best use ever I can of this chance, Mister Smith. I shall try to – to be everything you'd approve. I swear I'll pay you back, every penny. And if ever my skills may be of use to you, they will be at your service. For ever.'

'Don't swear promises you aren't sure you can keep, lad,' Mister Smith said, softening. 'Just you work hard and be a good lad, come back a skilled man. You can do that, I know. He'll be wanting you not long after Michaelmas, I reckon. You can be ready by then. Just mind your boots are in good order, you'll be walking all day. Can you pay the cobbler, or shall I have a word with him?'

Faithful, Franklin called that dog. It took him a while to stop naming dogs earnestly; his next one, a decade later, had been called Patience. He'd loved Faithful with all his heart: they'd shared a bed, their suppers, their work, their days and nights. Mister Smith must have looked around for some time to find him, for foresters' dogs needed to be good scenthounds. Every moment he'd had free, Franklin had practised with Faithful. At first, it was all he could think to do to repay Mister Smith – and then he did it because he loved working with dogs more than almost anything in the world.

Faithful, rest his doggy soul, had been a good tracker. But Soots – ugly, laughing, loll-tongued, devoted Soots – was better.

By the time the cantering horses drew in sight of the Smiths' cart, it was clear where they were: on the road to Tinsdowne, where Corbie had once been at home, which his older brother was now too aged to hold.

Soots wagged her tail, feeling she'd done a very good job for the master. She was a little surprised when he veered off, saying, 'Come on, girl, back home! Time to track Mister Smith!' The master had seemed very eager to catch up to the cart – but the other man was heading off towards it, and it was driven by the noisy guest Soots knew the master didn't like, so perhaps he'd changed his mind. Soots was quite happy to oblige: the master knew everything, and besides, Mister Smith always had a scratch for her.

Stan loved his father Dunstan. He'd never understood the hostility that bristled from Jedediah Smith, who sniffed at every offer the Mackems made as if for poison, when for pity's sake, the man was a Mackem himself. Stan had always regretted not knowing Uncle Corbie better when he was young; his father and his Uncle Sweep were much alike and had a hearty enjoyment of each other's company, a warmth that overspilled to their children, wives, nieces, nephews and everybody else who'd share a laugh with them. As far as Stan was concerned, another uncle would have added to the merriment, even if Corbie was seldom mentioned – and when he was, the men spoke of him with a certain pity as the fool of the clan, and the women said very little. But there was his son Jedediah – the whole name, by all things holy, too fine even for a nickname – with his Gyrford voice and his ragged clothes and his stubborn refusal to look even a little bit like the rest of the family . . .

Yes, that was a young man's resentment; Stan could accept that now. He didn't want to admit it, but there was no point lying to yourself. Jedediah Smith had reason not to like his father very much.

Jedediah's father.

Stan had a father of his own – for pity's sake, the Smiths should understand that, else why had they taken these Thorpes under their wings?

Stan drew level with the cart, calling out, 'Hey now!'

'Hey now, hey now!' Corbie was driving in quite good cheer – or at least, his face was covered with the beekeeper's mask but the set of his shoulders was cheerful. It was the first time Stan had noticed how alike their voices sounded.

What he would have said to Corbie next, he couldn't say; he was saved by a new voice, thinly hoarse, the way boys' voices are when they're on the edge of breaking. Slurred, and extremely angry.

'He could have *killed* me!' it said. Stan reined in the horse and turned, bewildered: a bundle in the back of the cart was, it appeared, attempting to hit him.

Corbie reached back, gave it a hard pat. 'Shhhh,' he said.

'I hear you, Stan Mackem, and you let me out this second, or I'll scream for every fey in hearing – I know that drowse Uncle Corbie forced down me: folks *die* if they drink too much of it! It's got hemlock and mandragora in it! I'd have *died* if I hadn't spat so much of it out! It tastes *terrible*! Godfa Tom worked for *six months* on it with Grandpa, and they tested it on themselves *four-and-twenty times* before they had it right! I'm about to be sick,' the sack added, with less alarm than accusation, 'and if you don't let me out and put my head over the side, I'll be sick on you, *on purpose*.'

'If you want him to understand you,' John observed a little later, wiping his mouth, 'you'd do best to speak to me and let him hear it half-slant. He takes some things in like that, at least. Though I reckon he pretends to understand less than he does. Or chooses to, perhaps, for if—'

'You need to instruct less and listen more,' Stan interrupted. He was driving the cart now, although Corbie kept wheedling the horse to turn them back Tinsdowne-wards. Perhaps that Franklin Thorpe could have helped if he hadn't raced off to find Jedediah, but as it was, Stan was exhausted from the ride and the shocks he'd undergone, and the thought gripping him with outraged fingers was, *I am too old for this*.

'You're not my elder,' John pointed out, sniffing hard. 'My elder's my grandpa. I don't always agree with him, but I mean to honour his teachings before others for the credit of my clan.'

Corbie gave John a prod, indicating silence, which John tried and failed to swat away.

'Uncle – Fa – Corbie,' Stan said, feeling a little hysterically that this was really not the moment to be obliged to settle on what to call the man, 'I am sure you hear me, or part of you does. You cannot steal children, and you cannot go to Tinsdowne.' He didn't mention Constance; he didn't want to think about that. The man must have grabbed her, frail as she was, and forced the drink down her throat. If they could just get him back to Gyrford without the subject of Constance coming up, the Smiths had a bedchamber with a locking door. It should be possible; all they needed to do was stay off the subject. The boy didn't know, and Corbie didn't know they knew. 'We'll back to Gyrford,' Stan said, with all the firmness he could muster, 'and you must mind them.'

The mask swung from side to side.

'*Elder Mackem speaks!*'

'He'll speak all day at this rate,' John said.

Stan, whose nerves were already frayed to their stitching, turned to him angrily, but John shrugged. 'My grandpa says it's no disrespect to give a man sound advice.'

'Do not mention your grandpa to me again,' Stan said.

'Do not elder me about,' John replied, in the exact same tone.

Stan made an effort to cuff him, but Corbie stopped the blow and tucked John under his arm with the air of a man shielding his chicken from a bad dog.

'Let me go or I'll bite you,' said John, wriggling out of his grip. 'And I may still have hemlock on my teeth. Elder Stan Mackem, if you think he's grown more reasonable overnight just because somebody told you he's your father, I'd like to know how.'

Jedediah's teaching laid more emphasis on patience than was the Mackem custom. Stan was a grown man and could do his best. But it wasn't helped by the fact that young John Smith did not have any plan of holding his tongue.

'Where did he learn to think of fairy-servants?' John demanded. 'We wouldn't have them in Gyrford. Grandpa says you end up picking the master out of the servant's teeth when folks try that.'

'Oh, he does?' said Stan. He wouldn't admit it, but his respect for Jedediah Smith was rising just a little. This boy was *impossible* to discipline. Stan quite believed the rumours that the lad was fey; he might not have been able to say for sure – testing would involve trials the Smiths would be tiresome about – but he was surely wild-willed enough. And yet he insisted on obeying his grandfather. Stan had no idea how Jedediah had done it.

'Well,' John shrugged, 'that's his short way of saying it. What he means is that the People weren't put on this earth to serve us. And besides, they're not all servants; some might take to the idea, but others are fey that somebody trapped, and that's not a servant, it's a slave. Grandpa reckons it's our business to stop cruelty, whether it's to folks or fey.'

'He says that, does he?' said Stan, still more curious about the boy's deference to Jedediah than about Jedediah's politics.

'Well, it's what he *means*,' John said. 'I reckon you could learn from that – but that's not the point, though: how would a man get a fairy-servant? A real one, I mean? We don't have them in Gyrford. Grandpa won't let anyone try. No one's tried for as long as he can recall.'

'That's what reading does to you,' said Stan with disgust. '"As far as he can recall" indeed. There's a memory that goes back generations. The man's still alive!'

John stopped talking. He was silent for a long moment, while Corbie started working sigils around him that would bind a fairy-servant to its master. Stan felt he should intervene, but it was more important to keep the cart moving.

When John spoke, he did not sound ashamed. 'Mister Mackem,' he said, almost casually, 'I don't reckon you ever heard tell of a man with a fairy-servant near the border between our holding and yours? I mean, before Grandpa's time?'

Stan snorted. 'You mean Peter Alder? Well, there's a man who came to a bad end. That'd be in your great-great-great-grandfather's time. Not so long ago, if you don't keep your brains in your books.'

'We don't write books,' John said. He spoke very quietly; this must be it. He wasn't sure how yet, but this must be. Ab must have come from somewhere. Dada told him there was a man in a grave, stabbed to the ground with cold iron, and Ab was pinned down with him.

The man must have come across Ab somehow. Ab must have been somewhere before it was staked with the buried man.

How many great-grandfathers ago? Clem was his great-great grandfather, so great-great-great had to be one extra generation.

Elder Samuel, Dada had called the buried man, the man of Clem's generation, and if he was elder of any trade, he'd said, it couldn't have been licit.

Elder. Alder. It wouldn't matter which, if you wrote it down; a lot of folks spelled their names different ways. But even if you didn't write it . . . whatever Stan said, things could go astray in the spoken record, and besides, the Tinsdowne and Gyrford accents weren't quite alike.

If he was right . . . if he could make Stan explain without losing patience.

'We know the families in our holding,' John said, 'right up to the borders. There aren't any Alders.'

'Well, there wouldn't be *now*,' Stan said. 'The People swallowed his son up before he could marry. That was the end of them.'

'I don't understand,' John said. He spoke very politely, showing the full deference to an elder farrier. 'Would you please tell me the tale?'

Stan snorted. 'Would you remember it if I did? Memory's a muscle, lad: you don't work it, it weakens, and you Smiths keep your memories in your inkhorns from all I've heard.'

'Well, you didn't hear it from a Smith,' John answered back, and then remembered he was being respectful. 'Do you mean you have a memory-chant for it? Is it sound after sound the same as the swine – you know, the poet pig we keep in the pen?'

'Do you go to mock me, lad?'

'No!' John was honestly a bit surprised at the question. 'No, I just thought that was how Mackem chants went.'

'Don't you Smiths know *anything*?' Stan demanded, by now too exasperated with the boy's ignorance to be suspicious of his motives. 'You change your forms over time, lad. That's part of how you remember what happened when: if it all sounds the same, it's easier to mix up. This is how folks had it in my great-grandfather's day, all right? No rhymes, no sound-echoing, it's all in the beat. Open your ears; let's see if you have any memory at all. And don't go adding or changing words in your memory: you listen to what I say *exact*.' And, with a flick of the reins and a dour glance and Corbie, Stan Mackem sat back to share an old clan memory-chant with a small and irritating Smith boy.

> Now Peter Alder was a learned man
> With too much in his head to do him good.
> By guile and boldness, stealth, and lack of ruth,

He thought to steal a fairy from its court
And make of it a servant and a carl
To weave his nettle-flax to garb of silk.
No fairy-smith he had to aid his work:
What could he do but coax his way beneath
The hollow hills to fairy-courts within?
He cared not how the People like a bright
And coloured trinket to entice their eye,
But, thinking night the proper time for fey
Did gather to him animals of black
And set them on to coax his way beneath.
For first, he set a snare to catch a crow
And, teaching it to chatter like a man,
He stuffed its crop with pleading words that cried,
'Oh, let me in, for I am cold without!
Be good to me, fair neighbours, let me in!'
For second, Peter then a poppet stitched
With hair he'd stolen from a simple girl
Who wandered through the woods, and left behind
Black skeins of hair a-tangled in the briars.
These Peter gathered up, and worked so fine
The thing of rags just might pass for a girl
To those who'd never seen a girl before.
For last, this Peter Alder took a web,
New-woven that May morn, still wet with dew,
And, chasing off the sooty spiderling,
He laid it on the poppet's naked back,
As if to show how ragged went the soul
That cried, crow-voiced, before the People's door,

'Oh, let me in, for I am cold without!
Be good to me, fair neighbours, let me in!'

With these entrapments Peter climbed the hill,
And there, upon the People's greening step,
He placed the bird and web-cloaked beggar-maid.
No force for forty generations since
Had pried apart the People's mossy door,
But there, as cried the crow, 'Be good to me!'
The gate of earth did open up.

At this
Did Peter slip, dark-cloaked and hood on head,
Between the shadowed architraves of earth,
And while his kindly hosts did stroke and shake
And beg an answer of their poppet guest,
Thus Peter snatched a fairy-servant up.

Beneath his cloak, the speaking crow was pent,
But once the fairy-slave was in his grip,
Then Peter oped the cloak, and out, in pain,
Flapping and shrieking, came the battered crow.
With pinions crushed by Peter Alder's grip
The crow could only thrash and plaint and cry,
'Be good to me, fair neighbours!' So the fey
Did turn aside from Peter's knotted bait
And ran to find whose voice did weep so harsh,
And with their eyes turned so aside from him,
Thus Peter Alder fled the People's court,
And to the breathing surface brought his slave.

For seven years and seven days, the fey
Was bound to Peter by a chain of iron,
And wept, and did his will, and gnashed its teeth,
And changed and changed and changed about its shape
To try and find a way to slip its bonds.
But shackled as it was, the captured thing
Could change its outer shape, but not the wrist
That Peter kept, tight-manacled in iron.

Yet iron rusts without a farrier.

For seven years and seven days, the fey
Did wish and pine and cry aloud for home,
And on the last of all those many days,
The shackle on its changeless wrist cracked wide,
And in a blink, the fairy-thing was gone,
And never seen again upon this earth.

Now Peter had a son called Samuel
Who lived a farmer. Led a blameless life.
Nay, not for Samuel was his father's way
Of trickery and captive fairy-kin.
Yet though this son had no desire to please
His father through the learning of his ways,
Still Peter, who had once held the command
Of wind and water, earth and leaf and beast,
So fretted in his heart that this, his boy,
Could not be ordered into loving him
Not only as a father, but a man
Whose wisdom was the key to all the world

That when old Peter felt Time's chilly breath
Upon his neck, and knew that he must turn
To see the years a-creeping up, and know
That Death will have his due of mortal man,
He set his thoughts upon another plan:
To leave his son a fairy-slave behind
Who this time, would not pant to 'scape the bond.

Again did Peter Alder gather up
The crow, the spiderweb, the poppet bait,
And only this change did he make: the crow
He taught to cry aloud, 'Oh, I was wronged!
The man's to blame! Be good to me, fair sirs!'
And well enough he knew the angry fey
Would more than likely rip the bird apart
In vengeance for the theft those years ago,
But while the feathers flew, and bird-bones broke,
He'd sneak within, and snatch up for himself
Another fey, and leave it to his son,
A legacy to serve him in its turn
And for his Samuel, stand eternal proof
That Father Peter had the right of it.

Thus did confide the man unto such friends
He had, and they thought Peter Alder mad.
And yet, Midsummer night, they heard the cries
Upon the hill, and when they ran to see
What wailed aloud beneath the staring moon
They found no Peter Alder.

In the dark
Was nothing but some scattered shreds of flesh,
And, there before them, kneeling on the ground,
Wept Samuel, and raised an orphan's cry.

Thus ended then the life of Peter. Thus
The line of Alder closed upon the world.
For Samuel betook him to his farm
And closed his doors to neighbours, pined away,
Or fled the county, or perhaps was snatched
To slave within a fairy court beneath
The shouldered earth that braces 'gainst the folks
Who breach its secrets with a rite unkenned.
Samuel Alder took no wife, begot
No son, and left no name.
His farm was sold, and none saw him again.

So ends the tale, as sorrowful as true.
Cry now for Alders. Folks will ask you, 'Who?'

'Well, lad?' Stan said, his voice apparently none the wearier for the long recitation, 'how much of that do you reckon you can say back?'

John sat in thought for so long that Stan suspected him stunned.

'I don't expect you to say it all from one hearing,' he conceded. 'Even trained, that'd be asking a lot.'

'No,' said John, 'that's not it. It's just that . . . no, never mind.'

'Oh, don't be like that,' Stan said. 'You must have got some of it.' It was a longish chant to drop on a lad unprepared, which felt like a mean trick; he should have started him with something shorter. It was just hard to put up with the boy's Smithish airs. John needed some lessons in his own limitations, Stan mentally defended himself – sharing, in that moment, more common experience with his half-brother than he'd ever have guessed.

'*Peter Alder was a learned man with too much in his head to do him good*,' John summarised, sounding oddly preoccupied, 'And *set a snare to catch a crow*, teaching it to cry, "*Be good to me!*" He fled the People's court, and *to the breathing surface brought his slave*, and was thoroughly cruel to it in a way it sounds like the Mackems might have found out about sooner if they'd been paying attention, and put a stop to it. But he *fretted in his heart that this, his boy, could not be ordered into loving him* – which was stupid of him, nobody can love you if you aren't kind – and decided to *leave his son a fairy-slave behind, which this time would not pant to 'scape the bond*, although I notice your chant doesn't say how he thought he'd bring that about.

'You know, that's the trouble with your chants: if you have to remember them *exact*, you can't improve them. If whoever came up with this one had let his listeners ask questions instead of chanting at them, he might have had fewer gaps in it.

'Anyway, he made a mess of it, and then himself, leaving behind some *scattered shreds of flesh, and, there before them, kneeling on the ground, wept Samuel, and raised an orphan's cry*. And whoever forged this chant doesn't know what happened to Samuel after, and didn't like to admit it. You'd think he could have just said so, you know:

And after that, I don't know what befell
Young Samuel: that's all I have to tell.

'But thank you. That's . . . very helpful.'

Stan closed his gaping mouth with something of an effort. '. . . All right,' he said, resolute. 'You remembered bits of it, that's good.'

'Well, I won't say the whole thing back now,' John said with alarming off-handedness. 'My question is, is that *all* there is to know about it? Do you have any other chants that say *where* exactly all this happened? It talks of hills and grass and moss, and that could be anywhere.'

Stan cleared his throat. He'd have to hand the boy over to his father when they got back and no doubt Matthew'd have something to say about it if Stan thumped him. 'That's not in the tale,' he said, 'because it's not the lesson.'

'Well, if the lesson is "Don't trifle with the People unless you know what you're about," ' said John, and Stan felt a great weariness settle upon him, 'then you'd think you wouldn't need all those lines to teach it. I think the man who came up with it just didn't know where it took place. I reckon he heard the tale at second- or third-hand – and that says to me it didn't happen in his holding.'

Stan clicked to the horse, suddenly too exhausted to argue any further.

'Don't take it to heart that I found fault with the tale,' John went on with maddening kindness; 'I'm sure you have better ones. And don't worry about it either. I can solder the gaps, I'm pretty sure. I've all but worked it out.'

Stan found himself gaping again, and he very nearly asked the boy what in the world he meant – but if he did that, the boy would keep talking.

The three of them sat in silence a little longer. Corbie, who had a sack of Smith tools with him in the cart, had failed to trap John within a fine chain pentangle. He was now absorbed with rubbing iron filings into the lad's sleeves, or possibly his wings. Between the boy's chatter and Corbie's conviction, Stan himself was starting to lose his certainty.

'My Auntie Pell's house isn't far,' John announced suddenly. 'She can take me the rest of the way. I don't like Uncle Corbie's mauling me.'

John hadn't forgotten Pell's message saying that she'd left her cottage, but he was pretty sure Stan wasn't aware of it. It had come in the form of a letter, and Stan didn't read.

'I mean to take you back to your father,' Stan said. They were passing a small woodland; it was fenced around with iron, sharp-tipped palings that, he had to admit, were thoroughly good workmanship. Plainer than the Mackem style, perhaps, but no denying it: they were pretty in their way. Some Smith had gone to a lot of trouble to make them – and that meant there'd be something in the woods that Cousin Matthew wouldn't thank him for dropping his only son right beside.

'My father would set me down here,' said John, without so much as a blush.

'I'm not your father, lad, and I won't.'

John sighed, looking genuinely regretful. 'Well, I'm sorry about this, then,' he said. 'But sometimes needs must. Grandpa says a farrier has to do what has to be done.'

'What do you mean . . . ?'

But before Stan could stop him, John had whipped the covering off Corbie and from under his shirt, produced a pair of cutters – Corbie's cutters. At what point in his starings and mutterings the boy had got into his tool sack and abstracted them, Stan didn't know, but he'd done it without so much as a clink.

'You'll mark I'm wielding iron in a most un-fey manner,' John told Corbie, almost cheerfully, and with a set of slashes so fast and deft Stan later blamed the men who'd trained him to be neat-handed, John cut the centre out of Corbie's wicker mask.

'That's your face in view,' he told Corbie, 'and if you look to your right, you'll see that's Auntie Pell's wood. The crows have hidden all over the county, and that's one of their favourite places to hide. You remember the tree in there, don't you? You lived in it a long time.'

Corbie was out of the cart, hands clutched over his face and running away from the wood before Stan had time to do anything. He stumbled, evidently not able to see very well; all that mattered to him was getting away from a wood full of crows – a place that remembered what he had done to Ab.

Stan jumped down and took after him; he needed to catch the man before he broke his neck.

He barely heard the sound of a lighter body leaping down beside him and a youthful voice saying cheerfully, 'Well, God by you. Sorry about this.'

But by the time he had Corbie back to the cart – though not settled in it, Corbie kept hitting him – John was nowhere to be seen and Stan's hands were too full to do anything about it.

★

When Jedediah Smith returned to his home, Corbie Mackem was already locked in a Smith bedchamber with iron fittings across the door. He banged against it, chanting and chattering, screeching like a raven.

Matthew took him aside and the two of them spoke quietly in a closed room. Nobody wished to disturb them. They came out grave, pale, equally quiet. The two of them had never shared much family likeness – it was Louise Matthew resembled – but there was between them a shared rhythm, like birds in a flock or fish in a shoal, that made them on that day look curiously alike.

Corbie wouldn't lose the idea he was penned in a bird house, so after some hours, Matthew brought Anthony Brady over, for Corbie could understand him. He stood outside with Stan and Jedediah, silent and watching.

'Sir,' Anthony said, a little uncertainly. He was still anxious to make amends for his freeing of Left-Lop, and he would do pretty much anything Franklin asked of him anyway, but he was a man of compunction. 'You must remain within there, sir. It's known you made an attempt to poison a woman.'

Corbie's banging stopped. There was a deep, black emptiness. Then he banged again. 'I don't know what you mean,' he said. 'I drowsed a fairy-bird – I never touched any other physic.'

'I speak of your wife, Constance,' Anthony said, torn between misery and anger; the discovery that his own brother had been a violent husband shamed him, and he felt the shadow of that shame whenever compelled to think about such men. 'You forced hemlock and mandragora down her throat, sir. By God's grace she's survived, brought round by the good care of Mister

Tom Attic – who, by the by, sir,' Anthony said, turning to Stan, as to a man easier to confront, 'you've wronged and should beg pardon of. You should not have taken her from his house without his leave, sir.'

Stan, who didn't have an especially high view of this uncomfortable young man, didn't reply.

'You should, sir,' Anthony insisted. 'It was ill doing by a good man and his good wife. I'm sure you think better of it now you see the result, but you do owe him your contrition, sir. But you, Mister Corbie Mackem,' he said, turning round with his resolve apparently braced by this practice on a lesser sinner, 'you forced the same drowse on our John as on your wife, sir. You are to remain within, and if you cannot make less noise, you'll have to be put somewhere worse.'

Corbie punched the door. 'I never did,' he said. 'Not my fault if an idiot finds a bottle and drinks from it. Don't put that to me.'

'Sir,' Anthony said, apparently to Stan as well as to Corbie, 'the good woman lived four decades with Mister Tom Attic with physic all around her and never came to a drop of harm. She lived most safe and comfortable with Tom Attic.'

'Don't put that to me!' Corbie roared.

Matthew looked at Anthony in a kind of grief. He never again wished to sit through such a watch as they'd had over Constance, and while he wasn't foolish enough to deny the testimony of his own eyes, his heart rebelled at the thought that anyone could have done such a thing without shame. He'd hoped for a little penitence, just a little. It would make it easier to bear the fact that on the other side of the door was his own grandfather.

'Don't you put that to me, young man!' Corbie shouted again. 'That woman never had the wit to know cherry from nightshade!'

Matthew couldn't bear any more. 'Come on, Anthony,' he said, jerking his head since he couldn't pat anyone's shoulder. 'I think we're finished here.'

'A-are you all right, Matthew?' Anthony looked at his friend in concern; Matthew looked so wretchedly unhappy. 'I mean, I'm glad Constance is better, but – but at least he can't try again.'

Matthew sighed. 'I think . . .' he said. 'Well, I don't like to think it, but if he's a man to poison, he's perhaps not a man of conscience. But he sounds so *sure*.'

'You don't think he's innocent, do you?' Anthony was sure Corbie wasn't, but Matthew had a generous nature that he hoped wasn't about to be abused.

'No,' Matthew said. He looked at Jedediah's face. It was still, mute, frozen as cold iron. 'No, I think he's guilty as Cain. But I think he feels he isn't.' He didn't like any of these thoughts, especially not to Anthony, who had his own history of hard men, but he couldn't leave his father alone in his understanding. 'He feels,' Matthew pressed on, 'that she *might* have poisoned herself by mistake, and so the fact that it was him shouldn't be weighed against him. Or something like that. He blames her for being, well, the way she is. Blames her mortally. There's folks like that, when it comes to touched souls. It's just . . . it's a bad thing in itself, and worse when one's a farrier.'

Stan cleared his throat, but said nothing. Back before his wits had gone a-wandering, his father had talked of how Corbie had taken it hard, finding himself married to – well, to Constance. *Think twice before you marry, lads*, he'd said, *but wives have their faults, and remember they don't choose them just to vex you.*

'John said he ran when John cut the mask,' Anthony said to Matthew, 'but not before. He didn't think anyone in Gyrford would arrest him for – for Constance.'

Matthew's arms hung heavy in their slings. 'I reckon he thinks us birds, and too foolish to see it,' he said. 'Or else that no one would miss her enough to hang him for it.'

He was silent so long that Anthony put an arm around him and said, 'Well, she didn't die. And John'll come back. I know it's been a long day, but he will come back.'

'He will for certain,' Jedediah said. His voice was hoarse. 'First light, I'll go for him.'

'Are you sure I shouldn't, Dada?' Matthew said. 'I can walk fine.'

'You guard Corbie,' Jedediah said. 'If I stay in this house, I can't swear I won't break down the door and kill him myself.'

All his life John had been kept out of Aunt Pell's wood, though he'd longed to see it; it had been his one real grudge against her that she somehow always knew when he was trying to get in there. He still didn't know how. If it had been his Great-Aunt Mabbie, who Dada said could talk to birds, then that would make sense. There were always birds around to see him and sound an alarm. But he'd never met Aunt Mabbie, so it couldn't be that. Aunt Pell was a cunning woman, that was clear, and had tricks of her own.

There had always been a slowness to those trees, and slower

still were the spaces between them. Even from the boundary, John could tell that things fell soft in Aunt Pell's wood. The trees shed and the birds flew, but they had always done so with a kind of clarity: you could see the stretch and spring of beating feathers, the tip and spiral of drifting leaves, as if you had endless time to stand and stare. The world moved, but it moved as if time was thick around it, and it took a little longer to push through.

Now John climbed the fence and nothing stopped him. He didn't want Stan Mackem after him, so he high-stepped branches and worked his way around thorns as fast as he dared, and it was only when he was properly within that he stopped, scented the place out and started to feel the oddity of it soak into him.

It had been a slow place once, with a deep drag to it. That would have been Ab's tree: a spirit so powerful pent up so small must have stepped in and out of time, and time softened around the tree to cushion it.

But Ab was out of the tree now, and the softened pace of the world hadn't been enough to absorb the shock. The wood felt *crumpled*, like a dropped rag. In places it pleated up, so that when he moved his hand through the air he felt a luxurious ease, and no matter how hard he tried he couldn't make his muscles push fast. In others, life was frantic: he climbed over one log where the toadstools pulsed on the bark like frog-throats, and while John tried to climb carefully, he was over the other side and staggering for balance before he'd even had a moment to notice he was doing it.

He reached out, touched a tree trunk. It was in one of the

racing places; he could feel its bark aching beneath his touch, stretching out to grow fast enough for a mortal hand to feel.

'You'll settle,' he said. 'Not so fast as a pool, but the ripples will die down, I'm almost sure. In tree-time, perhaps. Earth-time. A decade, maybe? I'm almost sure you'll smooth out. Could be we'll come back with iron and speed things along, if Grandpa agrees.'

He walked, skewing, staggering, for time wouldn't keep pace with him. In some places the trees were growing, their trunks fattening like risen dough; in others, he could hardly move or think. And the further he walked, the worse a problem the frozen spots became, because his mind slowed in them too; thoughts happened, but slow as stone, and in the time it took to get through them it was like trying to remember the same idea for days at a stretch.

By the time he made it through those moments, he found that he'd forgotten where he was.

He turned, looking around for an eye-mark, some kind of guide. If he could remember something simple, he wouldn't keep getting confused. But he couldn't find one, and it was dawning on him that he might be getting somewhat pixy-led. The People weren't dancing him in circles, not on purpose, but the aftershocks were ringing everywhere, and he had finally to admit that he was lost.

When he heard the rustle overhead, at first he thought it was a crow. He'd seen them all along the way, huddled together between the lumps of time. And the sharp-tipped gleams, he thought for an instant – or perhaps a few minutes, it was like that around here – might be beaks.

There were loops of something glistening above, too, something that might have been sagging time – but no: time had no colour to it; it was what colour happened within. These loops shimmered, soft prisms serried row on row, a million little tubes of rainbow.

'Smooth out the air and bring to No One's yearning maw the swift of scamper and the careless of eye.' It was a whisper, a dry flute-note across a spitless throat. One sharp foot appeared, then another, then another, pointed as daggers, furred as paws. Many eyes, big as fists, gazed down at John in bleak self-pity. 'Shutter the air and unpleat the moment, or what shall the trees do for pretty gulps?'

John Smith had his faults, but by the mercy of God, as his father would probably have said, he was not afraid of spiders.

Jedediah had never given a detailed account of his own past and Matthew's knowledge of No One the spider had been absorbed in early childhood. It was a story his mother liked to tell him, about how when she'd been a young woman with hard work and no kin abound her, she'd had a best friend called No One with eight marvellous legs, who could spin silk thick as twine and say funny things about you and smell with its knees and taste with its feet, and one day Matthew's Dada had ridden up like a bold adventurer and rescued the spider from a terrible fire. The tale was one of their favourites. Louise hadn't wanted Matthew to be afraid of spiders, and he'd grown up to admire her skill in teaching him not to be; for that reason, it was one of the tales he had passed on to Johnny.

So John's understanding of the spider No One came from his father rather than his grandfather, and Matthew remembered it as a cosy childhood tale. The reality of No One was rather hungrier-looking and fuller of hard edges than John had quite pictured. The hunting had evidently been good in these woods, and where once No One had been the size of a badger, it was now the size of a cow. But when it came to fey things, John was nothing if not quick to absorb new ideas.

'Well, good day to you, kind friend,' he said. 'By any chance, are you No One the spider, who once was a friend of my Grandmother Louise?'

'Louise of the webless hair and leather-blinded feet,' No One sighed, with a kind of husky nostalgia. 'Ah, for the flesh unbitten of creamy blood and kindly motion!'

If John had known his Granny Louise he might have felt more proprietorial about No One's thoughts on her potential deliciousness, but as it was, his attention was entirely caught. Like his father, he enjoyed spiders: they had a kind of *instantaneousness*, a sense of pastless bristle that felt pleasing to him. They had spent many happy moments watching this or that striped spinner twang its fine threads, and meeting No One, to John, felt more or less like meeting a friend – a friend that might eat him if it got really hungry, probably, but still a friend.

'Yes,' he said, with a bit of regret, 'I've heard she was kind. She died thirty-some years ago, I'm sorry to say.'

No One's mouth parts tapped together, like the fingers of a thinker trying to unweave a difficult problem. 'Bones within silked hard together and a shell of pulp,' it objected. 'Still the air holds pretty thoughts, so what can be without Louise?'

'Oh.' Thinking about it, spiders probably didn't have a very deep concept of death; No One seemed to be having trouble picturing a world without Louise in it. John considered an explanation, but there was no need to be upsetting.

'Well, that's a way of looking at things,' he said a bit vaguely. 'In any case, I'm one of her – her manlings. So, No One, how are you in this wood since the blast?'

'Oh, for the still air and steady slow leap of squirrels.' It was a quavering threnody. 'Snapped and rumpled are the strings of air, and ill-wove is the gullet of thirsty time!'

'Yes, I can feel that,' John agreed. 'I don't suppose you'd like to come out of these woods and help me deal with the cause of it?'

'Crash of wood and shatter of birds!' No One protested in a voiceless whimper. 'Scatter of sharp-edged dust of living bark and the slice and rend of all things kindly sticky!'

It looked ready to go on, then a thought struck it. It clenched its legs beneath it and went very still. 'No One is not here,' it whispered. 'Boy of Louise cannot see what is not here, and No One unmoving is gall and nodule and not for the notice of eyes. Booted with stillness is No One and without taste.'

'What's your trouble with boots? John asked, temporarily intrigued. 'I don't see through my feet, and I don't reckon you do either or you wouldn't have all those eyes. Should I take off mine? Is that why I'm lost? Only it's splintery underfoot.'

'Supperless will be the deaf feet of harm, for No One is not here.'

'You listen with your feet? On the webs, I suppose? No, no, never mind,' John said with a sigh, recalling his mission. It would have been very convenient to have a giant silk-weaver's assistance, but he had just been inveighing against Stan Mackem about making slaves of fey things, and this was one of those times when Grandpa would say you had to live by your words. 'Look you, am I heading right for the broken chestnut? I can't find my way.'

'No One is not here,' came the breathless murmur. Its eyes wouldn't meet his, but it raised a talon and pointed south-east. 'Boy of Louise and tangles heads to the broken place such as pretty leg of bare oak marks, and No One is not here to speak help or hindrance.'

John looked. Yes, he could see it: a jagged bolt of oak branch, stripped of its leaves and broken at the tip like a fingernail. He could keep his eyes on it; it could mark his way. 'Thank you,' he said. 'Thank you very much.'

And there it was, broken apart, the iron chain fallen around it. The tree that had held Ab and Corbie and the crows. Shreds of bark and pulp were scattered everywhere; nearby trees had been smashed apart, jagged chunks and broken branches covering the ground.

John gazed at this place that had been a prison. He'd expected to find it fascinating, a-thrum with fairy life, but that wasn't the case. It was empty, cracked open and thrown aside. The first thought that came to his head almost surprised him in its mundanity: *What a mess.*

'Are you a horse scattering feed?' Grandpa used to say. *'Pick that up.'* Mess made Grandpa uncomfortable, and John had been drilled in neatness since he could walk. A tidy place was pleasanter to be in,

once you had the knack of cleaning it, he thought. If someone taught you.

He clambered to the gutted chestnut. It had been a fine tree once; now it was just a headless trunk with spicules jutting skywards. The space within it was very small. John might have squeezed inside it, and perhaps a crow or two if he'd stuffed them under his jacket, but Uncle Corbie would never have fitted. Not in normal circumstances, anyway.

John rested his hand over the gap, feeling it out as if testing water for warmth. There was a spaceless echo left behind: the place within it had nothing but a blank confusion. He hadn't stood over it long before he started to feel lonely.

There was no reason to cry.

He wasn't alone. He could go home any time he chose, and all his family would be there.

Within the cavity, the tree wasn't splintered but worn, dry, with an endless series of marks upon it: little ovals, tilted every which way, the centres of them drained to dust, as if some empty mouth had gummed and sucked upon the wood.

There was no reason to cry.

John wasn't sure how long he stood there. Perhaps he'd stepped into a piece of pleated time, or perhaps he just couldn't stop thinking how dark it must have been inside the tree, but how safe it would have been if the crows had loved you. Only they couldn't, because you weren't theirs.

What was it the mist-mother had said to Ab?

Shoo now. You're not mine.

And Ab had cracked into lightning and thirst, turned itself drowie and drunk the mist-mother down – the same drowie that had drunk the life out of the midwife, the woman who had protected Aunt Pell and locked the windows against Ab.

No, this wasn't what he'd come here to do. John crouched down, searching among the shavings. The earth beneath was just as dry as the tree, gritty as midsummer, as if all the water had been drunk out of it.

The first thing he found was a stone and the second was a clump of soil that disintegrated between his fingers, sifting down to nothing. He was usually good at searches like this; it was a fey place and he could settle into an absolute interest too deep to be called pleasure – but now he was starting to panic. He shouldn't; he just needed to be a little patient, and there was no reason to feel that he was hungry and thirsty, that his chest was empty and there was no one in the world to—

Ah. There it is. John picked it up, held it in a delicate grip. His fingertips were tough – handling heavy tools and hot objects grows thick skin – but the bristles still felt sharp, as if they were questing into his flesh, trying to nestle. In a second, he had it broken open – one of the chestnuts immediately fell from his grip and lost itself in the debris, but he had a firm hold on the other.

They'd rot now, those chestnuts Ab had grown from the tree and packed full of knowledge so that any beast that ate them would hear the thoughts of others – or the wishes, at least; the worries and requests. It worked well enough for a foraging pig to hear a frantic voice calling, *Unchain me – let me out. I'll give you wings if you'll get me out. I must find my friend.*

They'd probably have to dig the earth over with iron at some point, else every toadstool and fern would have something to say for itself.

John placed the chestnut beneath his nose and inhaled. It was bright brown and gleaming; it would have been quite easy to let it touch his mouth. He held it there for a long moment.

No, he decided at last. No, what folks thought and felt was complicated enough without hearing it unspoken. If he got any of this into him, probably his head would burst. Grandpa always said, *Let folks think what they like; it's not your business as long as you do right by them.*

John slipped the chestnut into his pocket. He'd got what he came for. He should have been feeling pleased with himself, but when he looked up, the sorrow of the place seeped into him again. The empty tree, its trunk full of suck-marks; the broken woods, scattered about like the aftermath of an exhausted, inconsolable tantrum.

'Hey now,' said a voice. 'No need to cry.'

It was a long, dizzying moment before John was able to realise that wasn't his own voice speaking his own thoughts aloud.

He turned. Jedediah stood in the blasted clearing, a plain, thin figure with sawdust all around his feet.

John rubbed his eye. 'I'm not crying,' he said. 'I'm too big to cry.'

'No such thing,' said Jedediah. His voice was soft. 'You either know how or you don't. Better to know.'

John couldn't think of an answer to that.

Jedediah didn't press him. 'Want me to take you home?' he said.

'You should have been home before,' John told him, a bit accusingly. 'Where were you?'

'With Aunt Pell,' Jedediah said. 'Don't fret, they've told me all about Uncle Stan. And Granny Constance is all right.'

'What? Why shouldn't she be?'

'Oh.' Jedediah cleared his throat. 'Uncle Corbie gave her some of the same drowse he gave you, but much more. Your Godfa and father pulled her through, though she came close.' His jaw was taut. 'Wasn't the first time he attempted her life. I just . . . I didn't think he'd be so open about it.'

'Well – well then, Mister Thorpe should take him to the sheriff! I know you don't care for hangings, Grandpa, and I don't either, it's a bad thing to do to someone, but when it comes to Uncle Corbie, well – well, I'm sorry to say I think he's a wicked man.'

Jedediah stood for a long, quiet moment, Then he said, 'I won't quarrel with you on that, Johnny lad. We do have to do something. I thought I'd talk to you and your father before we settled on what. It's a heavy thing, to hang your own kinsman. We – we should decide together.'

That thought brought John back to his present circumstances, which now felt rather pressing: he'd only been in the woods a couple of hours, but several days' worth of events had evidently happened behind his back. 'How did you know I was here?' he said.

At that, Jedediah snorted, a sound so familiar John started to feel warm again, though he hadn't known until that moment he was cold. 'Because I'm not a fool,' he said. 'Stan said you ran off by a railed woodland, so where else would you be? You've wanted to see in here all your life, odd piece that you are. And you never did stop till you had an answer.' His gaze on John wasn't angry, and he said the word 'odd' with a plain, flat acceptance that was like being held. 'Just wish I had more answers for you, lad. I've found some things out, but not enough.' He stepped forward, crossing the shattered ground to reach John. 'Sorry, lad.'

John had plenty to say: he'd worked out a lot too, and Grandpa would be obliged to admire him when he explained how much. He picked his way across the spikes. 'Thanks for coming for me, Grandpa,' he said. 'We do need to talk – but can I give you a hug? I think I need a hug.'

Jedediah put his arms around John without a word and John hugged back, leaning against his grandfather's chest. Bone and sinew: a comfort as familiar as his own skin.

'Have I been gone long?' he said, a little muffled by the shirt.

'Two days,' Jedediah said. 'And it was a little after sunrise outside the wood, so most likely it'll be dawn next day by the time we get out. Trust you to go a-walking through bent time.' He rested his hand upon John's head.

'I'm glad you're here,' John mumbled. 'I didn't want him to take me to Tinsdowne.'

'Of course I'm here,' Jedediah said, a little crossly. 'You're my boy, aren't you?'

'Yes, and on that point,' said John, disengaging with a sudden enthusiasm, 'let's talk things over. I've got an idea.'

'All right.' Jedediah let go without comment. Sometimes the highest reward children give your love is taking it for granted. 'Let's walk at the same time, though. The others'll be worried, us gone so long.'

'I'll tell you what,' John said, 'you can talk first, because you're the elder and I spent the whole cart-ride telling Stan

Mackem I had to respect you – *don't* look so surprised, it's not polite. I just need to ask you one thing first, is that all right?'

'Go on.' Jedediah said, resigned to patience.

'All right,' said John. 'You knew Clem Smith, didn't you?'

'Yes, he was my grandpa. Died when I was about your age.'

'Well, don't you go and do that,' said John sternly.

'As you order, sir.' Jedediah said, trying not to look moved. 'Don't tell me that was the question?'

'No, the question is: did he like children? Little ones?'

They stepped over a flayed chunk of tree-flesh.

'I reckon so,' Jedediah said. 'I remember him kind to me, and I suppose I started as little as most. He was a good man, whatever the Mackems might say of him.'

'See, that's what I thought,' said John. 'It explains why he never tried to kill Ab himself. No doubt he wore down, and when Uncle Corbie came along, he couldn't stop him – I mean, Uncle Corbie isn't easy to stop, and I suppose he was harder still when he had all his wits. By the by, he can't have been a very kind father, Grandpa.'

'He wasn't,' Jedediah said dryly. 'Never you mind, though. We won't let him beat you.'

'Well, thank you. But if Clem was kind, then I know why he let Ab go on so long – we'd have known it ourselves if he'd made a chant of it and taught you to pass it on. The Mackems aren't all wrong about that: we could do with more chants.'

'Suppose you prove yourself a skilled chantsman, then,' said Jedediah, raising his voice a little, just enough to recall the boy's attention from wherever it had wandered, 'and come to the point, eh?'

'Oh.' John took the meaning, if not quite how his grandfather had intended. 'All right.

'Clem didn't like to do the kind friend harms,
For no kind man will hurt a babe-in-arms.'

'I – what?' Jedediah kept walking; they needed to get out of the wood as soon as possible, for Matthew would be afraid something had happened to them. Only his ability to ask a sensible question had broken their stride.

'A cunning man had planned to get a slave
And wished it to be quiet and behave.
He'd tried it once before, but couldn't keep
That captured fey—'

'Johnny—' said Jedediah, with the hard-tested endurance of a man who has been very worried about his grandson and is trying not to think about how peaceful life had been in the hours he was gone, 'I didn't mean rhyme at me. Just tell me plain what you mean, if you please.'

'Oh dear. Do be careful, Grandpa, you always say the People take puzzling words in puzzling ways; we can't have you hurt.

'But it's quite simple. Dada told me the tale of Samuel Alder – though in our account, someone mixed his name up and called him Elder Samuel. Why didn't the Mackems and Smiths ever put their tales together, by the by? We'd have settled things long ago.'

'Well,' said Jedediah slowly, 'the clans don't meet that often.'

'Can't we meet more? Elder Stan Mackem wasn't respectful

to you, not as he should have been, but he did know lots of chants. I should learn more of them, I reckon.'

'Was Stan respectful to you?'

'Oh, no, he tried to elder it over me, but don't worry, I wouldn't have it. You're my elder. I told him so. But I do reckon we'd know more if we met them more, Grandpa. Can't you take me to visit them? I could pick up their chants pretty quick.'

Jedediah pictured himself sitting around a table with Stan Mackem and his lads, John beside him, piping up, asking impossible questions, offering candid opinions, honestly trying to help. Stan's face would be a sight to warm him on cold nights. *Why don't we try this? I reckon the People want that. That's just silly. No, don't hush me, I have a thought!* A certain glow rose in his chest.

'That one's easy enough,' he said. 'Before the clans married, the Mackems didn't share any of their histories with us. Afraid we'd write 'em down and stain custom with ink.'

'Well, that's not very sensible,' John said, and Jedediah covered his smile with his hand. 'Also, I reckon that Uncle Corbie's father must have been very eager to get rid of him if he was up to things with his sister-in-law. But anyway, I meant about why Grandpa Clem wouldn't kill the kind friend.'

'You did.' Jedediah grinned.

'All right,' John said, a little hurt, 'I do have a point.' Jedediah patted his shoulder and John accepted the comfort: Grandpa had come to look for him, after all. 'So the point is, this Peter Alder stole a fey from a fairy court somewhere and kept it for a slave, until it escaped. Then he made up his mind that the next one he stole wouldn't get away so easily. So he took another one that wouldn't know how, because it was too young. He took a baby.'

At that, Jedediah did stop. 'What's that, now?'

They stood in a mossy clearing where time ran across them like a river, the springy green beneath their feet turning tiny, craving tendrils up towards the light.

'He thought it wouldn't know how to get away,' John said, 'and it didn't. It doesn't know what it is at all; it didn't have anyone to teach it. It's all just shapes and wanting – that's why it comes and goes so much: it takes naps, I reckon. Mama says babies sleep a lot. But you remember how it says, over and over, that it must have its friend? I thought of it when I saw Cousin Lissy – she wants her mama, and she sucks at everything that comes near her mouth until someone brings her to Francie. She doesn't know what she's sucking at, I reckon; she just tries whatever she can find. But it's her mama she truly wants.'

Jedediah was staring at him with a face so still that John worried he'd offended him by lecturing him on infants, which, after all, were not as new a thing to Grandpa as they were to John.

'It's only,' he said in conciliation, 'that I never held a babe before. No one asked me to – folks don't do it to boys, have you noticed? So when Cousin Anthony did, that was the first time I had a baby to look at properly. And that's what Ab's like, Grandpa. It wants its friend, but it moves from friend to friend, sucking them dry. I reckon it was snatched away so young, it hadn't learned how to say – maybe even how to say to itself – that it wanted its mama.'

*

Stan Mackem sat smoking his pipe out in the Brady garden. Francie, who was fond of deep scents, had planted it with lavender and rose, honeysuckle and rosemary. This late in the year there wasn't much to show for it, but it hardly mattered: it was a dark night, cluttered thick with stars.

Franklin left him alone for a while. It might not be his place to interfere, but if they were to protect Constance and John and anyone else Corbie's eye might light on, a decision should be taken. He could bring Corbie Mackem to the sheriff now, testify plain that the man was a poisoner, and Corbie would have a rope around his neck before the year's end. Franklin hated hangings; he prospered as a forester because of his tracking and surveying skills, but he'd never rise to the highest rank because of his habit of letting poachers and fugitives go – those fugitives who weren't a danger to their fellow man, at least.

He could take the decision off Mister Smith's hands and just arrest the man, and that might be the kindest thing to do. But he was balking at the thought of it. It wasn't just Corbie Mister Smith had to think of, but Stan Mackem as well. The two of them still hadn't talked, not properly – neither knew where to begin – but if one hanged their father without the consent of the other, that rift would never close.

If they hanged their father at all. Franklin felt no more inclined to forgive Corbie than anyone else, but to hang your own father . . . He thought of hard-handed Joe Thorpe, his anger filling the room from wall to wall. There were days he'd prayed for his father to die, but he knew that if he'd been the one to kill Joe himself, he'd have been scarred: with that death on his hands, he'd have walked away for ever from the freedom to say, *This man is no longer my responsibility.*

Franklin took his pipe and headed out to the garden, Soots at his heels. He wasn't much of a smoker, really, but it was one of those things men did to calm themselves and if you did it alongside them, it could make things easier.

Stan was sitting on Francie's stone bench. Franklin, without a word, sat down beside him. Soots greeted Stan with a polite wag of her tail, sniffed the fist Stan held out and then, at Franklin's finger-snap, sat down beside her master and rested her chin on his knee. The two gazed ahead for a while, saying nothing.

'You know,' Franklin said after a while, 'you don't know me. If you make yourself foolish by talking to me, it costs you nothing.'

Stan looked startled; he evidently hadn't had to learn Jedediah's trick of wearing his face like a mask.

Leaning back, Franklin addressed himself with calm abstraction to the stars. 'I had a father,' he said, 'by blood. I had another man who was far more of a father than he could ever have been. I grieved when my father died – as much for the man he wasn't as the man he was – but it's the other man I'll weep for, come the day. God keep it far off.'

'A man of cheerful outlook, I see,' said Stan, dryly. He was not about to cry on anybody's shoulder, evidently – or at least, not a Gyrford man's.

Soots raised her head and when Franklin didn't signal her back, she wandered over to condole with Stan. After a few tactful nudges with her nose, he conceded to pat her.

'I won't tell you to like Mister Smith,' Franklin said to the light-crumbed sky, 'but I reckon you haven't seen the best of him.'

Stan snorted. 'Oh, I don't doubt he's a better Smith than he is a Mackem.'

Franklin said nothing. He wanted to say, *Once, when I was smaller than a dog, a man found me stealing food. He took me in and warmed me by the fire, and he gave me a sweet apple. He could have given me bread alone; he didn't need to give me the apple as well. He was eighteen years old and he looked at my arm and saw one bruise, and he knew everything he needed to know about my father. Don't resent him. You've been the lucky one.*

But Stan was carrying enough already, a burden Franklin wouldn't wish on any man: the lead-shirt weight of being ashamed of your father.

Then Stan laughed. The sound was harsh, bitter, but not without real amusement. 'Here I came, thinking I had it all to rights,' he said. 'He always did gall me, that Jedediah of yours, here in this smithy with but a couple of men and madness in his line a fathom deep, holding his head up like a king as if he's too good for his father's name. Well, it's my ballocks on the anvil now. He has me. Have to give it to him: he has me.'

'What's that?' Franklin stroked Soots, being very careful not to stare.

'The eldership,' Stan said. He didn't sound surprised that a man outside the clan didn't understand the weight of it. 'There was never any question of mine. Dunstan Mackem, son of Dunstan, son of Dunstan, and all that: the elder's eldest son. Well, that's not who I am, is it? By rights, the eldership goes to Esau.'

'Esau?'

'My brother – my father's son – Dunstan's son, that is, and no question of that: Corbie was well gone before he got started.'

Franklin went still. 'Doesn't the eldership go to whoever the elder names?' he said. 'After all, Corbie was elder here and he wasn't Mister Clem Smith's son.'

'The Tinsdowne elder names a Dunstan,' Stan said. 'God help us, Esau'd have to change his name.'

He sighed. 'We get on, Esau and me. I'll tell him – I'll have to tell him. We could make it work between us. But' – he spelled it out as if to a layman too untrained to follow the intricacies – 'it's one thing within the smithy walls. I never had sons of my own, so Esau's Danny – that's young Dunstan Mackem to you – will inherit after me anyway. It's another thing to blazon it to the world that I'm the bastard son of a poisoner. Folks'd listen to any who told *that* tale.' He said it almost as flat as Jedediah might have. 'Which, if I don't oblige, no doubt your Jedediah will do. And to my pa.'

Franklin blinked. His first thought was to say, *Mister Smith wouldn't extort anyone.* His second thought was that with someone to protect, Mister Smith definitely would, and so would Janet, God bless her. But he didn't think that was what was afoot here.

'You reckon,' he asked, 'your pa didn't know?'

'He didn't.' Stan spoke with flat certainty. 'He liked to talk of how alike we were. My grandpa must have known – he set up the marriage – but he wouldn't have told anyone.' He paused. 'He was like that, my grandpa; wanted us all to get along.' He gazed sightlessly into the garden, staring at memories. 'One time I overheard something, some customer's private talk, when I was an apprentice – not my business, but I repeated it to him in front of others. Didn't know any better. He slapped my arse right then and there, said God made ears to stay open, but mouths can be kept shut.'

'Well, then,' Franklin said. It was hard listening to men speaking casually of slaps in their childhood, and he wrestled briefly with himself, but Stan obviously remembered the proverb more than the blow. 'I reckon . . . You might find Mister Smith more of a Mackem in that than you think.'

Stan didn't look at him.

There was a noise, footsteps, and Janet came into the garden. As well as attending to Francie upstairs, she'd been supervising Shibbie, who was, she thought, getting a little too enthusiastic about instructing Molly.

'Well, my fellows,' she said, not quite divested of her elder-midwife voice, 'no doubt I interrupt you, but you'll just have to endure it. Have you forgiven me for finding your father yet, Stan Mackem, or have I made an enemy of you?'

Stan grunted, not eager to be having that conversation with Matthew's Janet, who was almost as bad as her John when it came to talking too much, but she sat beside him with an air of auntieish authority particularly galling in a woman more than two decades his junior.

'There's a man you and Father must see hanged or not,' she said, almost consolingly. 'I reckon it's time for differences to be set aside. By the by,' she added, with no hint in her tone that she might be deploying a strategy, 'Shibbie tells me you keep no chickens in Tinsdowne. Would you care for some of ours? We have enough and more to spare. Your pa was out by our coop for hours this afternoon, laughing away at their play. I never knew there were so many jokes one man could make about cocks, and I'll tell you, I thought I knew plenty.' She brushed aside a lock of hair, smiling with resolute innocence. 'He had a fine time. It's good, you know, when folks start to wander in their wits a little, to be with birds and beasts. Makes them happy. Don't worry,' she added, 'he wasn't cold. We gave him blankets, poor dear.'

'Don't you "poor dear" him, woman!' Stan snapped.

Franklin would have been startled at the sudden outburst, except he was too busy regarding Janet with suspicion. That last remark was unlike her: one of her fiercest rules of nursing was that you never talk down to the sick.

Stan was truly angry now. ' "Poor dear," indeed!' he shouted. 'My father was a legend in his time, Matthew's Janet, a *legend!* He's the man who nailed down the Hill-Skin Door; he killed Jack-o'-the-Flood! There are six-and-forty songs about him. *Six-and-forty!*'

'That's a pity,' Janet said. 'Corbie can't bear him. We've locked him in a bedroom, but most likely he'll find a way out sooner or later. He has ideas against Old Dunstan.'

'He won't do a thing,' Stan said, rising. 'I'll go and have it out with Jedediah *right now* if I have to.'

Stan might be upset, but he was an intelligent man and he caught the slightly smug look Janet cast at Franklin.

'All right, all right,' he said, sitting down again. It was too tiring to be angry; he had enough heavy feelings on his back without. 'If you thought it was time I spoke to him, you could have just said so.'

'And deny you the satisfaction of doing it by your own word?' Janet grinned at him.

Stan was not overly fond of clever women, but evidently this was yet another Smith tradition: they all were mad enough to prefer women with more opinions than anyone needed to hear. Louise had been another of the same, the one time he'd met her: a secretive smile that made him feel mocked; a distant poise that made him feel snubbed; entirely wrapped up in his aggravating cousin, who had done nothing Stan could see to deserve so pretty a girl.

Clever women and touched ones. Gyrford wasn't a rookery but a cursed henhouse.

But that thought brought him to another he'd wanted to avoid. His mama, Annie Mackem: his grey-eyed, yellow-haired, restless mother, who had loved to be the first to hear a piece of gossip, who had always been the one to volunteer when a message was to be run from smithy to customer, who had danced her children round in laughing circles whenever a fiddler played, who had sighed when her husband spoke of duties and responsibilities. Annie Mackem, who loved her children, who would gossip about anyone – except unfaithful wives. Annie Mackem, who was all for a bit of fun.

She had died thirty years ago. He still missed her.

'Tell your father-in-law,' he said slowly, 'that I wash my hands of this. Settling a crime in your holding is farrier work, and I don't work for Jedediah Smith.'

Janet sat very still for a moment. They might have won, in a way, but it was no satisfaction. With a weary heart, Janet rose and dusted off her hands. 'I'll tell him,' she said. 'Let us know how many chickens you'd like to take with you. Call it a gift from kin to kin.'

No one spoke for a moment after she'd gone.

'Do you have a wife?' Stan said, his voice still a little angry.

Franklin shook his head. 'I lost her – oh, a decade ago. May she rest in peace.' His Sarah had been very dear to him; he loved that Francie was so like her in temper. Perhaps Lissy would be too; she certainly was a promisingly sweet baby.

Stan was a decent enough man to say, 'I'm sorry about that.' He was fond of his own wife: Sal was the right kind of woman. He wished he was with her now.

Franklin said, very lightly, 'Is your mother living?'

'No,' said Stan. He looked away and took to the Mackem proverb: a man knows when to shut his mouth.

Then he said, 'Thorpe, is it?'

'Franklin Thorpe.'

'Well, Franklin Thorpe,' said Stan, returning to the tone of a fairy-smith: plain, authoritative, his heart his own, 'you may, so please you, mind your own business.'

It had taken many years for Franklin to learn not to be afraid of men; he still wasn't sure he always managed it. There was nothing in Stan Mackem's words that suggested he'd reconsider; it was just the way the words came out, and the other things Stan could have said and didn't, that made him realise he liked the man.

'I can,' he said, 'and with the guidance of God, I will. I'll be off now to mind it elsewhere.' He stood, dusted himself down, and with a bit of a grin, knuckled his forelock, as was proper to an elder farrier, and went off to mind his own business.

*

Later that night Old Dunstan Mackem woke in the dark. It happened more and more as time went on, and he couldn't always remember what he was supposed to be doing. At home, if he went for a wander, he'd soon enough run into one of his children or grandchildren and they'd make him laugh and put him back to bed; it was all right once he got past the part where he was awake and afraid and he didn't know why.

When he woke in the dark of Anthony Brady's house, he was more frightened than he could ever remember. There was a man asleep in the bed with him, shaped like one of his sons, but the room itself was wrong: the walls were in the wrong places, and the ceiling loomed too high, and there was a window in it that looked out onto a moon so bright that it might not have been the moon at all, but the sun that lit some other, colder, unholy world.

The body in his bed snored, or possibly snarled at him.

Dunstan crept out and went looking for his family. They were sound lads and lasses; they knew what was what. It would be all right when he got to them.

But the doors and stairways led to more wrong places, and then one of them betrayed him by leading out into an entire new land: a cobbled square, treed all around and lit by the dim glow of a night-time forge – but the forge was on the far side of the square. Safety was retreating from him.

Dunstan had to get to his family, but something was taking them away from him, floating his bed away from the forge with Stan and Esau and his young ones.

'Stan!' he called, stumbling towards the forge on freezing legs. 'Esau! Boys, where are you?'

There was a silence, and nobody answered.

Dunstan, starting to wake up properly, was having the fearful sense that he'd forgotten something – but he didn't know what it was. Maybe the fey things floating the smithy in the dark had taken it from him.

Nobody came, long second after long second. Dunstan Mackem sat down and cried.

He was still weeping when something appeared at his side. Possibly it was an imp, so he made the sign of the cross, warding it away.

'Well, bless you too,' the imp said with a sleepy yawn. 'You woke me up. I'll go and wake Dada and Grandpa in a moment, unless you'd like to take my advice and go back to bed now, but there's no need to cry about it.' It patted him, almost experimentally. 'Never mind,' it said. 'I'm sure you'll feel better soon.'

Dunstan stopped crying and was trying very hard to make his memories come together. The imp-boy, or possibly just a boy, was one he'd seen before: it was dark out here, but the imp-boy had a head of curly hair like that pretty Janet girl who made such good jokes. If it didn't mind blessings, then possibly it was just a boy. But he wasn't sure what its name was.

'There you are,' it told him in a whisper. 'No need to cry. It'll only wake folks and then they'll be out of temper tomorrow, and we have a great deal to settle then. Do you know what room you were in before you came out here?'

Things might have been settled peacefully, except that at that moment there was a sharp crack from above their heads.

Dunstan cowered towards the imp-or-maybe-boy; it was at least friendly, and if this uncanny new world was splitting apart, it might help him jump to one of the larger pieces.

'Hey!' exclaimed the imp, 'you are *not* to break our windows! You can't climb out, it's too small, and you'd only smash on the ground anyway. And if you smash tonight you'll probably go to Hell, which Parson Green says is a bad idea, so I'd think you'd want to avoid any further sins and try repenting and so on. I'm sure they'd let you talk to the parson about it. Dada'd be delighted, he loves forgiving folks.'

Dunstan held on to the imp-boy's hand, which, reassuringly, it didn't withdraw. 'I think I should go for Nuncle Stan,' it said. 'That's what Dada reckons we should call him. Cousin Shibbie says she's glad to see at least some folks listen to what she says.'

Then Dunstan was alone in a black world, stuck on a cold stone bench and the imp wasn't there to help him. He started to cry again.

'Well, now.' It was a whisper from above. 'How are the mighty fallen.'

Dunstan looked up, but he couldn't see anything but a house with a window open at the top of it, and above, a flurry of cold stars and a moon bright enough to scorch you. It was possible that the next door he opened would be into Hell; the imp's talk had certainly implied that. Dunstan reckoned he'd been a sinner like anyone, but he'd tried to be good most of the time. He'd worked for his neighbours, said his prayers, gone to church, stayed true to his wife, honoured his parents, fed and taught his children – he thought he'd done pretty well. But perhaps that was pride and now he was damned for it. He cried louder.

'Ah, Dunstan.' The whisper came again. 'Time came for you, didn't it? Not a word for me did you speak, even after you knew what I was shackled to. Not a word now, I'll be bound: chained to a demon and hanged for trying to free myself, while you were a king, my brother. Well, it's my nestling will come after you – never knew that, did you? Ah, you and Sweep were all to work on that chalk man, scraping at his head with the villagers and ruling over them like grand men – felt like kings of the world, you did, while I was down on that chalk cock with your Annie. Thought your Stan was the image of you, you always did. Well, my man—'

Dunstan was crying so hard by now that he didn't entirely understand what the voice was saying, but it was talking of demons and kings and ruling over all, and it was so likely that Hell really was on the other side of this next door that when the tall figure appeared before him, he struck out wildly at the thing come to drag him down.

'Last rites!' he shouted. 'I didn't die yet – I want my last rites!'

'Hush, Pa, hush, hush, it's all right.' The figure's voice was affectionate, soothing; he felt a hard palm on his head, stroking his hair with no unkind touch. 'It's only your Stan, Pa. Don't be afraid, Pa. You walked in your sleep, that's all.'

Dunstan tried to reach out in the dark, but the monsters were still there: at the words 'your Stan' the fiend above gave a cackle – and the imp-boy was standing there, too, staring – holding hands with another imp, except that this bigger imp was that pretty Janet – and then the one standing before him was indeed his Stan, his fine son. The demons might be after him, but they wouldn't get Stan; he might have been a faulty sinner, but Stan was a good lad.

'Well,' said the figure that was Janet, 'I'm not sure I think someone deserves to be kept out of the noose, but there you are.'

'I'm not either, Mama,' chirped the imp, 'but it's not about that. I reckon it's about how Grandpa and Dada don't deserve to be the ones put him into it. Could be Nuncle Stan, too, if he pulls himself together. I know you've had a shock, Nuncle' – the imp turned to Stan, who had stepped protectively in front of Dunstan – 'but I reckon we need every man. You don't have to hang him; I've thought of something else.'

'Oh you have, have you?' said Stan. He sounded annoyed, and Dunstan took hold of his arm, but Stan sat down beside him, saying, 'Never mind, Pa, never mind. It's all quite all right. We'll get back to bed, eh? Settle down warm and safe.'

'Yes, I have,' the imp announced. 'Well, I'll say it was "we", for I told you I act under my grandpa, and he and I and Dada and Mama and Molly and – well, we all had a talk, and now we have a plan. I thought of most of it, but Grandpa says it's worth a try. So you don't have to hang your fa—Um . . . your *uncle*,' it corrected itself, 'and your pa will be safe, and so will you. Don't worry, it's farrier work. Mostly. And after that *most uncalled-for* bit of unkindness up above' – it cast an accusing look into the fractured sky – 'I reckon you might be with us in this, Nuncle. I know you said you didn't work for Grandpa, but when I say things like that because I'm out of temper, folks tell me not to be silly, and I don't see that being older makes it any less silly in you. There's a long time to say things that hurt folks between now and a hanging, you know, but with our way, we could settle it tomorrow. And that should suit you, for I reckon what you want most is to guard your pa.'

'Oh, you do, do you?' Stan sat braced against his father, glaring at the shadowy boy before him.

'You know, you needn't repeat back and back like that,' the boy advised him. 'Grandpa says an elder farrier can say what he thinks – as long as it's needful.'

'If I have to hear you tell me one more time what your grandpa says,' Stan said, 'then I might find that I cannot work with you.'

'Oh, good,' said the boy. 'I thought you'd say yes in the end. Mind you, you'll have to work like a Smith. I reckon you can stomach it once you get started. It's not so bad. Grandpa grew up to like it, after all.'

John rose early the next morning, crept into his sisters' room and shook Molly awake. He always loved getting up in the dark, especially on Clementing day, which was drawing ever nearer. Molly was not such a dawn enthusiast; she was of an age where morning sleep is hard to escape. But she struggled silently into wakefulness and the two of them crept downstairs barefooted, being careful not to rouse those still sleeping.

Jedediah was already sitting at the kitchen table. He looked just as he always did. John was coming to appreciate, with the world as upside-down as it had been of late, that somehow his grandfather had the ability to be his usual self, no matter who was going mad around him. John had felt for a long time that there was something knackish and gifted about Molly's ability to create order and food out of mess and ingredients. Grandpa's normality, come what may, was something the same: he was like a stone the world bounced off. Except he wasn't a man of stone, but of flesh, and he had feelings – so exactly how he did it, John wasn't sure.

'I've made porridge,' he told John and Molly. 'You've time to eat. As long as we leave before first light, we'll be fine.'

Molly was too attached to Grandpa to be as curt as she would have been with her mother at such an hour, but her whole head was sodden with sleep. 'Not hungry,' she said with a yawn. 'I can't eat this early.'

Matthew might have pressed the issue, but Jedediah let it go. 'Takes longer to open your gullet than your eyes?' he said, quite kindly. 'Pack yourself some bread and cheese, then. It'll be long work and you shouldn't do it empty.'

The night outside was so cold it felt personal, or at least, it did to Molly: cold scraped her cheeks with intrusive nails, crept under her scarf like questing snakes, gripped her ribcage even under all her layers, squeezing hard breaths out of her that steamed in the dark.

'I don't know why you won't shiver,' she said to John. She did truly wish to help, but it was hard to be sensible all the time, and John and Grandpa minded it least if she complained, just a little. 'It'd freeze cream out here.'

'Whisht,' Jedediah said, not harshly. 'Let's get a little way out of Gyrford, and then you can repine, lass.'

'Cold's just cold,' whispered John – a statement he felt enlightening, apparently, but which didn't make Molly any warmer.

'Besides,' he went on, in a kind of hushed, light-tipped murmur so she could hear his words clear from close up but would have heard nothing even a couple of paces away, 'you mean to be a midwife, no? Midwives get up all hours and weathers.'

'I didn't say I wouldn't do it.' Molly hadn't mastered the farrier's hiss; perhaps, she thought, Johnny would teach it to her. She was waking up now, and things were beginning to feel exciting. She found she was grateful to him – there was nothing like a wrangle with Johnny to get you on the alert – and a grin was starting to tinge her grumbles. 'I said I'd do it shivering.'

'Whisht,' Jedediah said again, putting a hand on their arms and guiding them towards the path that led out of Gyrford towards the Lenden farm and Aunt Pell's wood.

The colours of dawn began muted, as if seen through blurry eyes: red light striped the horizon, melting into grey above; the tree branches were flat black against the dull blue, and no birds cried out their dawn chorus.

The sun rose, spilling saffron light upwards into a silent sky.

Molly might not have a strong sense of things when it came to fey places, but she knew a blasted spot when she saw one. Aunt Pell's wood had been off-limits to her as much as to John; she hadn't minded, for the People were trouble as far as she was concerned. She still wasn't entirely sure she wanted this encounter, but for a skyful of birdsong, for a smithy without Uncle Corbie and his hot, probing eyes, for Grandpa to smile at her with his shoulders dropped and his arms held loose – yes, she'd do it for those.

Even through her boot soles, the broken chunks of tree pressed their sharp edges.

'Grandpa,' she said now, 'I'm not sure I can . . . well, I don't know if I'm good at persuading.' She wouldn't have spoken that thought aloud, not back in the smithy, but it was a fear of hers. Celdie and Vevie were bright-haired and laughing, immersed in the sunny pool of each other's eternal approval; they winked at boys and learned new skills for fun and then grew bored and forgot them, leaving no scratch upon their gleaming surfaces. Mama could talk to anyone and John was never short of chat, and even Dada, for all he was shy with strangers, was big and handsome and folks thought him impressive just by the way he took up space. Molly's life was that of the ordinary one, and that didn't feel like much to go on.

'You'll be fine, lass,' Grandpa said, with a reassurance so habitual it had rather lost its meaning in Molly's world.

'You always say that,' she said. Her skirt caught on a snag of broken tree; that, she felt, was the kind of thing that usually happened to her.

'Haven't been wrong yet, have I?' Jedediah said. It was still shadowy, the day not fully broken, but as he looked at her, he saw a kind of weary doubt. She had her grandmother's lovely face, but that look of hers had never been Louise's.

'Look you.' He stopped, rested his hand on her shoulder. 'You and John and I, we'll work this together. I'd not have asked if I didn't trust you. Have you ever known me suffer a fool?'

'Yes,' Molly said, softly defiant, 'all the time. You say what you think, and then you go right on and help them.'

'Well, all right, then.' He looked embarrassed at being caught out. 'So what I think is that we'll work this together, and I'd not have brought you if I wasn't certain you could. My John and my Molly know what they're about. I didn't breed soft-headed children.' Then, since he seemed to be going all lengths anyway, he added, 'My young ones are all I could wish.'

Molly bit her lip, embarrassed in her turn. They stood opposite each other, not quite sure what to do.

At which point, John added, with true helpfulness, 'Besides, Molly, Grandpa couldn't do it alone. He's afraid of spiders. Oh yes you are, Grandpa. I wouldn't tell a lie on fey ground if I were you.'

'No One! John called up the ash tree. It was a long way from Ab's prison and its branches rose high and sturdy. A gleaming weft of threads strung in elegant circles from branch to branch, so interwoven that the whole crown of it shimmered silver. Here and there, sucked dark and dry, the corpses of squirrels hung like mistletoe.

Light prismed, striking colours off the tree, but there was no response.

'Hey! Spider!' Jedediah shouted. He kept his elbows very close to his sides. John had announced his fear of spiders plain as plain, though the lad had never mentioned it before. It might have been sensitive of him, except that he'd chosen to reveal it just before they went to coax a giant spider from its web.

'We know you're there!' he insisted. 'Don't give me trouble. I helped you before and I'm not in the mood for nonsense.' John said the thing still remembered Louise, so it must remember him. His voice hadn't quite the force it had had at nineteen summers, but he could still make himself heard.

'Sense of the block and grind No One cannot bend pretty shell to nor hinge back the legs.' It was a plaintive sigh and Jedediah had tensed before he could help it. He had the dismal feeling that his father had been right about one thing all those years he was growing up: he was easier to see through than he wished.

'Shimmer and float is the skein of thought to gullet, and fluid taste of flow and sate,' the whisper went on. 'Boots of poison and heart of stricken snap, and what shall the air do for sweet things? No One is not here. Movement is not and alone hang the sucked and drunken skins, and No One is but bark and still within the light of stretching reach.'

Jedediah rubbed his face, because it wouldn't be dignified to clutch his head. He agreed with the abominable thing: he, too, would much prefer it if it wasn't there.

'Hey now, No One,' John called up. 'If you're not there, then you might as well be not down here. If you're not down here, there's a face you might like to see.'

Molly Smith stood between her brother and her grandfather as a foot, needle-edged and glossy, took a shivering step down the bark. It was like an eye, she thought: it flickered from side to side, seeking and seeking a safe spot as if sometimes it didn't quite know where to put itself. That was a feeling she knew well.

Molly wasn't exactly afraid of spiders; they had a tendency to scuttle that could make you jump if you weren't expecting it – and somehow, you never were – but what she liked least was handling them. Their legs were so thin, their joints so tiny, that just the slightest wrong move and you could snap them. Then you'd have killed something, and it would be gone for ever and to no purpose; it wasn't your dinner, or a pest that would gnaw your house down, but just a small animal that you couldn't rebuild if you studied a thousand years. Folks said killing spiders was unlucky, but Molly felt it was more than that: it was sinful – and it was a sin that, because they were so small, you could do completely by mistake.

She cleared her throat. At least this one wasn't small. 'Good day, No One, dear,' she said, and her voice was almost tender. 'Will you come and talk with me?'

The foot paused. Then another one came tip-tipping down with a soft quiver, then a sharp grip as it found its hold.

'It must be easier to step on the web,' Molly said. 'I wish I could make webs to walk on. I always have to guess where to stand, and I never know if I've guessed wrong.'

The spider took this in for a second, and then committed one of the scuttles its kind were prone to, racing down the bark and gazing into Molly's face with every one of its gleaming eyes.

Molly managed not to take a step back. She'd seen smaller ponies than this beast. How it remained in the tree-tops without breaking the branches she couldn't imagine – but then, fey things seldom bothered to match their size to their weight. It moved as if it were no heavier than a common spider.

'Scentless of knee and blind of foot and without web is the Louise girl!' It was a lament, crackling with compassion. 'Empty is the air and placeless the girl of cream-blood and warm skin and liver clean and colour-sweet. Viscera of delicate scent and hair of stream-water and what shall the flesh do for placeless stepping?'

Molly was surprised to find herself a little comforted – no, more than comforted: *complimented.* Her parents told her she was pretty, but that convinced her about as much as a loving parent's word ever convinces a girl not yet out of her teens, and boys' comments felt like a down-payment on favours she didn't intend to deliver. No one had ever told her that her liver and blood were attractive – but she couldn't see them to find fault, and why should the spider lie? No One was rather nicer than Grandpa had led her to expect.

'Well, that's a kind thing to say,' she said. 'Thank you very much. I do like your shell, it gleams most beautiful.'

'Heart wet and twitching and goodness is to No One's poor feelings,' the spider hiss-crooned. 'Here the Louise-girl comes at last to friend and praise, for No One has been good so many years. Squirrel-husks hang witness to the chaste hunting of No One, for fox and rat and air-sparrow has No One drunk but never man nor beast of man, and has not the promise been kept by a good No One?'

'I'm sure you've been a very good spider,' said Molly, finding herself oddly tempted to pet the thing.

'So says the Louise-girl!' It was a whispered fanfare, hushing and triumphant. 'Year upon year has No One lived in virtue and beloved must be!'

John gave Molly a pat on the arm and then, when she looked at him, a wink of approval as of one crafty trickster to another.

Jedediah, on the other side, was as stiff as a man waiting for his tooth to be pulled. He'd said many fond things to her over the years, but the fact that he hadn't run away touched Molly to the heart deeper than any of them.

'I'm . . . not quite Louise,' Molly said. She found it went against her conscience to lie. 'She was my grandmother. So . . .' She considered the matter. Aunt Pell had said that if Molly liked to be a midwife there was no reason not to train her; the girl was bright enough and she'd have the manner if she'd just build up a little boldness with it. How would a midwife explain this? 'I'm . . . a little bit Louise,' Molly said. 'A fourth Louise, mixed in with other . . . bloods. But they say her flavour came out strong.'

John looked at Molly in frank admiration, and Molly felt buoyed.

'Scent of blood and kidney-meat,' No One confirmed. 'Dry-throated is Louise-love,' it then added with sad regret, 'for never a drop did comfort the gullet of leaf and paper that thirsted. But kind and scent is Louise-girl, and No One must be beloved and good, or what shall the gullet do for empty hearts?'

'You are *not* to bite my granddaughter.' Jedediah spoke in a tight burst, and Molly took his hand as No One cringed down.

'But a tree-gall and nothing is the innocent,' it keened. 'Iron of hand and thought cannot hurt gall and innocence.'

'We can still see you,' Jedediah said, his voice strangled. 'You're the size of a bull.'

'No One, dear,' Molly said, for it was time to come to the point, 'we've a very great favour we need to ask you. Louise would have wished it, and I – and I wish it, if you please. For love, dear, will you help us? For the – er – for the face and scent and sake of Louise?'

When Matthew arrived at the little house on the Lenden land that morning, he knocked with a pre-arranged rat-tat.

The birdsong from within went quiet.

'It's Matthew Smith, Aunt Mabbie,' he called. It was a bit peculiar calling a woman 'Aunt' when he'd never met her, but he'd been brought up to be respectful, and from all the tales he'd heard she didn't sound like someone to cross.

'Good morning, Aunt Pell,' he said as he entered. 'And thank you for your help, Aunt Mabbie, it's kind of you.'

Mabbie's head flicked a little, as if tossing aside the chaff of an idea. 'Ready for your lesson?'

'I am, thank you.' Matthew was shy by nature and had expected to feel himself rather nervous around this strange, fierce-sounding woman – and he did, in a way, but it was an odd kind of nerves. Not his usual awkwardness: more the caution you felt around a wild dog or an ill-trained stallion. There was no embarrassment at all; just the need to avoid getting kicked or bitten. Or, he supposed, pecked.

Mabbie blinked, her expression changing not at all. 'Your father says you sing well, but a bass hasn't the range to talk bird-speech. Unless we geld you this morning, we'll need other means.'

She stared at him with a look so intent that Matthew felt obliged to say, 'Er, thank you, I'd rather not be gelded, so I'll learn the other means, so please you.'

'Then it's head-dance and whistles,' Mabbie said. Her voice

was clean as a knife-cut. 'And you'll learn it precise, or you'll do no good with it.'

'Are you sure,' Matthew said, 'we shouldn't find John for this? I've heard him bird-call – he has the range for it, and the best ear I know.'

Mabbie flipped this suggestion aside, but felt no apparent need to discuss it. It was Aunt Pell who intervened. 'The lad can't be everywhere,' she said, her voice not entirely harsh. 'And he has the wrong hair. You've a head of black and that's to their liking. They've their own superstitions, crows: your mother used to feed them, and around these parts they hold that a dark head is more their kind than any other.' She nodded at his aching arms, which had kept him from working at his anvil, holding his children, embracing his wife, pushing back trouble. 'What's more, you've broken wings. Let them know what hurt you and the crows'll be on your side, no question of that. You've had yourself pulled about, so might as well make use of the wounds while you've got them.' She gave a grim smile. 'Crows don't like those who maul their wings.'

Mabbie gave a sound somewhere between a trill and a harrumph. 'We haven't time to waste,' she said. 'Work hard and you'll know a few words by tonight. That should get you by. Now, eyes on me and keep them there.'

John was quite disappointed that they couldn't ride on No One's back. The rhythm of pattering feet must be interestingly different from a horse's, and to be caged safely amidst sharp-hinged knees was a view he would have enjoyed. Molly kicked his ankle when he tried to propose it, though; she and No One had struck up a rapport.

'Don't hurt No One's feelings,' Molly said, and that was that.

'What shall the air do for feelings?' No One agreed. It had extended a clawed foot and was palpating Molly's knees and elbows as if unable to accept that a girl so sympathetic had no scent organs there at all. Molly endured it, no trace of any fear that might wound No One's delicate sensibilities. The sight made John feel rather proud of himself: he'd always *known* Molly's good sense was special.

As the group set out across the fields, Jedediah looked like a man marching to his martyr's pyre, but that couldn't be helped. He had insisted on supervising John in this part of the proceedings, if for no other reason than he didn't want the spider talking the lad into getting himself eaten out of pure curiosity as to how painful it would truly be. No One dashed from hedgerow to hedgerow in a bristling scuttle, its mouth parts prattling together like a scholar's fingertips, making Jedediah regret very much that he'd insisted on breakfast.

No one should have been out this early, but they spotted young Sarah Dawes creeping home along the drovers' lane. She saw a boy, a girl, an old man – and a spider the size of a horse, its talons drumming the soil as if testing the stretch on a web.

Before she'd managed to get out more than one scream, Jedediah snapped, 'Now stop that, Sarah Dawes. It's under our authority, so suppose you get yourself home and leave folks to their work?'

Sarah, ashen, made a mute gesture to Molly, who she'd always thought more normal than this.

'Leave us to it, there's a dear,' Molly said. She didn't usually say 'there's a dear', but Mama often said it when she had to order folks around and didn't like to upset them, and Molly was starting to think that sort of thing might be useful. 'I wouldn't scream too loud either, if I were you,' she thought to add. There had been a dance last night and Sarah must have been out at it, where she wasn't supposed to be: she was courting with Mark Ware, who was pleasant and honest, but he had an eccentric family and no property and the Daweses didn't approve. 'I won't tell your mother you sneaked off,' Molly assured her, 'but if you scream, she'll hear you herself.'

That rallied Sarah and she ran off without another word.

Jedediah patted Molly's shoulder. 'Good work, lass.'

John looked impressed and Molly flushed. When Grandpa said such things, it was the last word in praise.

'Scratch and scrape of air, and preyless she keens!' No One complained, sounding offended.

'Come on,' John told it. 'We've a hollow hill to find.'

The whole family had been consulting and disputing, and finally agreed to John's idea. And it was even a good one.

'But can't you think of something else, John?' Jedediah said. 'You were right,' he went on. It might be hard to admit, but he couldn't go forward without saying it aloud. 'It's true. I am afraid of spiders. Foolish, but there you are.'

Nobody laughed – or even stopped talking.

'I'm sorry, Grandpa,' John said, patting his arm. 'I've thought it through, and every other plan I came up with is worse.'

'I could go with Johnny instead,' Matthew offered. 'I'm fond of them, myself. You could go to learn bird-speech from Aunt Mabbie.'

'Nay.' Jedediah shook his head with a ferocity that was fighting the echoes inside it, not the folks before him. 'Nay, you . . . you have your mother's face. Let the spider see Molly and it'll get fond memories. See two of you and it might get confused and just squat up the tree feeling sorry for itself. Besides, Mabbie asked for you and it's as well she did, for you always had the better voice. I'll go with the spider.'

'That's most bold of you, Father,' Janet said, patting him much the same way John had. 'But Johnny, love, what makes you so sure the spider can find out where Ab was stolen from?'

'Well, it must have been stolen from near the Lenden lands,' John said, enjoying the opportunity to rehearse his thinking, 'for that's where the Alders lived, and it was Alder the elder – hah, *Alder the elder, Alder the elder* – all right, all right, Grandpa – it was they who stole a fey first. And the Mackem tale says it was stolen from a fairy-*court*, and I don't think they'd have said that if they weren't sure of it, for they're too stubborn. And I know we see little fairy-courts in ditches and conker-shells and so on, but the Alders weren't fairy-smiths, so I reckon they'd look for the kind you hear of in lay tales, which means under the hollow hills. And if we want to find hollow hills, well, we can't dig up the county, it'd take too long, and we can't knock on them and see if they echo, for we haven't the hearing feet for the job. But a spider does: they listen with their feet for their supper. It told me so itself, more or less. So if we can get No One to foot it along the land, it'll find the hollow hill, then we'll know where to put Ab back.'

'Heavy the earth and sharp-crack chalk and what shall the dance be with no walls to tack light to light?'

'All right,' John said, undeterred. They had tried every unironed hill in reach, to no effect. 'Let's try westwards, back the other way.'

'Why?' Molly asked, feeling the urge to shield No One's status as expert.

'I don't know.' John chewed his lip, gazed at the sky. The sun was past its peak, a prick of white half-hidden amidst the clouds, and there was no wind to drive them along. He didn't know why he should feel like there was something gusting at him – not a storm, but a small tickling, as if his scalp and ankles were being traced by small fingers. He closed his eyes, turned himself around a couple of times, but he still felt the desire to journey west.

'Binding of self in air and breezeless wind,' No One reproached, addressing Molly more than John, 'and twirl of prey is not for iron, else how shall the dry throat hold itself fast?'

'If you can't keep from biting a lad because he turns himself in a couple of circles,' Jedediah said, sounding a great deal less measured than he usually did, 'then I'm sorry I put you somewhere safe to grow. No, don't you *dare* play dead, or I'll—'

'Grandpa, you've bitten my ear often enough about hollow threats to the People—'

'It's all right,' Molly said, raising her voice. No One was lying on its back, legs crossed in a resolute evocation of an arachnid corpse. She put her arm around Jedediah's waist and said, 'Never mind what he says, No One, dear. He's all leg-wave and no sting. Now, Grandpa, perhaps we'll let Johnny ask?'

Jedediah's image of himself as an unvenomed, posturing spider – conjured up by his pet granddaughter, no less – was very possibly the worst comparison anyone had ever made about him in the whole of his threescore years. The hug only barely padded it.

'Hard is the grateless kind, for man of shear and step holds now a nest of Louiselings, and what is No One but to thank?'

It was true, Jedediah thought; the notion checked his crawling skin. He had been afraid of No One and had tried his best to be kind because Louise loved it – and he wanted to impress her, probably; it wasn't much credit to himself. But if he'd just set fire to the thing, in accordance with any laws of common sense and bearable geometry, she might not have liked him. He wouldn't have – oh, God, spare him from the thought of his family all bundled up in webbing like a writhing egg sac – *a nest of Louiselings*. It would have been a comforting thought, if only it wasn't so full of spiders.

'Let's go west,' he said, as firmly as he could. 'One way's as good as another, and I suppose you're some reason, John.'

'Wait—' John whipped his hand up in the air, then stood frozen to the spot like a sighthound.

'No One attends, for what is not cannot hold vice nor sin, and has not No One been the most virtuous of—'

'*Whisht*,' John hissed. 'I'm thinking.'

The clouds were thinning, leaving behind a mild, pallid blue. There would be a skyful of stars that night, and most likely a frost: nothing would hold any warmth to the earth.

'No One,' John said, turning round from his frozen position so suddenly that the spider clutched its legs to its body in shock, 'you remember the Lenden place?'

'What of the place, for edgeless is the earth and skeinless names cut no margin from coil to coil?' No One whispered, sounding a bit defensive. It remembered Louise's name, John realised, but that had evidently taken up as much of its capacity as it had.

'All right,' he said, 'I reckon if you map places out by web rather than boundary you wouldn't know one farmer's land from another; that's fair enough. But I've another notion. You know the wood Grandpa placed you in?'

'Skeins under earth and echo of stone,' No One affirmed.

'All right,' John said, 'but what about the hill beside that?'

No One went extremely still. It didn't even protest that it was dead.

'You're sure?' John said, taking this for an answer.

'No One is husked, for grief cannot be drained dry and eyes not made for tears cannot lament enough the dangermenting of the hard of heart and soft of shell inside-outers!'

Molly went to console the spider, which all of a sudden had the manner of a dog seeing a raised stick, but John and Jedediah were looking at each other.

The day grew colder; only the lightest of wind touched the trees.

'Well,' Jedediah said, 'it would make sense.'

'I went up there before,' John said. 'I went into the henge. It felt like it pushed me out. It didn't want anyone in there.'

'Sure, though? We'd be looking for a hill that hadn't known farrier's iron.'

'Of course, but it never *did* know farrier's iron, did it? Just chalk on the hill across the way.'

'We'll have to test it. Bring the spider up, tap beneath the hills. And if it's a resisting place, we'll need more iron. Mustn't run ahead of ourselves.'

'I'm sure now I think of it,' John said, 'but of course we can test.'

'We'd never shift 'em, though. Not with the tools and the men we have at hand. They'd keep us out.'

'What would?' said Molly. This was one of those farrier conversations she usually kept out of, full of unspoken knowledge, but as long as she was to be spider-nurse, she felt she should have some idea what was going on.

'The stone wolves,' John said, turning. His face was alight, not quite looking at her. 'You know, that sarsen circle just west of here. We never knew if it was folk or fey that made it – well, now we do. I reckon it's a fey one – the only trouble is that Corbie went and chalked it, so that's a problem we'll have to solve.'

'What?' In that moment Molly Smith truly committed to her decision to become a midwife, and not just a midwife, but an *expert* midwife – maybe even a cunning woman. She'd deal in flesh and blood, in things that made sense, and above all, that made men pale when you spoke too frankly. The next time she was in a conversation like this, she would be the one who knew what was what – and she'd do it in front of Johnny, too. She'd make sure of that.

'The sarsen wolves, lass,' Jedediah said. 'There's been trouble around them for generations, on and off. When I was a lad the trouble got too much: used to be they'd creep around at night, and Corbie would have it settled, so he had me draw a huge wolf, and it was cut into the hill facing the henge. The stone wolves saw it and they sat down like a pack with a new master. They haven't crept since then.

'John thinks the stone wolves mark a hollow hill, and if you can't stay within the circle – and John says it's hard to stand there without falling out – then it must be they're there to guard the entrance.

'We'll need to get Ab past them, but if it truly is from the court under the hill, then they won't keep us out.'

'They might even open the door for us,' John put in. 'But just now they're frozen in place and that means they keep *everyone* out. Grandpa, what was it you said about a pack with a new master?'

'Just that,' Jedediah said, frowning. 'What else do you want?'

'*Ohhh!*' said John. 'Oh, of course! That would make sense of it.'

So delighted was John with his apparent epiphany that it was a moment before Jedediah said, 'Well, suppose you share your sense with the world, lad, unless the rest of us are to stand here like fools.'

'Oh, don't feel foolish, Grandpa – you didn't have the chance to feel it,' said John with unwelcome reassurance. 'And you had the right of it with what you said in any case. I was up there before on my own – it was the way they pushed me out, you know. I mean, they didn't get up and push, but they gave me that feeling. See, they're cowering to the wolf on the hill, and the wolf on the hill wasn't drawn to tell them they could let Ab back in; it was drawn to tell them to *stay down* – so they stay down and keep out *everyone*, because they're too cowed to do otherwise.'

His words were coming almost faster than his tongue could form them. 'That was wrong, Grandpa, whoever called them stone wolves. That's most likely what gave Corbie the wrong idea. He made you draw a wolf, so of course they're too afraid of it to do anything but squat down and bounce everyone out. But they didn't hunt folks ever, did they? Before the chalk wolf? I mean, not beyond their bounds? They just did things to make folks fearful enough to stay away, maybe hurt them a bit if they went too close, but not hurt them to death.'

Jedediah didn't question John's definition of 'a bit'. 'They stayed in the field, yes,' he said.

'Well, that's not a wolf pack, is it?' said John, grabbing his grandfather's hand in excitement. 'If folks had just called them the stone *guard dogs*, maybe Corbie'd have known better. Of course they fear a wolf! What dog wouldn't?'

'Well, all right,' said Jedediah, trying not to look like a man who was having to rearrange multiple generations of geographic history in his mind on short order. John was so delighted at his acknowledgement that it felt harsh to point out the obvious problem, so the best he could do was a man-to-man discussion. 'All right, John, that's . . . fair reasoning. But even if the spider found the hollow hill, we can't just do away with the chalk wolf: that's two years' worth of grass to grow back at least. And we can't re-dig the shape of it, not before nightfall, even with men to help. It's too big.'

John rubbed his forehead. Jedediah did too. There wasn't much family resemblance between them, but the image of unity warmed Molly for a moment.

Also, it made her feel a little left out, so she decided to have an idea herself.

'No One, dear,' she said, her voice showing nothing but soft encouragement, 'how much silk can you weave in an hour?'

The sun slipped down behind a tangle of trees. Across the fields, the cropped wheat turned fox-red against the soft, dark earth.

Matthew knew the iron palings around Aunt Pell's wood as well as he knew his own hands. He hadn't been afraid of the woods when he made them. He'd been thirteen years old and dreaming of journeyman status as something high to aspire to when Dada had told him, quite casually, that it was 'about coming on time' he made his piece, with nothing at all in his bearing to suggest he was giving Matthew anything more than his common due, and Matthew had been so struck with pride and gratitude he'd hardly found the breath to say 'yes'.

He hadn't known then that there had ever been any question about Jedediah's own journeyman or master status. It wasn't the sort of thing that you made an issue of, not in the Smith home: you gave someone his rank because it was time. When Matthew had tried to thank him, Jedediah brushed it aside with a swift, 'None of that, son. You're ready, and that's all there is to it. Thank me with good work, if you like, and then the world'll thank you.'

That hadn't surprised Matthew; his dada had never liked to be thanked for doing what folks needed. He seemed to feel it degraded them to think he might have chosen not to.

There it stood, the long line of prickles he'd worked so many days to shape, every tip as consistent as ever he could make them, but each a story of its own, the swift negotiation of time as the red cooled to black, the precise angle of strike and the infinite slight mistakes to amend and amend until it was as perfect as he could make it. Under the dimming sky they stood in steady rank, the trees immediately beyond them crowded with crows.

Matthew hopped the fence and landed on the earth beyond – and it was like missing a step: his iron had kept the crumpled-up time bound, but within those borders, everything was creased out of place. No wonder the crows preferred to sit nearer the iron. Ab wouldn't like to enter this wood, but Matthew wouldn't wish to go deep inside either.

These, Mabbie had said, were the boldest of the crows; the others were hiding wherever they could. But if he could persuade these to join him, he knew where he could find some more and that should be enough.

Matthew pinched his lips and gave his best attempt at a crow's shriek.

It was a good impression by man's standards, but Mabbie had said a crow would regard him as a lisping simpleton. Still, that couldn't be helped. All he needed to do was get their attention; the only word he had to speak in Crow was, effectively, *Hey!*

The black shapes in the trees did not immediately flock to his aid. A few wings flicked out, as two or three crows considered taking off, then decided against it.

Matthew tried again: *Hey!* His tongue ached with the tension.

Some narrow heads cocked down. Men did sometimes make strange noises at the birds, but they didn't usually say the same very badly pronounced word twice in a row.

'Mabbie,' he said. From under his shirt, he drew out a knitted wool scarf and wrapped it around his head. It was Mabbie's; she wore it every day she walked these lands, she'd told him, so that anyone at a distance might mistake her for Pell.

Matthew wrapped Mabbie's scarf around his black hair, tipping his head at the best angle he could to contrive the message: *Friend.* The gesture made his shoulders ache.

They'd ached all the time since Ab had pulled them from their sockets. He'd tried not to complain, for he didn't want to worry anyone, but he was weary, and he was frightened. He knew men who lived well enough with a limb or two missing; possibly it was sinful to repine when his arms might still mend. But he'd hammered iron all his life: it was how he'd knocked grief into safety; it was the rhythm by which he'd shaped a life in which there were some things at least he could make better.

He let his arms drop and they hung loose by his sides, tired under their own weight. With real meaning, he looked up at the crows. This was a difficult whistle, but Mabbie had taken pains with him.

He looked at one of his arms, then the other, tautened his mouth, put what he could of his voice behind it and sent out the call: *Someone hurt me. Danger to us. Someone hurt me.*

A crow rattled down from the branches, tilted its head to attend. Then another. Then another.

The notions of justice, for men, are difficult and painful. But within the bounds of their understanding – their towering, wind-tipped, starve-edged bounds – there is justice in the crows of the air.

An hour later, Tom Attic looked up from his garden and saw his godson jogging up the darkening path, winged with crows. The flock massed either side of him and the sound of their cries was a fiddle-bow struck against a dozen jarring strings.

Tom put down his trowel and smiled. 'There you are, old dear,' he said. 'Dickon, open the shed, there's a good lad.'

'All right, Grandpa,' said Dickon, as composed as any boy could be while watching a host of crows hovering over a man.

The crows around Matthew dropped from the air; sudden silence rang out.

Matthew pointed with his head and a dozen crows marched themselves into Tom Attic's physic stores, where a hundred more had hidden themselves away since the day Ab burst from the tree.

Tom waited, watching Matthew standing alert as a sentry, just where the birds had left him. Jedediah had explained what they had in mind, and had, as usual, apologised for being a trouble.

'How,' Tom had said, 'are you a trouble for getting the crows out of my shed? One of these days I'll tell you that you *are* a trouble to me, and then I'll go to Hell for murder, for I reckon you'd die of the shock.'

★

It was night, with a coin-bright moon lighting their way, when Jedediah and Molly Smith came to the hills of Hawton Down. The trees, to Jedediah's eyes, were a horrible tangle of nasty-legged branches and scuttling twigs, while the grass twitched and skittered in the breeze. Only the stars overhead were clean and clear and blessedly free of legs.

The chalk wolf stretched out beneath them. Up close, the white ground was dusty but clear; the folks from Hawton village nearby were assiduous in their weeding. He'd order them to stop the annual clean-up if tonight went as they needed; any fey effects, they'd find a different way to deal with – though if Johnny was right, the stones might be more settled in any case, now folks like the Alders had stopped plundering the courts below.

No wonder they'd gone a-creep, with People being snatched into servitude right out from under them. That was what men had done to the People here: broken up their families, then cowed them out of protesting.

No, this chalk wolf had never been right; this gouge in the earth plucked lifeless every year. Time to let the scar grow over, let the grass and the weeds take it back.

But that was for another year. Tonight, they needed something else. He looked across the valley to where the stone dogs pointed their bereft muzzles at a blue, unhelping sky.

'No One,' he said.

'No One attends the juiceless earth, and stone of bodiless flesh and thirst is sadness to the eyes, and where shall the web tack from home to home on a hill bellying over so empty an ache?'

'So there's a hollow? Is it beneath the stone dogs? Can you feel the hollow?'

'Under the thrum of guarding and checked webbery,' No One confirmed, its whisper as dry as a parched mouth, 'and all below, what can be but grief and heart-thirst, and how are pretty thoughts to skein aloft under the down-drag of such lamenting?'

'No One,' Jedediah said again, but he couldn't carry on. How could he tell No One to stop complaining? The thing was revoltingly limbed and had far too many eyes, but it was sad in a world where it couldn't quite tell where it ended and other things began. No One thought the air hurt when it did. He'd grown up taking blow after blow in silence to keep the air silent around a woman who thought that she hurt along with it.

The thought hit him hard and he didn't know how to go on. He could think all this, and still, immovably, ridiculously, he couldn't change the stupid, ordinary fact that he hated spiders.

He looked at Molly, and she took his hand in the cold.

'No One, dear,' she said, 'you've been the best of spiders and a marvel of cleverness and pretty kindness. Well done, dear. Thank you very much. Now, will you do us a good thing?'

No One hunched back on itself. Legs thick as timbers and sharp-kneed as axes clutched up around its bobbing abdomen like startled shoulders.

'Flowing . . .' it whispered, too stunned to say more than that; a single word of thanks. Silk flowing into webs, perhaps; the easy swing as it lowered itself through the air. The melted innards it loved to flow down its throat. Jedediah couldn't feel much better for knowing how spiders described joy, but No

One was definitely expressing its happiness with Molly's praise. 'Flowing!' it carolled.

'You're welcome,' said Molly, feeling rather grown-up. 'Most welcome. Now, darling, we have another plan for this chalk wolf. If my grandpa – if Louise's man – draws it on the ground, can you feel it with your, er, pretty toes, and then weave? Kick up some grass to cover the bits we want hidden and spin your, er, shining webs to add the parts we want added?'

'Never is to doubt the might of thinking tips and spinneret's yield. Flowing and viscid is the good charity and beauty-knowing of No One, and thanks upon the pretty air!'

How do they do it? Jedediah thought. How did John and Molly, even Matthew, spin words into the air like webs without counting the risk of every syllable? He must have been a good father to have such folks as his own, but he wasn't sure, even standing here with the bare-boned hill at his feet, quite how he'd done it.

With a light-prickled scuttle, No One was away, a fan of liquid spreading out from its pointed tip. Back and forth, back and forth, with dancing sway and spitting silk, No One wove over the tail and limbs and jagged mouth of the wolf he'd drawn so many years ago under his father's eye.

You could have put a cock on it, though, Jedediah. Wouldn't have killed you. Just for sentiment's sake.

No One kicked up grass with a bristling claw. The scent of earth and green was clear as water in the back of his throat.

No one ever handed me a baby. Folks don't do it to boys, have you noticed?

Under a skin of gleaming white, the muzzle of the wolf

softened. The tail was covered already; a new one, drooping soft and careful, hung down at the wolf's hindquarters.

Who do you think you are, Jedediah Smith? Just who, pray tell, do you take yourself for?

The reflecting silk glittered back the moon's light in a thousand prisms, a field of coloured stars winking at the silver specks in the sky above. There it stood, calm-headed and white and raising no dread: not a wolf, brandishing his tail and baring his fangs, but a she-dog, hunched in tender care over a litter of suckling pups.

There now, Jedediah thought, gazing down at the stones. *Let them find anything to fear in* that.

'You are truly the best of spiders,' Molly said, and Jedediah heard a scrattling noise sounding like mouth parts clapping together. He didn't look.

Below, on the opposite hills, the sarsen dogs turned, just a little. They moved the way shadows move across the ground, changing proportion ever so slightly until suddenly you see, all at once, that what you saw before has changed before your very eyes.

Jedediah and Molly stood on the hill, watching the results of their labours. The stones shifted, moving in a heavy, implacable circle. They didn't move like creatures; it was so slow that you thought your eyes had tricked you – and then you looked again, and they weren't where they had been. But they were on the hunt, now, or on the search. And what they sought wasn't there.

One after another, they held their jagged muzzles to the sky and howled.

Jedediah and Molly both felt it: the booming grief of the earth was ringing along their bones, finding out the brittle white within them, the chalk under their flesh. They stood, deafened to the last fibre, calcified with the echo of that stone-throated sorrow.

They couldn't outlast it; they'd start to crack if it didn't stop.

'No One,' Jedediah said, his teeth rattling against each other. He'd been prepared for this: it was the ugliest of safety measures, but it should protect them. 'Can you take off our ears? Quick?'

It would mean letting the thing touch him, but flesh wasn't made to bear this sound. He turned, ready to submit—

The hill behind them was empty. Down the far slope he could see a glimmering thread, and at the bottom of it, a giant and absolute coward of a spider sailing down and scampering off to safety.

Jedediah clapped his hands over Molly's ears. It was a long, shivering moment before he saw she was saying something, but he couldn't make it out; his own ears were too full of stony howls. It was only when she pushed his hands off that he understood she was saying, 'Cover yourself, I'll cover myself! Don't be *silly*, Grandpa!'

Molly under the moon was grey, the soft glow of her daylight skin drained into the shadows – but was she growing greyer? Jedediah could feel the skin of his hands pressed against his face: hard calluses, dry, ageing palms – but too hard, too dry. They were setting. The stone was getting into his skin, his and Molly's.

He looked wildly at Molly's beautiful face. It wasn't Louise's;

he wouldn't see that till Doomsday, though here was Louise's jaw, Louise's eyes, Louise's soft black hair – but there were traces of Janet, too: the neat-set ears, the bridge of the nose just a little too low. And a shadow of him, too, in the cast of the features: but it all added up to her own dear face. Life had given it to her, and she would have to make what she could of it – if she outlived this instant.

But her lips were starting to flake, and it wasn't Louise's dryness. Dust was gathering around her eyes; a strand of her pretty black hair had turned stone-grey. Then another. And another.

Jedediah staggered forward – he could run down the hill and clamber up the other side. The dogs were seeking something – or someone. He would throw himself to them; that was all he could think to do. It would pay a price, and perhaps the pack would tear him apart, but he'd leave behind a granddaughter of flesh, not of stone, and a family unbroken.

His feet were heavy, his joints stiff, but he'd not got more than a dozen paces before there was a silence.

The howling had stopped. Something had sucked them out of the sky, and when Jedediah looked around, he saw the sarsens had stopped their dirge and sat still, poised.

Over their heads flew a whirling circle – or no, the air itself was circling, a spinning storm of emptiness and undirected want. The birds couldn't sail this wind; all they could do was try desperately not to fall. They tumbled round, blown stiff as sycamore seeds, bestormed in their natural element.

The voice that reached them was very quiet, but it struck sharp as a needle. *I must have my friend*, it said.

Jedediah stared wildly down the hill. He could see Matthew

there, frantically trying to conduct the birds. He'd done his part all right; he'd called up a frenzy of crows, enough to wake Ab from whatever nap it had been taking in some other part of the cosmos.

Ab was calling now, wanting to be picked up, but it didn't know the way through the circle – how could it, when it hadn't been old enough to remember? All it knew to do was cry and hope that somebody would set the world to rights again.

John could open the door in the hill, Jedediah was sure of that. They'd agreed he'd bring Corbie; Johnny said that was the simplest part of the plan. Corbie still thought him a fairy-servant, even if, since the wicker-mask incident, he thought him a perfidious one. John could offer to lead him to safety, or, if he was afraid, he could threaten him. He could get him to arrive at the stone circle, and then . . .

'John!' Jedediah called. 'Where are you? *John—!*'

The stone dogs gazed up at the whirlwind of birds and Jedediah's cry was swallowed up in the choking silence.

Limbs stiffening, flesh growing cold, Jedediah pressed closer to the sarsen stones.

Fetching Corbie was the sort of job usually taken on by Matthew; in his absence, it fell to Stan and Franklin. Anthony Brady had offered, but had been declined on the grounds that he shouldn't abandon Francie mid-lying-in. Or at least, that was the reason Janet gave him; Jedediah had private doubts as to whether a man unfamiliar with fairy-smithing would be much use in a crisis, but the fellow meant well and there was no need to hurt his feelings.

There was one more fact to consider: they would have to get Corbie out of the smithy, across the square and out of the village unseen.

'I could arrest him,' Franklin had offered, 'if I had to. But . . .'

'No.' Jedediah and Stan spoke at the same time, and then glanced at each other in irritation: Stan felt he had more to lose than Jedediah if the full truth came out, and Jedediah felt that Stan had no right to order Franklin about.

'Folks'll think we conspired,' Jedediah said, firmly taking the conversation into his own hands. 'It's known you're one of us, Franklin, and I can't remember the last time you took a man to the sheriff instead of warning him off. Nobody'd believe him a poisoner. They'd believe you corrupt.'

'I'm not eager to have folks believe him a poisoner,' Stan remarked, aggrieved. 'Perhaps you don't care what anyone thinks of your clan, but mine hasn't been known for its killers and madmen.'

'In which case,' Franklin intervened, before Jedediah could express his views of this remark, 'it'll be a question of coaxing. We can shackle him once we're out of view, and if we travel after dusk, odds are we won't be seen. But we'll need to take him out of Gyrford by persuasion. John?' He turned. The lad looked keen and alert. 'Do you reckon you can get him to follow you?'

So as the spider wove a wolf away, Franklin Thorpe and Stan Mackem unlocked the door of Corbie's imprisoning bedroom.

The Smiths had given him a chamber pot before locking the door, but the room had an ominously clean smell that suggested he'd been pissing out of the window. That was all they had time to notice before Corbie hurled his shoulder at the opening door, broke past, and ran downstairs.

'John—' Franklin yelled, 'Johnny! He's headed down, mind out!'

'*I could arrest him*,' Stan muttered. 'Hurry, man!'

Franklin turned and raced down.

John should have been waiting for him. That was the plan: John would greet Corbie inside the house, magpie about a bit and propose to become the fairy-servant Corbie wanted, if Corbie would just join him at Hawton Down to seal the agreement.

It was with horror that Franklin and Stan, clattering down the stairs, saw the door was unbolted, Corbie was already lifting the latch – *and John wasn't in the house*.

Franklin wasn't a fighter by nature. Mister Smith had taught him a little boxing and wrestling in his youth, saying blandly that it could help a man if the People ever laid hold of him and making no mention of the fact that sometimes a lad might need to get out of his father's grip. He wasn't as strong as Corbie, though, and he'd known all his life that the man wasn't to be crossed.

But there was nothing else for it. Years and decades pushed him forward.

'Stay where you are,' he said, stepping up. 'I'll drag you back by my teeth in your knuckles if I have to.'

Corbie raised his fists. Franklin braced himself.

The knee hit him hard in the crotch, and for the next minute he wasn't aware of anything very much except a profound sense that life was a vale of tears.

'Damn it,' Stan said. 'Thorpe, where's your dog? We can track him if we get her.'

'Anthony has her,' Franklin said, very faintly. 'If you – I'm sorry . . .'

Stan Mackem was in haste, but wasn't above the universal brotherhood of one man for another just kicked in the cullions. He crouched down, patted Franklin's back awkwardly. 'We'll have to catch him up,' he said. 'Will you be all right if I go for—?'

At that moment, there was a shriek from the square. Franklin sat up, grey-faced, and Stan stood in alarm. It was a ghastly scream, thin, grinding, shrill as a child. Whatever had made Corbie scream like that – or whatever he'd made scream – it wasn't anything human.

Corbie had got as far as the middle of the square as Franklin and Stan emerged, Franklin still gripping Stan's arm for support, but they saw with some astonishment that he wasn't running from the square; rather, he was backing up slowly, his eyes fixed on something.

It was only when they heard a friendly, 'Hey there!' that they turned and saw what was heading out of the Smiths' garden.

John stood there, calm and confident, if a little out of breath. Beside him, flaking brown needles and baring its large, champing teeth, stood Left-Lop the pig.

'Sorry to be late, Mister Thorpe,' he called, 'but I had a better idea. And I thought you might scruple to agree to it.'

John pointed and spoke in a whisper none but Left-Lop could hear.

'*This man is a menace to me and mine*,' he said.
'*Help us hunt him to Hawton Hills?*'

Left-Lop didn't waste time on a versifying answer. John Smith had bandaged its flayed sides; he'd visited its cage and fed it daily. Corbie had never so much as tossed it a scrap. It lowered its head, invoked the spirit of wild boars long past, and charged.

And when a full-fattened flitcher bristling with bile and outraged enmity has a mind to mash the marrow of a man – well, what can that man do but run?

It was a hard few miles. Several times Left-Lop had caught up to Corbie and given him a hard bite, more on principle than out of a real killing rage, but even the most conversational gnawing is nothing to joke about when it comes from the well-muscled jaws of a swine. John called out for the pig to save its strength and leave the man's legs alone, and by the time they reached the stone dogs, they were staggering tired.

Overhead, the sky was a black, shrieking turmoil of feathers, within which tossed little bodies plucked half-bare by the wind.

Only if you knew what you were looking for would you see it in the blackness: two eyes, unblinking, gazing down, helplessly craving towards the spinning disaster of dander and crow-meat.

Matthew stood beneath the circle. He was flesh and blood still, but his arms were frozen aloft, scarecrow-stiff, a gesture Franklin had seen a thousand times before: the unthinking, irresistible reach to lift a baby you can't bear to hear cry.

Even from a distance, you could see the wind was lashing Matthew's arms raw.

Matthew was singing a lullaby, Franklin realised, and the emptiness was swallowing it up, reeling the sound down into its ravenous depths; the song and the proffered embrace were holding the whirlwind in place, keeping it from unreeling and racing across the countryside to strip the skin from everyone.

The song was an old one; Franklin remembered Louise singing it when Matthew was a baby. He'd not grown up on lullabies himself, but seeing Franklin liked it, she had taught it to him. A slice of grief pierced him, and it deepened every time he looked at those starless black eyes. Mistress Smith had been so kind to him.

Matthew's voice was well-trained, but it was a little hoarse. How long had he been holding Ab in place? They weren't late, surely not – but Ab was here, and the stone was on the move, and Franklin thought with horror that the time must have passed here faster than it had in Gyrford.

'Matt, we're here!' Franklin shouted, and Matthew, making a ghastly attempt at a smile of greeting, gave his head an infinitesimal jerk towards the hill beyond the stones – where, frozen in a dash towards the sarsens, were two figures.

Molly was further behind, reaching forward an arm. She was trapped in place, the colour and motion leached out of her. She couldn't reach the man she was trying so desperately to call back.

Jedediah Smith stood near the top of the hill. Franklin could see the muscles of his arms, bunched and wiry; he could see his face, set and desperate, clear as carving on a body turned to stone.

*

Stan raced forward, appalled. He knew no charms for turning stone to flesh; there was nothing in the chants. He was almost there when he heard a cry behind him.

'Stan!' said a voice that stopped him where he stood. 'My Stan, why didn't you wait?'

Stan Mackem turned to see the old man behind him, shivering in the cold, wearing nothing but a shirt; his feet were bare and blackened with mud.

'Why did we run here?' Old Dunstan asked his son. And then, muddled, he said, 'I think I walked in my sleep again. It's all cracked up here.'

John didn't see his kin, not at first; he was too startled at the sight of Old Dunstan. Stan was frantically laying iron chain around his father's feet, fitting a torc around his neck, doing everything he could to shield him from the fey whirlwind up above, but it was slow work, for Corbie was there too, lifting up the chains Stan had laid and throwing them far from his shaking brother.

John meant to run and help, until Franklin shook him and cried, 'John, look – we were too late, time got ahead of us! What's to do, John?'

John felt the hand on his shoulder and heard the words, though they were half-muffled in the mangled air. He didn't have any answers. There was nothing in his throat but pain.

'John!' Franklin begged, 'come along – haven't you the chestnut? Didn't you have a plan? I know you did, and I know you're afraid and it hurts to see, I swear it, Johnny, but please . . . Johnny, you were always the clever one—'

John heard him, but when he tried to say, *I don't know*, the words wouldn't come out. Grandpa was standing there, frozen to sarsen, a dead statue of a man, blank eyes meeting his, with nothing about him left to hug. Molly was behind him, stiff and grey, and Dada was peeling down to bloody flesh, and Mister Thorpe didn't know what to do, and Grandpa – Grandpa—

He started to cry. He didn't mean to; he clamped his hand over his mouth, muffling the sobs, for if Ab heard him – but he kept weeping. He just couldn't stop.

There was a scratch at his calf. Left-Lop had slowed, now they'd reached their destination, and was nudging near him, frightened at what it saw.

'*Waste not your wits weeping amidst wolves!*' it pleaded. '*Save me from the stones that surround your sire!*'

If it had been a less self-centred plea, John might have just sat down and cried his eyes out and forgotten how to be anything other than a grieving boy. But his fury at the ungrateful beast – after *all* they had tried to do to keep it from the People's madness and the butcher's knife – sparked just enough fire in him that he stayed on his feet.

'Selfish swine,' he said, and then, because he heard himself talking, he remembered he could put thoughts together. He was still crying – he didn't know how to stop – but he could cry and work at the same time, and he was angry enough at Left-Lop to think of something.

'Left-Lop,' he said, and pointed at Corbie, 'knock down the knave lest he bite you back.'

Left-Lop, grunting in fear and indignation at the thought of a man's teeth finally meeting in its all-too-edible flesh, charged.

Before he could fight or flee, Corbie was on his back. The pig's teeth were bared, but before it could bite, John shouted out, 'What did you say?'

Left-Lop hadn't said anything, but the tearing wind above them stifled sound, and it was, after all, a verbose animal.

'*No time for talking 'midst trials and terror!*' it shrieked, not without some justification.

'*I'll bear down any butcher who'd bite me back!*'

Corbie Mackem heard the words 'bite me back'. And he was, by the grace of God, a stubborn man.

Left-Lop raised a grinding squeal as Corbie sank his teeth into its snout, biting so hard that a small scrap of the flesh came away in his teeth—

And before anyone else had time to know what was happening, man and pig found themselves assailed by a weeping boy. John clamped his hand over Corbie's nose and mouth, and with the other, knocked against his throat. It was an old trick for making horses swallow a draught – and the next second, the raw, bleeding pork was down in Corbie's stomach.

John sat on the grass opposite him, tears racing down his cheeks, his throat burning. He didn't think he was ever going to stop crying.

'I blame you for this,' he sobbed. 'If you were a better farrier, you'd have never stored up such trouble. You'd have *listened* to the land, you'd have *known* the stone dogs weren't wolves. You stupid, *stupid* man.'

Corbie sat up. Blood smudged his lips dark in the moonlight. 'What the – John. John Smith, that's your name. John Smith, what did you do to me?'

John wiped his eye. 'Ab made the chestnuts full of knowledge,' he said. 'Knowledge of what others meant. That's how it got out of the tree, and you with it. The pig ate the chestnut and it knew what the prisoners in the tree wished it to hear. I went and found another chestnut. I meant to make you eat it, but chestnuts are too good for you, *Great-Grandpa*. I made you eat a bit of the pig instead, and the pig's full of knowledge too. So now you know what others mean.'

The air wailed around them. Matthew's lullaby grew hoarser and hoarser, and Jedediah stood, frozen in sarsen, not quite within reach of his son.

Corbie shook his head. 'Dear God,' he said, 'but I've had a strange time of it. Stop that weeping, boy, I thought you had some spirit in you.'

'*No!*' John whimpered. He was trying to cry quietly, to keep his voice low enough to be drowned out by the crows, but it was truly difficult. 'Look what your mess did to Grandpa!'

Following John's pointing finger, Corbie turned. His son stood before him, stone in face and limb.

Corbie laughed. It was a shocked laugh, but it was a laugh, and it was a little wildly that he said, 'Well, that's him all over. Can't say I see much difference myself.'

John looked at him. 'Well,' he said, making a last effort to be steady, 'I reckon that settles that. I'd thought I might feel a little guilty for this, but I don't. All things considered, I think I'm being very, very kind.'

And he stopped trying to weep in quiet.

John opened his mouth and wailing, sobbed to the skies.

Old Dunstan covered his ears as Franklin tried to hug John,

tearful himself, but John pushed him away and ran towards the sarsens.

Over the sound of Matthew's lullaby and the screaming wind rose the sobs of a child who had lost kin, who was torn with the grief of losing those he absolutely could not do without.

And the whirling stopped, vanished; the eyes in the sky fixed on John, standing weeping before them. All around, exhausted crows rained down, landing hard on the earth.

Ab's eyes turned on John and the world filled with a whimper, so harsh and wretched that it echoed into the soil: *Where is our friend?*

John did not clean the tears off his face but let them reflect the dark and the stars, and his voice was very soft as he said, 'Give me back mine and I'll get you back to yours.'

The wind had stilled, but the air still rang. The sky quivered like a lip.

'Now be a kind friend,' John said, his own lips not entirely firm, and pointed at the hill, gargoyled with his beloved kin. 'Those two are mine, and I want them the way they were. Not better, not improved, just the way they were before. And I know you can do it, and if you do, I'll take you home.'

There was a hiccough. The darkness *gulped*.

John gathered up every memory of his father's voice, his mother's. 'Be a kind friend,' he said, soothing, firm, as gently undeniable as ever he could invoke. 'You can do it. Do it as a crow – remember? There is justice in the crows of the air – so be a good crow.'

Stretching out his wrist, he saw the dark sky lighten from

moiling black to common night. A thing shaped like a crow glided down. Mostly like a crow. It blinked at him with his own blue eyes.

'That's a kind friend,' John said. 'Now, let's tidy up the mess and get you home. It's – it's decades past your bedtime.'

The first thing Ab wanted to do was heal up the crows it had accidentally torn. Some of them were dead, smashed little bodies lying on the grass, but John wouldn't allow it to revive them; he knew enough to be sure you could get in trouble with heaven and earth crossing *that* line. Ab thrashed a bit, splitting the hill opposite into two smaller ones, but John stayed adamant, saying only, 'Well, my grandpa did say he wished the chalk wolf gone, and it's pretty broke up now, so you've troubled no one but yourself there.' He sounded more like Janet than anyone – she had great patience for tantrums – but Ab wasn't much bothered by that kind of echoing; crows could always copy voices.

Once the surviving crows were repaired, they sprang into the air in a mass and hovered over Ab and John, ready to mob them, but Matthew intervened, communicating with bleeding hands to the effect that this would be dangerous. It was a weak attempt; as soon as the storm had dropped his arms, they had fallen limp, barely able to lift above his waist. Matthew's face held a kind of bleak resolution: he knew he'd crippled himself for life.

'While you're about it,' John said, still sniffing rather, 'you can mend my father's arms, Ab. That wasn't a kind night's work you did there.'

'No, no,' said Matthew, hastily withdrawing, 'that's quite all right—'

'It won't do it wrong this time, Dada,' John said. 'I reckon it panicked with Clem because it knew he was afraid of it. It tried too hard to please him. Ab,' he went on before Matthew could question this leap of faith, 'I would like my father's arms healed to just what they were the first moment ever you met him, if you please.'

I want my friend, the something-like-a-crow said. It was still on John's arm, weeping boyish-looking tears from its bright blue eyes.

'You will behave,' John said, 'or I will – will be *most* disappointed in you.' That was Matthew's sternest threat.

Before he had time to object to the caricature, Matthew felt a rush of cool over his arms.

And he looked down to find them just as they had been: strong, whole and no more scarred and scraped than a farrier's arms ever were. Carefully, he rotated one shoulder, then the other and, for the first moment in what seemed like a lifetime, the ache was gone. He swung his arms a little more freely, and then lifted them right up. They didn't hurt. They'd never felt better.

'Do you need more help before I go to Grandpa and Molly?' John said, looking alarmingly at ease with the situation, even if he hadn't quite stopped crying.

'For pity's sake,' Matthew said, sounding much less patient than usual now the pain had stopped blurring his mind, 'how could you leave them stood there while you came here to fool around with me?'

'Because I need you to stop Great-Grandpa Corbie from running away,' John said, a little wounded at the ingratitude, 'and also because you were hurt and you're my dada, but I can give you a task if you mean to be like that.'

'Johnny,' said Matthew, remembering his son was still just a boy, 'I'm sorry, I didn't mean—'

'No, you're right,' John said, drawing himself up. 'There's much to do. But we have to keep Great-Grandpa Corbie where he is. Mister Thorpe's with him, but Corbie's remembered him from when he was a child and is saying things about how he still hangs on Smith hems and it's hurting his feelings. It's not called for. Can you just go and sit on him, Dada, while I go for the others?'

'Oh, I'll do more than *that*,' Matthew said, smiling with sudden satisfaction. He strode over to Corbie, who was making a gesture that looked alarmingly like squeezing someone's ballsack.

'Well, sir,' he said, 'my son reckons you can understand me now. Do you?'

'Well, sir,' Corbie said. He stood, squaring up, but it was only once he was fully on his feet that he realised he was facing something almost unheard-of: a man bigger than himself.

Corbie was a tall man, muscular and stocky. But Matthew, uninjured, was more or less an ox wearing a shirt.

'Well indeed,' Matthew said, taking him by the scruff of the neck. 'You and I will sit here, sir, and you will not stir a finger nor a toe.' Corbie struggled. It was like watching a hare fighting in the grip of a trapper. 'I never whipped my son in his life, sir,' Matthew told him, 'but I might not hold the same rule for a grown kinsman. I have *opinions* about those who hurt the ones I love, sir, and you are not the only father on this hill.'

*

Molly stood in the field, grey as dust, her hair streaked stony and her skin crackling over like dry mud. John found himself crying again at the sight of her, but it was probably all to the good: it would keep Ab's sympathies focused on him.

Jedediah stood ahead of her. Standing between them, John could only see his back, the strong, thin bones, the shoulders built by a lifetime of work.

He hesitated, and Ab said, *Shall Ab make him as this morning?* The words tasted blue on John's tongue, eye-blue, and it was a long second before he was sure of his answer.

'Yes,' he said, 'but mend my sister first. If I left her suffering while you tended to Grandpa first, he'd never let me hear the end of it.'

Ab sat on John's wrist, quiet and shapely, but as its attention touched Molly its wings began to melt like mist. Blackness ravelled away in oily twists of colour, shimmering dark and iridescent under the moon, until the thing John held was little more than wavering ribbons of smoke held together by nothing at the centre except a little spot of sorrow.

Ab can fix the girl, it said. *What great friends are we?*

It wasn't a cry of triumph, but a question; a pair of arms raised in the hopes of being lifted up and comforted.

'That's very good,' John said. How had he liked folks to speak to him when he was very little? 'You go on and do that,' he said. 'Show Johnny how clever you are. I'm sure I'll be most struck with you.'

Ab can fix the girl. The words tugged at his attention, a set of sharp jerks upon him that were exhausting, like carrying the weight of a clinging body upon your brain.

'Go on,' John said, feeling that he was very patient, and also that perhaps he'd marry late in life, to someone happy to do most of the childcare for him. This was harder work than he'd expected. 'Go on, be a good, er, a good fixer.'

Ab didn't leave his wrist, for it could work Molly from a distance. There was no sharp moment when it began; one second John was watching Ab; the next, his eye was caught by Molly as the crackled grey across her skin began to waver, unreeling like a drop of ink through water. Stone seeped out of her and her body quivered as if straining against a great weight – then she jolted a step forward, crashing straight into him and nearly knocking them both down.

'Johnny!' she panted.

'That's all right, Molly,' John said, bracing himself and hugging her one-armed so that Ab didn't take offence at being shaken from his wrist. 'I reckon you got stuck as you were running. You should be all right now. I guessed right, you see: if the stone dogs froze you, Ab's work should fix it fine, they're all from the same court . . .'

John was generally on the best of terms with his sister and not used to the sensation of her furious fingers grabbing him by the ear. 'Hey!' he protested.

'John Smith,' Molly said, still gasping for breath, 'Grandpa stands there turned to stone and if you don't stop your chatter and attend to him *this very minute* I will give you the thrashing he never did; don't think I won't!'

'Hey now,' John said, distracted and a little admiring, 'you sounded just like a midwife there – ow, all right, all *right*!'

John stood before his grandfather for a moment. The finer details of the man's face, the wrinkles and scars of sixty years, were shadowed in the dark; the statue was halted mid-stride. If they left it there, it would grow lichen and wear down over the centuries, its wide-open eyes and hard-set jaw blurring away until it was just a man, any man, frozen halfway up a hill, trapped in a sacrifice that took away all he was.

Can't say I see much difference myself, Corbie had said. John bit his lips.

Corbie hadn't entirely meant it, John could tell. He'd spoken as if he had other feelings somewhere, maybe even better feelings, but he just couldn't help himself. And John didn't feel forgiving. This thing here, this thing of stone, wasn't anything like Grandpa. It didn't look at you, that quick, sharp gaze that caught you in naughtiness before you'd even had a chance to get away with it, that glance that sized up and dismissed anyone who didn't love you. It didn't move neat and swift, showing hard-practised skill in every gesture, or catch you before you hurt yourself. It couldn't reach out and pat you, a day's praise in the light touch of hand on shoulder. Only the pose, the fact that he was running, that he'd run until his limbs petrified: that was the only thing in this piece of stone that spoke anything of his grandpa.

'Ab,' he said to the textureless fall of black that now drooped from his arm in weary tatters, 'set this right, so please you. There's a good one.'

Good one, Ab said, and the stone soaked itself into the night.

Jedediah Smith stood, up on one foot, and then there was the grind of rock on rock as he fought his way forward, slow and relentless, and brought his other foot to rest on the ground.

'John,' he said. The word came out through his teeth; the stone wasn't fully out of him yet. 'Where's your father? Is he hurt?'

'It's all right, Grandpa,' John said. 'Ab, wait there.' He set the vaguely birdy jumble down on the ground, where it crept onto his boot and sat there in determined attendance. John reached out, put his arms round Jedediah. The body smelled wrong, ancient rock and hour-old dew, but it was softening. 'Never fret. Dada got a little scrubbed, but he's fine now, and so's Molly. I reckoned you'd rather wake up to find them all mended. Nuncle Stan's here and his father followed after, but Dada's got hold of Uncle Corbie – by the scruff, I think – so they won't come to any harm. We only need set Ab on its path now.'

Jedediah couldn't quite bend his arms to hug the boy back; he felt a numbness at his core, although it was shrinking, slow and steady as sunrise. He'd been running to cast himself between Matthew and harm, then he'd been cold, and colder still, until the cold had stopped feeling like anything at all, and now he'd awakened to a world where nobody was upset – or at least nobody but Ab, huddling all its vague tendrils up against John's leather and laces. John's arms around Jedediah were warm, gripping him with a sincerity that called him back to himself as his mind woke up ahead of his bones.

After a long moment John let his grandfather go and Jedediah blinked at him, dragging his lids over dry, gritty eyes. The boy was a little smudged around the edges, or maybe Jedediah's vision needed a lot more blinking to set it straight. Probably that was why, in that moment, the boy looked so tall.

You've been elder since you could think and act, Pell had told him. *What's elder work, if not what you've been at all this time?*

He cleared his throat, no longer full of dust and shale; just a little hoarse. 'All right,' he said, 'let's get through the night. You do your part, and tomorrow we'll talk about your journeyman piece. Plan out what you'll make, set you to work on it. I reckon it's about that time for you.'

'Goodness.' John wasn't usually surprised by a tribute to his cleverness, but that did take him off-guard. 'Have you been planning the smithy's tasks while you were stuck in stone?'

Jedediah pulled himself together; he dragged his blood and bones out of their grey death as if rousing himself from a deep, unquiet sleep. 'I said you could make a journeyman piece.' His voice was almost its old self by now. 'I didn't say you could give me impudence. You'll make your piece, and you'll make it perfect, mind. I'll have no poor work in my smithy.'

'Well, of course not, Grandpa,' John said. Ab had crept up his leg with a suckerish scuttle and had now bound itself tight upon his hip, but his free arm, he linked with Jedediah's to walk him up the hill. 'I'm disappointed you'd think I'd suggest such a thing.'

Matthew was not, in fact, sitting on Corbie. Having subdued him – Corbie Mackem not being foolish enough to fight a losing battle – Matthew sat back and watched. Left-Lop's knowledge should be working through him by now, so he must be starting to see the wants of others.

'How do you feel, sir?' he said after a while. 'Do you know me?'

Corbie met his eyes. His own were scrunched, as if there was a headache beginning to press upon his skull.

'What makes you love that little monster?' he demanded. There was still a kind of wronged humour in his tone. It sounded habitual, yes, but a habit clung to. Corbie's glare, between pressed eyelids, was hard.

'If you mean my son, sir, then, well, he's my son. I know he pressed touched food down your throat, but I hope you'll admit, now you see things differently, that he had cause.' Matthew was struggling to stay calm. He didn't like folks calling Johnny names.

'God help us, you're another monster-lover,' Corbie said. He was looking at Matthew clearer-eyed now, but his expression gave Matthew a feeling of sick disappointment. Matthew had hoped – no, more than that, he'd had faith – that a dose of Left-Lop's insight might be enough to make Corbie stop – just . . . stop hurting those around him. But it was dawning on Matthew that Left-Lop would still maul if it felt itself enough provoked. One could know the way another man felt without taking on his cares.

Now Corbie stared at him. Granny Constance had passed through Matthew's thoughts, her limp body as he and Aunt Agnes struggled to keep her alive. He couldn't think of them without a flicker of affection; that was just what they were to him. That was what Corbie had seen.

'Sir,' Matthew said, trying hard, 'or Grandpa, I suppose. I hope we may come to an understanding.'

'How in Heaven,' Corbie demanded, as Jedediah crossed Matthew's mind, 'did he get a son as sturdy as you?'

Both Corbie and Matthew were taller than Jedediah, but Matthew didn't think of his father as small. Jedediah was one of those men whose height folks would be hard-pressed to remember, being neither tall nor short enough to startle you – but for Matthew, there were also years of memories, when his father had been tall as the sky and had lifted him up to view the world from atop it.

It was too complex to voice. 'My mother was tall,' Matthew said, 'and Dada's no small man.'

'What befell her, then?' Corbie demanded. 'I heard tell she was a fine-looking lass.'

Again, it was roughly asked, but Matthew could feel something new beneath it: a genuine wonder about the feelings of others. Matthew had outlived the shock of his mother's passing, but it would always be sad. Corbie's comment about her looks felt almost like an attempt to pay respects.

But he could have called her a good woman, at least. Everyone spoke of her as a good woman.

Matthew looked away to where Franklin was sitting in attendance over Left-Lop, examining its tattered greenery with professional concern. 'She was,' he said. 'She was a good woman, kind and clever, much loved and respected. She died of fever three-and-thirty years ago.'

'That long?' Corbie said. Matthew's discomfort was clearly getting to him, but the agitation it provoked was coming out in aggression. 'Why in God's name have you no stepmother, man? Don't tell me nobody would take him in all that time?'

'I didn't choose to.' That was Jedediah's voice. He stood with his arms around his grandchildren, Molly at one side and John at the other. 'Some of us loved our wives.'

'Well, heaven help us, some of us got to choose them,' Corbie said, an instant snap-back that stood at odds with the gathering frown on his face.

Left-Lop's ability to see folks' meaning was filtering through now. He could tell that his grandson wasn't comfortable talking to him, and it was frustrating – but it didn't prepare him for Jedediah.

Corbie's son stood, a grandchild at each side, his face as blank as ever. There was no difference, except what Corbie could hear behind the blankness.

'Dear God,' he said, and his voice really shook. 'What did I ever do to make you dislike me so?'

Jedediah sighed. There was no answer he could give. Or perhaps there was, just this once, while Corbie was almost listening. 'I never wished to dislike you,' he said. 'I wished to love and be proud of you. It angered me that you had to make it so hard.'

'God help us,' Corbie said, the words getting away from him. 'That's the first time in my life my son ever felt what I was feeling. Don't you know what a stiff-necked lad you were? Oh, don't bring up your mother again,' he added, as the thought crossed Jedediah's mind. 'You had a wife you loved. Some of us didn't.'

Jedediah's face twitched, and Corbie looked as shocked as if he'd been slapped.

'What's *wrong* with you?' he shouted. 'God damn it, Jedediah, I was easy enough with you – didn't I do what I could?'

He looked at the faces around him. Moonlight showed little of the expressions on any of them, but he didn't need it.

'What have you to fear, Franklin Thorpe?' he shouted. 'When did I ever lay a hand on you, all the while you crept in and out my kitchen like a mouse, eating my food and distracting my son? And you, lass, what's your name, Molly? God help any man who turns his eyes to you! Jedediah!'

John had been resting against Jedediah; it was comforting to feel his muscles settling into their usual resilience, and the dank stone scent was changing to something more familiar, the daily smell of Smith skin that was similar between Grandpa and Dada: salt and chicory and the underlying tang of iron.

Now he had a moment of alarm that Grandpa was turning back to stone again.

'That's enough,' Jedediah said. He'd held an arm around each grandchild's shoulder as if shielding them from a vicious wind, but now, slowly, he loosed them.

'Oh now, don't give me any of that,' Corbie said. 'You've been too old to whip for more decades than either of us recall.'

'That's *enough*.' Jedediah's voice was very quiet.

Molly and John looked at each other in a moment of fear. Grandpa had spoken blunt to them times without number, but there was something now that wasn't even iron in him. It was older than that, colder: a sharp, dark flint, knocked to an edge by blow after blow until it formed the head of a weapon.

John reached out and took Molly's hand; Jedediah caught the motion out of the corner of his eye without turning from Corbie.

'Never fret, dears,' he said. 'It's all right.'

'All right indeed!' Corbie exploded. 'Dear God, have you murder in mind? Is that it, Jedediah Smith?' He had a raging bluster, the wildness of a man who couldn't believe he was where he found himself – but the threat in his voice was real. 'Bring me to an empty hill and set your pack upon your own father, is that it?'

'I thought of murder,' Jedediah said. He spoke very plain and soft. 'And you know it. And if I hadn't the stomach for it, I'm not sorry. Makes me less like you. No, we've something else in mind for you, Father. Matthew hoped it wouldn't come to that. I reckoned it would. He was always a better man than me and I was glad of that. But if you speak another ill word to my children, we'll do it with the tongue cut from your mouth.'

Corbie started to say something, but Jedediah ploughed on.

'They're good men, Matthew and Franklin. They won't like it, but they'll help if I ask them. Folks liked you, Father, if they didn't know you. But there's no one'd fight for you.

'And me, well, I have a family.'

He said this last almost gently, and it slipped into Corbie quiet as a blade through the ear.

Corbie rose to his feet. His son stood before him: a man lighter-boned, growing thin with age, sixty years tired.

'Cut the tongue from me?' he roared. 'I've held it, I've held it! What did you do to me, Jedediah? Decades of you and your prodigies, plaints and whimpers all around me so I couldn't turn round but see . . . *what have you done that I can't shut it out?*'

He lowered his head and charged, a bull's charge, blind and furious, his hands reaching out for his son's face.

Matthew caught him; the force of the rush lifted him off his feet, but Matthew kept him in a wrestling hold, doing all he could not to bruise the man. 'Steady, I beg you,' he said, really trying. 'Take a moment to settle, please. I'd like to let you go. You may see things different if you just . . .'

Corbie craned and spat in his face. 'Let *go*!' he shouted. 'Don't you stain me with your pity, you – you wife-fucker!'

As insults went it was one that Matthew couldn't refute, but it wasn't that that made him despair. It was the other cry: *Don't you stain me with your pity*. His grandfather's spittle tracked a slow, chill path down his cheek.

Matthew looked to Jedediah. So did John.

'It's up to you, Dada,' Matthew said.

'I think it's the best thing for him,' John added, more as if he was giving practical advice than comfort. 'I don't see him stopping, pig-sight or not; he doesn't do very well with dislike. In truth, I think it's mercy; we can't have him kill Granny, and this way he might even like – more than he likes this, at any rate. Still, you're elder, Grandpa, and you're the one knows him best.'

Jedediah would have liked to wait, to take a long moment of thought before he answered, but Corbie was kicking at Matthew's legs and Molly was still holding John's hand, each trying to shield the other.

'A man won't learn a lesson that he won't endure,' he said. 'And I know you're fond of mercy, Mattie. All right, John, go on. It'll be your holding one day; let's see how your notions hold up.'

John gave a quick nod of acknowledgement before he turned back to the wavering blackness clinging to him. His voice was soft, friendly. 'Quill up, there's a good Ab,' he said. 'Here's a man to bring you home. Never fear, Johnny'll see to it he delivers you right.'

The blackness coalesced, and then Ab was on his wrist, crow-bodied and alert, cocking its head towards Corbie.

'No,' Corbie said, shielding his face, 'no – I'm just a crow. Tell the bird, great-grandboy, tell him I'm just a crow!'

'Now then,' John said, almost comforting, 'it's wrong to lie to an infant. Here, Ab, see him? He learned all about birds for you. Do you remember what bird he is? He's a cuckoo.'

Matthew kept Corbie in his hold, saying, 'Now, now. Johnny won't see you hurt.'

'Cuckoo,' said John to the bird on his wrist. It was yearning up towards him, opening its beak as if to be fed; the words slipped down its throat and it gulped and opened up for more. 'Think of that. Isn't it lonely to be dropped into another bird's nest?'

Ab swallowed the words. Its throat pulsed, and John felt the ripple through its body like a heartbeat.

And it must have been that Corbie felt it too, for Ab lifted up and flew to Corbie, shedding its crowness as it spanned the few feet of space between them; feathers unplucked themselves from its skin, vanishing before they could touch the ground; its beak wore away over a few seconds of forward flight.

By the time it landed itself in Corbie's shocked arms, the crow was gone. What remained was earthen, a kind of chalky grey. It lacked fingers, ears, a nose, and John remembered the old tale of how a bear-cub needed to be licked into shape before it quite knew it was a bear. He didn't believe that; he'd never seen a bear, but they couldn't be so very different from kittens and foals, and their mothers licked them by way of kisses and cleaning.

But on the other hand, how could you know how to be in the world if no one cleaned you up and gave you a kiss?

'Ab,' he said, 'you need to go home. You're not finished, young thing. So here we have a nursemaid for you. He'll know when you've reached the right place, because he can tell what you mean now, a little, anyway – and I'll go with him to make sure he does it right. Can you just ask the dogs to let us through?'

Corbie's mouth opened, but he didn't ask what in heaven's name John meant. He didn't need to; he could see what John meant without asking – but that wasn't why. As soon as John had named him, Ab had turned its eyes upon Corbie's face.

To begin, they were blurred pebbles, blinking lids translucent as flint-heart and searching, everywhere at once, for a gaze to meet its own. As they settled on Corbie, though, they gave a plaintive twitch and blued themselves over. A clutch of red hair flickered into life atop its muddled head. The hair itself was a little confused – some of it was more in the nature of glowing charcoals than anything more fringy – but it was a very earnest attempt.

Jedediah, watching his grandson at work, knew he himself would have been appalled if it had been nestling in his own arms, pleading for affection he wouldn't know how to give, not to something so imitative and so wild. He wouldn't have seen an infant; he would have seen a changeling.

But Corbie had swallowed Ab's insight, the meat of nut and

pig that had put out into the world the thing's hunger to be heard.

Everywhere he looked, there were folks who hated him or feared him and wanted nothing of his company. He could fight, but he couldn't drown it out, not any more.

Corbie's eyes, looking at the men around him, were terrified. He'd never had to hear another soul feeling anything that he couldn't shout down, and because of this, he had never had to learn the knack of bearing it.

Matthew did have a preference for mercy; he'd been raised to it. But Jedediah, looking inside himself, realised something with depthless clarity: whatever ability he'd had to forgive his father died the day they chained his mother to a tree. If he'd been a better man, he might have more chances left in him, but he wasn't, and he didn't. He'd run, near the end of his life, into a thing he just couldn't do.

And looking at Corbie now he did feel, just for once, a distant flare of pity. Corbie had been in another world for a long time, and now he had to live in this one. If Jedediah had had to face a world where his son couldn't forgive him his failings, he wouldn't want to live in it either.

Corbie saw this in him and looked around in panic. Above him was a sky, cold and white-starred and empty of reassurance. All around him were faces unable to hide their lack of welcome. But when he looked down, something longed up at him. There, in his arms, lay something that wanted his love, that would dote on him beyond all reason if he would only say that he was its friend.

He jiggled his arms. The creature within them was earth and

illusion and it wanted its mama. It wanted to go home. It wanted someone to care for it, no matter what it smashed.

Corbie gazed at it, eyes upon eyes. The wish rang through his bones.

'Who's a pretty babe?' he said. 'There now. Who wants to go home?'

A hand reached up to him, or something like a hand. It shaped itself fingers as it moved. They were rough and knuckled like a man's, not a babe's chubby folds of flesh, but they touched Corbie's face with real longing.

'Well now,' Corbie said, softening. 'That's something more like. You were right, my little friend. Who'd have thought it? You were right. Who needs birds? Is home a pretty place? Who likes a pretty place? Come along, funny one. We want to go home!'

He lifted it up onto his shoulder and walked to the sarsen circle.

The stone dogs, slow as nightfall, lowered their muzzles to greet him.

'Open up!' Corbie said, a servant bringing the little master home.

The sarsens bowed. The earth churned – not the whirlwind gasp of Ab's longing, but a soft, smooth motion like sand swept aside by wagging tails.

And the earth underneath was smooth as a paved path, an open chamber ready to walk within.

When they were planning, Matthew and Jedediah had both raised objections to John going under the henge.

'If you're right, Johnny,' said Matthew, trying to debate man to man because he knew it would get him nowhere to tell John he was too young for such a risk, 'then what's the need? Won't Ab guide him?'

'They're both unsteady,' John had said helpfully, 'so someone needs to make sure nothing fails at the last minute, else we'll have trouble for another half a dozen generations.'

'We'll have more than that if you get yourself killed, lad,' Jedediah said, as practically as he could. There was no point inflicting your own terror of losing a child on the child himself. 'You're our heir, remember, and we need you to have sons. I'm not about to trade off one of your sisters to some other clan's boy; there's been enough of that for one century.'

'You could train Thomas,' John said, equally practical. 'He's not two years old yet, and he's a cousin, more or less. I'm sure Francie wouldn't mind. But I won't be killed, so that's all right. Or at least, someone's got to do it, and, with much respect, Dada and Grandpa, I think I'm the least likely to get horrified down there. And that'll matter. I don't say you aren't brave men, but – well, Ab's touchy, and I reckon his People will be too. I don't think they'd like a man in there who isn't happy to visit.'

'Johnny . . .' Matthew started.

Jedediah turned away. He couldn't bear the sight of Matthew crying.

'What'll we do without you if they trap you there?'

'Well, I don't know, Dada,' said John, going over and giving his father a hug. Then he went and hugged his grandfather too. 'Let's hope for the best, eh? But if I'm killed, I'll tell God it wasn't your fault and that you were always good to me. I don't reckon I'll have time to say goodbye come the moment, so let's agree that I said so now. Oh, now, don't fret, Dada, I'll be fine.'

It should have been dark as Corbie carried the stolen fairy babe into the tunnel. The night was black above and only a few steps in, the earth was arched above their heads and the shadows wrapped around them. The world of men might never have been.

John could see, though; it just took a little staring. The tunnel had a kind of light to it – it wasn't that it glowed, or not quite: the walls were perfectly smooth and perfectly round, as if trodden on all sides by small, shapely feet, and they had the quality of earth under sunlight. The brightness came from nowhere, with no sun to illuminate them, but nevertheless, even without a source, they held their own daylight.

Corbie gazed around, drew in a wondering breath. 'Well, my cherub,' he said to Ab, 'I never saw the like.'

His face was so entranced that John was convinced that he was seeing something else, something influenced by the self Ab had poured into his eyes. 'What's it like in here, Uncle?' he asked. 'I can't quite make it out.'

'Well now,' said Corbie. His voice echoed off the tunnel, sounding back on itself in a quaint, chiming harmony. 'There's gold beneath our feet and silver over our heads, boy, and precious jewels too – I've never seen the like! It's a treasure-chest of earth here – why, you could make this step sapphire' – he moved one foot forwards, marvelling at the soft tap his bare sole made – 'and here, I could gather up rubies, and there's everything I need to grow pearls, a barrel of pearls beneath my feet. Why, my cherub, I've never seen the like.'

John felt the earth with his own bare feet; you couldn't bring iron into a place like this, which meant taking off their hobnailed boots. He'd always liked getting mud between his toes; it was a kind of tickle-game between himself and the soil. But this was too smooth, almost slippery, without a pebble or a tussock to tell you where you stood.

Perhaps Corbie was right: gold and silver and precious jewels did all come out of the earth, so it could be they really were surrounded by the raw materials to make any kind of treasure. He wasn't sure, though; gemstones weren't his trade.

'Do you mean to make jewels out of this?' he asked. His own voice echoed back too, but it wasn't the same: no harmonies rang with his words. Ab wasn't beckoning him in.

'Dig it up?' Corbie said, bewildered. 'Smelt it down to one thing, when it's all *everything* here? What kind of foolery would that be?'

John didn't have an answer to that, except that Corbie clearly wasn't so changed by Ab's embrace that he had to feel too guilty: he'd always been the kind of man who preferred to keep his options open. Or perhaps, more kindly, he might be looking at a world of chances: a second, third, hundredth chance under every footstep.

They moved deeper; the tunnel was widening, now, the floor descending. The earth was full of nothing and nowhere: light with no source, shape with no texture, a place that chose its own echoes. Corbie might see a wonderland here, but this wasn't a place for him. It was a strange kind of perfect, the sort he'd never seen before, where you had no flaws to tell one thing from another. He felt lost in it, and achingly homesick.

John swallowed, thinking that if he felt this way down here, Ab must have felt just as lost up there, where every blade of grass was its own straggling self and you'd never find two acorns just alike. No wonder Ab had never found a form to suit it: nothing could fit in the mortal world that wasn't a little raggedy.

The downwards path led to a circling tunnel, smooth as water and carved with a precision no mortal workman could ever achieve. John considered asking if they should go left or right, but Corbie dandled the babe in his arms and turned left without a moment's hesitation, saying, 'Off we go, my pretty! Let's see more pretty things!'

To John it felt as if they were travelling on the same circular track for miles, going round and round the same path, but he knew that couldn't be, for the echoes were changing. The sounds were receding now, taking longer and longer to come back to him; as his feet tired, he tried singing two notes in quick succession – and they took so long to return that they rang back to him in a chord.

So they must be getting somewhere. He recognised that it was a kind of maze: you walked the same path over and over, except that it never really was the same path.

Corbie was so occupied with the bright colours he might be

seeing that he didn't notice the opening when it began – but John felt it coming over them in a rush: three steps forward and the roof above them peeled back, far too fast – and there they were, in the open. The earth was lit as if by daylight, but above them was a night sky unmarred with stars, smooth and empty and open to anything you might wish to imagine within it. Only the moon remained – but not the mortal moon: there were no smudges on the surface, no mottled grey across the brightness. It hung perfectly full, dead overhead at the absolute centre of the sky, white and smooth as a sun.

Corbie, of all men, went down on one knee.

Farriers weren't supposed to do that – that was John's first thought. The dignity of the trade was not served by getting down on your shin-bones, Grandpa said. You bowed if you had to – the grand folks could get tetchy if you didn't – but even then, if you spoke for the smithy, it was better just to knuckle your forelock.

But there was, before them, a shifting sea of cloaks, and Corbie was kneeling in delighted fealty.

The cloaks weren't cloth; they were more like the obscurity of a storm-cloud, opaque and blue-shadowed and promising wild weather. They stood about like a court – but no, there was something in the middle of them – not a throne, but a bed, made of leaves round as coins and white as snow and piled high into pillows. There upon it sat a figure, holding out its arms to the empty moon.

John could feel it now, the weeping reverberated through the earth; slow, pulsing sobs. His stomach cramped, sickening with the rumble of something's grief.

He remembered, all of a sudden, the thought he'd had with the mist-mother, that moment of utter wretchedness when the thing didn't want him: *Mama, love me, Mama, please, I need you, please, don't take the world away.*

He hadn't thought it made much sense at the time, but now he remembered being a baby, toddling to his mother's lap for comfort whenever the world felt too much. She was a hazy figure in his memories now, solid earth to stand on, shelter against a sky that was otherwise too tall for him to stand beneath.

The People under the earth had been waiting. Time didn't move for them as it did for men. Their guard dogs had been frozen with fear and couldn't let them out, so what could they do but shade their faces in grief and wait for something, anything, to bring their baby back?

Corbie knelt and held up the bundle in his arms. 'I've brought back my little friend,' he said, and he sounded enchanted – and more than that: comforting. His voice was delighted, filled with the absolute bliss of coming home.

Ab's voice rang from his arms, quiet now, tentative. *What friends are we?* it said.

And the figure on the bed stirred, lowering arms thin as roots, its shaded head coming down. One white leaf fell from its bed.

'Here's my little friend,' said Corbie again, his voice rejoicing. 'Haven't I been a clever fellow?'

And after that it was all flurry: the white leaves dissipated in a whirl of power as the thing on the bed leaped forward.

John jumped back in shock, but nothing was interested in him. The hard, narrow arms closed around the stony babe and snatched it up. John felt himself draw a breath as Ab was smothered against a breast of rock. The earth stilled, its sobs subsiding down to nothing as Ab was muffled against the body of its mother.

The air was changing: he'd been cold, but now the place was warming and the figures that had stood guard were all around him – or no, they weren't seeing him. Some of them had stretched out hands pale as chalk and narrow as talons to Corbie, patting him on the shoulder, drawing them in amongst them, and as they did so, the stormy cloaks were melting, a gathering tumble of billows, as if they were making their own weather down here and after a dead, uncertain vigil, the sun had at last come out.

John heard Corbie say, 'Well, by goodness, that's something a little more like.'

He had to get out of here. They'd kept the air still while they waited, but now they wanted it for themselves, for their little one – for Corbie too, since he had the breath to laugh. But the place was darkening and John was having to fight hard to get any air into his lungs. What there was didn't nourish him.

This isn't for me, he thought in anguished confusion. *I can't stomach their milk. I have to go home.*

But he didn't have breath enough for the walk. He was going to smother down here.

What could he do? He had no iron on him, no weapons or

tools. Up above, the stone dogs held their guard; maybe they'd let him out – or even chase him out, he didn't belong here – but he couldn't find them. They were too high up, and he couldn't breathe.

John cast around, his chest burning, wondering what he had that might help. He doubted he could swim up through the earth – it was all things, that's what Corbie had said, and all the stones would make it impenetrable.

His pockets were empty of iron. All he had was the chestnut, the one Ab had filled with hearing, back at the tree in Aunt Pell's wood. He hadn't eaten it himself; he didn't want what it had. He'd meant it for Corbie. If he ate it, would the People down here take him in – was that what was left to him, a life down here in fairy-servitude?

It would be better than drowning.

But he'd promised he'd get back home.

Every kind of stone. That's what Corbie had said: a treasure-house of everything.

John grabbed the chestnut and closed his eyes so that he couldn't see what he'd seen before, just plain earth, trodden smooth, with nothing of sarsen in it, and he pressed the chestnut to the floor before him, pressed so hard it sank into the earth.

'Earth eats what falls upon it,' he said. 'Time and rot, eat this chestnut! Tell the stone guard dogs I'm here – let them know what I feel. I don't belong here and I want to go home. Be sarsen, earth, just for this moment, be sarsen. Tell the dogs to cast me out! I want to go home!'

His chest thumped, twisting on itself in the airless tunnel. He was buried; this was his grave. His head bristled with noise, his ears full of rushing, but there was nothing down here—

—and then a paw of stone broke through the roof, bringing cold air with it, filling John's lungs with a tearing gasp.

'Thank you,' he whispered, heaving for breath. 'Good dog.' And he found himself gripped, really quite painfully, between two ragged jaws of stone and dragged upwards, back to the place where the stone knew he was supposed to be.

The Smiths sat in the dark, waiting. Their small lanterns cast little light, and it was very cold.

'*You fathers fear to find out*

'*That the sarsens swallowed up your son*,' Left-Lop remarked, with the air of a pig that really wished to be helpful.

'*Never gnaw your nails now:*

'*The stripling was certain he'd skip back to safety.*'

'Do you hear him below?' Matthew asked, trying not to let his voice shake. He'd sworn to trust John, but he hadn't sworn not to worry his heart out while he did it.

'*Deeper and darker are the depths he dived to*

'*Than even the hopefullest hog can hear*,' Left-Lop apologised.

'*But hold your heads and hearts high,*

'*For the fellow was full of fearless faith.*'

'Of course he was,' said Jedediah, a little hoarsely. 'He always is.'

'*Then count yourself a kindly king to your kin!*' said Left-Lop, apparently bewildered that Jedediah wasn't satisfied with this.

'*Your weanling doesn't weep; he welcomes the world!*

'*Isn't this all you intended to achieve?*'

Jedediah was in the habit of holding his feelings close. It had begun with not wanting to be hurt himself, and grown into not wanting to hurt others. To hear his life's aspiration – children who weren't afraid of him, who could face the world and feel welcome – boiled down to a few alliterative lines by a moulting pig was so ridiculous that for once, Jedediah laughed.

He laughed out loud. He'd lost the ability to cry, years ago, when he was younger than John, and he doubted he'd ever get it back. There was more than a little hysteria in his laughter – but it was funny, after all, painfully, heart-shakingly funny. Where a giant fey spider had fled in terror, his strong young grandson had walked into an underworld with nothing by his side but a mad fairy and a murderous lecher, and he'd done it with the cheerful interest of a squirrel finding new nuts. He genuinely thought that when you fell down, someone would always pick you up.

So when the stone dog dived – falling down to the earth with a crash, and then keeping on falling, down into the blackness out of sight – it was such a shock that Jedediah didn't know how to stop laughing. In a few seconds, surely, he'd be able to gather himself – but a few seconds was all it took. John had been down in the fairy realm for less than five minutes – and then all of a sudden, fast as a blink, there was a dark fountain of earth, splattering them all with dry, rough cold, and before they could get to their feet, there was a thud and a scream.

Matthew and Franklin jumped to their feet, ready to fight whatever ghastly foe had burst from the darkness.

'Oh, sorry, Molly.' It was John's voice, a little muffled and entirely friendly. 'Well, no, I'm supposed to be truthful: I can't say I'm altogether sorry I landed on something softer than earth, for that stone dog threw me pretty hard. But I'm sorry to knock you. Are you all right? Can you breathe, dear?'

Molly was sitting up, struggling to drag breath back into her startled lungs, and John Smith crouched beside her, patting her shoulder solicitously, not a hair of him the worse for his absence.

'Johnny!' Matthew ran over to him, lifted him up and, torn between the need to hug him and to check his arms and legs for breaks, turned him upside-down. 'Johnny, love, are you well? Are you hurt?'

'I'll be fine, Dada, if you'll be so good as to set me on my feet,' John said. 'No, I mean it, Dada, let go; I'm glad your arms are better now, but you've forgotten how hard you can grip and I can't breathe.'

'John Smith,' Molly said, now she was able to, 'I swear, when I'm a cunning woman, I'll make you bow to me. You can *bow*, John Smith!'

'Oh, I'm sorry, darling,' Matthew said, reaching out to check her too. 'Are you much hurt? Poor Molly, that wasn't fair to you.'

Jedediah couldn't get up, not for a moment. He was old, he knew it, but he'd always been strong. Now, though, his legs wouldn't lift him. He stared in the thin lantern-light at his son, his grandson, his granddaughter, clutching each other with relief and laughing.

He felt a hand before him and Franklin was there, reaching out. He didn't say anything as Mister Smith took his extended arm and stood, a little shaky. Jedediah patted Franklin, which was as much as he knew how to do at that moment. He'd have to trust it would suffice.

'Glory be!' said Old Dunstan Mackem. Stan hurried protectively to his side, but Dunstan stroked his son's head, then gestured him away with something like authority. 'Well, *that's* some farrier work I never did see! Who's the elder here?'

There was a small, tense silence.

Then Stan flicked his hand and said, 'Jedediah Smith. You remember your nephew Jedediah, Pa?'

If it had been daylight Dunstan might have been more confused, for time had worn Jedediah's face. But the shape of him in the moonlight wasn't so different from what it had been when he was young, and his voice was much the same as he said, very cautiously, 'How do you, Uncle?'

'Ah, well, there you are, Gyrford man,' Dunstan said. 'You were a headstrong one, you were. Well, never mind; young men will have their way. It's good to hear you call me Uncle again. So, my foolish brother made you master at last, did he?'

Stan watched Jedediah. To Stan's increasingly familiar annoyance, his face gave nothing away. 'He wasn't in the humour,' Jedediah said tonelessly. 'I've held the forge for decades, though.'

'Well, that's a bigger fool than I thought!' Dunstan said. The memories of a red-haired man snarling at him in the dark were being pressed out of his mind by memories greater: a day when he was a younger man with the world before him, when he'd done his best to be an uncle to a guarded youth who was tiresome about accepting it. Well, the lad looked to have cheered up a little now. Maybe time had been good for him.

'Not a master, indeed!' Dunstan said, as cheerful as if he were, indeed, a new-made elder himself. 'That was some fine work together, you and your lads; if no one else'll call it a master-work then I will, and gladly. Come round to our forge, lad, we'll stamp you the new brand any day you like.'

Jedediah held himself together. Then he bowed. 'I thank you for the kindness, Uncle,' he said. 'I'll take the calling and be glad of it. Never mind the brand, though. Our ways are different here.'

'Well, then, Grandpa, I told you I'd be back,' said John. It should have sounded cocky, and it did, if you didn't know him. At the thought, Jedediah started laughing again.

'No need to make merry,' John went on, a little offended. 'I've been down in the depths and you may like to know that I conducted myself with much resource and courtly wisdom and your father is quite safe away, and Ab with him. I think they'll be pretty cheery down there. He saw chances every which way; perhaps with enough of them he might get himself right. Besides, we owe them a servant after all the Alders did to them. Men, I mean, we as a whole, we owe them a servant, and he was out of time anyway, so . . . Oh, also, I talked to the earth with a chestnut and made think itself all sarsen, and nobody taught me how to do *that*.'

'You didn't . . .' Jedediah was still laughing. 'You didn't consider that maybe you could make it think itself iron? Such as a farrier uses? That didn't cross your mind?'

'Well, I was rather flurried,' John said with dignity, 'but no, that would have been a worse idea anyway. The People down there don't mean trouble to us, so I had no business bringing iron into it. It would have been *very* bad manners. I'm a little surprised at you, Grandpa.'

Jedediah was laughing so much that he had to lean on Franklin's shoulder while Franklin held him up. 'Well, well,' he said, and brushed away a tear that had overspilled his eye, 'all right, Johnny. That's me told.'

EPILOGUE

It was two days before Clementing that the village of Gyrford woke to find the rumour spreading from door to door: Elder Mackem was gone. His brother Old Dunstan was still staying with the Brady family – little Thomas Brady had taken to him enormously, and the two of them spent hours in the garden pulling faces at each other – and Stan Mackem, the elder of Tinsdowne, was with them.

But Corbie Mackem had been called away in the night. Something had smashed up the hill at Hawton Down, threatening to drag the whole world down with it, but the Sarsen Shepherd, hero of the county, had cast himself into the depths to save them all from a maddened fey.

Oh, for Johnny's unscratchable conscience, Jedediah thought. But Jedediah didn't have that, and if he didn't, well, he'd just have to do without.

What's elder work? Pell had said. Sometimes it was carrying your own wishes close to your chest so that others could have what they needed. Or if not all of what they needed, enough to get by.

'He was a brave man,' Jedediah said when folks condoled him for the loss of Corbie. The words were hard to say; they twisted in his gullet. But he wouldn't have to say them again after this, or not too many times. Folks would tell the tale to each other – so often, most likely, that the Smiths would never have to explain it again.

It was, after all, a tale easily told. Corbie Mackem had been a man of exceptional character and charm, so forceful that he could even herd violent sarsen stones. So the village of Gyrford called upon him when their own elder farrier was crippled, and Corbie came, married the beautiful daughter of the Smiths and locked the plaguey fey up in a tree. Years later, a dreadful beast arose in the skies and broke the tree apart, releasing the fey to torment the country once again.

(Exactly what the beast had looked like was a matter of some disagreement. Those who hadn't seen Left-Lop's flight favoured the idea of something griffon-like with the head of a hawk and the body of a lion – or at least what a lion probably looked like, as extrapolated from local barn-cats. Others thought a flying wyrm more likely, a dreadful serpent with wings as sharp as a bat and talons dripping blood – or tree-sap, according to the more practical-minded. It was something suitably spectacular, at any rate. There was a certain amount of argument, but the few who had seen Left-Lop weighed in on the griffon side, and nobody's memory allowed that it might have been a flying pig; that was an entirely unsuitable foe for the great Sarsen Shepherd.)

Everyone did agree, however, on what had happened next: the dire fey had blighted Corbie Mackem, blinding him to the knowledge of his nearest and dearest, and no crueller tragedy could have struck so noble a man. It was only when his loyal son Jedediah took him to the scene of his greatest triumph, the sarsen circle he had cowed with a chalk wolf, that Corbie finally remembered – and, in an act of astonishing courage, dragged the fey down under the earth with him, where they would wrestle for eternity.

Possibly one day he'd come back when the community most needed him, rising up through the earth like the return of spring. That was the initial thought, but Janet Smith, who was a wise woman by trade and a shameless one by nature, dropped hints with the chattiest of gossips that it was more likely that he'd wrestle the ghastly fey until both were so exhausted that they would fall asleep, locked in each other's arms, and to wake one would be to wake the other. If he did come when called upon, then Heaven help the country, for some battles were best kept beneath the earth. In fact, Janet reckoned, there was no need to be rash, and for her own part, she reckoned that the best way to honour the man's sacrifice was to refrain from ever mentioning his name again.

Clementing came upon them fast, and there was more to prepare than usual.

To begin with, there was Clem's grave, which had been disturbed and needed to be bedded back down again and his gravestone set firm in the earth. Matthew Smith, taking immense pleasure in his new-mended arms, dug it back into order. Just in case, he told folks, they thought they might set a grille of iron over it to be particularly sure nothing ever troubled Clem's bones again. The grille would be a good project for young John anyway, as Elder Jedediah Smith had decided it was about time the lad made his journeyman piece.

It would take a while, but at least the grave was tidied up before Clementing. Matthew had planted flowers upon it as well, explaining that Clem had been a worthy man who had borne his misfortunes with Christian resignation, and that in particular, Matthew felt they must always honour a man who was kind to children.

Molly and Janet cooked frantically for the feast, and even Celdie and Vevie remained to help. Of the four of them, only Molly was a competent cook, but she was feeling less resentful than she had in previous years. Aunt Pell said that a good midwife knew her herbs and salves, and that there was no need to look so doubtful, girl: a woman who could cook was a woman who could make a potion, and anyone could tell you that Molly Smith knew her way around a cauldron. So Molly prepared pottage with a will and seasoned it with unusual care, and Janet chopped vegetables under her direction and sang at the top of her voice. Celdie and Vevie were surprisingly invested as well; they were prone to being charmed by novelty, and this year's Clementing feast definitely was a novelty, for they somehow had to feed the village without a pig to roast.

Cissie Lenden had come all the way down to the forge to apologise very much to Mister Jedediah that the pig she'd fattened for him had gone so talkative and run away; she didn't know such a thing could be, and if she could make any amends to him, any at all, she'd be only too glad. They had other pigs, of course; he could take his choice, and she'd be glad to let him have whichever he thought best.

The Smiths looked at each other for a moment. Then Jedediah gave Matthew a shrug and a gesture indicating, *Go on. I know what you want to say.* And, in honesty, he didn't feel much like pork this Clementing either.

'That's most kind of you, Mistress,' Matthew said. 'I think that perhaps this year, though, we might feast on other things. We've Left-Lop under our care now and – well, it feels like bad manners. Perhaps, if you have any of those fine beans of yours to spare . . . ?'

They'd been worried about Left-Lop for a while. The pig was quite resolved against a free life in the wilderness: it insisted that it was a brave boar, but not barbarous, and indeed, it was not always kind to set a domestic animal loose in a world it hadn't been bred to bear. On the other hand, it wasn't healthy to spend the rest of its years in a fey-cage in the Smiths' back garden, either – and besides that, the pig still had a tendency to look into folks' hearts and poetise about what it saw there. It might have its uses, but as Jedediah had raised his boys to appreciate, a farrier needs to know when to keep his mouth shut – and Left-Lop most certainly didn't.

They were still fretting over the issue when Anthony Brady came into the smithy, Aunt Pell on his arm and Thomas toddling by his side, extremely proud that he'd managed to master the art of walking. Lissy was swaddled to Anthony's chest; as he spoke, his hand kept rising to stroke her small back.

'Mister Smith,' he said to Jedediah, knuckling his forelock to the elder farrier, 'I hope we find you well this day?'

'Anthony Brady,' Jedediah said in greeting. 'Yes, we're well enough. Auntie, good to see you. What can we do for you?'

'You can bring that pig out, young man,' Pell told Jedediah, with no more ceremony towards his threescore years than she'd had when he was Thomas' age. 'Our Mister Brady here has used such wits as God gave him and thought to talk to me about that pig of yours.'

'Oh, no,' Anthony said, looking a little uncomfortable at taking undue credit, 'it was something Father said. You know, being a forester, he has a notion of planting and such, and he said to me that Left-Lop's back looked in need of water – that it had been drying out, and that perhaps it'd be healthier if watered like a flowerbed. That's all. I just – no, Thomas, back to Dada, please, that's a hot forge. Thomas – Thomas, be a good boy – thank you, Matthew,' he added, as Matthew picked up the toddler under one arm and handed him back to Anthony before heading out to fetch Left-Lop.

'And there's some sense,' Pell added. 'You're good with iron, Jedediah, I'll give you that, but you never were much of a herbsman. Your friend Tom had all the sense there, I reckon. Had a pig in your garden with greenery all over its back and never thought to water it?' She shook her head. 'Men don't know how to care for things.'

'Tom's a man,' Jedediah objected, but Pell was not to be deterred by such paltry things as evidence in favour of his sex.

'What your Anthony's too shy to say,' she said with a click of her tongue, 'is that it's time you passed that beast over to me,

Jedediah. You can't have a creature chattering away in your smithy, especially one that knows when folks lie. If a farrier can't lie to his customers, the trade's done for, and if folks can't lie to the farrier and get away with it, they'll never set foot in the smithy. You'll give that pig to me, Jedediah Smith.'

Jedediah felt a rush of relief. It wasn't just the prospect of someone taking the intrusive animal off his hands; Pell knew a problem when she saw one, and glory be, this, for now, was the worst problem they had.

When Matthew returned with Left-Lop, the pig was in the middle of telling him that a simple slurry of scraps would suffice if he'd hold a helpful heart towards Left-Lop's hunger.

'Ah, now, Pig,' Pell said. 'Left-Lop, I hear they call you. You like that name? You're to come and live with me. I call it a good, sensible name, but you can change it if you like. I'll get your back to rights. Bit of water, maybe a bit of manure, you'll feel much better. We'll get along fine together.'

Left Lop gazed at her.

'*Fine and fierce one, have you fodder?*' it said. For all the bristling wilds on its back, there was something homely about the wet eyes and pink snout it turned so hopefully upon Pell.

'*You're willing, wisewoman? You truly want me?*

'*Shield and shelter me, shrewdest of shes!*

'*Left-Lop would like it,*' it added, rather shyly, '*if you'll lend me your love. Just a little.*'

'Well, that's settled, Left-Lop my lad,' Pell said, giving the pig a pat on the pate. 'I wouldn't say I was lonely out there, but a companion'll do me a world of good. Let's you and me head home, my hog.'

'Wait a moment,' John objected. The subtler nuances of adult relationships were still a bit beyond him, but he knew the facts of life and nobody works in a smithy without hearing some gossip about young folks who've been up to what they shouldn't. 'You're a midwife. If folks feel shy of us, wouldn't the women feel shy of you? Mama says a midwife needs to know when not to pry.'

'True enough,' Pell said, giving him just the smallest of nods, which John received with a burst of pride. 'And when the girls come, the pig won't be in the house. But the days when a lad swears he never touched the girl he set carrying and walked away from? Ha!' She gave a fierce smile. 'I'd like to see their faces when I bring Left-Lop to meet *them*.'

The morning of Saint Clement's Day, the Smiths rose early. Janet and the girls headed down to the kitchen rubbing sleepy eyes; there would be plenty of bean pottage to feed the village, but there were still some cakes to finish and Godfa Tom, who'd spent the night, had been very firm that they were to begin first thing.

'Some dainties need time and attention, my lasses,' he'd said, 'and if we're to honour our forebears that day, I won't have my sainted father turn in his grave at the thought of us serving up poor pastries.'

The kitchen was rather crowded, for Aunt Agnes was there as well, and Granny Constance sat nestled between her and Tom, not willing to be parted from either of them. Nobody could explain to her what had befallen Corbie, not without upsetting her too much, but Jedediah told her that he'd gone away again and wouldn't be back, and she saw no reason not to believe 'little one'; everything else he'd ever promised had come true. This had been a kitchen of bad experiences for her in the past, but Constance went far more by the temper of folks who filled a room than by the room itself, and this felt like an Attic place: the many selves around her thrummed in a harmony that didn't drown out her thoughts. Constance had a spoon of her own and dished out scoops of honey with proud precision, smiling bright as marble when the women praised her for her skill. A grinning death's-head, you might have thought if you didn't know her, but the Smiths did, and that wasn't what they thought.

Stan Mackem took a smaller part in the preparations. The last time Constance had seen him he'd been a young lad standing by his father while Dunstan overlooked Constance, and he'd been rather uncomfortable about meeting her.

'I won't turn against my father for it,' he told Jedediah, before Jedediah even had time to raise the subject. 'He meant well. It wasn't his clumsiness that did for her ear. That man's been paid out.'

Clumsiness. Jedediah could have said much, but he didn't want to; it was an ugly memory, and Stan was a stubborn bastard about giving Mackem men the benefit of the doubt.

'Ear or not,' he said, 'it was plain cruelty to frighten her so, and if your father wasn't so changed inside and out, don't think for a moment I'd let him within a stone's throw of my mother. Just be glad she won't know him.'

'Cruelty my eye,' Stan snapped. 'He wished to help. He didn't know how used to mad women you are in these parts.'

Jedediah crossed his arms at this – but no, he didn't need to retaliate. He confined himself to saying, 'If you prefer your women dull, that's your own problem.'

Stan crossed his arms in turn. He was fond of his wife. But no, he should stick to the subject; besides, it wasn't right to goad a widower. 'What I mean is, I'm not about to blame him. He meant well.'

Many replies twisted in Jedediah's stomach. 'By whom?' he said.

'I don't think,' Stan said, a rising edge in his voice, 'that that's a question you'd hear an answer to.'

'No, I wouldn't,' Jedediah told him. 'I've my own ideas there. I'll just ask you this: do you overlook folks yourself? These days, do you?'

Stan looked away, his jaw stiff. 'Of course,' he said. 'There's folks need it. If you mean have I done for anyone's ear, then no. I'm not all chants and lore, man. I know you think we go by customs, but it doesn't mean we can't think. Or that we don't learn from experience. Where else do you think customs come from?'

It wasn't everything Jedediah needed to hear, but it was all he would get. And it could have been worse. He drew a breath. 'I reckon,' he said, 'we'll be seeing more of each other in coming days. My John'd like to know his Mackem cousins better. So let's each reckon that the other man knows how to think.'

It was a cautious truce. Then, because it wasn't good enough, he added, 'So if I hear you've taken the ears off some poor soul, or frightened their wits out, I'll know of it.'

'And,' Stan said, frozen in care, 'certain facts will reach certain ears, I reckon?'

'Nay,' said Jedediah, waving the threat of blackmail aside with an irritated shrug. 'I'll just knock your head off.'

It was a long pause before Stan nodded. 'All right,' he said. 'Fair enough. I'd say you could try, but there won't be any need. You've more to learn of our ways than you think, Jedediah Smith.'

Neither of them quite smiled, but the tension was going out of them. 'As to my mother,' Jedediah said, 'don't fret. She won't recognise you either. I'm sorry to tell you this, my man, but time does its work on most of us, and you don't look quite the way you used to. Sorry if that wounds your pride. You look pretty good for your age, but you do not look two-and-twenty.'

The air was silken-cold that Clementing morning as the three Smith men headed down the lanes, ready to lay the iron wreaths on the graves of their forbears. John held Jedediah's hand while Matthew carried the wreaths, clinking in his arms delicate as bells.

'That's pretty work,' Jedediah said, looking straight ahead into the rich darkness. 'Well done, Matthew. John, mind you keep watching your dada work. You'll have years of care before you're the match of him for wreaths.'

John was usually eager to defend his own skills, but he was clever enough to recognise a plain fact. 'I know, Grandpa,' he said seriously. 'It'd be poor business if a journeyman worked better than a master.'

'Journeyman-in-prospect,' Jedediah said, more amused than

surprised. 'Oh, don't fret, I've no doubt you'll do your piece well enough. But you're an apprentice now, however far you think ahead – and there's no shame in that, either. You've been – a good apprentice. On the whole. When you've used your head.'

John's smile was visible even in the darkness. 'Tell our forebears that,' he said. 'Mind you do, Grandpa. And I'll tell them myself, it hasn't been so bad. I'd rather you an elder than – well, we shan't name him. But I'm sorry he wasn't kind. You should have had a father more like you and Dada.'

That remark took Jedediah so unprepared that he stopped in the lane. Matthew turned, watching him with a little concern.

'I don't know why I should have said anything surprising,' John said. 'Even as a bird he wasn't much of a father. There are birds that dote on their nestlings, and he didn't. It must have been fearful to be around him when you were little.'

It was a child's comfort, and it wasn't the words that reached Jedediah's heart. It was the way John said 'you', as if Jedediah were unconnected with cruelty; as if his childhood with Corbie was a kind of aberration: not his *real* life, his real self, but a bird dropped into the wrong nest until it could find its way out.

'Well, never you mind,' he said to John in the end, and took his arm again. 'I'm all right now.'

The gunpowder struck fountains of light and the anvils held, strong and ready for another year's use. Folks laughed and shrieked at the explosions, and Lissy Brady cried and had to be taken out, but that was all right; her mama had a good hold of her and her elder brother Thomas followed, patting her with earnest concern, if a slight air of doubt as to her wisdom and maturity. The men joked with each other and the women sighed at the giddiness of men and returned to their kitchens to finish the cooking.

Molly Smith, discovering that they were a little short of certain herbs, announced that she'd better make a trip to Aunt Pell's garden.

'That's all right, sweetheart,' Janet said, smudging flour across her forehead, 'you get some fresh air – it's hot enough to smelt lead in here, and you've worked very hard.'

'You'll remember to turn those over?' Molly said, hesitating over some particularly temperamental dainties.

'Get you gone, lovie,' Godfa Tom told her with a pat on the shoulder. 'I'll keep your mama under orders, never fear.' He was in excellent spirits: Stan Mackem was being extremely respectful to him these last few days. Matthew had had a word with Stan about calling him a pagan, and Stan had taken it seriously.

Jedediah had informed him, straight-faced, that Matthew's pious testimony about what a good godfather he'd been would have impressed any man, and Tom had affected to believe him with a face equally straight. And no doubt, Tom reckoned, Matthew had sincerely testified to his character, good lad that he was. Nobody was about to hurt Matthew's feelings or Stan's dignity by commenting how much more impressive testimonies to your character are when delivered by an enormous man whose arms are now able to back up their owner's opinions.

Of course, Tom knew, there were men who wouldn't be told, but Stan Mackem probably wasn't one of them; he'd even asked Tom's opinion on the planting of St John's Wort yesterday.

There were few things more satisfying in this life than giving helpful advice to a man who was not allowed to pass comment on you. Tom's father had never fully converted, whatever he said in public, but he had taught his children the secret enjoyment of heaping coals of fire.

'You go on,' he told Molly. 'It's a busy enough life for hard workers. Celdie Smith, if you steal any more of that honey, I shall *judge* you,' he added. He'd lived many years with Aunt Constance and had long ago acquired the knack of making threats that wouldn't frighten her. 'I shall form *opinions* on you, my lass, so you leave some for the community and your darling granny. We'll see you later, Molly love.'

So Molly got her walk. She only wanted thyme, and that grew in thick in the Smiths' own garden, but Godfa Tom was always willing to conspire with a child who needed a break. She didn't usually take advantage, but today she felt the need to clear something in her own mind.

Aunt Pell's woods were still a mess of bark and shatter, the trees all over sawdust; only the damp of recent days had started to settle them down. If it was a wet winter, chances were they'd wash clean and look much better come spring. Another season or two of autumn leaves on the ground and moss starting to grow on the broken lumps of wood, and it would look better yet. John had said time here was crumpled like cloth, but Molly did the washing and could have told him that if you hang a damp sheet over the line, its creases start to smooth. Time would uncrumple itself here under its own weight, eventually.

But right now it was still an unsettled place. Molly picked her way carefully, speeding up or slowing through the ripples of stretched or compressed moments. You would get used to it in the end, she thought. It was like a boat she'd been in once, when Dada had travelled to Kidderminster to testify at an assizes, and he'd had brought her along for company. Some of the folks onboard got motion-sick, but she quickly found that if you stopped waiting for the ground to be stable and just rocked along with it, you didn't feel so bad.

She almost laughed to herself at her sensible thoughts; alas, she was a martyr to them. But this might be one that Johnny would enjoy. She must remember to tell him.

At the tree, she stood and called up, 'No One, dear? Are you there?'

There was a pause, then the furtive scratch of talon on branch betrayed its presence. For a giant spider, No One was very good at making itself invisible.

'Did you get home safe?' Molly said. Aunt Pell said she needed to work on her patient voice; well, practice was practice, wherever you did it. 'I'm not here to scold you, dear. I just thought I should make sure you were all right.'

'No One is not present to screaming stones and scolding heart-stones and the hurt of limbs and feelings.' It was a nervous little whisper.

'Of course not, dear,' Molly said. 'You did your part very well. You wove perfectly. We're very grateful.'

The sighing stopped. Silence held sway again – or at least, woodland silence: far off, a single robin piped, and the twigs rustled together overhead like skirts.

'Grateful to weaving spinner and chaste thirst and pretty

thoughts of stretch and gleam,' No One hinted. Molly could see its legs now; they were just extending a little, like a tentative hand reached out to take yours.

'The prettiest of spinner and thinkers, and the most virtuous of hunters,' Molly said. They didn't keep animals at the smithy except Dobbs the horse, and also the hens and chicks and the sea of cheeping cats that swept in and out of their garden according to the tidal pull of Janet's feeding. And No One wasn't entirely an animal, of course; it would be underestimating it to think of it as a pet, and Grandpa always said that to underestimate the fey was the quickest way to get yourself hurt. But still, here she was, out in the woods like a wilder girl than she really was. It might be winter-cold, but she felt a warmth lifting her lips into a smile.

'Gleam of Louise-Molly and pulse of clean and tasty blood, and what shall the air do but for pretty-kneed Molly!' exclaimed No One, and now it sounded really pleased to see her.

'I had a thought, dear,' Molly said, 'a virtuous act you might do. Well, more than one, really. The first is that if I'm to midwife, I'll need bandages – Aunt Pell says you can never have enough of them. Do you think your silk might make good bandages? There might even be the odd feast in it for you.'

'Virtuous is No One beyond the skein of star and moon, and feasts of plenty and quenching!'

'Well, that's good news,' Molly said. 'There's another feast I'll be at tonight, but I'll see if anyone around has a treat for you. It's not lambing or farrowing season now, nor calving season, come to that, but I'll do you better come spring. I'm sure folks will have some culls, and they might as well go to you as to another use. Let's you and me have some pretty thoughts together, No One, and perhaps we'll both be the wiser for it.'

'Point to point and dancing swing, for wisdom may quench the driest and wettest together!' No One's front legs were rubbing, a little clap of joy.

'So that's good,' Molly said. 'And I had just one other thought. My grandpa has a scar on his wrist, you know, a Mackem brand. He never liked it much. He told me once that he'd never do that to his own flesh and blood – that it was an elder's task to *stop* his lads getting burned, not burn them himself. I think he'd be happier with his own scar gone. He told me you were very good at taking folks apart and putting them back together, dear. Do you think you could take his scar and move it somewhere he didn't have to look at it? The sole of his foot, perhaps, or his back? Could you do that, dear?'

'Pick and pick and stick again,' No One answered, and the satisfaction in its voice was so deep that the breathy husk had almost the sweetness of a flute. 'What shall the toes do but untack and shift, and . . .' A thought froze it; No One pulled in its legs and gnarled itself into a camouflaged bulge.

'Dear, I know you're still there,' said Molly. 'Please? Won't you come back and help my grandpa?'

'Iron and stone and fear of pretty legs, and man of Louise wounds No One of the weaving feet for liking not the skein and step. What can dainty knee and fine-strung waist do against the slash of iron dagger?' No One cringed at the thought.

Matthew had often told his children that spiders were more afraid of you than you were of them. *Well*, thought Molly, *it looks like he was right.*

'Oh, that's all right,' she said. She shook back her hair. This wisewomaning business was more fun than she'd expected. 'I know he's a little fearful of spiders, but he'll come if I ask him. And he'll hold still for you; he's a very brave man, my grandpa.'

The air above the village rippled like water in the rising heat as the bonfire tinged every house in Gyrford square with gold. They toasted Saint Clement as sparks tossed themselves heavenwards in brilliant handfuls. Mugs clinked, voices sang, and if the saint himself wasn't having a merry evening, it wasn't because the folks below weren't setting a fine example.

Shibbie Mackem proved to be an excellent dancer and was not about to let anyone think her otherwise. She danced with Molly, by way of showing her paces, and then with every lad of the village who asked her. The handsome ones were accepted with enthusiasm and the ugly ones with good grace, Shibbie holding the principle that it was beneath a woman of importance to withhold her attention from any who needed it. Old Dunstan Mackem had a joke for every boy she danced with, which embarrassed most of them, but Shibbie was remarkably forbearing about it for her age, saying with a toss of her head that if a lad couldn't see a respected man happy, then most likely he wouldn't be much joy to dance with either.

Molly also found herself asked to dance by quite a few boys. She still didn't want to use the occasion to find a sweetheart – a sweetheart might expect you to marry him, and being a wisewoman promised to be far better sport – but some of them were pleasant enough and a dance was a dance, so she skipped around with a will. As soon as the opportunity came to sit down, though, she settled with her best friend Mary Anne and the many younger Morgan sisters, whispering confidences and giggling almost like any girl her age. It had felt like a long haul these last few weeks, and Molly was being rather bolder about enjoying herself than she would have been a few months ago.

Janet Smith danced with her husband, then with her friend Franklin, and after that she took over dishing the pottage, telling anyone who complained about the absence of meat that saints don't admire the mockers and that poor drowned Clement would no doubt have been glad of a nice warm bowl down at the bottom of the sea. Matthew tried to have a word with her about whether she was being entirely consistent – there was a distinct gleam in her eye that might have led a stern judge to consign her to the mockers herself – but Janet sat in his lap and tucked herself into his new-healed arms, defying him to prove her theology wrong. Matthew had never been able to hold out against his wife when she took that line. For one thing, kisses were involved, and he found them very persuasive, especially after a period of careful inaction that had felt very, very long. Deep down, though, it was even more simple: Matthew was Clem Smith's great-grandson and he agreed with his old forebear: it was better when the girls were happy.

Pell Smith attended, which was usual, but what was unusual was that she brought a guest: her sister, Miss Mabbie Smith, who had not been seen in Gyrford since she was a child. Everyone asked her about what she'd been up to in the past decades, but Mabbie would only answer, 'This and that,' and then turn her attention back to the singing, and her voice was so beautiful that no one wanted to interrupt her. At one point her great-nephew John Smith crept up and whispered in her ear, and she whispered back, and he crept away giggling so hard he almost fell down, but he declined to explain what was so funny except the confusing remark that what words folks heard in the song and what words birds would take away from it were very different. Which didn't leave anyone feeling much the wiser, but then, he was a young lad, and youngsters do get the giggles pretty often when there's nothing worrying them.

Jedediah Smith sat gazing into the fire, not saying very much to anyone – but he wasn't frowning. Franklin Thorpe brought him food and drink, and they chatted for a while; still, those two were old friends.

'Is there anything more I can do for you?' Franklin asked

Jedediah looked into the dazzling heart of the fire. 'You've no need,' he said, an instinctive answer as automatic as shielding a wound. Then he thought about it, and said, 'Well, folks listen to you when they gossip. There's Stan Mackem: Corbie thought him a rook like me, but I'd say . . . I'd say he was confused – he saw a farrier and thought he must be kin. Doesn't say anything about blood. They'll believe that.' He rubbed his face. 'It's more or less true, anyway.'

'Is it?' Franklin spoke with more hesitancy than Jedediah had heard since he was a boy. Well, since both of them were boys, although neither of them had seen things that way at the time. 'I don't like to overstep, only – well, he thought me a treecreeper. I'm no farrier and he knew I was no son of yours, and I – I don't – but – no, surely he couldn't—?'

Jedediah put a hand on his shoulder before the panic could

take hold. 'Nay, nay, you're no son of his. Sorry to say it, but you do have a look of old Joe Thorpe about you, before drink and foolishness wore out his fine face, at least.' Franklin looked down, half-embarrassed for raising the subject at all, but Jedediah hadn't finished. 'And if he thought it over, he'd've known you're not mine either – not by blood, at least.'

He spoke that last with a light emphasis. Franklin was a warm-hearted man, grateful and affectionate; Jedediah had always loved that in him. But it was hard to forget the thin, skittish boy who was so easy to overwhelm.

'Nay, what I remember,' he went on, 'is that he liked to joke you were mine. I can't have been but twelve when you were conceived, and I wasn't that forward a lad, but he wasn't one to let that get in the way of a good laugh. And he always reckoned I judged him – and I did. He'd have liked it very well to believe me a hypocrite who got children before I was old enough to shave. I reckon he liked that tale so much that after a while, he half-forgot he'd made it up.' He patted Franklin's shoulder again. 'Ab didn't know what blood-kin meant; look how it fastened on any man or beast that was kind to it for half a minute. It just took away anyone Corbie *thought* was descended from him. And, well . . .' He remembered the day he met Louise. *Have you brought your son?* she'd said, asking if he was single, and he'd had to answer the question without crushing Franklin's hopeful heart. 'I liked you much better than he liked me, after all. He couldn't think of many reasons a man might be fond of a child. But he could see I was fond of you.'

Franklin blinked for a while. Then he said, 'So he'd have known Stan Mackem was his son?'

Jedediah shrugged. 'Well, he must have known why he was sent from Tinsdowne. I don't reckon he thought of him much, though. Stan got him cast out there, I got him tied down here. We . . . neither of us were a blessing to him.'

Franklin might have said something about that, but at this point Francie came to join them, and shortly thereafter, the village observed Jedediah Smith dandling little Lissy on his lap, holding her with a tenderness you wouldn't have expected if you'd only ever seen him hammer iron – but then, the little thing was more or less family to him.

Tom Attic talked with Mister Smith as well, but he was kept busy by the demand for his baking; even with the help of the tireless Agnes Smith, it was flatteringly brisk. Agnes herself was looking truly cheerful; she had always been fond of the children and here were all Matthew's young ones and the little Bradys as well. Thomas had taken a tremendous fancy to her: she could swing him into the air higher than anyone, so he had adopted her as his new best friend – or at least, his new best friend along with his Auntie Alice, when she could be spared from doting on her namesake Lissy. The two women passed him back and forth between them, laughing with each other, and Thomas laughed too by way of solidarity. He didn't understand much of what they said, but he was a sanguine little man and as long as people were giving him cake, he felt things were as they should be.

Most of the village stepped wide of Constance Smith. Her husband had recently been lost in a tremendous struggle with the mightiest of feys and while it was possible he might live for ever down there in the depths, she surely ought to be accorded the respect due a widow – but widows usually looked sad, and Mistress Constance did not. She was cuddling young Thomas, or stroking the hair of her great-grandson John, laughing with him over some private joke, or petting the head of Mistress Brady's new babe, or smoothing the fur of any stray cat that brushed up against her, or otherwise engaging in some act of merry widowhood that made the usual condolences feel . . . uncomfortable.

Well, folks agreed, her husband had been a living saint, not only to save Gyrford so many times but to marry a woman so simple-minded and protect her from the evils of the world – for look at her now, sitting there without a care! Folks sighed with satisfaction and agreed, with the deep contentment that comes from traducing the younger generations as compared with the old, that they wouldn't see Corbie's like again.

Matthew was having a good time; kisses from Janet aside, he liked his neighbours and seeing them enjoy themselves was always a pleasure – but it was a little on his mind that Stan Mackem and Jedediah were sitting on opposite sides of the bonfire. Of course, there was no gain in trying to force them to be friends; Matthew had always been firm with his own children that they must be kind and loving to each other, but Stan and Jedediah were too old for that. Probably. Still, Matthew was worried about Stan. The man hadn't known Corbie long, but a father was a father.

He erred on the side of prudence, waiting until Stan had drunk a couple of mugs before sitting down beside him. 'How are you, Nuncle?' he said. 'I fear it mayn't be as joyous a day for you as usual, and nor for your kin in Tinsdowne, for they'll be missing you. Not but that we're glad to have you with us. Can I fetch you anything?'

Stan considered him for a long moment, the firelight snapping in his eyes. 'You're a fine lad,' he said in the end. 'Your pa must be proud of you.'

Matthew smiled, a little shyly. 'I hope so.'

'Ach, he will be,' Stan said. 'Mind you,' he added, 'that one was proud before ever you were thought of. I reckon he'd have been proud of you if you'd been born with no face and two arses.'

Having said this he looked at Matthew warily. No Mackem would judge you for being loose-tongued on your third mug of cider, but this son of Jedediah's had struck him as a little pious.

Matthew laughed, though, and Stan relaxed into another swig. It was pretty good cider; that Janet of theirs might be too sharp by half, but Stan had to admit she could brew.

'Most likely he would,' Matthew said. 'I'd love my young ones either way. Though I'm glad of their faces, I'll confess it.'

'They're a well-looking set,' Stan conceded. 'Not much of the Mackem look to them, though. Stubborn to the balls, you Smiths.'

'Oh, no,' Matthew said cheerfully, 'skirt-led, that's what you want to call us. We look like our mothers.'

Stan regarded at his nephew, the bonfire painting his face bright, and with a great shrug, he laughed back. 'All right,' he agreed. 'I don't reckon we have that much in common, me and Elder Smithie over there' – he indicated Jedediah, sitting unaware of his sudden re-Christening on the other side of the flames – 'but I can't say I'd have done all that different if it was me and mine.' He chuckled. 'God help the elders. You just wait and see.'

'Oh, I don't like to think of it,' Matthew said earnestly. 'I don't wish to lose my father and I don't like to order folks about. I just pray my father lives a long life, and that come the day, Johnny'll be old enough to share the burden with me.' He looked into the fire and laughed again. 'That'll be some rare times.'

Janet, seeing Matthew attending to Stan, sat herself by Jedediah. 'How do you, Father?' She rested her hand on his shoulder. If you waited for Jedediah to start an embrace you might wait forever, but that didn't mean he didn't like one.

Jedediah didn't turn his head, which was how she knew he wanted to ask her something.

'No one's listening,' she said. 'Everyone's at their dancing and gossip.'

Jedediah rolled his pipe between his fingers. He was too warm to smoke, but it was a bit of a comfort to have it, nevertheless. 'Pell said something to me,' he said. 'I wondered if you agreed.'

'I might,' Janet said, quite lightly. 'She had the training of me, her and Sarah Thorpe, God rest her. What did she say?

'She said,' Jedediah didn't turn, 'that killing was women's work.'

There was a pause. Music rang between them.

'Oh, Pell,' Janet said after a while. 'I know what she means, but I wouldn't take it to heart. She hasn't the best view of men, but I don't think you're all so foolish.' She laughed. 'Not all of you.'

Jedediah did look at her then. Only if you'd known him for years would you see the bewilderment in his eyes.

Feeling a little sorry for him, Janet stroked his shoulder again. 'She means midwife work, I reckon,' she said, 'and mothering – I'd kill to guard Johnny and the girls, if I had to, and I wouldn't be sorry for it either. But then, I reckon you would too.'

She still wasn't making herself clear, for Jedediah's shoulder hadn't relaxed under her caress. 'I don't know,' Janet said, 'when she said it to you, but if I were to guess, I reckon she meant she'd rather do an ill thing than let you do it – and that's not women's work. That's just because she loves you.'

Jedediah looked down. He'd never known what to say when folks spoke to him like that.

'Look you,' Janet said. 'All those years after Mother Louise died, may she rest in peace – well, I know folks offered to take Matthew from you, give you an easier life. You must have been tired to your soul, and you could have done it, couldn't you? After all, you were your own master.'

'No.' The answer came before he could plan it. 'Matthew was.'

Janet smiled. 'And there's your answer. Pell would stain her own soul before yours, just like you'd stain yours before his.' She patted him again. 'Don't grudge us our little laugh at men,' she said. 'We've plenty to do that you can't join us in, and it's better to laugh than repine.'

'Yes,' Jedediah said slowly, 'if it's a real laugh, yes.'

'And it's all right if you're mourning.'

Jedediah looked at her sharp. 'Mourning?'

'For your father. For what you lost, and what you never had. You're not made of iron, Father, however hard you try.'

His fingers tightened around his pipe. 'You know what he was,' he said.

'Oh yes – I'd have pushed him into the Byde and left him there. But he wasn't my father. And besides, there's Stan beside the fire there. He's a new thought.'

Jedediah shook his head. 'Dunstan Mackem was his father,' he said. 'He's made up his mind on that score.'

Janet shrugged. 'Well, there's many a man born with a little softening around the truth of their conceptions,' she said, 'and they're not the worse for it.' She gave him a look.

'What's that?' Jedediah asked. Despite the fire, his hands felt cold.

'Well, Matthew's birthday is in March,' Janet said. 'If I have this right, you were married at Michaelmas, weren't you?' Her smile had more compassion than he'd expected. 'I've brought babies that early, but they didn't live – or if they did, they didn't thrive.' She raised her eyebrows just a little. Of the many ways you might describe Matthew, 'sickly' was not one of them.

Jedediah said nothing for a long moment. There was no need to point out the difference. Janet knew he'd loved Louise. Corbie hadn't loved any of his women, not as far as his sons could tell.

And Jedediah wasn't sorry. They'd had so few years together in the end, he and Louise. At least they'd taken their joys where they could.

'Does he know?' he said in the end.

At that, Janet grinned. 'He can count,' she said. 'And a man with four children knows the difference between nine months and six. I'll tell you the truth, though: I don't reckon he thinks about it. It doesn't matter, does it? You didn't raise him to judge the grass-got or the bastards or the children of cruel men, but to judge the kind or the unkind. I reckon Stan can be your brother or not; it's up to the two of you. But it was never Corbie's decision, nor Old Dunstan's, come to that. Men aren't their fathers, whether they want to be or not. So like him or not, as you wish to; you wouldn't be granting anything to Corbie if you did.

'And if anyone was a father to you, it was Pell. So go on and make up your own mind. You've had plenty of practice, haven't you?'

John Smith liked a party – there were sweetmeats and songs, two things he was very fond of – but the entire village was a lot to manage. You couldn't think quietly to yourself with so many folks together. He'd had all the greetings he could digest, and had been very polite to lot of folks, even when he was growing tired, and in the end he went to sit by Grandpa after Grandpa had finished talking to Nuncle Stan.

John hadn't wanted to take part in that talk – he still wasn't sure he liked Stan Mackem – but after Grandpa was came back, he relaxed on his stool, considering the flames. They glowed bright enough to dazzle, shaking their blonde tresses with a rustle like the beating of wings.

'Will I start my journeyman piece tomorrow?' John asked.

'You're eager for work,' Jedediah said mildly. 'Yes, if you like. You all right, Johnny?'

'Oh yes,' John said. 'You know, it was most interesting under the earth. Did you know that—?'

But before he could continue, there was a shriek: something white as a ghost had swooped over Shibbie, dipping through the darkness without a sound.

'It's a spirit!' Shibbie declared angrily, clutching her hair. 'It's a spirit, and us right beside the church! You're all mad in Gyrford – well, not you, Molly, *maybe*, but you're all a pack of hexers!'

'Now, now, dear,' Matthew said, coming over, 'no need to fret.'

'Shibbie, lass,' said Stan, standing up as well and looking askance at Matthew for comforting the girl who was definitely *his* kin to protect, 'what did you see? What ailed you – and if you think it worth laughing over, John Smith, ungodly little wretch that you are, then I hope someone will have a word with you.'

'You're right, Johnny!' Molly jumped up too, remembering the woods where No One hid, that fierce little ripple of sweetness that sang from the branches. 'I did hear a robin this morning!'

'Perhaps,' Stan said rather dourly, 'you have a thought you might like to bestow upon us poor sound-witted folks?'

John grinned and patted Shibbie with the full condescension of an amused cousin. 'It was a barn owl,' he said. 'Just a barn owl, Shibbie. Listen, can you hear the shriek?'

The sound rang out against the crackle of the flames: a shrill, merciless screech, hoarse as a goblin, sharp as a hinge. It was already flying away, but the gleam of wings, whiter than white, was beautiful beyond anything John could imagine.

John smiled again and elbowed Jedediah, who put an arm around his shoulder.

'Calm yourself, Stan,' Jedediah said. 'The lad means it's good news. The birds are back.'

The End

ACKNOWLEDGEMENTS

As ever, Sophie Hicks: agent, charmer, staunch ally and super-person.

Jo Fletcher – both a privilege and a treat to work with.

Everyone at JFB, particularly Corinna Zifko, Ella Patel, Ellie Nightingale, Ajebowale Roberts and Anne Perry.

If I've said something daft about Muslims or Moors, you can blame me; if I've avoided saying anything daft, we can thank sensitivity reader Theophina Gabriel, and my dear friend Lisa Holmes – the latter of whom also just gets kudos for being an awesome Constant Reader and lovely lady.

On that note, I'm grateful to a lot of friends! Shout-out to Claire Bott, Alyssa Gilbert, Jude Boyce and Ammy Griffith, Anoushka Yeoh and Margaret Young for particular cheering on; Catriona Mackay and Chris Naden for some excellent suggestions and humouring my etymology geeking; Ali Baker Brooks, Fiona Moore and Sue York for making my first conventions so much less daunting; LJ Sedgwick and Mark Norman for being excellent folk in both senses of the word; probably others I'll remember after this goes to the printers because there's so many nice people.

On the subject of conventions, everyone at ComicCon, FantasyCon and the book clubs for making me so welcome and being such fun. Also everyone in Folk Horror Revival, for so often brightening my day, and particularly the hard-working mods who keep it a nice place. And Alex Davis, fine fellow and awesome organiser.

Andreea Grigorescu, without whom I don't think I'd have had the peace of mind to write at all – just an absolute star.

My family, as always.

Gareth Thomas: husband, audience, Man Consultant and monster lover.

My beloved Nathaniel: I love you with all my heart.

And for this book, it feels like only manners to thank the rooks and the crows. I suspect something might befall me if I didn't, but even if it won't, I'll do it for love.